GILES EVERGREEN;

OR,

FRESH FROM THE COUNTRY.

"EXERCISE BEFORE BREAKFAST."

No. 1.

CHAPTER I.

THE SCHOOL ON FIRE!

HUNDREDS of throats were shouting out the fearful sounds, and hundreds of strong men and women, and even children, were seen rushing through the sparkling snow to the scene of this dread calamity and horror. The heavens seemed to be one immense pall of crimson, while a thousand sparks kept whirling up in the air in fantastic flight.

The establishment of Doctor Birchenough, situated in the town of Yaxley, was in flames. Fortunately the holidays had commenced, so that the greater portion of the students had left for their happy homes.

Fire! fire! fire! fire! was the agonising cry that rang through the town, and in a brief space there was scarcely an inhabitant but was hastening to the conflagration.

At that time there were only five pupils in the house, the doctor, his sister, and four domestics.

The pupils were named Giles Evergreen, Tommy Jolter, Norman Campbell, Terence Flaherty O'Flanagan, and Alfred Ravensborne. With the exception of Tommy Jolter, they were all fine, tall lads; Tommy was what might have been termed stumpy. They all slept in a large, ventilated apartment, and they had been talking over their plans for the future, for their school days were ended, and the next day was to behold them bid adieu to Doctors Prosody, Syntax and Birchenough.

"Up, up, for your lives!" shouted Giles Evergreen, almost suffocated by the blinding smoke that was rushing in dark clouds through the room.

To spring out of bed and partly dress, and rush to the others, was but the work of a moment.

"Norman, Terence, Alfred, Jolter, make for the stairs! the house is on fire!"

The affrighted boys sprung up wildly, and for the moment scarcely realised the horrors of their situation.

Rushing to the door of the room, and trying to pull it open, Giles, to his dismay, found it securely locked.

Terence O'Flanagan had, with the fun and frolic of an Irish Boy, locked the door and hid the key.

"Who locked the door?" hoarsely shouted Giles, "and where is the key? Heaven look down upon us! We shall be burnt to death!"

There was no time to lose.

The shouts of the men below, the screams of the women, told them how rapidly the flames were gaining on them.

Giles groped his way to the fire-place, and in an instant had grasped the poker; then, bounding back to the door, dealt a vigorous blow on the lock, which flew in a hundred pieces.

"Murder! murder!" shouted Terence, "but you've smashed me fingers into the middle of next week."

Terence was tugging at the lock when the blow descended.

Speedily the door was opened; but Giles and his schoolmates plainly saw there was not the faintest hope of escape by the stairs.

"Shut the door," he shouted; "it will stop the flames from entering the room. Tie the sheets together; we must descend into the play-ground that way."

In an instant it was done, with the tact and strength that boys know how to use so well.

"Where's Tommy Jolter?" said Giles.

"He sprained his ankle the other day, and cannot stand."

"He shall be the first to go down. Where are you, Tommy?"

"God bless thee, Giles! I be here, standin' on one leg, like our old gander!" cried Tommy, shaking with fear.

Giles, seizing a blanket, fastened it round Tommy Jolter's shivering body, and then throwing the coil of sheets out of the window, Tommy Jolter seizing them with a firm hold—for his life depended upon it—was launched into the air.

It was a fortunate thought of Giles's to wrap the blanket round him, for the flames were blazing fiercely out of the windows.

"Cover your face, Tommy!" shouted Giles.

He reached the ground safely.

"Hurrah! hurrah! hurrah!" shouted the crowd, almost mad with excitement.

Up went the sheets, and in a few moments Norman Campbell had safely descended.

Again the wild cry of joy rang through the air.

Then Alfred Ravensborne was the next.

The flames had now reached the door, and sent a lurid light along the floor.

The two boys, Giles and Terence, were now alone.

"I'll let you down as aisy as if you were going to be hanged," said Terence.

"You'll go next, Terence," said Giles, firmly.

"No, no," said the warm-hearted Irish lad; "I locked the kay and lost the lock, and so——"

What more he would have said was not heard, for the blanket was covered over his head and face, and with a caution to hold tight, he got out of the window.

He had scarcely reached the ground when the sheets caught fire, and cut off all hopes of escape for the brave, devoted boy!

A cry of horror and dismay arose.

At that moment the door, which was of a thin material, fell in with a loud crash.

The flames ran leaping and roaring into the room!

Despair almost seized upon the heart of Giles, and he prepared to meet his fate with a bold, unshrinking spirit.

At that moment he looked up to Heaven to ask for mercy, when his eye rested upon the stone gutter that ran round the house. At the same moment he looked below, and saw lying on the ground a large carpet.

He was about to mount the ledge of the window, and, grasping the gutter, make his way to the iron pipe that extended to the ground.

"Hold out the carpet firmly," shouted he, "and I'll leap out."

A hundred pairs of hands secured it.

The fire had by this time seized upon the beds.

The room was one blaze.

"Leap! leap!" was the cry.

"Stand by!" shouted Giles.

He murmured a prayer for mercy.

Then, with a bold heart, he took the awful leap for life!

Swift as an arrow through the air his form was seen, and in an instant he had fallen safely into his "ark of refuge."

A wild hurrah rang through the crowd. He sprang up.

"Where is the doctor?" shouted he.

"Here, here, my brave lad," said the doctor, with streaming eyes, falling on his neck.

"Are all out?" asked the excited boy —and he glanced around. "Where is the poor deformed little servant girl?"

"Ah! where, indeed!"

"She is lost, I fear," said the doctor.

"Merciful Heaven! the poor girl is deaf and dumb, and cannot know her danger; and if she did, cannot call for help. She sleeps there," pointing to a window of the building close upon the ground.

Giles rushed to the window; alas, the shutters were closed, and closely barred from within.

He looked around, and in an instant saw the means of rescue.

The railings enclosing the playground had, by the excited mob, been forced down; he snatched up one, and, with desperate blows, battered against the shutters with almost superhuman strength.

Terence was alongside of him in an instant, and the pair rained blows upon the barred windows. At last one slightly gave way, so as to allow the iron bar to be inserted as a lever.

Away went the shutter into the room, and out shot the bright, vivid flame.

A moment more, and Giles sprang into the place.

There lay the poor "deformed one," crouched up in a corner of the room, the picture of terror and unmistakable horror.

The poor girl sprang up, and threw her arms desperately round Giles.

He held her firmly, and sprang towards the window.

"Saved, saved! Terence," shouted he, "lay hold of her."

"By the powers, as tight as though she were a bag of sovereigns. Hurrah! Pat's a darling boy."

And, so saying, he pulled her out in the open air.

"Come out of that," shouted he to Giles.

But that was a task not easily accomplished; blinded, and nearly suffocated with the smoke, Giles for a moment reeled, and fell upon the floor. With great presence of mind, he turned over on his face, and thus, for the moment, escaped suffocation.

Soon he sprang to his feet, and gained the window; a table stood beneath it, and, tottering, he got upon it.

He felt his hand tightly clenched.

"Hurroo for ould Ireland! I've got him as tight as an old bear sticks to her cubs," shouted Terence.

Kind, strong hands dragged him from a horrible death; scarcely had he gained the open play-ground when the roof came toppling down. Still the building went burning on.

The crowd gazed awe-struck at it.

The re-action had been too much for Giles; the efforts he had made to save himself and others now told upon him, and he sank heavily to the ground.

"Poor fellow, he has gone," cried the doctor.

"Whisht, my darling," said Terence; "he's been to a nice house-warming, and met a fiery reception; I'll give him a cool one," and, so saying, he seized the branch from the beadle, and, directing a stream of cold water upon Giles, he sprang upon his feet with his wonted alacrity.

"Thanks, Terence, thanks!" and, spite of the scene, he gave forth a merry, ringing laugh.

"You are as welcome as the flowers of May," grinned Terence. The crowd caught the infection, and laughed heartily.

"What's good for the gander is wholesome for the goose," muttered Terence, and turned the branch among the crowd; they, headed by the beadle, made a hasty retreat from such an unseasonable ducking.

By this time the fire was gradually dying out, and then came the kindness of heart so strikingly shown by the English people in the hour of distress and suffering.

The school itself was situated half a mile from the town; but every house in it was open for the reception of the unfortunate schoolmaster, his pupils, and household.

Great coats and shawls were taken off, and wrapped round the shivering forms of the poor burnt-out sufferers.

Large fires were burning in the principal houses and the inns, and everything got ready to relieve and mitigate the misery of the conflagration of the school of Doctor Birchenough.

"My brave boy," said he to Giles, "to you those lads owe their lives; and I hope, when they are men, and making their way through the world, they will always remember the coolness, courage, and daring you have this night exhibited."

"I hope you'll not say anything more about it, sir," replied the frank-hearted Giles. "I have done no more than my duty, and there isn't a fellow amongst us but what would have done the same."

It was a singular sight to behold the procession from the still burning school to the town.

The only engine belonging to the place (almost the eighth wonder of the world) had been found in an efficient state, and the large pond close to the house was ready without the aid of the turn-cock.

The building having now fallen in, the engine was no longer of any use; upon that they mounted the doctor and his pupils, and then some fifty men, having seized the ropes that were fastened to it, started off at a rattling pace towards the town, cheering as though a great victory had been won.

There was not a life, thank God! lost, they knew; the doctor was rich and well insured, and so the return from the fire resembled more a triumphant procession than anything else; all along the road were heard shouts coupled with the name of Giles Evergreen, the noble boy who had saved the lives of five of his fellow creatures.

And the shouts of joy lasted during that memorable night until the " rising sun" rose upon the blackened walls and smouldering embers of the once happy school.

CHAPTER II.

CHARACTERS.

BEFORE we proceed further with the adventures of Giles Evergreen and his schoolfellows, we must place before the Boys of England their several characters and dispositions.

Begin we with Giles Evergreen.

The father of Giles was a squire, residing in a distant part of England. Of him, Giles had but a dim recollection, for, at a very early age he was taken from under the paternal roof by a maiden aunt (his mother's sister), and brought up by her in an old mansion, so large, and so antique that almost every panel in the wainscot had a ghost legend attached to it. The only place that could not boast of such a thing was the cellar, that was quite out of *spirits*.

A year or two rolled away, when one day, Mr. Sheepshanks, his aunt's lawyer, waited upon her, and held a long consultation.

Upon his departure, Giles was sent for into his aunt's room, and told that his father had fallen off his horse while hunting and was killed; that he had died a poor, ruined man, and that aunty was the only friend he had in the world.

Time rolled on, and dear aunty was taken ill, and again Mr. Sheepshanks came.

A long part of the day passed away, and the shades of night were fast falling, when Giles was taken to her room.

Young as he was he saw the change. She was dying.

"Giles," said the old lady, "I am going upon a long journey, and shall not return to you. I've left you in the care of this good man, who will at a proper time inform you of many things. God bless you, my boy! Be honest and manly in all your transactions and you will have little to fear here or hereafter."

A few weeks after he had followed his last relative to her long home, and, shortly after, he was taken by Lawyer Sheepshanks, generally called "Tough Mutton," to the school of Dr. Birchenough, who soon found out the characteristics of the " desolate boy."

Manly, frank, brave, and generous in his nature, unsuspecting almost to a fault, so much so that they at times called him Master Green for ever.

And so time rolled on, with the usual school-boy's troubles and disasters. Twice a-year he went to the old lawyer's house, but when our tale commenced he was about to leave school for the " busy one of the world," and so for the present we leave him.

Tommy Jolter's father was a substantial farmer, with a large family.

A number of disastrous illnesses had reduced the farmer's family to two children, Tommy, and a sister, Suke; the difference between them was of a very marked description.

Tommy was soft, Sukey sharp; as Tommy grew up, his extreme softness was so apparent that he became the butt of all the boys of the town, and he generally went by the name of Soft Tommy.

If a quantity of pigeon's milk was required Tommy was sent to purchase it, and it generally took him a day to get, for he was kindly sent from house to house for it.

" I say, Tommy, my lad, wilt run to old Hardwelt's, the cobbler, for a pen'north of strap oil ?" said one of his tormentors, giving him a large jug.

He was told the cobbler sold it.

Tommy went as directed, but the " oil," instead of being placed in a jug, was well rubbed in on his shoulders with old Welts's strap, to the great delight of those who had accompanied him on his expedition.

A kind friend of the farmer's seeing all this, advised him to place the boy at school, and so " Soft Tommy " was drafted off to Doctor Birchenough's academy.

Twenty-four hours after his admission, a boy older then himself took the liberty of trying to curl Tommy's long red hair with a ruler.

To the surprise of all the " Soft One " resented this.

The embryo hairdresser measured his length on the ground.

A ring was then formed, and the fight commenced ; and here Tommy's hard knuckles and pluck came off victorious, and the " red head " was not molested again.

The head might be soft, but the heart was warm and generous, and a kind act done once by Giles Evergreen remained indelibly impressed upon the rough nature of the farmer's boy.

Tommy Jolter never forgot a kind action.

Norman Campbell was the son of an old tough Scotch practitioner of surgery, and was intended for the same honourable and great art.

Norman was as tough and unbending as a block of granite ; cool, calculating, and self-denying ; his blood appeared as though it had been frozen, and scarcely the trace of any emotion was to be seen in his face ; a gem of the brave Scottish nation.

It was only once when he and Terence O'Flanagan came to words that he forgot his usual coldness of disposition so far as to raise his hand in anger.

It is certainly trying to find one's pillow stuffed full of prickly pears or horse chesnuts, or to find, when the light was out, and you are springing into bed, that a large treacle plaster is spread over the sheet, and which you do not discover until it adheres closely to your skin.

The closeness of the Scot's disposition held out an excellent opportunity for the rollicking humour of the Irish boy.

It was one morning when the first

bell had rung that Norman Campbell opened his eyes, and beheld his coverlid covered with thistles, and a paper, upon which was written, "How's a' wi' ye? A donkey's breakfast."

The blood of the Scotch boy fired at this; he thought it not only an insult to himself, but likewise to "Puir auld Scotland," and he determined to avenge it.

Rising cautiously he took a handful of the thistles, and approaching the bed in which Terence lay enjoying a comfortable slumber, he stuffed them in Terence's mouth, saying—

"Your breakfast is ready, my lad."

Terence started up in bed, and in a moment guessed the truth of the matter.

"Ha! ha! by the powers, it's rather tough ateing," said Terence, "and a mighty queer breakfast; but where's your own, Sawney?"

"I've no appetite, my mon," was the reply.

"Then I'll give you a *whet* for it," and the next moment the contents of a large water jug were sent over Norman Campbell.

By this time the other boys were awake, and enjoyed the fun amazingly.

"He looks mighty like a Welshman just now," shouted Terence; "he's a *leak* from head to foot."

"Ha! ha! ha!" rung through the room.

"Bravo, young Shamrock!" shouted Giles.

Before another word could be uttered Norman had sprung upon Terence.

A desperate fight commenced.

Alfred Ravensborne taking the side of Norman Campbell, Giles Evergreen that of Terence, while Tommy capered about the room like a sprite.

The battle was not fated to last long, the unexpected appearance of (not the police, but the worthy doctor, with a cane in his hand) put an end to the contest.

Upon investigating the affair he decreed the punishment; Terence was to learn four pages of the History of Scotland, and Norman the same quantity from the History of Ireland, thus enabling them to have a better knowledge of each other's country.

In disposition Norman Campbell was a cool, shrewd, calculating boy, studying well the chances for and against matters; but his besetting sin was his inordinate love "o' the siller." Catch him spending an idle penny; and then, as Captain Cuttle said, "when found, make a note of it." His father, the old Scotchman, had never ceased inculcating in his son's mind that "it was gold and siller that made the man," and the son promised never to forget his father's advice.

Alfred Ravensborne was the son of the Honourable Plantagenet Montmorency Ravensborne, the seventh son of a greatly impoverished peer, and the allowance made by the earl to his youngest child came to just one thousand pounds per annum. Alfred's father had no "fashionable follies;" by making a book upon all the "great events" of the year, he managed to keep his head above *water*, and *tide* over many difficulties.

"Make no enemies, but as many friends as you can," was the motto of the father of Alfred. He was a subtle, cunning man, one who never hesitated quietly and unseen to remove any obstacle from his path, no matter by what means.

Alfred was the only son, and as Doctor Birchenough's was not only respectable but reasonable, it came within the scope of his father's means.

His mother died a few days after his birth, so that he never had the good advice and counsel of man's best friend, "his mother."

When Alfred and Giles first met, they looked fiercely into each other's eyes, and a feeling of hate arose in the breast of the former, and to which he could assign no cause; and when Giles advanced and frankly stretched out his hand, the first impulse of Ravensborne was to dash it aside.

Six months passed over, when one day, at cricket, a lesser boy than Alfred gave him some trivial offence. In a moment of rage, he made a desperate blow at the boy with his bat, but before the fatal blow could reach the lad it was wrested from him, and he found himself on his back.

He was soon again on his feet.

"How dare you interfere?" he said, eying Giles sternly.

"How dare you attempt to strike a boy smaller than yourself with the bat? Even with your fist, it would have been wrong, but with the bat—it was most cowardly. Think better of it, Alfred."

"Indeed!" and he looked scornfully upon him.

"Yes, *indeed!* Alfred Ravensborne. I say cowardly."

"And you call me a coward?" And Alfred's cheeks flushed crimson.

"Yes," was the cool answer.

Alfred Ravensborne was not deficient in courage, but he knew well the strength and courage of Giles Evergreen. He paused.

"Had you not better tell the doctor?" he said.

"I never tell tales, sir," was the reply; "but I should advise you not to use a cricket-bat about a boy's head again, or it will lead you into an awkward scrape."

"And if it does, I shall not ask Giles Evergreen to get me out of it." And so saying, he walked off, followed by three or four boys.

The rest stayed behind, and sent a hearty hiss after Ravensborne and his party.

Subtle in his nature, he pondered day after day how he should revenge himself upon Giles; but while at school no opportunity presented itself.

By the great majority of the boys he was thoroughly detested. This he knew; but he met it with a smile, while the demon Murder was lurking in his heart, and thirsting for an opportunity of wreaking his vengeance upon Giles and his friends. And so, like a crafty, subtle tiger, he waited until his spring could be at once deadly and certain.

Terence Flaherty O'Flanagan was commonly called Ted Flan by his schoolmates. He was the only son of a poor Irish gentleman, who used to say of himself that his paternal mansion was the healthiest in the country, for it hadn't even a *pane* (of glass) in its body, and that there was plenty of game, if you knew where to find it;

but it was not convanient to *reckon* in, for there was not a *slate* on the roof, and the cellar was *full* of *empty* bottles of wine, and that the fish-pond once gave excellent sport, but they dwindled down to one poor Jack, who, having lost his Jill, died of solitary confinement.

For seven years of his life Terence played the part of a "Wild Irish Boy;" occasionally the monotony of his life was relieved by the "man in possession," and, strange to say, the only time he cried, was when the man was *paid out*, and *went out.*

Terence's father having lived a fast life, had contrived to *gallop* to the "end of his tether," and the only means of subsistence he had was an annuity allowed him by his wife's sister, an Englishwoman. To all her kind entreaties that the boy should be sent to her he was deaf; he loved the boy, although he was addicted to putting hot coals in his boots, fine sand in his hat, and cayenne pepper on his toast. But one cold winter's day a visitor who will not be denied called and claimed him, and poor Ted Flan was alone in the world.

A few weeks after, he found himself residing in England with his good relative, and very soon after became a resident at Doctor Birchenough's. At first Terence's back and the cane became daily acquaintances, but, animated by the example of Giles Evergreen, he soon got well to his studies. His propensity for fun and larking nothing could subdue.

"I've got a bit of a sacret to confide to you, Giles," said Ted Flan, one after-noon; "but whisper, are you fond of grapes?"

"Yes; why?"

"Do you like them for supper?"

"Any time," said Giles.

"Then not a word to the cat; plase the pigs, this night we'll have an illigant desert—for supper."

"I think I perceive your plan, Ted," and Giles pointed to the splendid vine that adorned the front of the house, covered with a hundred bunches of luscious fruit.

"By the powers you're as wise as the ould pigeon who knew how many peas made five. Ha-ha! wait awhile, my darlin', and we'll have such a feast of grapes!"

"But I'm not quite certain that the act is a right one," said Giles.

"Batherashin! to the four corners of the airth with you and your act! It's no act at all, but merely a lark; besides, didn't the doctor say the other day that the grapes were like his *corns*, they wanted *cutting*."

"Who is to be in it?" said Giles, laughing.

"Yourself, myself, Soft Tommy, and Cannie Sawney; the illigant Master Alfred stays with papa at the hotel for the night, and——"

At that moment the approach of the worthy doctor broke off the conversation.

The night came, and an hour after all had retired to rest the plan of action had been decided upon. The best steel tongs were to be got out of the draw-ing-room, Tommy was to hold the stalk by them, Terence was to hold tight of Tommy, while Giles, having tied a penknife to a long stick, was to cut the bunch.

Norman declined having anything to do with it; he didn't see that any "siller" was to be made by it, and there was a risk, and so the three were left to do the work themselves.

The moon shone out brightly.

Soft Tommy leaned out of the window, Terence holding him by the leg, and seized a bunch, and just as Giles was about to sever the stalk, Terence uttered a cry of terror. A cat that had hid itself in the room brushed past the Irish boy's legs, and in his fright he let loose his hold of Soft Tommy's leg, and away went Tommy and the steel tongs, with a crash, into the playground.

"What ails you, Ted? You've killed Tommy," said Giles.

"It's myself that's killed, and murdered with fright. A ghost tickled me on the calf of my leg, and it's more than mortal boy could stand. Oh! what'll I do?"

"Do! we must get Tommy Jolter up at all hazards," said Giles.

"I'll throw myself after him," said Terence.

"Stuff! hold your tongue, Tommy," whispered Giles; "are you hurt?"

"Broke my neck!" replied Tommy, 'I mean my ankle."

"Nonsense! I'll lower a blanket. Lay tight hold of it, and we'll pull you up."

This was quickly done, and Tommy and tongs were again safely in the room; but all was not over; some old women, who had been to market and were returning home, saw something white dangling from the window.

Their screams rang loudly through the air.

Up started the doctor, and up went the window.

"What's the matter, you squalling beldames, eh?" asked the doctor, his head covered with a large white cap.

"A ghost! a ghost!" screamed the women.

"Where? where?" shouted the doctor.

"There! there!" replied the women, pointing to the window, which had been quietly closed.

"Stuff and nonsense! Go home and get to bed, and next market day don't drink such strong ale," and the doctor slammed the window down.

As soon as all was quiet, Giles went over to Tommy's bed, and, guessing the lad had sprained his ankle, he bound it tightly round with a handkerchief, and returned.

"What was it frightened you, Ted?" asked Giles.

"It must have been the inimy of us all," said Terence, "it was so soft. Oh, murder! my teeth are chattering in my head like a broken-winded horse, and I shake—quite—onnateral. Och, murder! no more grapes for Terence Flaherty O'Flanagan."

CHAPTER III.

AT NIGHT.

Two nights after the conversation recorded in our last number the house was destroyed; and, the day after the fire, all having recovered from their fright and fatigue, preparations were made for sending the young gentlemen to their several destinations.

Alfred Ravensborne and Norman Campbell were dispatched to London, the one to his father's club, the other to a lodging-house in the neighbourhood of Camden Town.

Their parting from their playmates was cold and formal, and the worthy doctor was grieved to see it.

Tommy Jolter was fetched away in his father's chaise by Sister Suke.

"I'll find thee out soon as I be well, danged if I don't. Thee saved my life, Giles Evergreen, and as long as I've got a brass farden, or a vether to fly with, I don't forget it; if I do, may feyther's cantankerous bull send me a flying. I zay, Ted Flan, don't thee forget tongs." With that, soft but grateful Tommy drove off.

Mr. Sheepshanks having heard of the catastrophe, arrived in the course of the day.

"What's all this, Birchenough, eh?" said the lawyer. "Rather a serious affair."

"Yes; might have been worse, but for that brave lad."

The tale was told.

"Ah," said the lawyer, taking a pinch of snuff, while his grey eyes twinkled again, "heard all about it; didn't believe it. Chip of the old block, without the rotten wood. Build the school up again, I suppose?"

"Yes; I've plenty to live upon; but I love the Boys of England."

"Right! stick to your last—I mean your cane."

"The fate, often wished by the boys, I daresay, has happened to it—it is burnt," replied the doctor.

"Ha, ha!—well well; I must be off. Assizes come on day after to-morrow—heavy calendar—forgery, murder, arson, burglary, and many other little eccentricities of human nature too numerous to mention. Now, boys."

"Well, good-bye, Ted Flan; we shall meet again, old fellow," and Giles warmly grasped his hand.

"Meet again," said the lawyer; "who said you were going to part?"

"What do you mean?" said Birchenough.

"Mean? I know Master Terence Flaherty O'Flanagan's aunt well; am her legal adviser. He goes home with me to-morrow; we have a little matter of business to settle. Now, then, boys, we've only got ten minutes to catch the train, and then a hundred miles to ride."

The two boys were ready, and that cheerfully, for they were going together, and felt happy and delighted that they were not parted.

"Giles Evergreen," said the doctor, grasping his hand, "you will hear from me. Never, never, shall I forget the heroic act of last night."

They parted, and some time passed over their heads ere they met again.

A few hours after, the lawyer, with the two boys, were seated at a capital dinner in his old mansion.

The cloth cleared, the old gentleman made Terence (for Giles stoutly refused) relate all about the fire, more than once.

The next day was a busy one for the lawyer; the assizes rendered him doubly busy, and clients were continually passing in and out.

Towards the middle of the day, the bustle somewhat ceased, and sending for the boys into his study, he bade them be seated.

"Master Terence Flaherty O'Flanagan, I address you first, because, being Irish, you'll take the longest to understand."

"You overpower me, sir; but I have a great objection to blarney," said Ted Flan. "Soft soap isn't an article I dale in."

"I think you'd make a capital lawyer, you'd bother the old one himself."

"Oh, thank you, sir, Is the old one your friend?—is he a client of yours?"

"What do you mean, sir?"

"Ah, sir, you see I am Irish, and don't know what I mane; I take a long time to understand."

"You are laughing at me, sir," said the lawyer.

"The divil a smile have I on my face, sir."

"Silence; I suppose you remember your aunt?"

"May p'ison be my drink if ever I forget her."

"She is going to provide for you."

"May her shadow never go out of sight."

"You start for London in a day or two."

"Oh, murder! I'll be taken in and done for. I've read of that same place, London. Is it true the paving stones are made of gould?" and Ted winked at Giles.

"Nonsense; you'll have to get your living."

"What at? Is it to be a hod living?"

"Listen, boy; you will have some time given you to decide."

"That's time enough; mayhap I'll be transported before that."

"I think it very likely," muttered the lawyer, "or hanged."

"What for?"

"Not for foolishness."

"Ah! sir, when your time comes, I know what it will be for."

"My time?—well, sir, what for?"

"For wit and common sense; you've got them in an eminent degree—powerful like."

"That will do; you understand me."

"He must have a head of stone that couldn't."

"You and Giles will go to London together," said the lawyer.

"What! Giles and I go together? Then it's a wapping big fortune we'll make; and the first thing we'll do is to build up the ould school again, if it ain't done before, and make you the masther. I wouldn't be a boy, for a larrupin' then, no, not for my father's ould house, that ought to be standin', only they pulled it down to prevent its falling. If ever there were two bits of sticking plasther, it's Giles and Terence —hurroo—Pat's a darling boy!" and here he became so excited that he began dancing an Irish jig.

"Be quiet, sir," roared the lawyer; "what will the people think?"

"A fig for the people."

"Will you be quiet, sir," shouted the lawyer.

"I am as dumb as a dead drummer, and as quiet as a milestone that can't spake. Giles," and he grasped his hand, "I'll never forget the night of the fire, when you made me go first; if I do, may——"

An expressive look from the grey eyes of Lawyer Sheepshanks effectually silenced Terence.

"And now, Giles Evergreen," said the lawyer, turning to him, "I have some few words to say to you. You are about to launch your boat upon the troubled waters of the world, and you must take care and keep a sharp look-out that you are not wrecked. You will have ample time given you to enable you to judge of a profession; so that when it is determined on, it must not be abandoned lightly. In the great metropolis to which you are going you will be exposed to many temptations; whatever their nature, do not let any consideration tempt you from the path of honesty."

"It never shall," said Giles, warmly.

"If he does," said Ted O'Flanagan, "I'll blow my own brains out first, and settle his hash afterwards."

Sheepshanks smiled.

"I don't think there is much fear of any harm coming to either of you while you are so united."

"I think not," replied Giles; "for though boys, we can take care of ourselves."

"Take care! by my conscience, while the rose," said Ted, taking the hand of Giles, and grasping it, "and the shamrock remain firm to each other, harm will be many a day's march behind us —especially," he said, with a sly grin at Sheepshanks, "when we've got the law on our side."

"That's what you call blarney, Terence."

"The deuce a bit, sir; it's a lagal truth."

At that moment a knock was heard at the door.

"My clerk, I suppose. Come in, Pounce."

The door opened; but instead of Pounce, Tom Jolter, the elder, Tommy, the younger, and sister Suke, stood at the door.

In another instant Tommy was along with his two schoolfellows, while Suke stood staring at the boxes and piles of papers in the lawyer's sanctum sanctorum.

"Well, Jolter, what do you want, eh?" said Sheepshanks.

"I want law, master," replied the farmer.

"Stuff, nonsense! I thought you'd had enough of that."

"Nay, nay, I won't give in while I've a brass farden."

"What's the matter? A row with Weale?"

"Yes; but this time it will be a reformation of car-rack-ter."

"That's very much needed for both of you. Defamation, I suppose you mean?"

"It's one and the same thing," said the farmer. "Just you read that," placing a newspaper before him; "and then there's another matter I want to ask your opinion upon."

"Ah, well, sit down—and you too, Miss Suke—and I'll look into the affair."

The farmer and Suke seated themselves in front of the lawyer, who commenced reading the alleged libel.

Now, at the back of old Jolter and his daughter stood a heavy, tall screen; behind that our three heroes had retired to talk over their own affairs.

"Were you ever in a lawyer's office before, Tommy?" asked Giles.

"Never, in my varsal life. It be a mortal queer place," and Tommy stared round with his eyes opened to their fullest extent.

"You may say that," said Ted Flan, winking at Giles, who at once perceived that he was bent upon some mischief.

"What do they keep in those boxes?" whispered Tommy, pointing to three large iron chests on the floor.

Ted Flan pretended to shiver.

"Habeas corpses," replied Ted.

Giles took the cue like a well-experienced actor in an instant.

"Eh, my dear heart!" and his red head bristled up like quills upon the fretful porcupine. "You don't mean dead bodies, eh? Let us get out of this," said Tommy, clinging to Giles.

"Stuff, batherashin! They won't hurt you, Tommy. They can't move until a judge gives them leave."

"And what be in the small uns?" and he pointed to those on the shelf.

"That one," replied Ted Flan, with a face as imperturbable as a brass knocker, pointing to one upon which a mass of papers was placed, "is full of apples and oranges; and such nuts, Tommy."

Ted and Giles knew the fruitful failing of the country boy.

Tommy smacked his lips and gazed wistfully at the box.

"Would you like some, Tommy?" said Giles.

"By the powers, his mouth waters like the River Shannon," whispered Ted.

"How can we get up there?" asked Tommy.

"We get up. By my conscience, Tommy, you're the boy to do that nately. Stand on my shoulders."

"Don't you let me go, as you did about the grapes, Ted Flan; it's lucky I didn't fall on my head."

"Oh, bother! you wouldn't have hurt then. Up you go, Tommy, or you'll be too late."

In another moment Tommy was on Ted Flan's shoulders, but then he could scarcely reach the box.

"Cling hold of the shelf," whispered Giles.

"Are you all right, darlin'?" asked Ted Flan.

"Yes, I be right," said Tommy.

"Then hold on tight," and, so saying, Ted slid from under him.

And there hung Soft Tommy, looking down with woeful face, frightened nearly out of his wits, but afraid to call out for fear of rousing the lawyer, whom he held in great fear.

"GILES EVERGREEN'S 'ACT OF BRAVERY.'"

No. 2.

"Lay hold of the cord round the box, Tommy," said Giles.

Tommy obeyed; he made a desperate clutch at the box, and grasped it, when down came the box, the shelf, and a mass of papers that had not been disturbed for years.

Down went the screen upon the farmer and Sister Suke!

The latter, springing up, and thinking the house was falling, uttered a piercing yell, and, throwing her arms tightly round the lawyer's neck, nearly throttled him.

For some minutes the clouds of dust rolled over them, so that nothing could be discerned.

When they had rolled away the room was empty, so far as Giles, Ted, and Tommy were concerned, but the cries of Farmer Jolter under the screen, the screams of Suke, and the half-strangled tones of the lawyer, resounded through the house, alarming all in it.

CHAPTER IV.

FUN AND ITS CONSEQUENCES.

TAKING advantage of the thick clouds of dust the boys steered off, and, in a few minutes, were safe out in the street.

The town itself was large, but rather straggling, and, it being market day, and the one before the assizes were to be held, was exceedingly full. Like many other towns, the market was held in the high or principal street.

Here might have been seen some outdoor amusements, in the penny show line, from the "Battle of Waterloo," to the penny play of the "Siege of Lucknow."

Giles and Ted at once had plenty of scope for fun, and, as their blood was warmed, they determined to enjoy themselves.

"It will be necessary to buy some pase and two pase-shooters," said Ted to Giles.

"A capital idea, Ted," said Giles.

"How do you feel, Tommy, my lad, eh?"

"Oh, I don't like it at all; feyther won't forget me in a hurry," said Tommy.

"What, with the stick liquorice?" said Ted.

So saying he went into the toy-shop close by, and shortly afterwards made his appearance with two pea-shooters of somewhat formidable dimensions.

Tommy was dispatched to purchase peas.

Being thus armed they looked round for the "unfortunate wight" upon whom they could commence operations.

Two itinerant showmen seemed to hold out the most attraction.

The old saying that "two of a trade can seldom agree" was in this instance verified. The tide of success seemed to set in upon the Battle of Waterloo (old as it was), and the unfortunate proprietor of the Indian Mutiny scowled darkly upon the fortunate manager of Waterloo and Bonaparte.

Ted Flan, therefore, faced the Indian; Giles, Waterloo and " Up guards, and at 'em !" or, as Ted Flan had it, " Up guards, and ate 'em !"

Suddenly the Lucknow (who didn't seem to be in luck now at all) manager started, and, dropping his trumpet, rubbed his nose with an awful vigour and ferocity ; at the same instant the rival showman exhibited the same fearful emotion, dropping a penny he was taking in the mud, and his luck at the same time.

" Wot's the little game now, Boneypart ?" shouted out Lucknow.

" Stash that game, my blood-red Injun, or the kon-see-quee-ences may be fatal !" retorted Waterloo.

At that moment a well-directed shot from Ted Flan roused the blood of the Lucknow hero, so that dropping the trumpet, and buttoning up his treasury-pocket, he rushed at his rival ; at the same time the " hero of a hundred fights " received a well-aimed shot upon his vermilion-coloured nose, that made it flow with " more than its wonted fires."

" You're not satisfied with taking all the trade ; but you must hadd hinsult to injury.   What's the extensive meaning of this, eh, Jemmy ?"

" I axes you the same kevestion, and I should advise you not to come any of your larks with me. Wait until the commercial business of the day is over, and we'll settle it, my pippin."

And so saying, he turned away.

A stinging shot upon the ears of both, and then, with a rush and run, Waterloo and Lucknow were engaged in deadly conflict.

The women shouted, the men hal_looed, the boys huzzahed, and more than one fight seemed imminent ; but the love of money triumphed over their injured honour, and when they arose from the mud, " dirtied but not disgraced," they mutually agreed to settle their differences " arter supper."

Casting their eyes around, they fell upon Soft Tommy, who was laughing and capering about, and enjoying the spree.

" That's the warmint ! " shouted Waterloo.

" Collar him !" roared Lucknow, in answer, making a dash at him.

Tommy, seeing he had, with his usual luck, become Phil Garlic, started off, followed by the infuriated showmen, and a mob of men, women, and children, highly relishing the fun of the exciting chase, Ted and Giles, as well as laughing would permit, plying the retreating mob well with grape pea shot.

Tommy was an excellent runner, as well as jumper, and kept pretty well ahead ; but perceiving a disposition on the part of a man to intercept him, he took a flying leap over an old woman who sat before two crates of eggs she was exposing for sale.

Tommy cleared it as cleverly as ever did steeple-chaser his fence.

Not so the two showmen—jump they couldn't an inch—it was too late to pull up, so, with a shout and yell of despair, the egg-vendor, Waterloo, and Lucknow lay floundering, kicking, and swearing among hundreds of smashed eggs.

The roar of exultation when they rose and faced the crowd, their faces and clothes streaming with the yolks of the eggs, was heard from one end of the market-place to the other.

By this time Tommy was safe out of the range of any further pursuit. The woman and her husband were waging battle with the showmen, while the mob heightened the scene by pelting each other with the sound eggs that the unfortunate roll and tumble had left.

Giles and Ted Flan, with the tears running down their cheeks from excessive laughter, moved off the scene in search of Tommy.

The cattle market was about a quarter of a mile from the spot they were then in, and so to that they wended their way.

Reaching it, they were discerned by Tommy, who soon joined them, and enjoyed a hearty laugh over the fun they had just caused.

The market itself was crowded with animals, and the attendance of the farmers and graziers was very numerous.

In the centre, tied to a post, was a fine bull, who seemed to be by no means pleased with his situation. He pawed and snorted, at times tossing up his magnificent head, and sending forth a tremendous bellow as though it were a trumpet of defiance to some unseen enemy ; and at times he tugged at the rope, that seemed to bend the stout post like a reed.

"Giles, my aarlin'," whispered Ted Flan, "that bull is a countryman of mine ; you know my country is celebrated for bulls."

"He is a fine, noble fellow," said Giles ; "but he don't seem to be in a very good humour. What do you think, Tommy ?"

"Why, I think," grinned Tommy, "that if he should get loose, the longest legs will stand the best chance."

At that moment the bull, who had been tugging and straining at the rope, was assailed by a dog, one of a mongrel breed.

The noble beast took but little notice of him.

But the crowd kept urging the dog on, and irritating the animal by shouting.

"Shame ! shame !" said Giles, to one of the foremost ruffians.

"By the powers, those fellows deserve a good bating, Giles," said Ted.

The leader of the mob jeered Giles and Ted.

"Do you call yourselves men," said the former, "goading and using the noble animal in that way ? You'll suffer for it, mark my words."

Scarcely were the words uttered, when the rope snapped.

The wild, untamed bull was free !

For a moment he stood surveying the crowd.

For an instant the terrified mob stood as though paralysed, then, with a cry of horror, they fled.

A charge of cavalry could not have cleared the place quicker.

Giles and Ted Flan rushed into a grocer's shop; the former, seizing an iron bar used to open hogsheads with, stood prepared to defend himself and friend, while Ted sprang like a roe into an empty sugar hogshead.

As though it had been the dead, still hour of night, the place was clear of human beings.

All had fled, leaving their goods and wares to the mercy of Ted Flan's countryman.

Soon a pieman's shop was seen flying through the air; then the stock-in-trade of a hatter was seen whirling about, performing the most absurd gyrations. Then, with a loud bellow, he stood surveying the " vantage of the ground."

A looking-glass maker's soon attracted his attention, and a splendid pier glass reflecting his wrathful visage in it, he roared a defiance; in a moment he was through the shop window, and everything lay in ruins.

Suddenly the sound of trumpets was heard in the distance, and bleeding from various parts of the body, the mad beast leaped again into the street.

Giles, with the natural courage and daring of the British Boy, emerged from his retreat in search of his companions.

" Ted Flan, where are you?" he said.

" Oh, I'm in a swate retreat," said a voice from inside the sugar cask; " I'm clean dead and kilt with fright."

" Come out, Ted, all is safe."

" Yes; as safe as a man sitting on a barrel of gunpowder."

" How do you like your countryman?" said Giles.

Ted's head was seen above the hogshead.

" Not a bit. The West Indies be praised for my deliverance !"

" Well, jump out; the fun is not over yet."

With that they peeped out at the door.

The sheriff's cavalcade, headed by the javelin men, had just entered the market place, ushering in the judges for the forthcoming assizes.

The trumpeter who headed it wore a red cap and cloak; the cloth that covered his horse was red. His trumpet rang out cheerily, and at the sound the bull sprang out of the plate-glass shop, and with a stamp of his foot, eyed him sternly, and then sounded his roar of defiance.

" By the powers ! I wouldn't give a pinch of snuff for the trumpeter's chance," said Ted.

The man, perceiving how matters stood, wheeled his horse suddenly round, and galloped up a lane like mad.

With a roar and a bound the bull was after him, and as soon as the market-place was clear the cavalcade made a quick retreat to the place of their destination, thankful for their escape.

Giles and Ted Flan, seeing the coast clear, rushed forth.

" Now for home !" said Giles.

" Let's be off, or the bull will be down upon us," replied Flan.

" You are right, Ted, for here he comes."

The door of every house was shut against them, and so escape seemed hopeless.

In the High Street, however, there were two inns.

They both had high posts in the front with their respective signs, the one the Crown, the other the Angel.

"We must climb up those, Ted," shouted Giles.

"With all the pleasure in life," replied the Irish boy. "By my conscience, we've done higher than that at old Birchenough's. Hurroo, Pat! the Angel for ever!" and up went Ted Flan like a cat.

"I'll stand by the Crown, as all British boys will," shouted Giles, and showing the same agility as Ted, he was soon up.

Scarcely had they reached the top when the loud shouts of the mob, but at a great distance, told them they had not been a minute too soon.

At the same moment a figure, completely encased in mud from head to foot, came running in the same direction.

There was a large heavy crate of crockery standing in the road, opposite the Crown; behind it the figure darted.

"Hurroo! more power to you, my lad!" shouted Ted. "Stick as hard to that same crate, as an Irishman sticks to the cratur."

"Conceal yourself, my lad," shouted Giles, "Mr. Pitch-and-Toss is coming."

"Be that you, Giles Evergreen?"

"Yes. Who are you?"

"Tommy Jolter."

"By the powers, instead of Soft Tommy you shall be called Black Tommy. Hold hard! my countryman, he comes."

A tremendous clattering of hoofs was heard, and the trumpeter's horse came galloping down the road—but without its rider."

"By the powers," said Ted Flan, "the trumpeter's gone to glory!"

"Or part of the way, if the bull has tossed him," replied Giles.

The horse had been at one time a celebrated hunter and steeple-chaser, and the old blood was still within him.

On the right-hand side of the road was a wall enclosing the house and grounds of a gentleman; it was about eight feet in height.

Over this the gallant horse went like a rocket, while his pursuer, blown and heated by a long chase, pulled up, and, gazing at the flying horse with astonishment, gave a tremendous bellow, stamping his foot upon the ground with rage and fury.

"Hurrah! hurrah!" shouted the excited British boys, as the gallant grey cleared the wall, and was lost to sight.

The infuriated beast looked up from whence the sounds proceeded, and he ran blindly at the sign-post.

"Hold on, Ted!" shouted Giles.

"As tight as a miser does to his gould," was the reply.

Almost tired out, the bull seemed about to retire from the contest.

The mob, hissing, groaning, and by other noises, irritated the poor dumb animal.

"Shame! shame!" shouted the two noble-hearted boys; "why not let the poor brute rest? It is through you he has been goaded into madness."

The only answer from the brutal mob was a loud jeering laugh of derision.

At that moment, Soft Tommy popped his head up from behind the crate.

In an instant the animal fixed his eyes upon him.

He uttered a roar of defiance, and,

lashing his sides with his tail, dashed at the crate.

The pots and pans rattled gloriously, but the crate stood firm as a rock.

Again and again the crowd shouted at him, which made him dash still more furiously at the obstruction between him and poor Tommy; but finding his efforts of no use he, altered his tactics.

He ran furiously round it.

But Tommy was up to him, and was on the other side in an instant, and thus they went on dodging each other.

Foiled in all his attempts to get at Tommy, he bellowed loudly with rage and mortification.

Again he sprang at the crate, and with such force that it seemed falling to pieces.

Tommy's life was in fearful peril.

Giles saw this, and his brave heart sank within him.

"Can nothing be done to save our dear old schoolfellow?" he called to Ted.

"I'd give all my pocket-money for the next twelve months to be able to do it," was the reply.

But suddenly the poor deaf and dumb girl, whose life had been preserved by the bravery of the British boy and the no less brave Irish one, appeared at the window of the " Crown."

She seemed to realise in a moment the horrors of the situation, and gave Giles a look of deep meaning.

She disappeared for a moment, and then as quickly returned, bearing in her hand a gun.

This she handed to Giles, and by signs informed him that it was loaded.

During this short interval the fury of the maddened animal exceeded all bounds.

The crate lay dashed to pieces.

Tommy would be at the mercy of his tremendous assailant; he was already weakened by his great efforts to escape and if he had had the chance, could not have run fifty yards.

"Giles Evergreen—Ted Flan!" he shrieked; "save me—save me! you did so once."

" And will do so again at the hazard of my life," replied Giles, nimbly descending, holding the gun in one hand, while he assisted his descent with the other.

"I'm an egg in the same basket," shouted Ted; "bull or no bull," as he swung down from his lofty position.

Giles, once on the ground, gave a loud shout of defiance from behind the post; Ted doing the same from his.

This caused the animal to turn round, as poor Tommy, utterly exhausted, sank on the ground. For a moment the animal gazed at Giles, and seemed to be gathering strength for the rush of death.

The deadly rifle was held steadily at the shoulder, Not a limb or muscle of the brave British boy trembled; the eye looked calm and collected at his enemy.

Then the maddened brute prepared for his deadly rush.

He was too late.

The murderous weapon belched forth its contents ; the aim was true ; the ball went through the star upon the animal's forehead with a crash.

The ponderous beast lay a lifeless mass upon the earth.

The mob raised a loud shout of exultation.

Giles and Ted Flan ran and helped up Tommy, who soon recovered from his fright.

Separating themselves from the crowd, who were brutally exulting over the dead carcase of the poor animal they had goaded on to madness, the boys made for home with all the speed they could.

The office being open they rushed in.

The lawyer, Suke, Jolter, clerks and servants, ran out in a state of wonder and astonishment.

"Who the deuce are you?" asked the lawyer of Tommy, not recognising him in his livery of mud.

"Soft Tommy," was the reply.

Suke screamed out.

"Don't squall," and old Tough Mutton grinned.

"Where have you come from?"

"From the bottom of the town ditch," was the reply.

At this announcement, and the sight of the figure before them, the whole party burst into a hearty laugh.

Tommy, to escape from the bull when it commenced its mad career, jumped over a low wall that bounded the black ditch that ran outside the town, and, sticking hard and fast in the mud, for a time escaped from the fury of the infuriated animal.

The lawyer ordered Tommy to be led away and undergo a process of soap and scrubbing previous to his appearance at the dinner table.

Shortly after the lawyer became aware of what had taken place in the town ; he felt inwardly pleased at the pluck and courage displayed by the boys, and was certain they would not disgrace him when they were working their way in the great metropolis, to which they would shortly hasten.

CHAPTER V.

A DINNER, AND ITS RESULT.

A few hours after, Lawyer Sheepshanks, Farmer Jolter, his son and daughter, Giles and Ted Flan, were seated round the lawyer's hospitable board.

A suit of Giles' clothes had been put on Tommy, and, considering they were somewhat too long for him, he looked remarkably well.

The lawyer, glad that he had escaped from the toil and trouble of the day, was in high spirits, and had carried out his father's views and dress, as upon all great occasions.

He wore a full court suit of the reign of George III.; a well-powdered wig with a long queue, or pig-tail, and a dress sword, completed the *tout en-*

semble of a gentleman of the old school.

The Jolter family had never been at a dinner party before, and looked upon all the arrangements of the table with wonder and amazement; the splendid cut glass, the dazzling side-board of plate, the paintings, and the whole appearance of the room, excited their astonishment.

Giles was seated next to Tommy, and Ted Flan did the honours to Suke Jolter.

"By my conscience!" Ted Flan whispered in Suke Jolter's ear, and pointed to the lawyer, "it's me own great, great grandfather that's walked out of a gould frame in a bad frame of mind. Oh, what would I give for a wig like that!"

At this Suke laughed outright.

Old Jolter frowned at her, and growling, muttered—

"Thee hadst best go home, if thee can't behave thyself better."

"No, no,' said the lawyer; "let all enjoy themselves in their own way, and do as they like."

"You hear that?" said Ted Flan. "We'll see about that by and bye," and he winked in such a peculiar way at Suke, that the soup she was swallowing nearly went the wrong way.

As it was, every mouthful she took brought the tears into her eyes.

Master Ted Flan had dosed it powerfully with cayenne, so that Suke's throat felt as if it had ten thousand fires in it.

Giles, of course, was not behind in his attentions to Tommy, and his face resembled a water-course.

"Blow the soup, it's like vire! I say, Giles, put a lot of cold water to it; it be burning a hole in my throat!" and Tommy gasped for breath.

"Stuff! nonsense. It's the fashion, Tommy."

"Blow the fashion!" said Tommy. "It be a main hot one."

Tommy pushed his plate away.

"That won't do, man. The lawyer won't be best pleased if he sees that."

And so Tommy, fearful of exciting the anger of the lawyer, pulled the plate back again, and with many odd contortions of countenance that more than once nearly upset the gravity of the mischief makers, he finished the contents, washing it down with such copious draughts of water as almost alarmed the old man-servant who waited at the dinner table.

The attentions of Ted Flan to Suke Jolter were of the same assiduous description.

She was a most extraordinary girl to look at.

She had an intense red head of hair, red cheeks which extended to the nose, red arms and hands, and, as she rubbed the tears away, she made herself look redder and redder, or, as Ted said, "like a bunch of radishes."

He recommended strong Chili vinegar to cool the soup, and mild mustard to mollify the vinegar.

"I ginerally take salad oil myself in soup; it was a custom of my father's—rest him!—and will do you good," said Ted Flan, pouring a quantity into her plate.

"But why," said Suke, "do they want to make it so plaguy hot, eh?"

"It's the custom in all cold countries.

Kape close to me, and I'll be the making of you. Take some more? Ah, that's jolly !"

At last the fish was placed upon table, and here the unfortunate pair were dosed with such a mixture of sauces as would have puzzled the great Soyer himself.

But the crowning act of the feast was the recommendation of the anchovy sauce and soy to the roast beef.

Tommy was delighted with it, and swallowed it greedily.

" I say, Giles, they didn't give us such scrumptious gravy as this at old Birchenough's. Ecod! I'll have some more." And more he had.

Suke, like a good whist player, followed suit with her brother.

Then followed many other good things —puddings, pies, &c., &c.—of all of which they partook to repletion.

The lawyer was a wealthy man, and kept a good table, a custom worthy of imitation everywhere.

At an early hour they all retired.

Old Jolter went back to the inn to enjoy his pipe and grog, Suke was placed under the care of the old housekeeper, while a large room at the top of the house had been prepared for the boys.

The lawyer himself retired to his study, having important documents to prepare, which would take him half the night to do.

In a room upstairs, Giles, Ted Flan, and Tommy Jolter had retired to rest.

Ted Flan had proposed a joke upon Tommy to Giles, but they were so fatigued with the excitement of the day that they were glad to resign themselves to slumber.

Giles, however, felt very restless, starting up almost every moment, fancying that the bull was rushing upon him, and that he had not the power of stirring or preventing it.

Ted Flan slept as sound as a rock, and Tommy snored heavily.

A light had been left burning in the room.

All at once Giles saw Tommy rise up in the bed, get out, and proceed towards the light.

He was about to call out, when he remembered that Tommy had, when at school, several times been caught walking in his sleep ; and such was the case at that moment.

Tommy was fast asleep, although his senses were wide awake.

The unfortunate habit that he had of somnambulism was still further increased by the hearty dinner, and the various mixtures he had partaken of.

Giles regarded him attentively, and, at first, thought of waking Ted Flan ; but, on second thoughts, knowing the Irish boy's propensity for larking, he did not do so.

Tommy proceeded with great deliberation to take up the light.

Then Giles heard him mutter something like the following—

" Sister Suke's currant jelly is the best in the world."

" Oh, oh !" thought Giles, " Master Tommy fancies he is at home, and is on an expedition to the preserve and pickle cupboard."

He slipped out of bed, and, putting on his trousers, he determined to follow

Tommy, and watch the result of this nocturnal adventure.

Tommy opened the door, and then carefully listened.

"Feyther and Suke be fast asleep," he muttered; and with that he went cautiously down the well-carpeted stairs, followed silently by Giles.

On the same night Suke Jolter, who likewise inherited her brother's propensity to wander in her slumbers, was considerably disturbed in her sleep.

She imagined that she was at home, but she likewise dreamed that somebody was going to the old stocking in which she kept her savings.

Suke was a most inveterate miser.

This, in addition to the dinner she had eaten, discomposed her so much, that her old fit of somnambulism came on her.

Finding, on reaching her bed-room, that her face was very hot—the combined effects of the cayenne pepper and other little matters—she had covered it well over with powder, so that, what with her long red locks, and the white night-cap she wore, it gave her a very spectral appearance.

A few minutes before Tommy had emerged from his bed-chamber, Suke had also walked from hers, and proceeded, as she thought, downstairs, to preserve the precious old stocking and its contents.

The old lawyer had been for some time engaged in a very important case of lunacy, in which one of the parties laboured under the impression that he was ghost haunted.

Although a strong-minded man, he was slightly tinged with superstition, and often in the dead of the night, when engaged in laborious study, fancied strange things haunted the room.

He was intent upon reading a letter in which the party described his feelings at witnessing the shade of a departed sister, and how she came regularly to his bedside in the dead hour of the night.

"Ah," said the lawyer, laying down the letter, "I can well believe what his feelings are. Grief for the loss, and study combined, have for a time clouded the reason; but as for ghosts, hobgoblins, and all that sort of thing—rubbish, stuff, nonsense!"

Did his ears deceive him, or was it the handle of the door that moved?

Look round he could not.

Suddenly he felt a hand placed upon the top of his venerated father's pig-tail, and it left his head, showing him as bald as when he was born.

A cold perspiration ran down him; then, by a desperate effort, he started up and saw to his horror—A Ghost!

His presence of mind deserted him.

"Murder! murder!" he shouted, springing up and rushing to the door.

The noise awoke Suke, who, shrieking at the position she was placed in, seized hold of the lawyer by the coat-tails, and was by him dragged from the room.

At the same time, from a room upstairs, were heard loud shrieks and cries.

Tommy, in his sleep, had entered the old housekeeper's room.

It was the keen sense of smell and taste for jam and jelly which led Tommy to the large cupboard in which the shelves literally groaned under the weight of the sweets of life, carefully gathered by the old lady.

But so it was; Tommy had just reached the cupboard, and was opening the door, when the good old lady woke.

In this very sanctum sanctorum she had deposited the savings of many years' frugality.

The very demon of dreams seemed to be hovering over the lawyer's house that night.

The good old soul dreamed that a thief was at her hoard of notes and gold.

She woke up and saw a figure in white tugging at the door.

Out of bed she was on the instant, and, grasping hold of the supposed burglar, shouted out at the top of her lungs—

"Murder! thieves! Fire! fire!"

At the same moment, the lawyer's voice was heard pealing out "murder" and "thieves" throughout the house.

The servants rushed out of their rooms, and one of them, seizing hold of a long rope attached to a large alarum bell at the top of the house, set it going with a clamour that alarmed the people in the town, and away started hundreds of them, followed by the engines.

Ted Flan was aroused by these fearful cries, and springing out of bed at the cry of fire, caught up a large pitcher of water, and rushed to the door.

At the bottom of the stairs were the lawyer and Suke struggling, while near them, on the ground, lay Tommy bawling for mercy, while the housekeeper was pummelling, and shouting out "Fire! fire!"

"Is it fire you mane?" shouted Ted; "then, by the powers, here goes for an extinguisher."

And he discharged the contents of the large pitcher fairly amongst them.

While Giles, sliding down the banisters and opening the hall door, admitted a motley group of country people, police, and firemen; the sight which presented itself to their amazed senses they could not at first understand, but, when they did, never in the old mansion of Lawyer Tough Mutton was there heard such ringing peals and shouts of laughter.

There stood the lawyer, Suke Jolter, Tommy, and the old housekeeper, gazing at each other, dripping from head to foot with water, while Giles and Ted Flan followed the example of the mob, and fairly screamed with laughter.

It was some hours before the mob had dispersed and quiet and order again reigned in the house of the lawyer.

CHAPTER VI.

THE COURT.

At an early hour the next morning— for the lawyer, like all men of sense and business, was an early riser—the several parties assembled round the breakfast table.

Both Tommy and Suke were awfully

alarmed at the thought of meeting the lawyer after the night's occurrences.

Giles, Ted, and the two sleep-walkers having met in the breakfast-parlour long before the lawyer had left his study, the former thought it a good opportunity to increase the fears and perplexities of the latter.

"I am sorry for you, Tommy," said Giles; "but the old housekeeper, they say, is not likely to get over the fright; and if she should die——"

"Die? Don't thee say that," blubbered Tommy.

"I say if she should die, why, it will be both murder and robbery, for they say your walking in your sleep was only a sham."

And Giles winked at Ted, while Soft Tommy, nearly frightened out of his existence, threw himself upon a sofa, and called out—

"Feyther, feyther, fetch I home, or they'll transport Tommy."

Ted Flan had, on his part, impressed upon the mind of Suke that old Tough Mutton's nerves had been so shaken by his spectral visitant that he was confined to his bed.

"By the powers!" he said, " there'll be a pretty row at the 'sizes; you'll be had up for 'salt and battery, Suke; but I'll be bail for you."

"No, you shan't; but it be my virm belief that you are at the bottom of all this."

"Me! Why?" and Ted put on a look of astonishment.

"Yah, yes," and Suke looked very spiteful.

"You'll spoil your good looks, Suke," said Giles.

"What be my good looks to thee?" was the reply. "That be my business. Tommy may be soft, but thee'll find Sister Suke growed up quite different. They can't hang us."

Tommy groaned awfully.

"Be quiet, yah fool," she said; " what are you grunting like an old pig for, eh? We've been nicely bamboozled, Tommy."

"Bamboozled! What do you mean?" asked Ted.

"As if you didn't know, eh! Master Wiseacre. You've been having a foine lark wi' us, haven't you?"

" 'Pon my honour, Miss Jolter," and Ted bowed with mock politeness; "I assure you——"

"Bah!"

"I assure you that I don't understand you."

"Don't you? As if you didn't know how many beans go for five. I saw you wink your eye at t'other chap."

"Wink my eye! Oh, murder! it's a thing I couldn't do if I tried for a month. Now, my dear Miss Jolter," and he approached her.

"Keep thee off, or I'll claw thee."

Giles laughed heartily at this.

"And thee too; there be six o' one and half-a-dozen of t'other. But thee shan't have all the fun to thyselves, I promise thee."

"What do you mean?" said the lads.

"I'll show thee my meaning. Yah! yer thought Suke Jolter was a green 'un, did yer?"

"More of a red one," said Ted. This allusion to the girl's flaming head brought things to a climax.

"If I don't redden thy face, Suke

Jolter don't know a turnip from a mangel wurzel."

And, so saying, she made a dart at Ted; but he with great agility, got out of her way. Then she turned upon Giles, and so the pair led her a good chase round the breakfast table.

Tommy, seeing this, jumped up.

"Don't thee be a fool, sister Suke; they had naught to do with it. Didn't they save my life, you flat?" and he tried to catch hold of her.

"Keep off, Tommy," she bawled out, "or it will be the worse for thee, I tell thee."

And again the chase commenced.

Giles and Ted dancing round the table, roaring with delight.

Tommy got hold of Suke, and tried to prevent her catching his schoolfellows.

"Leave I alone, Tommy," she bawled out.

But Tommy held on like grim death.

In the struggle they reeled against the table, and over it went with a loud crash, Tommy and Suke falling in the ruins of china.

At that moment the door flew open, and the lawyer, followed by the housekeeper, rushed into the room.

"What, in the name of the Common Pleas, is all this?" he shouted.

Then, as Tommy and Suke sat up, his anger left him, and he laughed heartily at the ridiculous figure they cut.

An explanation ensued, and the breakfast table having been put to rights, the meal was soon dispatched.

Then Tommy and Suke were started off to their father.

"I'll meet thee in Lunnon, Giles and Ted," said he, at parting from them, "and blessed if we don't have some larks—ha, ha!—we'll all be 'up from the country,' loike; and, I beg your pardon, Mr. Sheepshanks, and Mrs. Sheep—noa, I means Mrs. Housekeeper —for frightening her; but I couldn't help it; it be an awkward habit that of walking in one's sleep. Feyther says these be times when boys must be wide awake—ha, ha!"

"And I be very sorry for frightening you, sir," said Suke, blushing, so that Ted Flan couldn't help comparing her to a red cabbage.

"There, there, say no more about it," replied the warm-hearted lawyer; "but you did frighten me, and that's a fact. However, through life let us forget and forgive; and here, Tommy, there's a sovereign for you towards buying your watch; another for you, Suke, towards a new bonnet; and so now, good-bye. Get your caps, boys; I'll take you to the court with me to-day."

A short time afterwards they had all left the house.

When the lawyer and the boys reached the court they found they were at least half an hour too soon. So, leaving them in the court, Mr. Sheepshanks proceeded to the lodgings of one of the counsel, for the purpose of having a consultation.

Then two of the barristers' clerks entered, carrying red bags; they placed them at each end of the place reserved for the learned in the law, and then retired to discuss a matter over some mild porter.

"What's in the bags, I wonder, Giles?" whispered Ted.

" Plenty of mischief and misery," replied Giles.

" I wonder to whom they belong," and Teddy went on tiptoe to one of them, and read out the name—" Serjeant Botherum.　What's yours, Giles ?"

" Serjeant Plausible," was the reply.

" Then, we'll put Plausible's in Botherum's place, and that will bother them both, I think."

No sooner said than done.　Serjeant Plausible's bag and brief went into Serjeant Botherum's seat, and *vice versa*.

The exchange had scarcely been effected when the court rapidly filled, and, the solicitors' seat being small and very much crowded, the boys were taken up to the gallery, and that very soon filled.

Then the judge, followed by the high sheriff, took his seat on the bench.

Civil causes having to be first tried, one was called on, and a jury empanelled.

" My lud," said Serjeant Botherum, a little thick-set man, with a large voice, and a red nose, which stood out in fine contrast with the white wig, " my lud, I am for the plaintiff," and, diving his hand into the bag, he pulled out a ponderous brief.

" In this case, my lud," said Serjeant Plausible, a tall, thin man, with a nose like an eagle's beak, which was continually twitching as if it had the Saint Vitus's dance, " in this case, may it please your ludship, I am for the defendant," and with that, following the example of his learned brother, he pulled a tremendous brief out of his bag.

All being in readiness, Serjeant Botherum rose, and, darting a fiery look at Plausible, began to open his case.

Now, be it known that these two serjeants learned in the law were bitter enemies, and to such an extent did they carry their enmity as actually to fight outside one of the courts with their umbrellas, which gave rise to their being called the " Umbrella Orators."*

" May it please your ludship and gentlemen of the jury, I have the honour to," here he glanced at the brief which lay before him, and paused, " to appear in this case for the—the—the," here he took up his brief, flung it down, and beckoned his clerk to him, and held an angry conversation with him.

" Well, brother," said his lordship, " pray go on, and don't waste the time of the court."

" I have no wish to do so, my lud, but a most impudent, impertinent, abominable, and scandalous trick has been played upon me and the court by some contemptible thing !" and here he darted a look of intense scorn at the learned Serjeant Plausible, who at once sprang on his legs.

" Does the learned serjeant allude to me ?" he said, in a voice like the crowing of a cock.

" How dare you put your bag and briefs in my place ?" roared Botherum.

" And how dare you put your bag and briefs in mine ?" screamed Plausible.

" My lud," shouted Botherum, " my clerk will swear that he placed my bag here."

" And mine," reiterated Plausible, " will swear he placed my bag in its proper place.　Somebody," and he glanced at Botherum, " has been guilty

---

* A fact !

"'I'LL SWEAR IT!' SAID THE WIDOW, EMPHATICALLY."

of a contemptible trick by placing such rubbish here," and he raised the bag as if he was about hurling it at Botherum's head.

" If," roared Botherum, " the learned serjeant sends the rubbish back in that way, he will receive his own back in the same manner !" and he raised up the bag as high as he could.

" My learned brothers will keep the——"

The peace, the learned judge would have said ; but before he could get the word out the war commenced.

Plausible's bag went flying at Botherum, and Botherum's at Plausible, with this difference ; Botherum being, as we said before, a short man, the bag fell short of its intended mark, and, hitting another learned serjeant who had risen, knocked him backwards.

At this the whole court burst into a roar of laughter, except the judge, who, with difficulty, preserved his gravity.

Ted and Giles both enjoyed the fun, and laughed heartily with the rest.

Order having been restored, the judge severely reprimanded the two serjeants, who had so unseemly forgotten themselves.

" If I could find out the person," he said, in conclusion, " who has been guilty of such a scandalous joke, I would see if there was any law that could reach him. Proceed with the cause."

Now, Master Ted Flanagan O'-laherty had, while living in Ireland, been taught many accomplishments by an old servant, among others the art of imitating certain animals, and that of throwing his voice with such imitation into any part of a building, such as the crowing of a cock, the braying of a donkey, the cackle of a goose, the yelping of a dog, and many others.

He had often given specimens of these to his schoolfellows, and the boys always received them with great gusto.

Serjeant Botherum was in the midst of a grand appeal to the jury, when the supposed yelping of a dog in the gallery caused him to pause, and look up, like an enraged turkey cock.

" Will your ludship order that dog out of court ?" said he.

" Not the only one that ought to be sent away," muttered Plausible.

" Did my learned brother offer any observation? There is surely no relationship between them," and a slight sneering grin stole over Botherum's visage.

" I think it likely that it may be the unfortunate client of my learned brother in agony at hearing——"

" Turn the dog out, officer," said the judge.

Another yelp at the back of the gallery, a number of kicks, and it was supposed that the unfortunate cur had vanished.

Again Botherum went on, and had warmed into eloquence, when the growling of the dog was again heard.

Three or four females sprang up, screaming, and the whole court was thrown into a state of confusion.

" If that dog disturbs the court again," said the judge, angrily, " I will fine the sheriff."

During this Giles was in the agonies of pent-up laughter.

Ted Flan's face was as imperturbable as a knocker.

Scarcely had the court regained its usual gravity when the crowing of a cock was heard proceeding from the same spot.

This was too much for the judge.

"Officer, bring the person before me who is committing such a scandalous contempt of court."

"Yes, my lord," replied the officer, and, pouncing upon an unfortunate countryman who sat near the spot from whence the sound proceeded, he took him into custody, and hurrying the affrighted man into the body of the court, placed him before the indignant judge.

"How dare you disturb the court in that way, sir?" said he.

"I!—I!—I didn't disturb the court, please your majesty," said the affrighted man; "I only laughed with the rest."

"Oh, you did, did you?" said the judge; "then lock him up until the rising of the court, and I'll see what is to be done with him then. In order to put a stop to such goings on, I'll clear the gallery of everyone in it if it is continued."

And so the poor, trembling countryman, who expected nothing less than transportation, was taken from the court in custody, and the business went on quietly until the jury returned a verdict in favour of Serjeant Botherum's client, when the shrill tones of chanticleer were again heard. Then a body of officers rushed into the gallery and, without ceremony, turned everyone out.

Our young friends now left the court. Their attention was directed to a strange, fantastic being—the figure was that of a woman. At a glance they could perceive the poor soul was bereft of reason; the poor idiot had her head dressed with a quantity of ribbons, such as soldiers wear when recruiting. She had on an old, soiled soldier's jacket.

Her story was short, sad, and simple. When just on the point of marriage to a young soldier the regiment he belonged to was ordered abroad and he never returned, and so under this sad bereavement the poor girl's reason sank, and she went wandering about the country dressed as described, and fancying she was a soldier just returned crowned with laurels. She was known by the name of " Mad 'Liza."

Round this poor object was collected a mob (principally boys) jeering and teasing the poor idiot. They were led on by a young fellow dressed in the garb of a groom.

" Now, then, 'Liza, let's have the old song—' As they marched through the town!'" and he pulled one of the ribbons.

" March!" she said, vacantly, " who talked of marching? Ha! ha! Hark! 'tis the bugle's sound!—and they are going to take Willie from me."

" Ha! ha!—and a good thing too, old girl," said the groom. " Come, let us have a dance," and he pulled her about savagely.

" No, no! I cannot dance, and I cannot sing, when the heart is sad and sore."

" A dance! a dance!" shouted some half dozen boys, and they began to pull her about roughly.

The blood of Giles and Ted Flan was fired with rage at this, and they were about springing to the assistance of the poor crazed girl.

"If you won't dance," said the brutal leader of the rabble boors, "you'll at least give us a kiss;" and he threw his arms round her neck.

At this insult the scream of the poor girl was painful to hear; she looked round, and catching the flashing eyes and noble faces of the boys, she broke from her cruel persecutors and rushed towards them.

"You will not harm me," she said, clinging to Giles.

"No, nor shall anyone else," he said, and his eyes flashed a defiance around.

"And by my conscience I row in the same boat," said Ted Flan.

"Stand behind me," said Giles, "and we will protect you against insult."

"Indeed, here's a couple of fine dung-hill birds a-crowing!" and the swaggering groom tried to seize her by the arm. "I say she shall dance."

"And I say she shall not," replied Giles firmly.

"And who are you?" asked the fellow.

"That matters little; I won't see this poor crazed girl hurt." And Giles Evergreen cast a look of contempt at the mob.

"It is my own Willie who speaks!" and the plaintive tones with which she said this brought tears into the eyes of the boys; "you will not leave me again?" And she clung imploringly to them.

"I will not leave you until I see that you are safe from those bad-disposed fellows. Come with me, and I'll take you, at least for a time, to a place of safety."

"No, you won't; we always have a dance when we fall in with Mad 'Liza.

Come, leave the girl alone; it is no business of yours."

"But it is business of ours; and it ought to be the aim of everyone who possesses a spark of feeling or pity in their breasts, to protect those who have been afflicted as this poor girl has been."

And Giles looked defiantly round.

"I say she shall dance."

"And I say she shall not be made the sport and cruel jest of any of you."

"Ha! ha! who made you master here, eh?" And the fellow scowled at Giles darkly.

"That Being who has very mercifully blessed me with reason has sent me here to use it, and keep a poor, half-witted creature from insult."

"Ah! Willie! you have been long away!"

And the poor girl's head sank on Giles's shoulder.

Some of the mob drew back when they saw the determined, bold bearing of the boys.

This irritated the fellow who had thought to have it all his own way.

He placed his hand on the girl's shoulder, and tried to drag her away.

She clung frantically to Giles and Ted.

"I warn you," said the former, "to desist. Leave the poor crazed girl alone."

"Shan't! Who are you?" said the brute, and he aimed a savage blow at Giles.

But he had calculated without his host.

The blow fell short, Giles springing lightly aside.

Still the fellow pressed on.

Giles, therefore, leaving Mad 'Liza with Ted, sprang upon the fellow, and, in the twinkling of an eye, he lay sprawling on his back.

He was up again, and rushed at Giles, foaming with rage ; but our boy, who stood so gallantly forward to protect the oppressed, was as cool and collected as his cowardly opponent was the opposite.

Giles knew what he was about.

As he came reeling up, Giles planted a well-directed blow between the bully's eyes, and he went down as though he was shot.

In an instant the revulsion of feeling took place ; the mob cheered Giles and Ted ; for the latter, while engaged with the groom, had kept the rest back ;

and, at that moment a sergeant and some police coming up, half of them slunk away.

The baffled bully rose, and going up to Giles, looked him full in the face.

" I shall know *thee* again, and will pay thee for this."

And with that, as the police approached, he slunk away.

It was with difficulty Giles and Ted could disengage themselves from the poor girl ; but having placed her under the care of the sergeant of police, were soon after joined by Lawyer Sheepshanks, and they proceeded home, the rest of the day being spent in packing and getting ready for their intended journey to London, which was to take place the next day.

CHAPTER VII.

PLAYING WITH FIRE.

PLAYING with fire is rather a dangerous game, and is apt at times to burn the fingers ; the saying may be applied to other cases besides actual flame, as the present chapter will show.

The dinner ended, the lawyer and the boys drew their chairs close to the fire, for the weather was bitterly cold.

" My dear boys," said the lawyer, " you have now received all the advice that I can give you upon this trial trip to London. I think I know your hearts well. We lawyers are keen and searching anatomisers of human feelings, and seldom make a mistake. Be above a mean or dishonest action, and, above all, never play with fire."

" I confess I do not understand you," said Giles.

" He manes you mustn't lay hould of a red hot poker at the *wrong end*," said Ted Flan.

" There is a something in that," replied Sheepshanks, smiling ; " but it is not exactly that. My mind is, and has been, greatly disturbed by the foolishness of a lad ' playing with fire.' "

" I suppose," said Ted, " he's burnt his fingers."

" To the very bone," was the reply.

" And isn't there a cure ?" asked Giles.

" The remedy is a very sharp one. I'll tell you about it."

The lawyer was about entering into the narrative of "Playing with Fire," when he was interrupted by an altercation outside the room; voices appeared to be raised in supplication and deprecation alternately.

"Come in," called out Sheepshanks; and as the door opened, "What is the reason of this interruption?" he said, angrily.

"Well, sir, I told this lady that you would not be disturbed after dinner."

"And you told her very properly, James. Well, now, Mrs. Munro, since you have made your appearance in my drawing-room, pray be seated, take a glass of wine, and then your business."

The lady thus spoken to was dressed in widow's weeds, and bore upon her face the marks of unutterable woe and anguish.

Truly, suffering had marked her for its own.

"I cannot be seated," she said, in a low, tremulous voice, and waving her hand as the servant handed her a glass of wine. "With many thanks, I do not require that."

"Well, then, sit down. You can talk as well sitting as standing. Leave the room, James."

The man retired.

"I cannot rest," she said, "while this despair is clinging round my heart. Oh! if they knew (and she looked despairingly at the two boys)—Oh! if they knew the agony of the mother's heart!"

And here she sobbed aloud.

The muscles of the lawyer's face twitched and played about as though they had been electric wires, while the faces of Giles and Ted evinced the interest they felt in the widow's appeal.

"Well, now, what the—hem! can I do in this case? I have already told you so, Mrs. Munro."

"My son—my innocent son—takes his trial to-morrow for a crime he never committed."

"Very likely; that's the case always," said the lawyer, drily. "Everybody's innocent."

"I'll swear it," said the widow, emphatically.

"Pooh! stuff! How can you swear to a thing you can know nothing about? It would be flat perjury."

"It would be no such thing; it would be the truth, and the God of Truth knows it."

"The woman's mad!" growled Tough Mutton.

"I shall be if he is convicted. It is a false, deliberate conspiracy."

"Take care, Mrs. Munro."

"I'll take care that justice shall be done. Will you listen to me?"

"Yes; I was about telling these boys the danger of 'playing with fire,' and you come to illustrate it. Go on; but be calm."

"I will be as calm as the mother can who sees her only son on the brink of destruction. I will be as calm as the brave mariner who sees the 'last plank of hope' sinking from under his feet, and yet quails not, blenches not. You well knew the father of that boy who is now in yonder dark, foul prison, awaiting his doom to-morrow."

"I did," replied the lawyer; "and a more honourable man never existed than Jack Munro."

"The son, then, is what the father was. You know the villain who has coiled this net round him!" and the scorn in the widow's eyes shone out with an awful lustre.

"Be calm; he is my client."

"He is a consummate villain for all that."

"We can't always pick our clients, my good lady."

"No man is compelled to mix with villany."

"The widow will win by chalks," whispered Ted Flan.

"The man, this McHaffie, was the deadly rival of the brave heart I married. I tried the gold against the dross, and, thanks be to Heaven, I won; but I likewise won the undying hatred of the rascal, who is persecuting my dear boy to shame, and perhaps death; but," and her form seemed to crouch as though she were about to spring upon some unseen object, "there shall be blood for blood; satisfaction for wrong!"

"I say, my good lady," and the lawyer seemed rather alarmed; "this is——"

"The truth, and shall be carried out. Listen to me, kind, good man, for you are one."

"'Pon my word, I——"

"I have left the prison cell in which my son Robert is confined. I have been on my knees—but, on that cold floor—and heard what I am about to tell you sworn upon the holy, unalterable gospels. The son who opened his whole truthful heart to his almost heart-broken mother, was so great a master with his pen, as to be able to imitate anyone's handwriting."

"Playing with fire, boys," muttered the lawyer.

"You are right; and the flame has already scathed, and may, perhaps, destroy. In the office in which my boy was placed, there was a man by name Crawley (he is the principal witness), who was always praising this fatal attainment, and one day, in jest, persuaded the poor, unsuspecting lad to sign his master's name at the bottom of a slip of paper. The poor moth did so, and laughed at the wonderful resemblance."

"Aye, aye, playing with fire; dangerous game, signing another person's name to paper instead of your own."

"It is indeed," and the poor mother sighed deeply. "Imagine my horror—my agony—my despair—when, three days after, my poor boy was arrested, and charged with forging a cheque upon his master's banker for £100! The villain, Crawley, had got the unsuspecting victim of his own, and his employer, McHaffie's, villany, to sign what he thought was a blank piece of paper, but which was, no doubt, the cheque presented and paid."

"And which cheque will be most damning evidence against him. I was looking at it *an hour ago* in my room, and never saw such a wonderful resemblance to the signature of McHaffie. This has been playing with fire with a vengeance."

"And if that were lost?" said the woman.

"Why, then the whole affair would drop to the ground. I believe Mr. McHaffie to be—ahem, he is a client of mine."

" Then the devil give you joy of your bargain," said Ted Flan.

" Amen !" responded Giles.

" Silence, you boys. Well, now, Mrs. Munro, it's getting late, and——"

" And you can give me no hope ?"

And the mother clasped her hands in agony unutterable.

" Why, 'pon my word, don't I tell you that I am engaged against ? Would you have me sell my client ?"

" Yes, by the powers, and get rid of a bad, bitter lot," said Ted Flan.

" And ease your conscience. As I am an honest boy, I believe that poor fellow is innocent," chimed in Giles.

" Oh, bless you, bless you, my noble boys, for siding with the widow and the fatherless."

And she tried hard to restrain her tears.

" The widow and the fatherless !" cried the Irish boy, carried away by his feelings, " the man—no, the baste—that would oppress, should ride a steeple-chase upon a porcupine saddle with cobweb kickseys, and afterwards——"

" Ha ! ha ! Bravo, Ted ! bravo !" shouted Giles.

" Silence ! You talk of conspiracy, my good lady. What do you call this ?"

" Oh, Mr. Crawley, if I had you in Kilkenny, among the cats—och, murder !"

And Ted groaned.

" Be silent !" and the lawyer spoke with that tone of authority that enforced it. " Get the counsel whom you have employed, Mrs. Munro—and he is a clever man—to try and turn Mr. Crawley inside out. I don't care a pinch of snuff about this infernal affair, but I only know what I think."

" And that is, sir——?" said the woman, hopefully.

" Hem ! The least said is the soonest mended."

" That's what a countryman of mine said when he broke a window," said Ted.

" Bother your countryman !" replied the lawyer.

" Ah ! they're bothered enough, without any legal compliments."

" I'm glad you're going to-morrow, Master Flanagan."

" And I'm so delighted, sir, that I'll cry all the way."

" Cry, and delighted ?"

" Yes, cry with joy."

During this, Mrs. Munro had stood looking upon the group with feelings that can scarcely be described.

The two boys so forcibly reminded her of her own unfortunate son, that she could, with all a mother's fondness and love, have thrown her arms around them, and hugged them to her poor, agitated heart.

But another thought had struck her —a thought that, by some desperate expedient, she might be the means of averting the doom and disgrace that was impending over the head of her unfortunate child.

It might be dangerous ; but what is danger to the heart of the mother, when the child she has held at her bosom— gazed upon with all the rapturous joy that mothers only can feel—tush, tush ! there never was danger of peril seen in a mother's eyes at such a moment ; it is a daring courage of the most sublime kind.

" Good night, sir," she said to Sheep-shanks, " and many, many thanks for your kindness ; I feel assured that you believe in my boy's innocence. And you, dear, noble, generous youths,"—and, rushing to them, she tenderly, yet fervently embraced them—" may God prosper your course through life."

She kissed them, and silently left the room.

There was a pause of some moments, while the lawyer abstractedly was making lunges at the coals with the poker.

" Don't play with fire," said Ted Flan, " or you may——"

" Burn your fingers, " laughed Giles.

" Let this little incident be a warning to you, my dear boys, for the rest of your lives," replied Sheepshanks.

" A warning? A warning for what?" said Giles.

" Never to play with fire," dryly answered the lawyer ; " and now good night. You will start to-morrow for London, and all I wish is that you will pass through the ordeal unscathed ; so once more, good night."

And he left the room.

A few minutes after Giles and Ted had gained theirs.

" What did old Tough Mutton mane by warning, I wonder?" said Ted Flan, seating himself. " Did he take us for maids of all work ?"

" Oh, it's only his way, I suppose," said Giles. " I shall sleep very little to-night, Ted."

" Why not ?"

" Well, I can't get the thoughts of that poor woman and her boy out of my mind."

" Do you think she spoke the truth ?"

" I am as certain of it as I am of my own existence," replied Giles Evergreen, warmly.

" And so am I. I'd give a trifle to get hould of that Mr. Crawley. Oh, if we only had him among the boys at the old school, eh, Giles ? Well, I'll get to bed," and Ted Flan proceeded to undress. " I think we'd warm him mighty well. I wish they'd let me cross-examine him ; I'd bother him better than Botherum—ha, ha ! —I don't think he was mightily plased with the dog to-day—ha, ha !"—and, so saying, Ted sprang into bed. " Plase the pigs, I'll be in the arms of Murphy —I mane Morpheus—and who that is I haven't the slightest idea ; one of the hathen goddesses, I believe, eldest son to Peter, and—ah ! good night, Giles."

" Good night, Ted ; I shan't be long before I am in bed myself ; but that poor boy !"

Here he stopped, for he thought he heard a noise.

" What was that ? It sounded like a person sobbing. Nonsense, it's all fancy ; it's only Master Ted snoring more likely ; and yet——"

Giles opened the door of the room, and listened attentively, looking down over the banisters.

" Old Tough Mutton going to bed," said he, returning to his room ; " and suppose, Master Giles Evergreen, you follow his good example. I'll place the matches on the table, and so, if I can't sleep, I'll have a light and read."

And so saying, he proceeded to the fire-place to take the matches off the chimney-piece, where they had been placed.

By the side of that was a cupboard.

"I wonder what is in that cupboard? No ghost, I dare say. I'll have a look —ha, ha!—suppose one was to pop out —old Tough Mutton's father, with his old wig on—ha, ha! Ghost of a wig or not, I'll have a look."

And laying hold of the handle, he tried to open it.

It was in vain; it resisted all his efforts.

"Locked, eh? Well, never mind."

And so saying, he placed the matches on the table, drew back the window-curtains, and looked out.

"It's an exceeding cold night," he said, "and the snow is coming down right merrily. We shall have a famous journey through it to-morrow — to-morrow—ah! it's to-morrow when that poor boy's trial comes on."

And he sighed heavily.

Was it fancy?

He thought he heard another; and he looked anxiously round the room.

"It's curious," he said, "but I thought I heard a sigh answer mine."

He listened attentively and anxiously.

All was silent as the grave.

"Well, here goes for bed, or I shall fancy the ghost of some client of the lawyer's who was ruined in a chancery suit is wandering about the house, made a mistake, and got into this room instead of the lawyer's. Ha, ha! well, here goes. I wish I could let that poor boy out of his prison, that's all. What was that, the same noise again? Oh, this will never do!"

So saying, he blew out the light and sprang into bed.

It was in vain he tried to sleep.

An hour passed, and he was still awake; and so he lay, looking up at the star-spangled heavens, and mentally praising the mercy, goodness, and greatness of the Almighty Architect of this beautiful world.

Suddenly a dark shadow passed between him and the light.

"Who is there?" he said, springing up in bed.

"Crawley, you are a wretch," muttered Ted Flan in his sleep, "and I'll bate you!"

Not a sound was heard.

"What could that have been?" and Giles tried to pierce the gloom of the room. "I'm certain I saw something. Shall I wake Ted? No, it would frighten him, and he'd alarm the whole house. I must be dreaming."

And he lay down again, keeping his eyes fixed upon the window.

The moon now shone gloriously.

No warrior's heart was more courageous than that of Giles Evergreen, but for a moment he felt a sensation of fear creeping over him.

He kept his eyes firmly fixed upon the window.

Every object upon the table was as clearly defined as though the light of day was shining upon it.

Suddenly he saw a white hand pass slowly upon it.

For a moment he sank back in terror, and closed his eyes.

When he opened them the hand had disappeared and with it the candlestick.

He lay perfectly still.

Again the black shadow passed between him and the light, making for the door, and distinctly he heard the door open.

Then he rallied back his courage, and, getting quietly out of bed, slipped on his trousers, and made for the door.

It was open.

He had closed it before he went to bed.

The rays of the moon shone slantingly down the old staircase, and down the stairs went the figure in black.

And that figure was a woman's.

Giles' first thought was to alarm the inmates of the house, his second to reject it and follow this singular apparition.

Down the well-carpeted stairs they went without making the slightest noise, past the old lawyer's room until the ground-floor was gained.

Suddenly a light shone out.

And then Giles saw the pale face of the poor mother whose son was in gaol upon a fearful charge of forgery.

She raised the light, looking fearfully around.

Pale unto death was her face.

But there was an unshrinking courage in it.

A daring desperation was in her eyes.

Giles crouched down on the stairs.

Then she slowly raised the light and looked round until her eye rested upon a door which had the word " Private " written upon it.

She advanced slowly and cautiously towards it, and placed her hand upon the lock.

It was fast !

She fell against the side as though death had seized her.

Then, placing the light down, she fell upon her knees as if in prayer and thought.

After a pause she slowly rose, and, taking up the light, looked carefully and anxiously about the door.

By the side of it hung a key.

There was a smile of joy upon that poor wan face as she seized it.

Then placing it in the lock, she turned it without the slightest noise.

The door slowly opened, and she passed rapidly in, followed by the intrepid boy.

It was the study of Lawyer Sheepshanks.

She advanced rapidly to the table, which was covered with bundles of paper tied carefully round with red tape.

She took them up and looked at them one by one, with a troubled, disappointed look.

The document she was searching for was not there !

She placed her hand upon another.

A gleam of joy shone across her face.

It was the one she sought; it lay upon the lawyer's desk.

She was about opening it when a hand was placed firmly upon hers.

It was the hand of Giles.

She shuddered, uttering a low cry of dismay.

" What do you here, and what want you with those papers ?" he said, lowly, but firmly.

" My boy's life !" was the whispered answer.

"His life?"

"Yes, the only life precious to me in this world."

"You're turning thief," said Giles.

"I would do more than that to save him. Listen to me, boy. You were present when I told my tale to the lawyer; you believe me, for I had your sympathy."

"You had, for I pity the sorrows of anyone."

"I doubt it not, for you have a noble heart; it is written in your brave, open face. Have you a mother living?"

"Alas! no, I am an orphan!"

"That is a sad answer. Both gone? My poor, persecuted boy mourns the loss of his father only, and that loss is heavy enough, for it is a desperate fight for a lone woman to wage with the world; but I will not, with the help of Heaven, shrink from it!"

"You have a brave, unshrinking spirit!"

And Giles looked admiringly at her.

"Aye, and so have you; and in this world it is required, or I had not been here."

"And how did you gain admission into my room?"

"Listen; I must speak low. While I was in the room advocating the cause of the innocent, a thought struck me that if I could gain access to this room and secure the forged paper, I could save my boy. When I left the presence of the lawyer, I felt that nothing but a desperate expedient would save my son from degradation. I therefore determined to conceal myself in the house at all hazards—aye, though I perilled life itself."

"It was a bold resolve, and well carried out."

"A mother will dare much to save the child she has nestled in her bosom, even were that child crime-stricken and guilty. But what will she not dare when she knows that the object of her love is as pure as the undriven snow?"

Giles warmly pressed her hand, while a tear stood trembling in his eye.

"Thanks, thanks. I reached your room, and concealed myself in the closet, and waited with a trembling, but unshrinking heart, the time when I might issue forth; and when you tried the door I held it with the strength of a thousand giants. But when I heard your generous, noble-hearted sympathy for my child, then, and not till then, did I nearly betray myself. The rest you know; and, now, the fate of two lives rest in your hands."

"You pledge your word that your son is innocent?"

And Giles looked in her eyes as though he would read her very soul.

"I pledge the welfare of the immortal future, I pledge the dear cherished hope of meeting the loved object of my affections in that world to which he has been called; I pledge all these before and in the face of a just and all-seeing God, to the purity and innocence of my dear, dear boy."

"It is enough. Untie those papers and search for what you want."

The act was soon accomplished, although her hands trembled with impatience and anxiety.

"Suppose the paper is not here?" she whispered.

"Then it must be left in the hands

of Him who will not let the innocent fall," said Giles.

There were but few papers; but, apparently, what she sought was not there, and she looked at Giles, her face like chiselled marble.

"It is the cheque you want?" said Giles.

"It is," she answered, mournfully; "and, without that, he is lost."

Giles took up the papers, and, carefully looking, found the much-coveted document.

He placed it in the mother's hands.

"Thanks, thanks," she said. "My son is saved. Look, look," and she held the fatal paper before him, "the body of the paper is in another hand-writing, filled in by the infamous Crawley, the tool of a still more infamous employer."

Giles placed the light before her, and pointed to it.

With a deep look of gratitude at the brave boy, she held the accursed scrawl to the flame; slowly, but surely, it was consumed.

A light, bluish flame played around it until it became a black ash.

Then, carefully, it was thrown into the fire-place among a heap of old paper and cinders.

The papers were again fastened up as before; then, taking up the light, Giles led her to the hall door; it was carefully and quietly opened.

Then all the woman's daring courage seemed to forsake her, and she fell weeping upon his neck.

"God bless you; you have saved my boy," she sobbed, in broken accents.

"And baffled the villany of a pair of unmitigated scoundrels. God bless you and your son," said Giles.

The door closed, and she passed into the open air, the snow falling in thick flakes, the fierce wind dashing it in her face; but she felt it not.

She knew that on the morrow she would again hold in her arms her dear, dear child.

"Free—free—free—free!"

Everything having been replaced as before, Giles blew out the light, and, regaining his room, got again into bed with a light heart.

The last words he heard were—

"One for your nob, Mr. Crawley."

It was Ted Flan, fighting in his sleep with the baffled conspirators.

CHAPTER VIII.

THE RAILWAY STATION.

THE breakfast next morning was a very early one, for there was much to do.

The usual quiet of the lawyer's house was set aside for noise, bustle and activity; the servants hurried to and fro, and two large trunks, securely fastened, gave sufficient notice that travelling was the order of the day.

At the well-appointed table sat the lawyer, Giles Evergreen, and Ted Flan.

"Make a good breakfast, boys," said the warm-hearted lawyer. "There is nothing like it, especially when you're about to go a long journey; so don't spare it."

"You are not eating a good one yourself, sir," said Giles.

"Well, no; I've not had a good night's rest," he replied.

"Indade, 'sir; I've had rather a queer one myself," chimed in Ted.

"Nonsense, boys always sleep well; men only have care and trouble upon their minds."

"Then, if you plase, sir, I'll kape a boy all the rest of my days."

"I was dreaming half the night of the boy Munro, whose trial comes on to day," said Sheepshanks.

"My very drame, sir."

And Ted winked at Giles, who, while dressing, had informed him of the previous night's adventure.

"And a nice, ginteel drame it was."

"Mine was anything but pleasant. I dreamed that the boy was convicted, and sentenced to——"

"Oh, botherashin!" said Ted, "drames always go by contraries; therefore, he'll get off and have a hundred a year settled on him for the rest of his born days, and after."

The lawyer smiled.

Giles's thoughts kept him silent.

"Upon my soul, I hope it will turn out so; but the cheque is a black affair."

"By my troth, you're right; it's black as the ——. Saving your presence, it will be calling up a client of yours."

"Master Ted O'Flanagan!"

"Sir, I am your humble servant. But I'll tell you my drame. I dreamt that we were again at school, and that we had Mr. Crawley there. You must know there is a mighty fine pump there. Well, sir, we put Mr. Crawley under the pump, and nately washed all the sin and wickedness from him; and then—do you know what cobbing is, sir?"

Giles laughed.

"Cobbing? No; there is no such term in the law," replied the lawyer.

"It may not be in law, but it's to be found in justice, and a knotty point it is."

"Knotty point? Explain yourself."

"You see, we take a piece of rope— or, if rope's not handy, a stout handkerchief will do—and we make some illigant knots in it; the fortunate individual is then extended on his face, spread agle fashion, and justice is done to all parties.

"And so I dramed that Mr. Crawley, after being well pumped upon, was handsomely dried and mangled by the wholesome process of cobbing."

The lawyer, laughing heartily, rose from his seat.

"I have a favour to ask of you," said Giles, suddenly.

"What is it, my dear boy?"

"Ted and I would very much like to hear the trial of poor Harry Munro," said Giles. "We can start by the night train."

Mr. Sheepshanks paused, and for a minute a deep silence reigned.

"I think you had better not," at length he said.

"Why not?" asked the bold boys.

"The scene, if he is convicted, will be a most painful one, and I can't see any earthly reason why he should get off."

"Perhaps not, sir," said Giles; "but strange things have happened, and I've often heard of the glorious uncertainty of the law."

"Pooh, pooh! there is no uncertainty about this; the cheque will condemn him."

"Bad luck to the cheque!" said Ted, winking at Giles.

"So I say," replied the lawyer. "I wish it had been burnt."

"Playing with fire with a vengeance."

And the Irish boy laughed.

"Yes. However, if you like, you may go; it will be a lesson, for convicted he'll be."

"Be aisy; I have heard there is a mighty slip between the mouth and the pitcher."

"Very well, boys, get ready; I've only to put my papers in the bag, and then we'll be off."

And the kind-hearted lawyer bustled from the room.

"What a study his face will be when he misses the paper," said Ted Flan. "By the powers, the man who thought he had got a prize and found it was a blank, will be nothing at all to it!"

"Now, boys," shouted out Sheep-shanks, "come on. Tide and time, you know, wait for no man."

"True, sir," said Ted. "Are we going by water?"

And so saying, Giles and Ted Flan ran downstairs, and, joining the lawyer, they jumped into the carriage and were rapidly conveyed to the court.

During the ride, the muttered exclamations of the lawyer proved how utterly distasteful the whole affair he was going upon was to his mind, while Giles and Ted inwardly rejoiced that at all events, if there was no "flaw in the indictment," there would certainly be one in the evidence.

The excitement attendant on the trial of a boy for the grave offence of forgery was very great. His mother and himself had been long known and respected by all classes, and there was scarcely a person in the place but what had serious doubts respecting the guilt of the boy, because his previous character and habits had been of the most exemplary kind.

His father had been an officer in the army, and served with distinction and honour to himself and country.

But reward does not always fall to the hardest worker, and so, finding that promotion was a long day's march before him, he sold out, and, retiring into the country, devoted himself to agricultural pursuits.

For a time all went on well; but at last the sun of his happiness was suddenly clouded.

Three blooming children out of four were smitten down by a fell disease. A bank, in which he had foolishly and blindly deposited nearly all his savings, failed, and ruin and despair seemed to pour down upon him all at once. He sank beneath it—the heart of the brave soldier that would not have quailed at the cannon's mouth, at the "forlorn hope"—sank at the thoughts of beggary and so the grave closed over him.

The widow and her son had then to

"HEAVEN PROTECTS THE INNOCENT."

fight the great battle of life by themselves, and well and nobly did they do it. By giving lessons in music and drawing Mrs. Munro managed, with the wreck of her husband's property, to weather the storm, encouraged as she was by the devotion of her noble-hearted boy.

"Stop till I am old enough, mother," he said one night, rising from her knee, having finished his prayers. "Stop till then, and see how I'll work for you. You shall not have to put up with the pride and insolence of some of those you attend upon. No, no; I shall soon be able to earn a living for you, and then let me see who will dare bring a tear in my mother's eye."

His eyes darted fire, his nostrils dilated, while his clenched fist gave proof that the manly courage of the father had descended to the son.

And this was the boy that was to be placed at the bar of criminal justice for a crime that he was as innocent of as the heavens themselves.

The crowd outside the court were crushing and pushing to gain admission, for the doors had not yet been opened.

Through a private door, set apart for the accommodation of barristers and solicitors, Lawyer Sheepshanks, with Giles and Ted Flan, passed in, and a few minutes after the court doors were thrown open.

The rush was tremendous.

The screams and cries of the females —always a strong body upon these occasions—as they fought their way into the limited space allotted to them, were somewhat deafening; in a few minutes the whole body of the court was densely packed by an eager, anxious crowd.

The judge, a mild, benevolent man, took his seat upon the bench, while around him were seated a number of gentlemen and ladies of distinction.

And then was hushed the buzz of excitement.

"Place the prisoner at the bar," said the judge.

And then suddenly emerged from the crowd a female, dressed in deep mourning, who took up her position by the side of the dock.

From the back of that a door opened, and the head gaoler entered followed by a pale, interesting lad; as he advanced up to the front of the bar a murmur of sympathy ran through the spectators.

A flush mantled deeply upon his cheeks, as he looked round the court.

The next instant, a pair of loving arms were thrown round his neck; they were the arms of her who had so lovingly protected him in his helpless infancy, and who now stood by his side with a heart so intensely throbbing in all the agony of suspense as almost to deprive her of consciousness.

"Who is that female?" mildly asked his lordship.

"I am his mother, my lord," she replied; and she tried to draw her boy closer to her true, loving heart.

"Your feelings are a credit and an honour to you, but during the trial you must repress them, and not interrupt the court. Be seated, and rest assured your son's interest will not be lost sight of."

She would have spoken, and thanked

the man who addressed her kindly, but her emotion was so great that speech was denied her, so, inclining her head to him, she leaned against the side of the dock, clasping one of her son's hands in hers, and stifling all sounds of her pent-up agony and sorrow.

But what was the surprise of Giles and Ted Flan, to find, standing at the criminal bar, an old schoolfellow ?

"Why, that is Harry Munro, the boy that, after being six months with us, left in consequence of his father's ruin and death," whispered Giles.

"As like as two tin pase in a pod. I'll go bail they'll find out their mistake."

He was a fair-haired boy, with the light of truth and innocence beaming in his eyes ; the hair parted from the side, showed a forehead of great intellect and power, while the scrupulous neatness of his dress, the finely-turned throat, and the small, well-shaped hands, told the gazers on that he came of gentle blood.

"How say you, prisoner, are you guilty or not guilty ?" asked the clerk of the arraigns.

"Not guilty, as God shall judge me," was the reply, that rang like a trumpet charge through the court.

There were not six persons in that place that disbelieved him.

Then up rose the learned Serjeant Botherum, and began to open the case for the prosecution.

CHAPTER IX.

CHECKMATE.

HE began by saying his duty was a painful one at most times, but on the present occasion his pain was considerably heightened at beholding one so young in years yet so old in crime.

Here Mrs. Munro was starting indignantly forward, when the judge warned her by raising his hand.

"May I suggest to you, my learned brother," said his lordship, mildly, "that no crime of any description has yet been proved against the youth at the bar ?"

"But, my lord," blustered Botherum.

"One moment. While strictly advancing the facts of the case, it is hardly fair that the minds of the jury should be prejudiced by any statement which cannot be carried out by evidence. Has this lad no counsel to defend him ?" warmly asked his lordship.

"Yes, my lord," replied a young counsel, rising ; "I received a brief late yesterday, but I did not think it necessary to interrupt the learned counsel, because I feel certain the gentlemen of the jury will set a just value on his remarks."

"Just so, Mr. Anson ; I feel that the interests of the boy at the bar will not lose anything in your hands."

And so saying, the learned judge resumed his pen, amid the hum and buzz of approbation from all in the court.

This little stoppage to the eloquence of the learned Serjeant Botherum gave the greatest delight to Giles Evergreen and Ted Flan.

"I wish they'd let me give him a crow," whispered the latter.

"It is too serious a matter, Ted. Poor Harry Munro, what a brave boy he is!"

And Giles sighed heavily at seeing his schoolfellow in such a serious plight.

"Look at the lawyer," said Ted.

Giles did so.

Tough Mutton, evidently deeply puzzled, was busily searching among his papers.

Then he beckoned his clerk, who, after a little whispering, hurriedly left the court.

At length, after inveighing bitterly against the ingratitude and dishonesty of the prisoner at the bar, he finished by stating that it would be clearly proved, to the satisfaction of the court and the jury, that he was guilty of the very heinous crime of forgery, and that he should be able to prove indisputably that the cheque so drawn and paid was in the handwriting of the prisoner.

"Call Peter Crawley," said Botherum.

"Here!" answered a voice, and the person so called made his way through the crowd and ascended the witness box.

The low, cunning face of a villain was seen as he stood before the multitude; thin, lank hair hung down each side of his cat-like eyes and cadaverous cheeks, somewhat puffed out by the white neck-cloth that encircled his throat. He made a fawning bow to the judge, who, eyeing him closely, made no response.

He did the same to the jury, and met with the same reception; but, do all he could, he was unable to look the poor innocent boy in the dock in the face.

That face of honesty and rectitude would have caused him, villain as he was, and hardened in crime, to have trembled and shrunk back.

"You are the confidential clerk of McHaffie and Co., merchants, I believe?" said Botherum.

"The confidential clerk," was the reply.

"You know the prisoner at the dock?"

"Perfectly."

"Stop! What do you mean by perfectly, when you have not looked to see whether *any person* is in the dock or not?" said the judge, sternly. "Look and see if it is the same person or not."

It took a great effort on the part of the respectable Mr. Crawley to cast his eyes upon the spot the judge had directed him to.

But he did.

And a tremor ran through his frame as he did so, for he not only encountered the steady gaze of innocence in the injured boy's face, but the flashing indignation, contempt and withering scorn from the mother's eyes.

"Well, you have no doubt about it, I suppose!" said Botherum, with a sneer.

"None."

And he turned round, as though anxious to shut out the sight of them.

At this moment Sheepshanks' clerk returned and whispered a communication in his master's ear.

It had such an effect upon the lawyer that Ted Flan nearly laughed outright.

His eyes were open to their fullest extent, his lower jaw fell as though it was separating itself from the upper part, and he sank back in his seat a picture of blank dismay.

"You have often seen the prisoner write," continued Botherum.

"Often," was the reply.

"Often! and you can swear to it?"

"With certainty."

"Very well; now take this paper. Give me the cheque, Mr. Sheepshanks; we shall see about it now."

"By the powers! I think we shall. He is playing with fire, Giles," whispered the Irish boy.

"And will scorch himself," was the reply.

The lawyer had risen, and was speaking to Botherum, whose face suddenly blazed again.

"What, sir!" he thundered; "you can't find the cheque?"

Every person in the court seemed thunderstruck.

"The cheque supposed to be forged must be put in as evidence, or else there is an end of the case," said the judge.

"My lord," said Old Tough Mutton, rising, "I can assure you that last night I had the cheque in my possession; I placed it myself among my papers, and now— now——"

"Well, sir?"

"It cannot be found. I trust my respectability is——"

"Too well known to admit of the shadow of a doubt upon the matter; but if you cannot find the paper there is

an end of the case; the lad at the bar must be acquitted."

There was a loud murmur of applause.

"I will commit the first person who dares offend the dignity of the law," said the judge. "In justice to all parties I will adjourn this court for an hour, in order that strict search be made."

And his lordship rose.

The counsel for Harry Munro had hitherto kept silence.

But he now rose.

"Your lordship, may I be permitted to say a few words upon this most extraordinary case?"

"Certainly, Mr. Anson."

And his lordship reseated himself.

"I will save the time of the court, and so distinctly prove the innocence of the lad at the bar, that whether the cheque be found or not it will avail nothing."

Here Mr. Crawley's eyes caught sight of an object in the court, and rapidly descending from the witnessbox, he was hastily leaving the place.

"May I ask your lordship to intimate to that gentleman that it will not be convenient for him to leave the court at present; leave it he may, by-and-bye."

And with that Mr. Crawley was conducted back in the politest manner possible, while an attentive officer stood on each side of him.

"My lord, I charge that man, and likewise his employer, who, I am sorry to say, has left the town, with basely conspiring to charge that youth at the bar with the crime of forgery; a malignant feeling in the breast of McHaffie against Mrs. Munro was the origin of it. I shall be able to prove that the signature was signed by way of joke, and then that detestable scoundrel "—pointing to Crawley—" in conjunction with that arch-fiend, his master, filled up the cheque. The witness to all this is now in the court."

Here the long pent-up feelings of the crowd broke out in one long, loud British cheer, and none gave it heartier than the boys themselves.

" Here are the affidavits, and here the witnesses."

And here Mr. Sheepshanks returned into court.

The cheque could not be found.

" Gentlemen of the jury," said the judge, "you will acquit that much-injured boy at the bar, and he leaves it without a stain upon his character."

Over the dock leaped Harry Munro, into the arms of his mother, while Giles and Ted were shaking his hands nearly off in their joy and congratulations.

" See that witness is kept in safe custody."

And the judge pointed to Crawley.

" My lord," said a man who had placed a stern grip on his collar, " I have been five years looking after him and his pretended master upon five distinct charges of forgery. He is my prisoner, and won't easily escape from my clutches."

And so saying, he quietly slipped a pair of handcuffs on to the trembling wrists of the amiable Mr. Crawley, and led him from the court, amid the loud hisses of all present.

The judge had scarcely left the bench when from the gallery there arose the clear tones of victory from " bright chanticleer."

Master Ted Flan could not, in the joy of the moment, have resisted if he had been sent upon the silent system for a month.

Forth from the crowded court rushed the impatient mob; some half-dozen of them hoisted Harry Munro upon their shoulders and bore him home in triumph, followed by his trembling, happy mother, while the mass, making for the house of the respectable McHaffie, ventilated it by breaking every pane of glass, and well it was for him that he had received a timely warning, and placed many miles between him and the scene of his villany, or Lynch law would have been his doom.

The unexpected checkmate was brought about by the fellow clerk of Harry Munro, who had been sent to London upon a pretended business to get him out of the way, but who, hearing of the dangerous position of his brother clerk, soon made his way back to save him and hurl retribution upon the heads of the unprincipled scoundrels who would have destroyed him.

It was a narrow escape from " playing with fire," and was a lesson to all who knew the facts and witnessed the trial, and many days elapsed ere the town recovered its usual quiet.

When the lawyer reached home with his two protégés, he retired, taking them with him into his study.

He was evidently very much annoyed and disturbed in his mind, and after sitting in silence for some time, he rang the bell and ordered all his clerks into his presence.

After severely examining and cross-examining them he gave up the task.

"Who the devil," he said, in a rage, "could have taken the paper, for stolen it must have been?"

"Oh, pase and buttermilk, by the Cove of Cork, you've guessed it; he's got it!" and Ted's face looked as solemn as a quaker's.

"What do you mean, sir?" said Sheepshanks, sternly. "Do you know who has got it, eh?"

"Not I. Is it likely I'd trouble my head about a trifle like that? I only think that the gentleman whose name you mentioned might have come down the chimney and taken it."

"What do you mean?" roared the lawyer.

"That's just my maning."

"Why, you Irish blunderer. You ——"

"Whist! manners, sir! Don't make names, sir, because you might want some at your own christening. Did you ever hear the story of Larry O'Nailem."

"Larry O'Nailem? No; who was he?"

"Who was he? Well, I pity your ignorance, but I'll tell you. Larry O'Nailem—the saints save him!—was a little pettyfogging lawyer, and lived in the town of Ballymacslush, the clanest place in all creation if it wasn't for the heaps of mud. Well, sir, in that beautiful place lived and flourished Larry O'Nailem; what became of him no one could ever tell."

"Pshaw! I suppose he died."

"That's unsartain."

"Well, then he's living."

"That's unsartain."

"He must be either dead or alive, you blockhead."

"That's unsartain."

"What do you mean to say?"

"I mane to say that it's unsartain where he is at this minute."

"Did he run away?"

"Dare say he did, and that with his client's money."

"For shame, sir; as if any lawyer was ever guilty of such a dirty action."

The lawyer, Giles, and all present burst out into a fit of laughter.

"Well, go on, Mr. Ted Flan; have your length of rope."

"Yes, but I'll take care it's not long or strong enough for a swing. My father had it from Terry Hoolagan, the wandering piper. Ah, you should have heard Terry's music, it would have had such an effect you'd never get over it."

"I dare say; but keep to Larry O'Nailem."

"I'd be sorry to be near him now, anyhow. Well, this is how the story goes:—

"One night Larry was in his sanctum sanctorum; and beautifully furnished it was, wid a large fire-place and chimney a dozen might dine in and be convaniently comfortable, with a three-legged chair and a deal wooden table.

"Well, sir, during that day Larry had been serving convictions on the tinantry."

"Convictions! What's that, eh?"

"I beg your pardon—evictions. It's a sort of cure for that unpleasant, yet universal complaint they call poverty, because when they're starving in doors they turn them out to cure it.

"Well, sir, on that night Larry was alone by himself, when his housekeeper heard a loud talking, and with that—

not having the least curiosity in the world ; and what female ever had ?—she went to the door and listened.

" ' You thafe of the world, you have charged me with six-and-eightpence too much !' said a voice as husky as if it had lived all its life upon asthmatical fogs.

" ' Your highness, I'd scorn to do such a thing,' replied Larry, and his voice sounded as though he'd a seven years' ague.

" 'You villain,' said his highness (save us !), ' you shall come home with me, and see the bill.'

" With that a rumpus occurred, and the old woman ran away, and hid herself under the bed, and stopped till the morning came ; and then she called all the neighbours, and after a mighty deal of assistance from the crayther, they burst open the door of the sanctum sanctorum, and there, jammed in the chimney, was Larry O'Nailem's wooden leg ; and they were obliged to run from the place for the powerful odour."

" Odour ! Odour of what ?"

" I'd much rayther not say, sir," as Ted and Giles moved to the door.

" Odour of what ? Tell me instantly."

" Brimstone, sir," and away ran Giles and Ted, laughing at the very top of their voices.

When they met again at dinner, all the disappointments and vexations of the day seemed to have fled from the mind of the lawyer ; he laughed heartily at Larry O'Nailem and his wooden leg, and the odour. The dinner ended, the lawyer looked keenly at the boys, and then, placing his hand in his pocket, pulled out two handsome portmonnaies.

" Giles Evergreen, that is for you," he said, handing him one. " You will not open it until you have reached London. Ted Flaherty O'Flanagan, there is yours. Your travelling trunks are all directed, and when you reach London, fresh up from the country, you will find a person waiting to convey you to your destination. In your trunks you will find a few lines addressed to each ; endeavour to carry out faithfully what is there wished ; in any emergency come or send. I don't like parting with you, for you have wound yourselves round the heart of the old lawyer, but it is your destiny to go, and endeavour to pass through the ordeal unscathed ; and remember the lesson taught by ' playing with fire.' "

At that moment a knock was heard at the door, and the old servant entered, followed by the widow and her son.

Giles and Ted sprang up, and ran eagerly to them.

" Oh ! how glad we are to see you," they both said.

" Ha, ha, ha !" chuckled old Tough Mutton, rubbing his hands joyfully ; " I thought I'd give you a little surprise before you started for London. Sit down, Mrs. Munro," and he handed her a seat close to his own. " Let the boys sit together ; schoolfellows should never be parted, for when fighting the ' great battle of life,' and separated, they should never forget the happy days they passed as boys. Ah, dear me ! Oh ! the days when I was young." The querulous tone in which it was uttered made the boys laugh. " Ah, you dogs, stop till you grow old, and then somebody will have the laugh against you."

"We can afford to wait, sir," said Ted.

"And we shan't hurry, be assured, sir," chimed in Giles.

"Mrs. Munro, I dare say you were surprised when you got my note."

"I was, indeed," replied the widow.

"No more surprised than I was when I wrote it. The fact is, it's a matter of business."

"Business, sir!" she said with surprise.

"Yes; I wouldn't have had this day's affair turn out otherwise than it has—no, not for a thousand pounds."

"Oh, sir."

"Be quiet. A couple of infernal scamps have been unmasked; and about the cheque, it don't matter, although I confess that I—ah, well, never mind—burn the cheque!"

Here the widow glanced furtively at Giles.

"And there is an end of it. You see, my dear Mrs. Munro, I am going to lose those two mad-brained, rackety boys to-morrow."

"And, plase the pigs, we'll be a trifle more so when we return," said Ted.

"No doubt; no doubt; but now, my boys, what say you, Giles and Ted, to my taking Harry Munro into my office, and making a man and a lawyer of him, eh?"

"Oh, sir, will you do so?"

"By the powers, you are a lump of honey," said Ted.

"No blarney, Master Ted. What say you; madam?"

"Oh, sir, what can a lone widow say? She can only silently pray to God to reward them who assist the widow and the fatherless, and render their dark, struggling pathway one of light and joy."

And she fell weeping upon his shoulder.

"Bless my heart, Mrs. Munro, what are you about?" said he, affecting alarm. "If my old housekeeper were to see this she'd think the world had come to an end. There, there. Remember, Harry, you come to breakfast with those two boys before they start, and bring your mother with you, and I'll place you under my steady managing clerk, old Surepen, and, who knows, we may live to see you a judge yet."

And the good old lawyer laughed.

"But, sir, the money," faltered out the widow.

"Money! What money?" and the lawyer stared at her. "Who said a word about money?"

"I didn't; sure I wouldn't soil my tongue with the dirty word."

And Ted snapped his fingers in thorough contempt at it.

"Ha, ha! Bravo, Erin-go-bragh; not a word about money. Now, then, another glass of wine to drink success to Giles Evergreen, one of the Boys of England; Master Flan, a boy from the Green Isle; and the brave, hardy lads of dear Scotia. Success to them all in their journey through life."

When Giles and Ted laid their heads down on their pillows that night there was a feeling of sadness upon them that they were going to leave old Lawyer Tough Mutton.

"London. Up from the country to-morrow," said Giles dreamily.

"Yes," replied Ted, half dreamily, "where the paving-stones are wooden blocks of gold, and the buildings are built of marble, with the windows rale diamonds; and all the gintlemen with sovereigns in their pockets, and crowns on their heads, and——Och, bathera-shun. Good-night."

"Good-night!" returned Giles, and the two boys tumbled off to sleep, to dream of the glorious sprees to be enjoyed in London.

CHAPTER X.

THE RAILWAY STATION.

At breakfast the next morning all the parties that had met the evening before assembled.

At that happy meeting it was settled that Harry Munro was to be placed in the lawyer's office to learn the art and mystery of the law.

"But, my good lad," said the kind-hearted man, "don't get 'playing with fire,' because you see what may at times come of it."

"I shall be careful of it, sir," said the lad, "and if you doubt me, I——"

"No, no, I don't doubt you; a burnt child dreads the fire. I'll trust you, if it were only for your father's sake and your mother's affection."

"Oh, sir, how can I ever repay you for this act of kindness to this poor, fatherless boy?"

And the poor widow's eyes streamed with tears.

"By saying nothing about it," was the testy reply. "I'm a lawyer, and like everything brief."

"Like yourself—short, sir," said Ted Flan.

"Yes, like an Irishman's pipe," replied the lawyer.

"Ah, there you are upon my unfortunate country again. Have you forgotten Larry Nailem, how he disappeared suddenly and has never been heard of since, bekase he charged six and eightpence too much in his bill to one of his warmest clients? I'd rather not go that journey for six and eight-pence. Will I give you a bit of advice, bekase you'll not always have me at your elbows to look after you?"

"Ha! ha! Well, what is it?"

"Be careful and not charge too much in your bills, or when Giles and I come back mayhap we may have to act as ex-e-cutors. And with that I lave you my blessing and best wishes."

And so saying, he extended his hand with an air of great patronage.

The lawyer took it and pressed it heartily.

"Ted Flan, you are a wonder," he said.

"Aye, sir, that's what they told me in Ireland, where wonders are not thought wonders."

"Why not?"

"Bekase we are wonderful from one end to the other in consequence of our pace and quietness."

At that moment the servant entered.

"Everything is ready, sir," he said, addressing the lawyer.

"Right. Now, good bye, my lads; the carriage will take you to the station; on your way to town you will peruse that letter" — giving one to Giles—"and you will learn your destination. It may appear strange, but I am only carrying out my instructions."

"Which shall be faithfully and strictly adhered to by myself and Ted," said Giles. "Rest assured, sir, that, whatever our career may be in London, there shall be nothing to tarnish our reputation or that of our kind, dear friend."

"Hurroo! he spakes like a book. Oh! if we had only a Parleyment in Ireland, I'd return him for my borough, if I only had one. Oh, what a splendid figure of spache is the art of talking!"

"Which you don't know anything about, eh?"

"The want of that, sir, and my nateral modesty, will be a graveous hindrance to my progress through the vale of tears, which, in all my country excursions, will be avoided by your humble servant."

And so saying, they descended the stairs.

Again and again were the kind adieus exchanged, especially by Mrs. Munro and her son Harry, who parted from his dear schoolfellows with tears of gratitude in his bright eyes.

The luggage was already on the roof; anxious faces were seen peeping out of the windows; the carriage door was shut, and Giles Evergreen and Terence Flaherty O'Flanagan were on their road to London.

For a time they were both silent.

Like all noble-hearted boys, they keenly felt the pang at parting from kind, valued friends.

Although bitterly cold, it was a glorious ride through the country to the station, some four miles distant, the large one for the town not having been completed.

The trees seemed breaking down with silver drops, glittering and transparent, while the fields and upland downs were one pure mantle of dazzling white.

The sheep, in their fleecy coats thickly encrusted with snow, their warm breath rising like a cloud in the cold frosty air, and huddled close together to catch a little more warmth, stood gazing over the chill landscape, looking for the careful shepherd, who, with his faithful watch dog, was seen trudging through the snow with their wintry food.

Ever and anon, some cosy farm, with its warm ruddy glow from the log fire, was seen sending forth, as it would seem, an invitation to the benumbed travellers to enter and share its warm hospitality, and not fear a hearty welcome; and its old thatch had for its covering a thick blanket of pure, unsunned snow, which still fell in large flakes.

And thus the two boys travelled slowly on, immersed in their own thoughts.

It was not in the nature of Ted Flan to remain silent long.

"By the strong joint of my grandfather's elbow, but this is pleasant travelling; if a band of music were here it's a jig I'd be dancing, if it were only to bring a little life into my poor dear, departed toes. I say, Giles, we got the best of the big wigs for Harry Munro, didn't we?"

"That we did, Ted," said Giles, " and we shall never have cause to regret it. I wonder what the letter says, eh, Ted?"

"Break open its mouth, and let its voice jump out," was the reply.

No sooner said than done.

And Giles read out thus:—

"MY DEAR LADS,—Upon your arrival at the Great Northern Terminus, King's Cross, you will be met by a servant, who will conduct you to the house where apartments are taken for you ; everything is paid for both of you for twelve months ; further instructions you will find in letters in your travelling trunks. Enjoy yourselves, but do not let any consideration tempt you to do wrong.

"I am yours,
"TIMOTHY SHEEPSHANKS,
"Attorney-at-law."

"Do wrong! What, in the name of Saint Patrick, does he mane by that? I've a great mind to go back and ask the question."

"He has his reasons, no doubt, Ted, for what he says."

"Raisons! There's raison in roasting eggs, although I never tried it. Do wrong? Well, he may be right; but if anyone else had cast such a slur upon the carakter of an Irish gentleman, descended from the ancient kings of Munster and——"

"Well, don't make such a *stir about* it, Ted. I wish the horses would stir a little faster; I think old John is asleep."

"Aslape is he," said Ted, "then by all that's wide awake I'll stir him up."

He let down the window glass of the carriage, and, leaning his head out, looked behind the vehicle.

"Murder, murder!" cried a voice, in great agony. "What do you mean by running over me like that, you sleepy vagabond?"

Up went the window again.

The cries awoke old John, who, lulled by the intensity of the weather, was quietly dozing ; he started up, and in his horror at having run over some unfortunate person, rose so hastily that he let fall the reins, and fell head first in the snow.

Ted and Giles were looking out of the window as if alarmed at the cries, but that was changed to shouts of laughter when they beheld the old coachman struggling to get out of the snow and upon his legs.

"Murder! murder!" said the voice again, but in low tones, as if they were sinking fast.

Luckily, the horses stood perfectly quiet.

At last the coachman got upon his legs, and waded through the snow behind the carriage.

"Wha—wha—wha—what's—the—the—mat—matter?" said he, trembling and shaking between fright and the cold.

"Why, John, whatever have you done?" exclaimed the boys, in the same breath.

"Done? Hanged if I know, young gentlemen," he said. "Did you hear anybody call out?"

"Call out? What do you mean?" said Giles.

"Aye, what do you mane? Are you draming, John?"

"Well, sir, I can't say I know."

And the man's face looked so puzzled

and confounded, that again the air rang with the merry laugh of the boys.

"I heard somebody call out as if I'd run over them, but blest if there's a soul here, unless they be buried deep in the snow."

And again he went all round the carriage to see if, by any accident, he had missed seeing the injured person.

"Nonsense," said Giles; "the cold sent you to sleep, and you dreamed it. Come, get on, that's a good fellow."

"Well, it must have been so."

And he prepared to mount the box again.

Scarcely had he got his foot on the step, when, to his horror—

"Oh, oh, oh!" was heard in a dismal, faint groan, expressive of great agony.

"There it is again," said the poor fellow, shaking with fear.

"By the powers, you've lost your senses. Are you going to kape us here until we are frozen into snowballs?"

And here Teddy seemed very angry.

"You see there is nobody about but ourselves, John," said Giles.

Up he sprang, and gathering up the reins, set off at as smart a pace as the road would let him ; but a loud shriek, as of vengeance, was heard saluting him as he left the spot.

Frightened out of his sleepy fit, he got his horses into a gallop.

"I thought," said Ted, "I'd wake him ; but I believe, in my conscience, I've roused old Tough Mutton's horses to a pace they never went before. Hurroo ! kape it up, my beauties."

In a very short time they gained the station.

A railway station is a very exciting sight ; but a railway terminus is a small panorama of the world.

It is something astonishing to see the confusion and babel of tongues, and to listen to the various noises, from the cry of the baby to the scream of the engine.

Yet all this riot and confusion is reduced in a very short time to order and regularity.

The brief time allotted to passengers is up, and in a few minutes all are again in their respective seats.

The whistle sounds, and almost in the twinkle of an eye the once noisy station is as silent as a cemetery.

The porters lounge back to their snug berths, the refreshment-rooms look like "banquet halls deserted," and everyone seems to subside into silence and ease, except the unfortunate passenger who has been left behind, and who is angrily expostulating with the station-master, who kindly informs him that he will forward him by the parliamentary train in three hours' time.

Inside the station all is comfortable and snug, outside all is comfortless and snow.

Signal-posts, trucks, engines, carriages, and the solitary pointsman, all appear as if they had been converted into samples of the Universal Flour Company.

The only bustle is in the telegraph office, and there the needle is hard at work, telling the station-master that he may look out for a special train upon urgent government affairs, and that the line is to be kept clear of all trains until that has passed ; it may be some time yet, but it must have precedence of all others, so the passengers who are waiting for their especial trains—must wait, must wait!

That is the answer to the angry and indignant expostulations of some forty or fifty persons gathered together from different parts of the country, and, anxious to reach London, they will have to wait specially until the "special" has rushed like a whirlwind through the station, and in an instant is out of sight.

Such was the state of things at the place when the boys arrived at it.

They had given old John a present, and charged him with many loving messages to the lawyer, and warned him not to fall asleep again.

"No, no," said he; "I'll take care of that; it be a matter of five miles further round, but I don't go that road again!"

"Why not?" they asked, laughingly.

"Well, I'll tell ye. It be jest agin the lane that leads down to the crossroads, where, in a fit of jealousy, a young man murdered his sweetheart and then afterwards blew his brains out. They buried him there by torch-light, and put a stake in his inside."

"A stake," said Ted, raising his eyes with affected horror. "What's the use of a steak to a man when his brains are blown out?"

"You must make a mistake," said Giles.

"No, I am certain sure about it, because our cook was told by the housemaid, who was told by the waiter at the inn, who heard the ostler say that old List, the tailor, had it from a travelling tinker, who passed the spot the day after."

"Well, then, all I can say is that if they put steaks into men after they are dead, it's a great waste of good mate."

And Ted winked at Giles.

"That's what I said. Good bye, young gentlemen, and a pleasant journey to you."

And away drove the simple-hearted old coachman.

A porter having taken their trunks, and placed them in safety, Giles and Ted walked into the refreshment-room.

Now a refreshment-room at a railway station when there is no train waiting is a very dead-and-alive affair, and on this occasion it certainly partook more of the former than the latter.

There were not above twenty persons in the room, and they were scattered about at the different tables.

The front of the fire, and its sides, of course, were entirely taken up by about half-a-dozen thick-set men called drovers.

Remonstrances with them would have been useless, so Ted and Giles took their seats at a small table close to the bar.

In the bar were two females, young, and rather prepossessing; but evidently, from their dress and looks, in their own opinion they considered the passengers as rather "inferior animals."

Ted and Giles could see at a glance that there was no love lost between them; they occasionally cast looks of contempt and bitter defiance at each other; and the shrewd boys could at once perceive that it only required a little gentle fanning to set the smouldering embers into a fierce flame.

"We mustn't let them go to slape here, Giles," whispered Ted.

"By no means," was the answer.

"The waiter seems as proud as the Grand Turk's paycock that had four tails."

"What for, Ted?"

"One for each pint of the compass. Here, waiter! (I'll open the ball, Giles) we'll trouble you for some soup."

Of course the waiter did not attend to them.

"Did you hear those boys?" said one of the girls.

"Oh, yes; I'll attend to them shortly," replied the waiter.

"Some soup, my dear," said Ted, "and send plenty of Cayenne with it."

"My dear! Well, I'm sure!"

And the girl tossed her head until the ribbons rustled again.

"As if you didn't like it, Selina Jones," said the other girl, with a grin.

"Selina Jones will thank Florence Pepper to attend particularly to her own affairs," replied the other, curling her lip with an air of domestic drama.

The boys' eyes twinkled like stars at the approaching fun.

"It would be as well," chimed in the waiter.

"Keep your distance, Augustus," said Miss Pepper, "and your talk for that young woman," pointing with the "finger of scorn" at Selina Jones.

"Young woman? Who do you call young woman?"

And Selina's eyes shot fire.

Suddenly there was a call of roast beef for two from that part of the room where two old ladies sat; off bustled Augustus to them.

"Anything with the beef, ladies?" asked the waiter.

"Beef? What do you mean, sir? We never taste beef!" was the indignant ladies' reply.

"You certainly called for beef, ladies," said the waiter.

"We did nothing of the sort, you impudent fellow! Where is the master of this place?"

"Well, I beg your pardon, ladies, but certainly the order came from this quarter."

And, somewhat amazed, Augustus left them.

At last the soup appeared on the bar of the counter.

"Here's the soup for the boys," said Selina Jones.

"Manners, young woman!" said a voice behind her.

"I wish you wouldn't interfere with me, Miss Pepper," said the indignant Selina.

"I never opened my mouth to you," was the reply.

"It's a downright falsehood!"

"I know anything that comes from you is!"

"Do you mean to say that? Why, you frightful mean thing, I'll——"

Here war was about commencing, when the appearance of the master suddenly suspended the hostilities; but the looks of the two girls highly delighted Giles and Ted, who had their revenge for the discourteous treatment they had experienced from them.

"THE ENGINE, WITH ITS TERRIBLE BLOOD-RED LIGHT, CAME RUSHING ALONG."

The soup, when brought, was found to be such a mixture that even they, as boys, could not be induced to take more than one spoonful; it reminding them very much of the physic they were often compelled to take when at school, where one pill or draught was a dose.

But into a large piece of paper unobserved, Ted put a quanity of Cayenne pepper, and screwed it up tightly.

At this moment loud murmurs arose in the room at the shameful manner in which other persons were excluded from the warmth of the fire.

All this was of no avail; the men seated round it only laughed and jeered.

Telling Giles to sit still, Ted suddenly arose and carelessly strolled towards the fire; passing a small spirit-lamp on the counter, he lighted the paper he held in his hand, and, unnoticed, dropped it under the chair of the man in the centre, then wandered back to his seat.

In a few minutes the fumes of the burnt pepper mounted among the occupants of the fire.

Then came an amount of violent coughing and sneezing, extending itself all over the place, and, in less than five minutes, not only the fire-side was clear, but the room itself, the visitants preferring the cold air without rather than the risk of being choked within, all parties—except the gentlemen disturbed from their warm seats—being delighted at the clever trick played upon the uncivilized fellows, who did not care a rush for any one's comfort and convenience but their own.

The well-regulated official, the station-master, soon had all matters arranged, and the half-frozen travellers returned to the room, this time the fire-place being kept perfectly clear so that all could experience some slight portion of its genial warmth.

He informed the train-bound passengers that the special would go through in about an hour, and then they should be speedily on their way to their several destinations.

"You young gentlemen," he said, addressing the boys, "may go into the ladies' room, if you feel inclined."

"Many thanks, sir," replied Ted; "but we are highly delighted with the ladies here," and he glanced at the two girls at the bar. "My mother, who is an Irish baronet, in her own right, would like to have a couple of handsome, well-behaved females like those about her."

The station-master smiled; he saw what the shrewd boy meant.

"I have an aunt," said Giles, "who would like to have two of the same sort."

"Will you be kind enough to take for the—eh, what do you call that stuff you brought us, waiter?"

"Stuff?" and the dignity of Augustus shone out boldly. "It's real mock turtle."

"Rale mock turtle, Giles! Did you ever hear the likes of that afore?"

"It's a real mockery, he means," replied Giles.

"And can you tell us where it was growed, my good man?" asked Ted, with a beautiful air of simplicity that completely set the clever Augustus off his guard.

" Well, you see, I can't precisely say, but I think I've heard in some of the Channel Islands."

" In the Canine Islands ? By the powers, I thought so ! The flavour was so delicious ; what say you to some more, Giles ?"

" Well, not at present ; I don't like too many delicacies at once. We'll pay, waiter."

" Yes, *short* reckonings," said Ted, looking hard at the waiter, who was a small specimen of his species, " make *long* friends."

" Yes, gentlemen," and he bowed and cringed in a most alarming manner.

It was the sight of Giles's handsome, well-filled portemonnaie that caused the great transformation in the man's manners.

" Two soups, two breads, and—ah, let me see——"

And Augustus paused.

" Two basins, and two spoons," said Ted, looking hard at him.

" Beg pardon, we don't charge for them. No sherry ?"

" Well, no ; we don't want poisoning all at once. Gently does it, my man."

" Ha, ha ! Very good."

" What, the soup, my man ? I hope the difference of opinion will not cause a civil war, my friend ; but in my country they make a better soup than that that comes from the Canine Islands out of nothing at all."

" Indeed, gentlemen, how is that ?"

" Why, they put a peculiar stone into wather and boil it until——"

" Until what, sir ?"

" Until it becomes soft," said Ted, tapping his forehead.

Then rising, Giles and he went out upon the platform.

They had not been there many minutes, when the arrival of more passengers attracted their attention, but their surprise was very much increased when among them they saw Alfred Ravensborne, who they thought had proceeded to London.

Giles and Ted advanced with outstretched hands to greet him.

" You will excuse me, Giles Evergreen, from shaking hands with either you or your companion."

And, folding his arms, he stood surveying them with a smile of ill-disguised contempt.

" Indeed ! What for ?" said Giles.

" What for ? For many reasons," was the reply.

" Oh, I suppose it was because I prevented you from committing an action at Dr. Birchenough's which you would never have forgotten. Tush, tush ! think better of it, Alfred."

And again, with a manly frankness, he held out his hand.

Ravensborne fixedly contemplated him for a moment.

" I will be very candid with you," at length he said ; " from the very moment I cast my eyes upon you I hated you."

" Oh, murder, there's a beauty !" muttered Ted.

" I felt that in our passage through life you would in every respect be opposed to me."

" Ridiculous nonsense !" said Giles.

" That remains to be seen ; but I warn you to be careful how you oppose me ; there may be other reasons why we cannot at any time be upon speaking terms, let alone friendship. Follow me, Dick."

And so saying, he walked towards the refreshment rooms, followed by the individual he addressed.

Giles and Ted Flan looked at each other with great surprise and astonishment, and, then, at last, unable to resist it, the latter burst into a loud laugh.

"By the powers, he's coming Captain Grand over us, Giles," said Ted. "What does it all mane?"

"I can't for the life of me divine the cause, except you know we never agreed at school; but see how that fellow he called Dick is eyeing us; it's the man I knocked down for his unmanly treatment to the poor crazed girl."

The individual so called was standing at the door of the refreshment room, and was intently regarding both the friends with a peculiar scrutinizing gaze.

He was dressed in a costume partaking alike of groom and jockey, and in his general bearing there was no mistaking that he belonged to either the one class or the other.

His forehead was low and retreating, while the shaggy brows that hung over his eyes could not conceal from the keen observer that they combined the sharpness of the lynx with the cunning of the fox and ferocity of the wolf; small in stature, but well formed, his frame seemed capable of enduring great fatigue.

Round his well-fitting coat he wore a broad leathern belt and on the well-brushed hat there was a cockade, showing that whatever he was in position, he belonged to a person of some standing in society.

Seeing that the attention of Giles and Ted was intently fixed upon him, he scowled upon them, and then lounged carelessly away to that portion of the building known as the Tap connected with the waiting-rooms.

"I don't like the looks of that gentleman, Giles," said Ted.

"He appears to be the servant of Alfred Ravensborne; but his good or bad looks are a matter of perfect indifference to me," was the answer.

Not so Ted Flan; he treasured up the look, and it was a long time before the recollection of it left his mind.

Beyond the station, for about one hundred yards, there ran a bank from which the snow had melted, and from whose bed a splendid array of primroses peeped forth; Giles and Ted, in order to keep their blood in circulation, kept walking up and down the platform, and as the time for the special train to pass rapidly approached, the platform became more and more crowded.

"Stand back, everybody," called out the station-master; "the special will be through in a few minutes."

Suddenly there was a scream heard, and a lady, handsomely dressed, rushed out of the waiting-room, followed by a female servant whose pale face told a tale of agony and horror.

"Where, where, is the child—my darling Hilda?"

And the agonised mother rushed wildly about seeking for her.

The people, bustling about the platform, stood still for a moment and gazed in blank dismay at this appeal.

"Merciful Heaven!" said the frantic mother, "I see her not! Wretch!" And she flew at the frightened servant. "Where is she?"

The girl, alarmed at this outbreak of fury, sank on her knees, screaming, and exclaiming—

"Sure, madam, I don't know; she was standing beside me not a minute since."

And the girl and the mother both ran about the platform in search of the child.

"Oh!" screamed the servant, pointing to the opposite line, "there she is."

Our hero, Giles, who had been looking towards the bank where the primroses were growing, saw the figure of a girl, about thirteen years of age, gathering them, and evidently unconscious of the peril she was in, or the dreadful death that was awaiting her.

"In the name of Heaven," he said, "whose child is that?"

And he pointed to the bank of primroses.

The lady looked forward and uttered an appalling cry.

"Mine, mine!" she gasped out, and was springing forward, when, in gurgling accents, she exclaimed, "Sa—sa—save, save her!" and rushing forward, she was forcibly held back by the station master and a porter.

"Stand back, ma'am, you will be killed," said the porter.

"My child!" shrieked the mother.

At that moment the warning bell rang, and within a short distance could be distinctly heard the rushing noise of the engine of the special train, speeding along with the velocity of light upon its urgent errand.

"It will be death to anyone who attempts it," frantically called out the station-master.

"Here goes to try it," shouted Giles, rushing along the platform to the embankment.

"There are others quite as brave," shouted Alfred Ravensborne, who had joined the people on the platform, and he was after him like an arrow from a bow.

"Ireland for ever!" shouted Ted, and he also sprang after them.

The race was one of fearful excitement; the people held their breath in wonder, awe, and amazement; numbers rushed back into the waiting-room, placing their hands over their ears to shut out the appalling sounds and shriek of death.

On sped the three brave lads; they had often run the mimic race for fun and fame in the play ground, but here it was for life and to escape a fearful, horrible death.

The engine, with its terrible blood-red light, came rushing along, sounding its whistle, a scream almost beyond human endurance.

The driver saw it all, but knew his power was of no use; to shut off the steam was useless and would not have saved their lives.

Giles had reached the girl first, and, in an instant, she was in his arms.

"Run, run!" he shouted, and they reached the end of the bank.

"Leap, Ted, Alfred!" and suddenly the three disappeared from view, as the train shot past.

The driver and stoker, the guard and government messenger, saw the whole affair, and sent a ringing shout as they flew past, and waved their caps with frantic joy until they had disappeared.

The moment the special had rushed through the station men and women ran down the steps towards the bank, and gazed tremblingly down the embankment.

It was barely ten feet down, and there at the bottom stood Giles, holding the scared girl in his arms, Ted having Alfred in his arms, for in leaping his foot had caught some obstruction, and he was flung heavily down upon his forehead, the blow of which had rendered him senseless.

Luckily the snow was so thick that it reached nearly up to their waists, and so there at the bottom they stood like pillars of salt.

In a few moments they were again on the line of rail amid the shouts and boisterous congratulations of all the people, taken up by those upon the platform, whose horror-stricken faces, in the anticipation of a fearful tragedy, had changed suddenly to joy and gladness when they saw that they were all in safety.

A strong porter, bearing Alfred Ravensborne in his arms, rushed into the waiting-room with him, and by aid of strong stimulants, he speedily recovered consciousness.

Kind hands would have taken the bewildered girl from the arms of her preserver, but no mortal power could have done that with Giles, who held her to his breast with all the loving tenderness of a brother, and who only gave up his darling charge when the almost frantic mother rushed forward, and, placing her tenderly and respectfully in her arms, he walked away with Ted without waiting for the thanks the tongue could not speak, but which welled in tears of gratitude from the eyes.

The excitement at the railway station was intense; it was useless for Giles to try and conceal himself, for, with the modesty inherent in all great and good minds, he strove all he could to keep himself from the crowd that followed him about, and poured their admiration of his daring courage upon him.

But when the mother of the rescued girl approached him he went up to her, and taking the hand she held out, tenderly kissed it.

"Believe me," he said, "I do not want, nay, do not deserve thanks; myself and Ted and Alfred were all equal in the race, only I am lucky in being the swiftest, and gained the dear girl first."

"But that would not have been the case only you jostled me on purpose," said Alfred Ravensborne, scowling upon him; "but that's only on a par with your pitiful tricks."

The cheeks of Giles Evergreen flushed deeply.

"You wrong me, Alfred," he warmly replied; "I ran fair, and never touched you."

"You did not," cried Ravensborne.

"By the powers! but he did!" said Ted, warmly. "What matters?—we all tried to do our best, and the best won."

"I am sure you did; and my thanks

are equally due to all. Will you favour me with your names and addresses ?"

And the lady took Giles's hand.

" My name is Giles Evergreen; these are my schoolfellows. This is Alfred Ravensborne."

" Ravensborne ? Any relation to the earl of that name ?"

" Grandson," was the reply.

" Then I claim you as a kinsman, and am proud of your courage. The girl you tried to save is your third cousin, Hilda St. George. And your address ?" she said to Giles.

" I cannot tell you; I don't know myself," was the reply.

" And this young gentleman ?" pointing to Ted Flan.

" I am Master Terence Flaherty O'Flanagan, of Irish extraction; but, being Irish, it counts for nothing."

The bell now rang, for the train which they were to travel by was slowly entering the station.

" You are three brave boys, and shall travel with me in the same carriage, that I may know more about you."

" Excuse me, I shall not travel in the same carriage. Follow me," said Alfred to his servant, and touching his hat to the ladies, walked away.

" He has the bad blood of the family in him," said the lady. " Never mind him; you shall tell me more as we proceed on our journey."

By this time the station was crowded by persons who had heard of the daring act, and when Giles came out, leading Hilda by the hand, followed by her mother and Ted Flan, a ringing volley of cheers rang through the station.

" Curses on him, I'll see if I can't be even with him for this, as well as many other favours I owe him," muttered Alfred.

And throwing himself back, he pondered on his plans as the train proceeded rapidly towards the great metropolis.

CHAPTER XI.

FRESH FROM THE COUNTRY.

THE train sped swiftly on its way to London, and during its progress Lady St. George again and again warmly thanked Giles Evergreen and Ted Flan for their daring conduct and bravery in saving the life of her beloved child, Hilda.

Hilda, with a sweet, childish simplicity, and eyes beaming with love and gratitude, seated herself between the two boys, and clasping a hand of each, kept every now and then bestowing a

warm kiss upon them, expressive of her deep and lasting gratitude.

" You must again and again accept my thanks for your saving my only child from such a fearful, horrid death. It is astonishing at times what ruin the carelessness of servants may involve you in."

" It was not Smithson's fault, mamma. I was foolish to wander from her while she was reading; but the beauty of the primroses attracted me, and I could not resist gathering some, especially as I knew you were so fond of them."

"You must be more careful for the future, my dear. And so you say your name is——"

Giles Evergreen," replied Giles; "and I shall never forget this day, that made me the humble means of saving Miss Hilda."

"Are you a son of Mr. Evergreen of Scarsdale?" asked the lady.

"Yes, my lady."

"He is well, I hope?"

"He died some years since; I have neither father, nor mother, nor relative. My last relative, an aunt, died some time since."

"Yes, you have a relative, although a very distant one, in myself; yourself and Alfred Ravensborne are kinsmen," rejoined Lady St. George.

"By the powers, my lady, I am sorry to say there is no love in the blood of Master Alfred Ravensborne for my friend Giles; but it's a matter of great indifference to Ted Flan."

"And pray what are you going to London for, and alone? It's rather dangerous. I think you'd better make my house your home."

"That's more than we dare do. We have a guardian angel in the shape of a Lawyer Sheepshanks, but better known as Old Tough Mutton. Saving your ladyship's presence, it would have done your ladyship good to have seen the old gentleman's face in a court of justice upon a certain occasion; I never saw an elderly gentleman so astonished before in all my life."

"I know the worthy gentleman," was the lady's reply; "if you are under his care no harm can befal you. But where are you going when you arrive im London?"

"That we don't know," replied Giles.

"Ha! ha! Well, it's a most singular affair, two boys going up to London and not knowing where they are going to."

"We'll be a couple of nice babes in the wood fresh from the country; greenhorns, I think they call us."

They were now rapidly nearing London, when for a time they would have to part.

Lady St. George handed Giles a card.

"My dear boys, that is my address; you will call on me to-morrow, at any hour; I shall only be too anxious and happy to see you."

"We shall be but too happy," said Giles.

"I'll not sleep a wink to-night at the thoughts of it, my lady; for, you see——"

Ted Flan's speech was cut short by the rushing of the train into the terminus, and they were in London.

The moment they emerged from the carriage a servant in livery approached them.

"Mr. Giles Evergreen and Mr. O'Flanagan," he said, respectfully touching his hat; "your luggage, gentlemen."

"Quite right," said the guard, and in a few minutes their boxes were placed before them.

"May I inquire where the young gentlemen are going?" said Lady St. George.

."Certainly, madam; there is my mistress's card," and he handed her one.

"Mrs. Wilson, No.—, Gower Street. It bears the stamp of respectability upon it. Good evening, my dears; let me see you early to-morrow."

Her ladyship had entered her carriage, and again warmly embracing the preserver of her child's life, she drove off.

The boys entering a handsome brougham, into which they were shown by the servant, soon followed, and were driven rapidly towards their new home.

For the present we'll leave them to follow the persons in the hansom cab that likewise drove out of the terminus —Alfred Ravensborne and his confidential friend and valet, Dick Martingale.

The reflections of Alfred Ravensborne had not been very pleasant ones during the journey; he had great difficulty in keeping under the passion working in his breast.

He had always hated Giles Evergreen from the very first moment he saw him; why, he could scarcely tell, but it was a deep and deadly hate; his grovelling mind saw in Giles his superior in personal accomplishments— he outshone him in his studies.

There was scarcely a boy in Dr. Birchenough's establishment but would have done anything to serve Giles Evergreen, while they openly showed their dislike of Ravensborne; he went to the school imagining his rank would make him the head of it, he found his rank went for nothing at all, and he was miserably deceived.

Then, again, the incident in the cricket-ground rendered his hate of Giles deeper; but all culminated when the affair at the railway happened, and he found himself foiled and Giles was again the victor.

"You don't seem well, Master Alfred," said Dick, as they rode along.

"Don't pester me, Dick; I am busy thinking."

"Yes, yes; I can see that; but yours ain't pleasant thoughts. It's all owing to Giles Evergreen."

"How do you know that?" he said, sharply.

"How do I know that? Ha, ha! Well, come, I like that! Why, I can see with half an eye that you hate that chap almost as much as I do."

"As you? What cause can he have given you? You are dreaming, Dick."

"Am I? I'm not in the habit of dreaming or dozing. I hate him and all his race, and I have good cause."

Alfred Ravensborne looked hard at his companion as well as the passing lights would let him.

"You? Tell me how, Dick."

"No, I can't tell it now; but I'll tell you thus far. Have you ever mentioned his name to your father?"

"Have you been drinking, Dick Martingale, on the journey to London? What the deuce do you think my father cares for such a parvenu as Giles Evergreen?"

"A little more than you think, Master Alfred. I know a little more about your father's secrets than he is aware of, just the same as I know I have the honour of your confidence."

And Dick Martingale gave a peculiar

curl of his lip, quite unobserved by his companion.

"I trust you just as far as I like," was the reply.

"That, and the rest I can pick up," muttered Dick, "will make me your master."

At that moment the cab stopped at the club.

Upon inquiries Alfred was told the Honourable Mr. Alfred Ravensborne was confined to his house by an accident he had met with while hunting.

Thither they drove.

The distance being short they were soon there.

"I say, Master Alfred," whispered Martingale, in the hall, "after you have dined, and when the wine is on the table, tell the Honourable what occurred at the station to-day."

"Oh, he'll get it all in the papers to-morrow."

"Yes, yes, I know that; but I want you to ask it, and do it when I am in the room."

"I think you have gone crazed, Dick."

"Well, I have had enough in my time to make me; but I keep my senses in order to carry out my revenge."

"What has caused all this, eh, Dick?"

"The sight of that boy at the station," hissed through his teeth, "and it's made my blood rush through my veins enough to choke one. Never mind, the day of reckoning is a long time coming; but it does come."

And, so saying, Dick Martingale made the best of his way to the servants' room.

The Honourable Mr. Ravensborne had a small house in Dover Street, and which he kept only, it might be said, for his friends.

He had had a very successful year.

His star was in the ascendant on the turf, and his run of luck at cards had been marvellous.

The private meetings at his house had been highly remunerative, and altogether he had been, as his friends expressed themselves, cruelly fortunate.

All was going on well, when unfortunately, in following the hounds, his horse swerved at rather a stiff fence, and the consequences were a broken collar-bone, and rather a severe shaking, so that when Alfred arrived home from paying a visit in the country, he found his father suffering severely both in mind and body.

The mind was ill at ease upon the past, and disquietude at the present, as it compelled him to put aside a little scheme or two that would have swelled the balance at his banker's.

"I am sorry to hear of your accident, sir," said Alfred, going up to the couch upon which his father was lying.

"Yes, it's an infernal accident, my boy," he replied, "for you see the season will soon commence, and half of it will be over before I shall be able to get out."

"I hope not, sir," said Alfred.

"I dare say you do; but I don't place much belief in it. If I was boxed up to-morrow it would be all the better for you, would it not, eh?"

"I had no such thoughts, sir."

"Don't lie, boy. You'd be your own master."

"Lie, sir !"

"Ah, well, excuse my rudeness ; the pain caused it."

"But, with gentlemen, no pain should cause them to forget themselves."

"Any news, Alfred ?"

"Very little, sir."

"I don't intend to send you back to Birchenough's ; I think I shall send you to Harrow. I suppose they are a very common sort at that school ?"

The door opened softly and Dick Martingale slunk into the room unperceived.

"Well," replied Alfred, "there was scarcely a boy I could associate with ; there were some of all sorts."

"And sizes," said the father, with a smile.

"But one boy was there that I hated beyond all the rest."

"Ha ! you have got the good old blood in you, boy. How was that ? What was the cause ?"

"Well,"—and Alfred paused—"I felt an indescribable feeling running through my veins when I first saw him. When he offered his hand I would have sooner grasped the fangs of the deadliest serpent. There must be something in it."

And he paused.

"Go on, you interest me. Martingale, raise this pillow, and pour out some Maraschino ; it stirs up the flagging blood, and sends new life through the dull, creeping veins."

Dick did as he was ordered, and handed the stimulating draught round.

"Drink, Alfred," said his father ; "it won't bite you."

The boy sipped it slowly and with the air of one who knew what he was about.

He had been used to these things when he was a mere child, and it was his wretched father's boast that he had the face of an angel with the cunning of the serpent.

Such was the early training of Alfred Ravensborne.

"Well, now, proceed. And so, I suppose, he was your master, not only in the school, but out of it ; the first at his Homer, as well as in the races—in fact, the Admirable Crichton of the place ? My poor boy, how terribly you have degenerated !"

He said this with such an air of pity, blended with contempt and sarcasm, as stung the boy to the quick, and roused all his fiend-like qualities.

He sprang to his feet, for the Maraschino was doing its work ; he was about hurling a defiance in the face of his father, when, with a self-command almost wonderful to behold, he sat coolly down.

"Ha, ha, ha ! Well, I think we are degenerated with a vengeance ; why you are turning quite an old man. A slipt collar-bone, a slight shaking, which a glass of brandy would have settled, has degenerated you into a poor, feeble invalid."

At first the man heard his son with the coolness and patience common to him ; but, as the latter warmed and returned sarcasm for sarcasm, and withering contempt for contempt, he raised himself partly up, and looked at him as though he would have annihilated him.

For a time they gazed at each other.

Neither father nor son flinched from each other's gaze.

At last the Honourable opened his lips, but it was done as though it had cost him some great exertion.

"Come hither, Alfred, I am glad you have taught me a lesson, and proved yourself my son. We shall understand one another better for the future—go on."

"Oh, never mind the rest, it's hardly worth talking about," said the boy, listlessly.

"Go on, sir, and that directly. I am not in the habit of saying that twice."

"Oh, very well, just as you please."

And then Alfred detailed the account of the fire, the bravery and heroism of the boy, and then told the daring exploit of the three at the railway-station.

The manner in which this was related warmed the listener to a great pitch of excitement, so much so, that he sat up as though all bodily ailment had left him.

"I would have given a cool hundred to have seen that race down the line with the engine tearing and panting after you; the shouts of the mob when that boy was the victor were worth five hundred Derbys or Legers; he must come of great and glorious blood, that boy. And so he saved the girl, jumped down an embankment up to his middle in snow, while you went rolling down to the bottom like a log. Why, Alfred ——"

"Accident, sir, accident; almost as bad as when you lost your seat in the saddle," said the boy, with a sneer.

"Good; fair hit, boy," and he threw himself back on the sofa. "And the name of this hero—this boy that nothing seems to injure— I must see him, although I feel I hate him. His name, his name?"

"Tell him now," whispered Martingale.

"Giles Evergreen!" was the cold, determined reply.

In an instant the sick man sprang upon his feet, with a sharp cry as though an arrow had pierced him; he appeared to be gasping for breath, for his arms were wildly tossing about as though combating some unseen enemy.

He tried to articulate the name that caused this agony and horror, but in vain; then, with a deep groan, he fell upon the floor as though the angel of death had stricken him.

CHAPTER XII.

THE PAST, PRESENT, AND FUTURE.

WHEN the medical men called in to attend upon Alfred's father had finished their consultation, it was laid down very strictly the patient was to be kept quiet, and that no excitement of any kind was to be permitted.

His valet and an experienced nurse were the only persons allowed to remain in his bed-room, and they were upon no account to answer any questions (suppose he could ask any), or in any way disturb him, as a slight paralysis had already set in.

So soon as Alfred could collect his senses—for the fearful situation he saw his father in had for a time rather alarmed him—he tried to recall anything which might have occurred in his boyhood's days connected with the name that had brought such a calamity upon his parent; it was in vain he pondered and thought upon the matter; he had no remembrance of anything connected with the name of Evergreen.

Thus, tossing about upon the sofa, a prey to a thousand emotions, he waited for his valet and confidential adviser, Dick Martingale.

That gentleman had left the house upon a little matter of private business of his own, and didn't feel inclined to hurry himself for anyone else.

Alfred, with his mind tossed about by a thousand doubts and fears, rang the bell impatiently; but, to all his inquiries, Dick Martingale could not be found.

At last, not knowing why or wherefore, he was about rushing out in search of him, when the door opened, and the object of his anxious inquiries appeared.

"Where have you been, you infernal vagabond?" said Alfred, his eyes flashing with fire.

The countenance of the jockey did not alter a muscle.

"Eh, what did you say?"

"Say?"

"Say, yes, say."

And he looked steadily at him.

The coolness of the fellow roused the passion of the young aristocrat.

He seized a riding-whip that was lying on the table.

"You'd better put that down," said Dick, coolly.

"Why?" was the reply.

"Because I've been better used to them sort o' things than you have; they do very well for a horse or an ass, but a man is not particularly fond of having them laid on his shoulders."

"Where have you been, then?" asked Alfred.

"Out."

"Out where?"

"Partly on your business and partly on my own."

"Indeed!"

"Yes, indeed. Now, look ye, Master Alfred, things within the last few hours don't look at all gay, and it will be necessary to watch the betting well to keep on the right side of the post."

And Dick looked at Alfred with a most significant expression of face.

"What do you mean? Why did my father sink down in that helpless state at the mention of that infernal name, Giles Evergreen?"

"Ah, why, indeed? It's years ago when all that occurred! I was a boy then, and I don't think you would have found a happier one.

"Ah, there's no time like it if we could only make up our mind to it.

"You see, Master Alfred, it was only a dame school they sent me to; but when I come to think of even that, I was as merry as a tadpole in the stream with the summer's sun glancing down upon him. Well, I hadn't many happy days of that sort.

"My father was a trainer of horses, a hard, unbending man, fond of making money, which he did, and at times he lost it just as fast; then there was no holding him. He carried out the old proverb, 'good luck comes by cuffing,' and there was scarcely a day but what the whip and my shoulders were upon intimate terms. What mother and I suffered in those devilish tantrums it is impossible to tell; but we did; until, worn out, she died broken-hearted, and the little feather-weight, Dick Martingale, was taken into the stables."

"Drink and gallop on, Dick," said Alfred, pouring out a glass for him. "I am anxious to come to Giles Evergreen."

"Aye, I dare say; but it won't please you much when you do."

"Out with it, then; this is torture."

"Well, you ought to know that the father was——" here Dick paused.

"Well, was what?"

"Well, I don't think I ought to tell you, because, you see, the guv'nor hasn't given orders, and I'd rather not do it without."

"Indeed. Just as if I couldn't see your motives! You want a little more palm oil; is that it?"

"No, I don't!" said Dick, savagely.

"Well, then, what do you want?"

"I don't want to break faith, and what's more, I won't until the time comes."

"How long will that be?" said Alfred with a sneer.

"When it suits my pleasure, Master Alfred."

"Indeed! I'll pay you out for all this some day, Master Dick."

"Ah, there's a day of reckoning, for all, sooner or later, and we hardly know whose turn it is first. But, now, keep yourself cool, and don't try to fasten a quarrel upon me, and I'll do you all the service I can."

"Much obliged to you."

"No sneering, Master Alfred. The lion was under great obligations to the mouse—at least, so I read at the dame school—and I've seen a good deal of nibbling myself since."

"I dare say; and have done plenty of it yourself."

"Not half so much as your father."

"You dare not say that, you scoundrel, if he were here."

"Ah, well, I think we understand each other about these little matters; at all events, we are not such fools as to quarrel."

"Indeed! Well, I see that you are determined to play a game with me; I shall not require your services any longer."

"Ha! ha! well, that's good!—the old blood. You will not require my services, but I suppose I require yours. I speak it very respectfully."

"Humph! You have been an old servant of my father's, Dick?"

"Yes, ever since I was a youngster, and I'm barely thirty now."

"And you refuse to satisfy me upon what I am the most anxious to learn?"

And Alfred eyed him keenly.

"You mean Giles Evergreen?"

Alfred nodded assent.

"I will only tell you thus far. In all your career, that boy will be the bitterest and deadliest enemy you will have."

"Indeed, and why?"

"Time will tell you that; it is a great expounder of riddles, Master Alfred."

"I dare say; and it will not be long before you will expound, for you are the greatest riddle I've met with for a long time. You can go now—in a few days, when my father recovers, you shall go altogether!"

"Ah, that remains to be seen. Good night; you'll think better of it by the morning."

Dick Martingale walked coolly to the door, when suddenly it was opened by the valet, followed by Doctor Glanville.

The doctor himself was a tall man, with rather a stern expression of face, and rather a brusque way of expressing himself.

"You are the son of the man who is ill upstairs?" he said, abruptly, to Alfred.

He rose from the sofa upon which he had been lying, and, looking the doctor from head to foot, said—

"I am the son and only child of the Honourable Mr. Ravensborne, the master of this mansion. Pray, who and what are you?"

The doctor was somewhat taken aback.

"I am Doctor Glanville, and have been called in to give my advice. Humph! have you no relatives to send for?"

"None that I care for, or shall send for," was the reply.

"Well, then, it is my duty to tell you that if ever he recovers consciousness, he had better settle his worldly affairs."

"Indeed! is the case so bad and desperate?"

"It is both," was the reply. "You seem to be a most extraordinary lad; you meet this affair with the coolness of a man."

"My race have always been celebrated for their coolness and contempt of danger. I will see my father."

And he moved to the door.

"You had better not at present."

"You will excuse me, Doctor Glanville, but at present I am the master here."

And so saying, and, giving Martingale a look to follow him, they left the room, followed by the wondering and astonished physician.

When Alfred entered the room in which his father was dying, he experienced, for the moment, a sense of awe and dread.

There had never been a real love or affection between them; the man of the world now lying there, had cared only for that world, and so had brought up the boy in the same way.

Love between parent and child there was none; it was the unseen monitor that caused the heart and pulse to beat a little faster.

Alfred approached the bed; he looked steadfastly upon the face of his father and spoke low and with a tender accent, but there was no answer—no recognition.

Dick Martingale stood silently by, looking on the fast expiring man.

Was that a smile that flitted across his face and lit up the cold grey eyes that seemed to have no gleam of sorrow or regret in them?

"TURNING THE TABLES."

" He is going fast, Master Alfred,"
he whispered ; " his last race is run."

" Be silent," was the stern reply.

There was an almost imperceptible
movement of the hand, as if in an endeavour to raise it towards his breast.

A quivering of the eyelids, a deep-
drawn sigh, and another of the proud, cold
race of the Ravensbornes was no more.

The physician stood gazing upon the
pale, stern, determined face of the son,
then, placing his hand upon his arm, he
led him unresistingly from the silent
chamber of the dead.

At that moment a loud knocking
at the door of the mansion startled all
of them, and a few minutes elapsed,
when a gentleman entered the room into
which Alfred and Dick had retired.

The doctor left the house.

Bewildered by the crowd of exciting
events that had followed so rapidly upon
him that day, Alfred took but little
notice of him.

" 'Tis your late father's solicitor, Mr.
Davy Close," said Martingale.

" Well, sir, your business ?" said the
boy, looking up.

" Well," replied Mr. Davy, better
known among the profession and his
friends as Dark Davy, " this is hardly
a proper time for business. I am so
bewildered and astonished by this sudden
and unlooked-for event, that I hardly
know what to say ; but, my dear young
gentleman, leave everything to me. I
will at once away and inform the earl,
your grandfather, and the rest of your
relatives. I was your father's trusty
and confidential (as far as he reposed
confidence in any one) adviser. Leave
all to me, leave all to me."

And he hastily bustled from the room,
and in a few moments from the house.

Tired and jaded out, Alfred desired
the valet to show him to his room, and,
without deigning to speak to Dick Martingale, he retired to rest.

" Ha ! ha !" chuckled Dick, quietly.
" I think, my lad, we shall bring down
those great airs yet. I wish Dark Davy
hadn't left before I had a word with
him. I wonder whether he will return.
The servants will soon retire to rest,
and then we could have the house to
ourselves. I wonder what that high-
mettled spark would give to have the
secret of Giles Evergreen ? I'll go
below and watch for Dark Davy."

So saying, he left the room, and,
taking up his station at the window ·by
the hall door, watched anxiously for the
return of the lawyer.

He listened cautiously and heard the
few servants, one by one, retire to rest,
and knew that all was safe.

At last his patience was rewarded.

He saw Dark Davy approaching the
house.

And before that gentleman could
ascend the steps, the door was cautiously opened.

" All right, Mr. Davy Close, I thought
I'd be on the watch for you. Come in,
and be as quiet as a mole when he is
hard at work."

" Right, Dick, right," said Davy,
quietly, " you are an invaluable fellow
to work with."

" Aye, aye, I dare say you know my
value ; but come in here."

And so saying, Dick Martingale
quietly, yet securely, fastened the hall
door, and led the lawyer into a side room.

The only light they had was that from the hall-lamp, and that was waning fast.

The door of the room was left partly open, and the men spoke in whispers.

"How did this come about?" asked Dark Davy.

"Well, you see, the guv'nor has been ailing a long time, and I heard the doctor say that any sudden shock would bring about a crisis. I ain't exactly up to that; but I suppose it means something, so I got the boy who fancies himself somebody to do it."

"What was that?" said Davy.

"Why, he mentioned the name of the man that I knew would sound like a death-knell to him, and down he went like a shot."

"Humph! it was a bold stroke."

"Yes, Mr. Davy, and a bold stroke very often wins the game. The boy that we all thought dead has turned up."

"What! Giles Evergreen?"

"Yes."

"The devil!"

"He is likely to prove one; but now to work. The packet of papers containing the screw that we can put upon both must be secured."

"Where are they?"

"In the room with the late owner; he has the key about with him somewhere."

"And who is to do this?"

"Who?"

And Dick looked hard at him.

"Who? Why, us!"

"Not for the woolsack," said the lawyer, "would I enter the room where a dead body lay."

"Why not?" asked Dick.

"I have my reasons. If they are to be gained in that way, why, then ——"

"I suppose the affair must drop through; but it shan't! The revenge of a life shall be carried out upon both. Will you stand outside and brain the first person that interferes?"

"Well, I'll stand outside and see about it."

"Ah! very well; stop you here a bit."

And he left the room.

"Don't be long; I don't like being in the dark."

But Dick was out of hearing and gliding down the stairs to his own room below, leaving Dark Davy to his own thoughts, not the most enviable in the light, let alone in the dark.

At last a faint glimmer of a light was seen coming down the passage, and Dick appeared bearing in his hand a dark lantern.

"Now, then, follow me."

And away he stole up the stairs, followed by Dark Davy, who shook and trembled at every step he took.

"What are you shaking at, lawyer, eh? He is in here quiet enough," and Dick placed his hand upon the lock of the door. "He won't knock anyone down again, and then kick him, will he? You stay here and watch."

And so saying, he threw open the door, and, entering, shut it after him.

Were this man's nerves made of iron that he walked calmly and coolly up to the bed where the corpse lay, and, casting the full light upon the face, rigid and pale as marble, gazed upon it?

"Who's got the best of it now?" he muttered.

And with that he carefully took up the black ribbon that just appeared round the dead man's neck, and detached a small patent key of peculiar construction from it.

"I have got the lead, now, and I'll see and keep it."

Quickly, but carefully, he left the bed, and, going to the farther part of the room, looked carefully round until his eyes rested upon a green leather dispatch box.

This he carefully placed upon a table, and, applying the key, opened it.

It was full of papers, but, for the moment, he seemed disappointed at not finding the particular one he sought.

"Ah! here it is," and he held the light close to it, and read—

"Papers relating to Giles Evergreen."

"Ha, ha! that will do," and he thrust it into his breast pocket, buttoning his coat securely over it. "Suppose I take the rest," he said; "they may be useful."

The dispatch box was soon emptied, placed again in its former place, the key fastened again to the ribbon, then, opening the door and looking out, he observed **Dark Davy**.

He held the light up, looking at him full in the face, and, with the other hand pointing to the room, he said—

"The papers are not there!"

CHAPTER XII.

THE LODGING-HOUSE AND ITS SPIRITS.

IT was rather late in the evening when our hero, Giles Evergreen, and his dearly attached friend, Ted Flan, arrived at their destination "fresh from the country."

They were received at Mrs. Wilson's upon alighting from the very handsome brougham that had been sent for them, by the worthy hostess herself, and a remarkably sprightly-looking servant girl.

"My dear young gentlemen," said Mrs. Wilson, "I am more than delighted to see you."

"And, 'pon my word, ma'am, the feeling is what we say in my country before we commence a scrimmage—reciprocal."

"I perceive you are Irish," said the lady, ushering them into an elegantly-furnished room.

"Yes, madam, my friend comes from that peaceful portion of the globe," replied Giles.

Here Teddy observed the girl get behind her mistress.

"May I ask if there is anything particularly objectionable in that spot?" asked Ted, with great gravity.

"Oh, no, my dear sir! Why?"

"Why, bekase I saw the young famale lady there move behind you as if the great say sarpent had suddenly risen from its ocean bed."

" Susan, I am surprised at you ! Show the young gentlemen to their rooms ; and after they have rested——"

" Oh, we do not require any rest," replied Giles. " We'll just refresh ourselves with a wash, and then we'll have dinner, madam ; and I think we will have some tea first. And see there's plenty. I've read of a person being hungry as a hunter, but on this occasion I've got the appetite of all the huntsmen and the hounds into the bargain."

And so saying, they left the room.

" Well, I never !" said Susan.

" Go with the young gentlemen directly," said· her mistress, sternly ; " and no talk."

" Talk ?   As if I ever talked !"

And, tossing her head, Susan passed Giles and Ted and ushered them upstairs to their respective rooms.

It was not long before they descended again to the sitting-room, where they found Susan in waiting at the tea table.

While upstairs they had mutually agreed to ascertain the names, habits, and peculiarities of the several parties residing at Mrs. Wilson's.

So, when the tea had been handed round, Ted, winking his eyes at Giles, opened the ball.

" I think I heard, to the best of my hearing, the worthy lady of this hospitable domicile address you by the epithet of Susan ?"

" Yes, sir, Susan is my name, to which may be added Flipper."

" On my conscience, an iligant name !"

" Thank ye, sir ; it's seldom young women born in humble spears——"

" I beg your pardon."

" Humble spears, can boast of such a name."

" Are there any more of you, bekase I'd like to know the rest of the family ?"

" Thank ye, sir.   I am sure you're a gentleman born and bred ; and so are you, sir," dropping a curtsey to Giles ; " but, as I was saying, there's reason in most things throughout this extemporary path of life.   I was called Susan after the great heroine of the Downs because I was born at Deal."

" By my conscience, Giles," whispered Ted, " we've picked up a great card."

" Yes ; let us know what the rest of the pack consist of."

" Have you lived long here, Susan ?" asked Giles.

" All my born days.   I was left an orphan at Deal, and was sent to my uncle, a carpenter, in London, and was put into the charity, and came here directly they got me out."

" And your mistress ?"

" All that a 'art can wish for—only too fond of spirits."

Here Ted and Giles lost their gravity and laughed outright.

" By my conscience, a tippler ; is it the crayther she's fond of ?" asked Ted.

" I beg you not to slander the absent who are not present."

" A bit of a bull, Giles," whispered Ted.

" Rather a quieter one than the last we had anything to do with. I am sorry to hear that, Susan."

"I don't mean bottled-up spirits; I mean them that come on the table," said the girl.

"Well, that's the sort of way to do it; you bring them from the cellar on to the table."

"No; I don't! You don't catch me in the cellar without a light, and then not after dark."

And Susan began to look rather alarmed.

"Nonsense, Susan, what harm can they do if the spirits are corked up?"

"As my friend truly observes," chimed in Ted, "it's only when they are uncorked they do the mischief."

"Well, all I wish is, that they had not brought them here. I wish somebody would come and exercise them."

"Ha, ha! what do you mane?"

"I've read of it, but I don't know the meaning. I'm fond of reading—oh, yes! I thing it perverts the mind."

And she elevated her head.

"Divert, Susan," said Giles.

"One and the same thing—identical and similar to each other, I believe, sir. Have you finished tea, gentlemen?"

"I'll take another cup; I'm fond of my tay, and follow in the steps of Doctor Johnson, who always went in for a couple of gallons."

And Ted grinned.

"Cups, sir," said Susan, indignantly, pouring out some.

Suddenly, from underneath the table, was heard a sepulchral voice—

"Hulloa, where are you?"

Down went the tea-pot into the sugar-basin, and, with a scream, falling on her knees and flinging her apron over her face, Susan piteously asked for mercy.

"Why, what in the name of wonder's the matter?" asked the boys in the same breath.

"You might have called out scaldings before the hot water went over."

Ted had begun his ventriloquial powers again.

"Didn't you hear the spirit, gentlemen?"

"Nonsense! get up. There, don't be foolish."

And each taking an arm, they raised her.

"Please let me tell missus."

"Pour out the tay first."

Poor Susan began again; her tormentor had not done with her.

"Put it down," sounded a voice under the table.

"That I will! Murder!"

And, rushing to the door, Susan was out of the room in a twinkling.

A roar of laughter followed her exit, and before it had ceased, Mrs. Wilson appeared on the scene.

"My dear young gentlemen, what is all this?" said the lady.

"Well, madam, perhaps you will enlighten us," said Giles.

"Throw a light upon the darkness, if you please, madam, like a gas lamp on a foggy night. I am rayther of a narvous temperament, madam."

And Ted Flan's face looked it.

"Susan, come here directly," called out Mrs. Wilson.

After some delay the girl appeared at the door; but no persuasion could induce her to enter the room.

"What's the matter with the girl?"

" What's the matter with the room, marm ?" said the girl, shaking like a leaf in the wind. " They're all over the house !"

" 'Pon my conscience, I'll never slape then. Oh ! Giles, we're kilt !"

And Ted clung to him.

" It's very unpleasant, certainly," replied Giles.

" It's only her fears, my dear young gentlemen. The fact is, we have held some very extraordinary ' séances ' here, and——"

" Ah ! yes, it's the skyances that's done it," said the girl.

" But they are held in another room. The silly girl came to one, and has fancied nothing but foolish things since."

" The foolish things commenced it, perhaps, madam ?" said Giles.

" What was that noise that sounded so like a saw going through a rough knot of wood ?"

" What's that, madam ?" said Ted, clinging to the table. " Och ! murder ! the house is haunted !"

Susan uttered a low groan, clinging to the door.

" They're coming before they're summoned !" said Mrs. Wilson.

" Are they ?   Then I'm off !"

And Susan, rushing from the room, made the best of her way down to her own place.

This little piece of fun over, the parties retired to dress for dinner.

Upon the occasion of the arrival of Giles and Ted, the dinner table was set out with a little more than ordinary splendour.

The room itself was one of those good old-fashioned ones, that even in these modern days of improvement delight us.

At the table were seated Mrs. Wilson and three other ladies, a gentleman named Walmisley, and our friends Giles and Ted Flan.

The dinner passed off very quietly, very comfortably.

There was little to notice, and very little to afford fun to the boys ; it was reserved for a later portion of the evening.

Some time after dinner—the usual dessert had passed off—the elder portion of the party left the room.

" My dear young gentlemen," said Mrs. Wilson, " perhaps you would like to retire to your rooms."

" By no manes, ma'am," replied Ted. " Railway travelling at times is remarkably 'asy, it gives you time for thought and reflection.   What is it——"

" We shall attend with great deference to anything you may propose, madam," said Giles.

" You have not been alarmed at anything that has occurred here to-night ?"

" Not in the least."

" I am rather a believer in spirits."

" I hope not, madam, they are very exciting.   I remember my poor father, madam, he was an ardent——"

" Ah ! I see—I can excuse the ignorance of youth."

Here Ted gave a grin.

" I don't mean the spirits you mean."

" Then what do you mean ?"

" I mean—well, will you attend our séance ?"

"If it's anything good we will attend," said Giles.

"Especially if good wholesome spirits are there," said Ted.

And with that, rising from their chairs, they retired from the room.

About an hour after that the whole of the parties assembled in a room on the basement of the building around a large table; it might be then twenty minutes before twelve, and at the head of it sat Mr. Walmisley.

Ted O'Flan and Giles had previously gained all the information they required respecting the habits and dispositions of the parties, and were well prepared to carry out their fun.

The room was very dark, and the little light cast from the burner hanging in the ceiling shed a peculiar shadow upon them.

"Young gentlemen," said Mr. Walmisley, "in asking you here it is to be hoped you will not be alarmed."

"No fear about that, sir; the divil a thing can alarm us. What's coming? Bekase if it's anything desperate it's as well to be prepared," and Ted, turning to Giles, said, "it's a pity we didn't get revolvers."

"No, no; nothing so bad as that," replied the president, for so we might call Mr. Walmisley; "only you see ——"

"Oh, yes, we see," said Giles; "but boys are not easily alarmed. Ted, how do you feel?"

"Well, I may say, with an 'asy conscience, that I am like a celebrated coffin dangling between this and that, but I'll trust in my conscience, which I believe is as clear as a trout strame

after a storm. When do you commence?"

"Well, now; we have nothing to fear."

"I hope not, sir. Is the insurance paid?" said Ted.

"My dear young gentleman," and Mrs. Wilson looked at him.

"I beg your pardon, madam, but you see there is a trifle of luggage that ——"

"I paid the insurance yesterday."

"What a comfort that we are here to-day."

"I will trouble you to lay your hands upon the table," said the president, solemnly.

It was done.

As soon as it began to move, a slight grumbling noise was heard, and a rap was heard.

"That's a rap-r-a," whispered Ted.

"It will come to a rap-r-t," answered Giles.

"When the mahogany moves fast, look out," said Ted.

And sure enough, as the table moved faster, the Irish boy shifted uneasily in his seat.

"Keep your hands firmly on the table," said Walmisley.

"It's 'asy to say kape your hands still, but who is to do it?"

"This is wonderful," said Walmisley, solemnly.

"It is indade." Ted and Giles were working the table rapidly. "Och, murder! it's knocking me over," and away went Ted and Giles over their chairs, like a couple of acrobats, on to the floor.

While on the floor, a voice was heard in a sharp treble tone—

"What want ye?"

"It's my grandmother's voice, Giles," said Ted.

"What does she want?" was the reply.

By this time they were again seated at the table.

"My dear young gentleman," said old Walmisley, who certainly was somewhat astonished at this, "will you allow me to ask the spirit in my way?"

"Yes, but keep it in the madium," and Ted O'Flan, leaning on Giles, said in a faint voice, "oh, that my grandmother should follow me from Knocklofty semitry to Gower Street. Go on. I'll be bound she'll answer, for the dear ould crater never could kape her tongue from wagging and bragging. Och, hone! this is fearful."

"Be comforted, my child; all will be for the best," said Mrs. Wilson.

"I hope it will be; for I can't understand it. Oh, get me out of this suspending suspense."

And Ted sank on his knees, still keeping his hands on the table.

"Who are you?" said Walmisley.

"What's that to you?" was the reply, behind him.

There was a rap under the table.

Giles was playing the confederate.

"What do you want?" asked Mrs. Wilson.

"Ted O'Flan, my grandchild," was the answer.

"I am here, grandmother, rest you," replied Ted, lifting his head.

"Where's Ted Maloney?" was the next question; "he that stole the pig."

Down went Ted's head.

"He died in public, and was buried at its expense," was the answer.

Another rap under the table and groaning.

"What do you want, now?"

"Have you any of the craythur?"

"No; we are all taytotallers."

"Och, murder! Where's the money I left your father?"

"It followed the pig."

"And which way did it go?"

"Botherashin! who can tell which way a pig will go? Don't bother. Are you unhappy?"

There was a whirring noise under the table.

"Poor soul! Ask her what she wants, sir?"

"What do you want, my poor dear?"

"Och, murder! I know you."

And then there was a wailing.

"What do I want?"

"Yes."

"The gould in the thirteen per cent.—reduced."

"Reduced? Who reduced it?"

"The thafe of a stock-broker who ran off with it."

"It's a mistake; such a thing never occurred in the world."

"A mistake, is it. By the powers, that's as good as a lie. Let me get at him."

Now behind old Walmisley's chair were a large pair of folding doors.

There, then, a noise occurred, like the crashing of them in.

This certainly was out of the medium, and a general rush was made to the other door.

The elderly ladies, headed by Mrs. Wilson, of course, were first; then followed the old stock-broker, who, not only afflicted with twinges of gout, had a great many of the conscience as well, hobbled towards it.

Ted, having given the general crash in of the doors, was close behind him, and seizing hold of his coat tails, said, in the sharp treble tone—

"Where's my thirteen reduced?"

It happened unfortunately that Susan Flipper, with the inherent curiosity of her sex, had placed herself upon her hands and knees, outside the door.

The door being suddenly opened by Mrs. Wilson, that good lady and those following were precipitated upon her, causing a scene worthy of any farce in the world, heightened as it was by the unearthly howling of a dog.

And when peace and quiet again reigned in the mansion of Mrs. Wilson, in Gower Street, dear Giles Evergreen, and Ted O'Flan, with their noble hearts, their generous feelings, straightforward principles, and love of proper fun (and when should any boy be without it?), retired to their rooms. They laughed heartily, when Susan said—

"Oh, dear, young gentlemen, how shall we sleep to-night?"

"Beautifully, my darling, and in high spirits."

Then all retired to rest.

CHAPTER XIV.

A MIDNIGHT MODERN CONFERENCE.

THE hoarse whisper of Dick Martingale to the crafty man called Dark Davy, communicating the loss of the papers, did not call forth any particular emotion in him, but he kept staring upon the jockey with a wondering gaze, as if asking the meaning of the information conveyed to him.

"It arn't no use searching any further, and so we'll lock the door and leave the guv'nor in peace and quietude."

And so saying, he turned the key in the lock, and followed Dark Davy, who was really better pleased that he was going down stairs than up.

They reached the hall.

"Well, now, I'll get a cab, and make the best of my way home, Martingale," said the lawyer.

"Just as you please; but I was thinking."

"Thinking about what?"

"Well, a great number of things; but one in particular was that, perhaps, after this night's adventure, a little drop of something nice and hot would do neither of us any harm."

"Well, I don't think it would, Dick."

"I should think not. I never saw a man want it more than yourself; blest if your face arn't like chalk—a deal whiter than the one I've just left there."

And Dick pointed with his thumb up the stairs.

"There, there, never mind him," said the lawyer, nervously. "But I don't see any place to——"

"Be comfortable in. Lor' bless you! there's more secrets in this house than you knows anything on. Follow me, and I'll show you the private sanctum of Mr. Richard Martingale."

"Aye, aye, let us get out of this confounded cold hall, my teeth fairly chatter with cold."

"Or something else," chuckled Dick.

Leading the way downstairs, he went through a long passage that led to the back of the house, at the further end of which was a small door.

"Hold the light a moment, please, Mr. Davy." And Dick handed it to him. "Don't shake it about so."

"The cold, Dick; the cold."

And the lawyer looked nervously round.

"What are you looking about for in that way?" said Dick, while he was searching for something in his pocket. "You're enough to give a fellow the horrors."

So saying, he pulled from his pocket a key, and, applying it to the lock of the door, he threw it open.

Dark Davy, the lawyer, was somewhat surprised at the sight that struck him.

The room itself was of moderate size, but comfortably furnished.

Taking the key out of the door, Dick locked it in the inside, pulling down the little bit of brass that completely covered the keyhole, and letting fall a heavy curtain over all, effectually kept all cold and curious listeners out.

Throwing open a cupboard, he placed a couple of decanters upon the table, glasses, sugar and lemon, and stirred up the fire.

Then filling a jug from the kettle that was singing merrily on the hob, he put a box of cigars upon the table, and, flinging himself into one of the easy chairs, pointed with his hand to the other, for the lawyer, amazed at all this, had stood looking round him with a face of incredulous astonishment.

"This fellow means mischief," muttered Dark Davy.

"Sit down, Mr. Davy," said Dick, "and make yourself at home."

The lawyer sat down.

"'Pon my word," he said, rubbing his hands, for the heat of the room was rapidly calling back the truant blood, "this is a comfortable snuggery."

"Pretty well," replied Dick; "not more than I ought to have," and, mixing himself a glass of grog, lit a cigar.

"Lay hold, Mr. Davy," and he handed him the box.

"Never smoke, my dear fellow," was the reply.

"Just as you like; I never persuade one way or the other. This is the first time you have been here; I mean in my apartments."

"Why, yes, and 'pon my word, I must say——"

"That they are tolerably comfortable; but I'm afraid it's too good to last."

"What do you mean? Going to leave?"

And Dark Davy looked cunningly at him.

"That's as it may turn out. You've been in the guv'nor's confidence a long time, and I daresay you know a thing or two about him," and Dick looked carelessly up at the ceiling.

"No, very little; I have managed to be useful to him once or twice, all in the way of business, you know.

"Of course, only that I said to myself when I recommended you——"

"You?"

And Dark Davy stared hard at him.

"Yes; he came to you one day respecting a little transaction about an I. O. U. for a thousand, won by him of that young ensign."

"And the foolish young man disputed it, but I made him pay."

And the lawyer took a good pull at his glass.

"No, you didn't, Mr. Davy; you'll excuse me."

"Why, what do you know about it?"

"Know? Ha, ha! Well, come, that's a good one."

"My late client told me that it was honourably lost at play, and——"

"I daresay he told you so. I should have thought him a great fool if he had done otherwise. You know that the claim was resisted."

"Pooh, stuff! They hadn't a leg to stand on. The relatives threatened to defend the action."

"Yes; but the boy's prospects would have been injured for ever; and so, rather than that, they paid what he no more lost than I did."

"And do you mean to tell me that ——"

"I don't mean to tell you anything; I want you to tell me something. Fill your glass; you are hardly warm yet."

The lawyer, anxious to learn what his entertainer wanted to know, mixed himself another.

"Anything consistent with my duty to my late client and my conscience ——"

"Ha, ha! yes."

"I shall be happy to——"

"Tell me. Well, then, did you make his will?"

"No."

"The dev—ah, well, are you sure of it?"

"Sure."

"Humph! that's strange. Did he ever mention the name of Evergreen to you?"

"Evergreen? Let me reflect. I've heard the name before; but I don't think in connection with him. What was it, eh?"

Dark Davy thought he'd caught him.

Dick looked at him with a cunning leer of his eyes.

"Ah, that's it," he said, puffing out a cloud of smoke; "because it was the mention of that name that caused his death."

"What, the name of Evergreen?"

"Yes."

And Dick looked fixedly at him.

"But what could that mean?"

"That's what I want to know; you seem to be as wise as myself."

"Not so wise, my friend, Richard Martingale."

"Ah, now you are joking."

And Dick gave a tremendous yawn.

"Well, suppose we both put our wits

to work and try and find this mystery out, eh?"

And the lawyer looked round, as though he feared someone was listening.

"I've no objection; but don't be afraid of anyone overhearing us. In the first place, there is no one up here but ourselves ; and, in the next place, I'll defy anyone to do so through that double door and curtain."

"Ah, well, it's as well to be cautious."

"I always am; so much so, I often fear I cannot trust myself, especially when with those with more brains than my own. Have you ever seen much of the lad upstairs?"

"No. What's he like?" asked Davy.

"It's difficult to say; but I think he'll turn out a true chip of the old block."

"I hope he will," was the dry reply.

"Why?"

"Because we may get something out of him."

And the lawyer thrust his hands deep in his pockets, as if the imaginary sovereigns were already there.

"We! Well, I think you'll be puzzled. Another glass?"

"No; it's"—pulling out his watch—"three o'clock, as I'm a sinner!"

"There's one thing you can do at times, if you like."

"Ha, ha, what is that?"

"Speak the truth; you did it just now; but perhaps it was done by accident."

"Capital. Well, are we to work together?"

"Yes; but you must do all under my directions. I owe a long score to one or two persons, and I mean to pay them off."

"Right. Shall I see you again?"

"Perhaps. Where are you going?"

"Out—home!"

"Not that way," said Dick.

And he pulled aside a curtain opposite the door he entered at.

"There is more than one entrance to this house. We—that is the 'silent one' upstairs, and myself—found it very convenient at times."

He then unlocked the door that a curtain had so well concealed, and disclosed a long passage.

"You see, at times, a good deal of business was done upstairs; you understand?"

Dark Davy nodded his head, and, with his hands, imitated the shuffling of cards and the throwing of dice.

"Right."

"What about the young one, eh?"

"Leave him to me."

And so saying, Dick cautiously opened the door at the end of the passage they had been walking along.

"You are now in the street at the back of the house. Many a man has gone out with a heavy heart, but a light pocket. Good night, or rather morning; I dare say I shall soon see you."

"Aye, aye, don't forget."

"I never forget."

And he closed the door.

"Forget," he muttered, as he entered the room and made all secure. "No, no."

And he sat down and gazed moodily into the fire, as though faces and phantoms were dancing and leaping in the flames.

"It ain't likely a man can forget losing the only fond being he ever loved; losing her by treachery, fraud, and de-deceit. Oh, no, it ain't likely a man will forget being horsewhipped within an ace of death's door; and here, here it is all!"

And, thrusting his hand into his breast-pocket, he pulled out the packet he had taken from the dead man's chamber.

"Aye, aye! Ha, ha! My eyes so leap for joy, I can scarcely read!"

And he glared at the superscription as though the frenzy of madness had seized him :—

" *My own private papers and those of Evergreen.*

" P. M. Ravensborne."

" I've got you tight enough, my lordly lad, upstairs, and I'll goad you on, although you don't want that much, to kill that Giles Evergreen—my curse upon the name! I feel the stinging blow yet that boy gave me. Strange, that both father and son should—ah! let me not think of it, but compass their ruin. Yes, yes!"

He drained a glass of spirits, then, seizing one of the lights that was burning on the table, and extinguishing the rest, he passed into another room.

CHAPTER XV.

A RENCONTRE.

The last funeral rites have been paid, and the man so suddenly stricken down placed among the kindred dust of his ancestors, without one tear of sorrow, or a sigh of reget shed over his re-mains.

Cold hearted, without a feeling of sympathy save for himself and his own plans of fraud and deceit, he had passed away, and, in a few short hours, the Right Honourable Plantagenet Ravens-borne was forgotten.

The old earl, his father, had, as a matter of course, followed his remains, and much useless pomp had been be-stowed upon the lifeless clay, but, be-yond that, no one could have detected any paternal sorrow.

A long estrangement had deadened every feeling of affection or esteem.

The mourners had all assembled to hear the will read, which, only on the morning of the funeral, had been dis-covered.

The day after the "midnight con-ference" between Dick Martingale and Dark Davy, the family solicitor had taken upon himself the sole manage-ment of the affair, and commenced a search among the papers of the deceased man for the testamentary document.

None could be found until within a few hours of the funeral, and then, in moving a number of volumes of the "Racing Calendar," one volume speci-ally attracted his notice.

It was tied round firmly with a piece of red tape, and bore, in four different parts, the grand armorial seal of the deceased, and, strange to say, a paper closely attached to it bore an address to the Lady St. George, his cousin.

Then, when the funeral party had assembled in the drawing-room, the lawyer, producing the volume, handed it to that lady, who, with an astonishment that could not be disguised, received it.

" It is addressed to your ladyship," said the legal gentleman, " and may contain some paper or instructions ; you will please to break the seal."

The Lady St. George, with much hesitation, proceeded to do so, and, on opening the book, a paper, likewise sealed, fell to the ground.

It was the last will and testament of the deceased.

Its contents were short : He left most of the wealth he died worth to his son, Alfred Ravensborne, constituting the Lady St. George guardian to him until he attained his majority ; he left an annuity to his "faithful" servant, Richard Martingale, and a wish that he, the said Richard Martingale, should always be retained in the service of his son ; he further directed that all effects should be sold, and that his son should reside with Lady St. George. Legacies were left to his valet and housekeeper, who had been witnesses to the document.

He died rich !

How those riches had been gained we have partly spoken of, and that fact being pretty well known to the Lady St. George herself, she felt the greatest repugnance in accepting the trust, full well knowing the wild, unbridled passions of the lad whose future welfare was entrusted to her care.

But her goodness of heart made her cast aside all selfish feeling and accept the trust ; and the evening of that day saw that lady seated at her villa at Richmond, with Alfred Ravensborne, moody, disconcerted, and morose, with Dick Martingale in attendance upon him.

A few mornings after that, Alfred strolled forth, followed by Dick ; the two made their way to the hill, where they could converse unobserved.

" I am not at all satisfied with your conduct, Martingale," said the former.

" Why not, sir ?" replied Dick. " I thought we were running well together."

" Oh, yes ; you think I can't see through you. You're playing a nice double game, you infernal hypocrite ! Why don't you tell me where I can find that Giles Evergreen ?"

" How can I tell ? I want to know myself. He and his precious companion are living somewhere in London."

" Somewhere indeed !"

And Alfred sneered at him contemptuously.

" Yes, somewhere. If you knew what you were about you'd soon find out. You're only half——"

Here Dick's coolness was fast leaving him.

" Half what, sir ? "

" You are playing fast and loose with me, you cur !"

" Cur, am I ?"

" Yes, cur—whipped dog !"

"THE EYES OF ALFRED FLASHED FIRE UPON THE PAIR."

No. 7.

Dick's countenance turned completely livid.

He remembered a circumstance that lashed him to fury.

"Oh, yes, I was a whipped dog once !"

"Ha, ha! I thought so. When was that, you whelp ?"

"When Giles Evergreen's father could have sent yours to the gallows !"

Scarcely had the words passed his lips when Alfred sprang at him, and, like a raging tiger, seized him by the throat.

But with all his courage—and he had plenty—he was no match for the jockey.

Dick shook him off easily, and held him at arm's length.

"Be quiet," he said hoarsely. "Do you think you'll gain your ends by this ? Be quiet, I say ; you'll have a crowd about us."

And so saying, Dick smoothed his necktie, and walked away whistling.

Not so with Alfred.

He was so appalled by the words the jockey had uttered, that he sank back on a seat, almost senseless.

Suddenly he started up, for a hand was placed lightly on his shoulder, and he stood face to face with Dark Davy.

"I witnessed that affair, sir," he said. "Can I be of any assistance to you ? I served your late father upon more than one occasion."

"No ; I know you not," was the haughty reply.

"Have you forgotten me ? My name is Davy ; Dark Davy I am more generally called by my friends."

"Well, what do you want with me ?"

"I saw the altercation between you and Dick Martingale. May I ask the reason of it ? I am not asking from any idle curiosity."

And Dark Davy looked seriously at the boy.

Now, Alfred Ravensborne, lad as he was, had a great deal of his father's cunning and caution.

He glanced at the man who stood cringing before him, and, pausing a moment, he sat down.

"Be seated, Mr. Davy," he said.

The lawyer rubbed his hands quietly together, and sat down.

"I have hooked my fish," he muttered, to himself; "be cautious and play him well, and you will land him safely."

"You knew my father well ?" said Alfred.

"Few men better ; I was in his entire confidence "—Dark Davy could draw the long bow at times—"as I trust I shall be in that of the son's."

"That will depend very much upon circumstances. I suppose you knew some of his transactions ?"

"Nearly all."

"Indeed ! Any particular one involving his life ?"

"His life ! You are jesting, my dear sir ; there was never anything quite so desperate as that."

And Dark Davy looked wonderingly upon Alfred.

"You are sure ?"

"Quite. Why do you ask ?"

"Merely from curiosity. He knows nothing after all. Did you ever hear him mention the name of Evergreen ?"

And Alfred slightly quivered.

"Never. I have heard the name in connection with some transaction ; lately, too," said Davy.

"Indeed ! with my father ?"

"No ; let me see."

And the lawyer appeared for a moment lost in deep thought.

"Ah ! I have it ; that was the name of a brave lad, who, at the risk of being crushed to death, saved the life of a young girl. I read the account in the papers ; all London rang with it."

"Did it ? and made no mention of anyone else ?"

"Yes ; two other lads ; but did not state their names."

"Well, I was one of the other lads."

"You ? Allow me to congratulate you."

"Upon what ! Upon being foiled in everything I ever attempted by that lad, Giles Evergreen, and his Irish friend, O'Flanagan ?"

"Ha ! Then I suppose there is not much friendship existing between you ?" said Davy, drily.

"Friendship ! Ha, ha ! I hate him, and would give much to injure him and gratify my hate."

And his eyes flashed fire.

"All goes well," muttered the lawyer. "There wouldn't be any difficulty in doing that."

"In what way ?"

"In a thousand."

"Name one, and I——"

Here he was interrupted by the appearance of Lady St. George and Hilda, while at a distance Dick Martingale was following.

"We are interrupted," said Alfred. "I must see you some other time."

The lawyer thrust a card into his hand.

"My address. Happy to see you at any time."

"I shall soon call."

And Alfred rose and joined the ladies.

It was not very long before Dick and the lawyer were seated on the same seat that Alfred had left.

"What brought you down here, Mr. Davy, eh ?"

And Dick looked at him very earnestly.

"Well, partly to see you. What's going on ?"

"Going on ? Nothing down here ; too quiet by half."

"It was not so just now, 'when his hand was at your throat."

"Oh, you saw that then ?"

"Yes."

"Did he tell you the reason !"

"No. He is as close as his father was. What was it ?"

"Oh, nothing very particular. He is not only as close as his father was, but he's got his hot temper as well. He didn't mention anything, then ?"

"No."

Dick eyed him suspiciously.

"What have you been talking about, then ?"

"Why, the fact was——" said Davy, rather taken aback.

"Well, what was the fact ? Out with it !"

And Dick looked him hard in the face.

"I merely asked him about—about ——" here he paused.

"About—about what ?"

"The state of his health."

"Humph! His health must be of very great importance to you, eh? Have you secured him as a client, Mr. Davy?"

"Me? Why, bless your soul, I ——"

"Ah, never mind that. I can look after my health myself. You are playing a double game, Mr. Davy."

"Me. What do you mean?"

"Exactly what I say, neither more nor less; but, in case your hearing is bad, I'll tell you once more. You are playing a double game."

And Dick Martingale's voice quivered with passion.

"Nonsense. You have had a quarrel with the youngster, and have not recovered yourself. Perhaps you want to quarrel with me?"

And, in the slight laugh that followed, there was a mockery that did not escape the penetration of the jockey.

"Well, suppose I did, what of it?" replied Martingale, defiantly.

"Oh, not much, only I think we could work much better together. You are in possession of a secret, and——"

"You think so?"

"I know so. Do you think you can hoodwink me?"

"I could easily, if I tried."

"Try."

"I have something better to attend to at present."

And so saying, Dick moved away.

"Oh, very well. I'll wait your leisure; but supposing, instead of your playing the fool, you acted the part of a wise man?"

Dick burst into a hoarse laugh.

"Ha, that's better. Now, at four o'clock to-day, I am going to dine at the 'Talbot.' I don't care much for dining alone, suppose you join me; I owe you a treat for that last night we spent in the house in Dover Street. Eh, what say you?"

"I think I'll come," said Dick.

"Think, say you will."

"Well, then, I will."

"That's hearty. Give me your hand, Dick; it is not for our mutual interests that we should quarrel. When the time arrives, and you feel inclined to do so you can trust me with the secret, but don't hurry yourself; I have plenty of other persons' secrets in my keeping."

"All right; and I'll give you a bit of advice."

And Dick grinned; he had regained his usual coolness of disposition.

"Give me advice? That's altering the state of things altogether."

"How?"

"It's for me to give you advice."

And Dark Davy gave a pleasant sort of chuckle, which his intimate friends knew, when they heard it, meant mischief.

"Well, now for the advice, friend Martingale."

"Well, you shall have it, and I won't even charge you six-and-eightpence for it."

"That's very kind. Perhaps it's not worth it, eh?"

"You shall judge. You said just now that you had plenty of other persons' secrets in your keeping. Well, my advice is to keep them as safely ——"

"As what?"

."As safely as I shall keep mine! Don't forget four o'clock."

And, placing his hands in his pockets, cocking his hat on one side of his head, with a knowing look, and whistling "I'm a young man from the country," Dick made the best of his way down the hill towards the town.

Dark Davy, for the moment, felt that he was foiled, and, sinking down upon a seat, he began to reflect.

"He's got the subtlety and cunning of an Old Bailey lawyer in him," he muttered. "Nonsense, he has a little more than that, because I am one myself, and he's beaten me by odds. I was a fool to let him see the cards in my hand, and then try to win the trick; humph!"

And the crafty old Act of Parliament bit his nails, and played a certain gentleman's tattoo with his feet.

"It's quite clear he has a secret, or else why did the father place him near the son? He was afraid to discharge him; then, again, the young one has a secret, and, for a lad, he's the coolest hand I've ever met with. And when I came up they had been quarrelling over it, no doubt. Curse it! I can't get to the bottom of it."

And he started up.

"Let me see what a glass of wine will do to clear up all these mysteries. Humph! Giles Evergreen! That was the name of the boy who saved the young Lady Hilda St. George on the railway. And he hates him. I begin to see a little clearer now; a glass or two of wine will take me safely out of the fog."

And so saying, in a few moments

Dark Davy had commenced adopting a specific for clearing away the fog; but which very often is the means of making it more dense and dark.

When Alfred joined the Lady St. George and her daughter Hilda, he had in a great measure recovered the coolness and reservedness of his disposition.

He mentally resolved, for a time, outwardly to change his tactics, and see what the issue of that might lead to.

He, therefore, when he came up to the ladies, held out his hands with such a charming frankness that the Lady St. George beheld it with pleased astonishment.

"Why, my dear Alfred, this is indeed a great pleasure," said that lady.

"The pleasure is mine, your ladyship," he replied, gallantly kissing the hand of Hilda. "I strolled out for a walk as far as the park, but, attracted by the splendid prospect from the hill, could not tear myself from the charming spot. What are our engagements to-day?"

"Well, after making some purchases, I think we'll take a drive with the ponies. What say you, Hilda?"

"With pleasure, mamma."

"It will do her good. I am afraid she has not quite recovered the shock she experienced at the railway."

And her ladyship kissed the beautiful cheek of her child, mentally offering up a prayer for her safety.

"It was a miraculous escape from death, and the boy who saved her a wonderfully fortunate youth."

And Alfred slightly compressed his lips.

"I shall never be able to sufficiently repay him," said the lady.

"Or I either. I'm sure I am thankful to all of you; you all exposed yourselves bravely and devotedly to save me, but Giles Evergreen won the race, and snatched me, a poor thoughtless girl, from a cruel death."

Here Alfred saw the pearly drops gather in her eyes, and he mentally cursed the fortune of his old schoolfellow, forgetting that his courage and presence of mind saved him from a cruel death when the school was in flames from end to end.

"To-morrow I intend to go to town and find those boys out. I really take shame to myself for not doing it before, but a pressure of circumstances has really prevented me, but to-morrow we will find out Giles Evergreen, and his attached friend the 'Irish boy.'"

There is an old saying, which we will not quote, it is too hackneyed.

At the very moment that Lady St. George uttered her intention of seeking Giles and Ted, they had gained the corner of the street leading down to the bridge.

Suddenly two persons turned the corner so quickly that they ran against Alfred, and nearly knocked him down.

Alfred and the ladies looked to see who the parties were, and stood face to face with Giles Evergreen and Terence Flaherty O'Flanagan.

The eyes of Alfred flashed fire upon the pair.

"My dear Alfred," said both in a breath, "pray accept our sincere apologies. We really did not see you."

"I dare say not," was the reply. "I know you are both remarkably clever, but still I did not expect you could see round a corner."

Hilda had grasped Giles's hand, and her mother had taken the other.

"We were just talking about you," said the lady, "and to-morrow you would have seen us in town. To-day you are my guests. And pray what good fortune sent you to Richmond?"

"The fortune we have just encountered—yourself, madam, and the Lady Hilda; we came on purpose," and the countenance of Giles beamed with a noble frankness as he uttered this. "We took the liberty of calling at your town house, and we were directed here."

"And I don't think in all ould Ireland there is a spot more enchanting; at least, if it falls off in the natural beauties of scenery, it is made up in the ladies."

And Ted Flan lifted his cap with the grace of a courtier.

"Ah, well, you Irish gentlemen were born with a compliment on the tip of your tongues. I am delighted at seeing you, and I think we'll make our way home to luncheon. Alfred, my dear boy, what are you standing so moody about, eh?"

He was standing at some distance apart from the ladies, with folded arms and lowering brows, looking anything but pleased with the rencontre.

"Oh, I—I was merely waiting until this pleasant meeting was over. I am merely a make-up in the play; the principal actor," and he pointed sarcastically at Giles, "is there."

"Well, now, that is really too bad,

Alfred. Come, come, old fellow, don't let this foolish nonsense exist."

And Giles held out his hand with frank cordiality.

"Nonsense, sir! I do not understand you. You will find me at home at luncheon, my lady."

And, lifting his cap only to her and Hilda, he walked slowly away.

This nearly upset Giles's naturally good temper, and Lady St. George was not slow at perceiving it.

"My dear boys," she said, "you must not take offence at this; he has lately lost his father, and his temper, not the best at any time, is somewhat soured. Come, let us go home. Mr. Evergreen, give Hilda your arm. Mr. O'Flanagan will, perhaps, honour me with his?"

"Well, my lady," replied Ted Flan, "I've read of an individual going up to the stars, and falling in love with the —Athens, I think they call them—but upon the present occasion allow me to say there is no occasion to go so high to look for goddesses."

And so saying, it was not long before the happy party reached the handsome villa on the banks of the pleasant, gliding, silvery Thames.

With a heart full of mortification and disappointment, his mind rankling with a hundred evil thoughts against the welfare of Giles Evergreen, Alfred Ravensborne took his way by the banks on the side of the river.

"His father could have consigned mine to the gallows, could he? I'll murder that Dick, if he don't tell me the secret of that."

And clenching his hands, he flung them about in the air, as though he was grappling with some unseen enemy.

"And then that fellow, Dark Davy, as he calls himself, what shall I do with him? I don't like him, and I won't trust him."

He stood still for an instant, revolving in his mind what course to pursue.

"I have it. I'll try what a smiling face and a smooth tongue will do with them. I've read there is more done with cunning than anything else; it may be useful in my case."

He gained the door of the villa, and rang the bell.

"Yes, yes; I'll play such a part that shall cheat Satan himself."

The door was opened quietly, and Dick Martingale stood humbly before him, touching his hat, and looking very downcast and penitent.

Alfred eyed him keenly for a moment.

"Well, Richard," he said, quietly, "are you a little better tempered than you were an hour ago?"

"Yes, sir."

"I am glad to hear it. What, in the name of wonder, made you utter such a lie against the memory of my late father, eh? It was a lie, I suppose?"

"Well, sir, passion leads a man to say and do many things that he, in cooler moments, regrets," was the reply.

Dick Martingale was playing the same game as the Honourable Alfred Ravensborne, and it will remain to be seen which of them was check-mated.

"It was a falsehood, then?"

And Alfred waited eagerly for the reply.

There was a pause for a second.

"It was," replied the jockey, slowly.

"You say that very unwillingly."

"Well, no man likes to acknowledge he is a story-teller; and although I am not, nor ever was, nice to a shade, yet I don't like to confess."

"Ah! then say no more about it, Richard; let it all be forgotten. Put that sovereign in your pocket; it will go towards buying you a new tie."

"Thank ye, sir."

"I hope no tighter hand will ever be round your throat than mine was. Follow me to my room."

"Yes, sir."

"Giles Evergreen is in the house," said Alfred, and giving Dick Martingale a look of deep meaning, he slowly walked towards the villa, and was lost to sight.

"Giles Evergreen in the house, Dark Davy in the town, and his make-believe reconciliation with me! Ha, ha! I can see through it all. But look out, my young game-cock, you're not the first flat I've sold. Keep your eyes and ears wide open, Richard Martingale."

And so saying, he hastened after Alfred.

CHAPTER XVI.

A NARROW ESCAPE.

THE luncheon was soon dispatched, and then Lady St. George proposed that they should go out for a ride, and see some of the beauties of the country and the environs round Richmond.

"I suppose," said her ladyship, "that you and your friend can ride?"

"I followed the hounds when a boy, upon my pony, and do not think that I shall disgrace your ladyship," replied Giles modestly.

"And I did the same thing upon an old staple-chaser of my father's," said Ted; "and when the ould horse, after following the hounds, was boiled down, and they made many a hearty male off him, why, then Phil O'Connor—but I am tiring your ladyship."

"Not in the least," she said, smilingly. "Go on, I beg of you."

"Well, then, Phil O'Connor borrowed an illigant animal called a Jerusalem pony, and he carried out an old proverb to the very letter."

"And that was?"

"'Slow and sure wins the day.' Oh, he was a beauty! The first time I mounted him I went flying over his head into a beautiful ditch, remarkable for the quality of its mud and the swateness of its waters. Oh, it was a grand sight when I was pulled out. I was in capital trim for a sweepstakes."

They all had a hearty laugh at this.

"Well," said her ladyship, when the merriment had subsided, "I can promise you something better to ride than that."

And, ringing a bell, a servant instantly entered the room.

" Send Martingale to me."

The man bowed and retired.

When the jockey had been transferred to Richmond, he had, in consequence of the death of her ladyship's groom, undertaken the charge of her ladyship's stables.

" Martingale," she said, as that worthy entered the room, " saddle a couple of horses, and put the ponies in the phaeton."

" Yes, my lady."

" The horses are for these young gentlemen. Alfred, you will drive Hilda and myself in the phaeton."

" With pleasure," was the reply.

" I must saddle Spitfire and Rancour, my lady. Spitfire, I think, would just suit that young gentleman," he said, pointing to Giles, and giving a furtive glance at Alfred, unobserved by Giles, who was talking to Hilda, but noticed by the quick eye of the Irish boy.

" Very well; let them be round quickly. Come, Hilda."

And the ladies retired.

Dick Martingale hastened from the room, followed by Alfred.

" If he mounts Spitfire, I wouldn't give much for his neck," whispered Dick.

" So much the better," replied Alfred.

" Why, I wouldn't mount him for a hundred " and, the jockey grinned, " I've crossed some queer ones in my time."

" I know he can ride well," whispered Alfred.

" I don't care about that, he'll never manage Spitfire, you'll see."

And he hastened away to the stables,

Alfred going to his room to make some change in his dress.

" I'll change horses with you, Giles; Spitfire will suit me," said Ted Flan.

" I'll have nothing to do with Rancour," laughingly replied Giles. " Spitfire sounds as if there was some blood in him."

" That fellow is the same ruffian that you knocked down for oppressing the poor crazed girl."

" I know that, and I'll serve him so again, if he does the like. What's the matter, Ted ?"

Ted's laughing countenance had a deep shadow of thought upon it.

" Well, then, I hate anything like concealment; there's some devilry brewing, and that's the long and short of it, and Master Alfred and that groom are at the bottom of it."

" Nonsense, Ted. Spitfire won't throw me."

" Well, as the marine said, when he was going down under water, ' When we get to the bottom, we shall see the end of it.' But keep a tight rein upon Spitfire."

" Aye, aye; never fear me, Ted."

" I don't fear you; but I've got a trifle of doubt about that same horse," was the reply, " and I wish you would let me——"

Here the conversation was interrupted by the return of Lady St. George and her daughter.

The Irish boy's affection was so strong for Giles that he was resolved that he should run no risk of his life if it could be prevented.

" I beg your ladyship's pardon," said Ted.

" Beg my pardon ! What for ?"

" Is that same Spitfire a quiet cratur ?"

At that moment a servant entered, and informed them the phaeton and horses were in waiting.

" Oh, I see what you mean. Send the groom Martingale to me."

The man bowed and retired.

Almost immediately the groom entered.

" Is that horse Spitfire quiet, Martingale ?"

" Quiet !" and he glanced at Giles ; " he is as quiet as most horses of his breed are ; he's tamed down wonderfully since he has been under my care. P'r'aps the young gentleman is afraid."

" No, he is not afraid," and Giles's eyes flashed like fire upon him. " And if he has any bad qualities in him, I'll ——"

" What, sir ?"

" Tame him as I have done other brutes."

And Giles gave him a look of such scorn, mingled with a deep meaning, that Dick Martingale, for a moment, cast down his eyes.

" But if I thought there was any danger," said the lady.

" Danger, ha, ha ! Why, one would think I never crossed a horse before ; he must be the most intractable brute in existence if he beats me. Have no fears for me, your ladyship."

" I've seen too much of your true noble courage to doubt you ; but really if I thought——"

" Will your ladyship favour me with your hand ?"

And so saying, he took her hand in his, and led her from the room, followed by Ted and Hilda.

There at the door was the phaeton and a pair of charming mouse ponies.

Alfred had already seated himself, and, by his satisfied looks, was evidently in a better humour than usual.

Spitfire and Rancour were being walked about in charge of another groom, and both seemed quiet horses enough.

Of course, to neither of the boys were their vices known, nor was the Lady St. George acquainted with them or their natures.

Handing the ladies into the phaeton, Alfred, without waiting until they had mounted, was about to drive off, but was immediately checked by her ladyship.

Ted Flan was soon in the saddle, for Rancour stood sullen and quiet enough ; but the instant Giles had his foot in the stirrup, Spitfire gave a snort, and reared up on his hind legs as if he was preparing for an aerial trip.

But Giles was in the saddle, and sat solid as a rock, and by the firm hand by which he was held, Spitfire felt that he had somebody on his back that it was not easy to dislodge.

Lady St. George, seeing this, called out anxiously for Giles to dismount, and go with them in the phaeton.

" No danger, your ladyship," said Giles ; " he is full of blood and tricks. We are ready."

And so they drove off.

The horse Spitfire had the mischief of Lucifer himself in him, and Rancour was very little better; but both the boys had been used to riding early in their boyhood, and felt not the least fear about them.

And so, with many curvetings and prancings, they followed the phaeton.

Both ladies felt a degree of nervous anxiety about them which they could not account for, which was shown by their continually looking back, much to the annoyance of the amiable youth who was driving them.

Any sudden or startling noise, and Heaven look down upon the youths, especially if they were not good, bold, and determined riders.

Their vices were alone known to Dick Martingale and those under him in the stable.

Immediately, therefore, that Giles, Ted, and the two ladies had left the room, he made his way swiftly out at the back of the house, and ran along the banks of the river as though he had committed murder and the avengers of blood were after him.

"Old scores will be paid off now!" he said. "And yet the boy sits the horse as firmly as I did when I was ——Ah! no matter."

He stood still for a moment, and looked up at the clouds.

"There will be a fine storm down shortly, and if the lightning and thunder are only strong, I wouldn't give much for their necks. You can tame brutes, can you? Ha, ha! you'll find your match there, curse you!"

More than a dozen times did Spitfire and Rancour endeavour to unseat their riders.

But in vain.

The coolness with which the boys resisted the attempts excited the admiration of Lady St. George and Hilda, not unmixed with dread that some accident would happen before they reached home.

The rearing up of the horses, who seemed acting in concert, caused a cry of alarm from Hilda.

"Oh, there is nothing to alarm you," said Alfred, with a sneer. "Didn't you hear him say what a wonderful horseman he was?"

"And so they are both," replied Lady St. George, indignantly. "Let me but get them safe home, and those two brutes shall not disgrace my stables an hour longer."

They were now at the entrance of a narrow lane, the bottom of which branched off right and left, the centre of it opening on to the river; on each side of the lane there were high banks, the tops of which were thickly covered with trees and impervious hedges.

Curbed and restrained as they had been by their daring riders, the animals had become somewhat more tractable, and Lady St. George had desired Alfred to pull up on one side of the lane that, when they came up, she might speak to them.

They were some distance behind the phaeton.

"I think," said Ted, "that we have pretty well tamed these high-mettled racers, Giles."

"Don't be so certain," replied Giles.

At that moment a loud shout was heard proceeding from behind the trees on the bank.

Up reared the horses, and before

Giles and Ted could restrain them they had started off at a terrific, headlong, fearful speed down the lane.

With the velocity of the lightning's flash they dashed past the phaeton, their maddened fury still further heightened by the shrieks of Lady St. George and her daughter.

With all their skill and exertions it was with the greatest difficulty Giles and Ted could keep their seats.

Alfred Ravensborne, when he beheld the affrighted animals dash past him, could with difficulty conceal his exultation.

He inwardly felt that the death of one or both was certain.

"At last! at last!" he muttered, his eyes gleaming with savage joy.

Alarmed at the fearful peril the boys were placed in, Lady St. George urged Alfred to drive swiftly after them.

Anxious to witness their destruction, he did so.

Had they looked back they would have perceived the face of Dick Martingale looking out from behind the trees with the malignant scowl of a triumphant demon on his face.

Onward they rushed, closely followed by the phaeton, and soon the river, studded with pleasure-boats, appeared in view.

Giles, who retained all his coolness and presence of mind, saw what would happen.

"Clear your feet from the stirrups, Ted," he shouted, "and when they spring into the river, jump off and plunge in."

At the instant the phaeton came in sight of the river, the ladies saw, with horror and dismay, horses and riders disappear in the rapid, rushing waters.

Ted Flan had faithfully acted up to what Giles had told him, so that when the maddened beasts plunged into the water, Giles and his attached schoolfellow sprang out of the saddle, and dived well down.

When they came to the surface they looked around; the horses were struggling towards the centre of the stream, and a dozen boats were rowing towards them, but they heeded them not.

Giles and Ted had been taught the noble art of swimming, and were as buoyant in the water as corks.

Before any assistance had reached them they had gained the bank.

A loud cheer, a real English one, broke from the persons on the river, as well as the hundreds who had rushed to the side on witnessing what all thought the "death plunge" of the poor horses.

They had made for the middle of the stream, and, carried away by the swift, resistless current, had got entangled in the weeds, and were soon lost to sight.

It would be impossible to describe the various feelings which actuated the breasts of those who witnessed this appalling scene.

Lady St. George and Hilda sprang from the phaeton, and rushing down, would have flung themselves into their arms.

"Kape off, my ladies. Don't you see we are mermaids just arrived from the bottom of the say?"

"Jump into the phaeton, and get home directly," said the lady.

"No, no, my lady.   A run home will be the best thing.   Here goes—first home, Ted, for a new hat," said Giles.

"Done !" roared Ted.   "By this time my hat is full to the brim."

And with that they started off at a pace that the crowd who followed, shouting and huzzahing at the pluck and courage of the two lads, vainly endeavoured to keep up with.

When they arrived at the villa, the first person they met was Dick Martingale, who, losing his presence of mind, reeled back as though they had been spectres risen from the dead.

Both boys pushed him hastily out of the way, and preceded by a servant, to whom they quickly explained matters, they were shown into a double-bedded room.

Quick as thought they stripped, and were as quickly between the blankets.

"By all that's good, Giles," said Ted, his merry, laughing face just peeping out upon his friend, "this bed is a trifle drier than the bed of the Thames."

"Right, Ted.   Did you ever have such a gallop before in all your life? Poor Spitfire's fire is put out."

"And Miss Rancour is beyond the reach of malice.   I'd give a trifle to find out the blackguard who gave us the Indian war-whoop."

"Some stupid fellow who——"

Here the conversation was put a stop to by the entrance of Lady St. George.

Immediately the boys started upon their race home, her ladyship begged Alfred to drive swiftly after them, for

Hilda was frantic at the fearful peril of his life her dear preserver had run, but the young gentleman did not seem to have any wish to hurry.

This so enraged the lady that, snatching the reins out of his hands, she speedily urged the ponies into such a gallop that somewhat astonished them.

Arrived home, and leaving Hilda in the care of her maid, she eagerly sought out the boys.

Sinking on a chair the moment she entered the room, the generous, noble-hearted lady burst into a violent flood of tears.

"Don't cry, my lady," said Ted. " Pardon an Irish boy for saying that we have had wet enough for one day, at least."

" Are you sure you are not hurt ?' she faltered out.

" Not in the least, my lady," replied Giles.

"Thank God ! I've sent for the doctor."

" Och, then we are kilt and murdered !"

" What do you mean, Mr. Flan ?"

" Mane ?   My maning is as clear as the young May morn. If the doctor comes, won't he send bolus, pill and draught ? and who knows, he may throw in a blister as a make-weight. I'd rather have another dip than the doctor."

" Ted Flan speaks my sentiments, my lady.   All we want is dry clothes," said Giles, " and to apologise for the trouble we are putting you to."

" If there is a gintleman that sells ready-made habiliments, and he would condescend to try and fit our illigant persons, we would return———"

"Say no more about it," said the lady, rising. "I will send you up something warm. That, and a little rest, will do you both good. By that time everything, I hope, will be ready, I think you had better see the doctor."

"I'll faint for a week, my lady, if ———"

Ted was too late, for the door opening, a servant ushered that all-important personage into the room.

He was a short, pompous gentleman, and evidently upon intimate visiting terms with himself.

He bowed profoundly to the lady.

"You have heard what has happened?" she said.

"It's the talk of the town. Wonderful escape—broken bones—ah!—hem! Your ladyship will permit me to—hem."

"Most certainly."

And the lady left the room.

The doctor approached the bed in which Ted lay concerting some plan of fun and frolic.

"Do you feel any pain, my boy?" said he.

"Awful, doctor—oh!"

"Where?"

"In my great toe."

"Ah!—broken—put it out?"

"I'd rayther not."

"Nonsense, boy; I insist."

"Oh, if you insist," and Ted popped it out at the bottom of the bed, "there it is—a Munster toe."

"Hum!—ah!"

And the doctor began examining it, and while so employed, he started at the sound of a couple of cats about commencing a battle under the bed in which Giles lay.

"Curse the cats! Why do they let them in the room for, eh? I hate cats, dogs, and rats!" said the doctor, ringing the bell as though he would raise the whole house.

Ted gave a hollow groan.

Giles was laughing under the clothes.

"What's the matter, my boy?"

"A cat sends me into con-vul-sions —oh! oh!"

The servant entered the room.

Again the cats were giving tokens of an approaching conflict.

"Do you hear those infernal animals, my man?"

The man looked perfectly astounded.

"Can't make out how they came in here, sir."

"Take the poker and drive them out."

The man looked under the bed, and rattled about with the poker.

To his astonishment, the cats had made their way under Ted Flan's bed.

Ted groaned under the clothes, and laughed till they shook again.

The man looked at the doctor, and the doctor returned the look.

"Out with them!" roared the angry doctor.

"But I can't find them, sir," said the man.

"Under that bed."

Here they were again heard under Giles's bed.

"Which bed?" said the man, standing in the centre of the room, poker in hand.

Then up jumped the doctor as if a

wasp had stung him, for the cat bounded close to his legs.

The man, wheeling round rapidly to strike the cat, caught the doctor a blow on the shins which made him hop and dance as if he was in training for the Tarantella.

"Surely the cats must have taken refuge under the drawers, for the noise is there now."

The man advanced cautiously towards them, when suddenly the snarling and snapping of a dog was heard.

With a rush both doctor and man made for the door, and in a second the room was clear.

Neither Giles nor Ted dare show their heads because they would, by their merriment, have betrayed themselves, but the agitation of the bedclothes plainly showed that they were enjoying themselves to their hearts' content.

At last Ted looked out.

"An aisy way of getting rid of the docthor without paying his fee, eh, Giles?"

Giles was about replying when the servant entered the room, followed by two or three others, armed with sticks.

"I tell you," said the man, "there are not only two cats in the room, but a dog as well."

"Well, then, we'll soon have them out; we shan't disturb you much, young gentlemen."

"Don't mind us, but drive out the animals," said Giles.

"If you can find them," muttered Ted.

Well, search they did, but neither cat nor dog could they find, and so they stood looking from the one to the other with amazement.

While so employed, the dog was heard yelping down the stairs.

After him went the men, to the infinite merriment of Giles and Ted.

Their laughter had scarcely ceased when the head footman again entered, followed by a person carrying a large parcel.

He had attended at the house, and taking the measure of the wet garments, now returned with new ones, for in Richmond, as in London, it is wonderful how soon you can be suited by all classes as well as tailors.

He began to untie the parcel, but before doing so went to the looking-glass to adjust his collar.

Ted looked at Giles.

"When you've done with your collar I'll trouble you for my shirt," said Ted.

"Certainly, sir."

And the man placed one before him, doing the same to Giles.

Then, placing articles of wearing apparel before them, he left the room.

Giles and Ted were soon dressed, the clothes fitting them admirably, and the man of cloth having again entered the room before going downstairs, Ted thought he'd play off a little fun upon him.

At the far end of the room, which was rather spacious, was a large swing-glass at which Giles was standing.

•They had so arranged it.

"May I be favoured with your card, sir?" said Ted.

"Certainly, sir."

And he handed one to him.

"THE CALM BEFORE THE STORM."

" Mr. Board, tailor," said Ted, aloud. " Are you any relation to the Sleeve-board family ?"

" Not any, sir," was the reply.

" I thought you might be."

" Mr. Board," said a voice from the other part of the room.

" Sir," said the tailor, running nimbly to Giles.

" I didn't call, sir," said Giles.

" Beg pardon, sir, but I thought you did."

And he was going back when the voice again called him.

" Here I am, sir."

" Upon my word, I did not call you."

Now, Mr. Board happened to have a very choleric temper, hot as his own goose at times ; and he looked hard at Giles, as though thinking it somewhat strange.

" I am here, sir," he said.

" Well, I see you are. What of it ?" was the cool reply.

" You called me then, sir."

" I did not. I never opened my lips."

" But I could swear——"

" Swear, sir !" said Giles in an assumed rage. " Swear, sir ! what do you mean ? We'll have no swearing here."

" I am a tradesman, sir, and——"

" I know it ; your card says as much, and your name is Board ; but you'll excuse me, but I don't want to be bored."

It was with difficulty the man kept his temper at this.

During this little scene Ted had gone and partly opened the door.

" Mr. Board !" sounded a voice from the outside, resembling that of the head footman.

Mr. Board started, ran nimbly to the door, opened it, and, lo and behold, no one was there.

He appeared so perplexed that it was with difficulty the boys could prevent themselves from laughing in his face.

His face became red at the thought that the servant was playing tricks with him.

He returned into the room to tie up the paper when again he was called to the stairs.

" Now, Mr. Snip, are you coming ?" said the voice.

This was too much.

He rushed to the door just as the footman pushed it open, he having been sent by her ladyship to Giles and Ted.

" What do you mean by insulting me ?" said the choleric tailor. " You ought to know your place better."

" My place, sir ! What do you mean ? What has my place to do with you, eh ?" said the footman, warmly, his face flushing.

The temper of the man in livery was very little better than that of the man of buttons.

" What do you mean by playing larks with me——a respectable tradesman, eh ? A fellow in your position !"

" Fellow ! Who are you calling a fellow ? Hang it ! a footman's a match any day for a——"

" What, sir, what ?"

" Well, a——"

" Out with it ! What ?"

"Well, sir, as my favourite poet says, 'A thing of shreds and patches.'"

Giles and Ted were choking with laughter.

"A thing!" screamed the tailor. "That is as bad as what you called me just now."

"I call you? It's a——"

"What, sir, what? I'll swear you called me!"

"You will?"

"Yes; and kiss the book upon it."

"Then you'll swear and kiss anything!"

"You called me Snip."

"If I did, it's only your right name."

"That's enough. Now I know you did it; you, a common flunkey!"

"You, a common tailor!" was the reply.

Here they laid hold of one another by the collar, and Giles and Ted looked on at the expectant battle royal that now seemed imminent.

"What is all this disturbance about?" asked Lady St. George, at that moment entering the room.

"If you please, my lady——" said Board.

"No, if you please, my lady——" said Jones.

"One at a time, if you please. Go on, Mr. Board."

"Well, please your ladyship, I attended here at your ladyship's request with certain things for these young gentlemen; while upon the point of taking my departure, that man called me to the door."

"If I did, my lady, may I——"

"Be silent! Go on, Mr. Board."

"When I went to the door he had hid himself. I came back to the room, when a second time I was called by a most opprobrious epitaph."

"A what, Mr. Board?"

"Epithet, I mean," and the tailor coloured like a red cabbage. "He called me Snip."

Here the good humoured lady smiled, and a broad grin stole over the faces of the boys.

"How came you to take such a liberty, Jones, with Mr. Board?" said her ladyship, looking severely at him.

"Your ladyship, he must be dreaming. I came upstairs to tell the young gentlemen you wished to see them, and I never opened my lips to a mortal soul."

"I was called the epitaph—I mean epithet—by you!"

And here the rage of the tailor made him speak thick and guttural, as though he had indulged in something stronger than tea that morning.

"I think you must be labouring under some mistake," replied Lady St. George; "if I thought that any servant of mine so misconducted himself, I should immediately look for his successor. Jones is one of the best conducted ones I have."

"But, my lady, I cannot distrust my own senses. Pray ask the young gentlemen."

"Oh, the young gentlemen were not attending to anything of the kind, you may be sure, Mr. Board."

"But, my lady, I was called Snip by someone," continued the tailor, bridling up again with passion.

"Mere imagination lodging in your head, Mr. Board. Let me have your account, sir. When you are ready, my dear boys, I wish to see you in the drawing-room."

And so saying, her ladyship left the room.

Giles and Ted lingered for a moment to enjoy the angry looks of the two men.

"Mr. Jones, I'll pay you out for this," said Board.

"And I'll pay you out for it," was the reply. "You nearly lost me my place."

"And I'll make it hot for you yet," said the tailor.

"You'd better make your goose hot," sneered the footman, passing out of the door.

Ted and Giles were standing close by as he passed.

Jones had got half way down when Ted Flan again caused his voice to sound as though proceeding from the footman, and called out—

"Snip!"

This was more than flesh and blood could bear.

Out rushed the tailor, and, laying hold of the footman, a scuffle ensued, and away they went rolling downstairs amid the roars of Giles and Ted, who stood at the top cheering them on.

The footman and the tailor soon found their legs, and both of them, fearing the displeasure of Lady St. George, made the best of their way to the servants' hall, where they setttled their differences over some cold beef and a tankard of ale.

On entering the drawing-room, they found her ladyship and Hilda waiting to receive them; the latter springing up, and, in the excess of her joy at finding them none the worse for the perilous ducking they had received, throwing her arms round their necks, and kissing them with all the warm, pure sympathy of a guileless heart.

"My dear, dear boys," said her ladyship, "I am truly delighted to see you looking so well after the narrow escape you had of your lives this morning. I have had no end of visitors and inquiries after you."

"May I be so bold as to ask your ladyship what became of the poor horses?" said Giles.

"The poor animals became entangled in the thick weeds that abound so in the middle of the river here, that they perished," was the reply.

"Then poor Rancour has gone dead in spite of envy and malice; and upon that particular point I may have something to say to your ladyship, and, in addition to the sum total, a trifle respecting that amiable vixen, Spitfire."

"Indeed! pray let me hear it."

At that moment the butler announced that dinner was ready.

"After dinner, then, you will inform me?"

"After dinner, my lady. I not only spake for myself, but for Giles, when I say that we have both had an excellent whet to our appetites."

And, so saying, they left the room.

Mr. Richard Martingale stood transfixed to the spot for a few minutes after Giles and Ted had pushed him, without much ceremony, out of the way.

He then walked off rapidly to the stables, and ascending to a room that was specially devoted to his comfort over the stables, sat down to reflect.

"What's all this?" he muttered. "Those accursed boys escaped—and where are the horses?"

At that moment the pony-phaeton returned to the stables, and he heard the voice of Alfred Ravensborne loudly calling him.

"I am here, sir," he answered.

"Very well; I'll come up to you," said Alfred, as he ascended the stairs and entered the room.

It was not quite so snug and comfortable as the one the jockey had inhabited in the house of his father.

Still his living there was entirely his own choice, and so he made the best of it.

He kept up his racy taste by adorning the walls with choice prints of the "cracks," and altogether it was a tolerably comfortable place.

It possessed another advantage; it enabled Mr. Richard Martingale to be more his own master.

He could go in and out when he liked, and that was all he cared about.

"Well, Master Alfred," he said, after that young gentleman had thrown himself into a chair, "the luck's against us this time, ain't it?"

Alfred did not condescend to answer him.

"I'd 'a' betted a thousand to fifty they'd never come home alive."

"And so would I, after what you told me respecting the horse Spitfire," replied Alfred

"How was it they escaped? Why, hang me, if I think they have got a scratch!"

"Not one; and instead of making things better, it's made them worse."

"How is that?"

"How is it? Why, after this day's affair, they will become greater favourites than ever with my aunt and cousin, and be the talk of the place, and where shall I be? Who was it frightened those infernal brutes in such a manner?"

And he eyed Dick narrowly.

"Aye, who was it? Can't you guess?"

"Oh, yes."

"Who?"

"You."

"Right."

And Dick gave a quiet grin.

"I never shouted louder in all my life, and never saw horses gallop like mad devils to death faster than they did, and yet they have escaped."

"Yes; but I won't be baffled. But they have got the cunning of a hundred serpents in them, Dick."

"Maybe, and so has others I could mention. But what's become of the horses?"

"Lying at the bottom of the river, between the Bridge and the Eel Pie House, on the ait. When the horses madly plunged in the water, those two fellows plunged in free of them. I knew all was over then, for they could float like corks; they were masters of the school at that game."

"And nearly all the others, I've heard."

"Indeed! But I'll find a game for

Master Giles, before long, that he shan't win at."

"I should like to get the fellow away somewhere."

"Ah! that's what I have been thinking upon. Break his infernal stubborn pride and spirit."

"Ha, ha! that would be glorious; it would pay off old scores!"

"You mean the drubbing he gave you for molesting the poor crazed girl? That served you right!"

And Alfred laughed in his face.

"Did it?" Dick sullenly replied. "Never mind, it's an astonishing long lane that has no turning, and a stunning good hand of cards if you can always win. It's not only for that blow, but an old grudge that I owe his father some years ago."

"His father?" said Alfred, with surprise.

"His father," repeated the jockey. "I know what I am a talking about. I never had the chance of serving the father out, but if I don't chalk up double scores upon the son, may I be shot."

"Well, what was it?" said Alfred, anxiously.

"I shan't tell you now."

Dick had got into one of his savage moods.

"Why not tell me what it was?" said Alfred, coaxingly.

"No," was the dogged reply; "the time ain't come yet. You shall know, never fear. It's what ought to have been paid with his blood, and, if I can't have it of one, I will of another, that's all. There is the last bell for dinner ringing."

"Never mind that. I shan't dine with them."

"Well, I haven't got any to offer you."

"That's kind. Upon second thoughts, I think I'll show my face; but her ladyship is in her tantrums, and, when she is so, she's got the blood of the Ravensbornes in her, and don't stand nice about trifles. I shall see you again by-and-bye, Dick—say in the evening. I'll come and smoke a cigar with you when Virtue and Amiability have gone to bed."

"Ha, ha! that's right, Master Alfred! And, mark me, but it shall go hard if we ain't first past the winning post yet. I know a man that will help us."

"Indeed! I think I know the man."

"You do? Not the one I mean."

"Yes; Dark Davy."

"Ah! yes; he was talking to you to-day."

"He was; and offered his assistance, and said he had served my father."

"Ah, he's a cunning fellow; but you let me manage him. He'll twist you round his finger as easy as——"

"He can you, eh, Dick?"

"No, no, he can't do that."

"Oh, he can't twist you round his finger, and yet you think he can me," said Alfred, dryly.

"Yes."

"And you think you can twist me round, eh?"

"I did not mean that exactly."

"Well, perhaps you will tell me your mni ng when I see you again, Mr. Richard Martingale."

And so, uttering a low, scornful laugh, he descended the stairs.

"That boy," muttered the groom, "would turn his father's head inside out, and he was rayther crafty. Well, those who live longest see the most, that is, if they don't lose their eyesight. Well, now for Master Dark Davy. So, so, he's been trying to worm himself into the confidence of the boy, has he? I'll dig a nice pit for you to fall into, my dark friend, if you come the double-shuffle with me."

He descended the stairs, and was passing out when a servant informed him that the Lady St. George requested his presence in the drawing-room.

Mr. Martingale was rather taken aback at this request, and was somewhat at a loss to understand what he was wanted for.

Immediately after dinner, Ted Flan had told the whole affair to the ladies from the beginning of their first meeting the groom in the country.

"And by the powers," he said, "you'll excuse me, your ladyship, but that gentleman owes a deadly grudge against Giles, and well knew that the illigant Spitfire was a baste not fit for any one to cross; besides, who was it gave the yell like that of a wild Indian, and set Spitfire and Rancour (rest their bones) galloping off like mad deers?"

"I see it all now," said her ladyship, "and will inquire into it."

And with that she gave orders for the appearance of the jockey before her.

Alfred had pleaded fatigue, and only joined them as the dessert was being placed upon the table. His manners were, as usual, cold and constrained, but they made no impression upon the others.

He was somewhat surprised when he saw Dick enter the drawing-room, and he glanced uneasily at him.

"Your ladyship sent for me?" said Dick.

"I did; I wish to ask you a few questions."

"Certainly, my lady."

"Were you aware of the fierce nature of the horses you saddled this morning?"

And her ladyship looked keenly at him.

"Aware of what, my lady?" and he glanced slyly at Alfred.

"I have already asked you the question, sir; give me a truthful answer."

"Certainly. I never saw any vice in the horses, that is, if they were ridden by proper persons. I could see that young gentleman," pointing to Giles, "wasn't fit to manage him, directly he got on his back."

"Indeed! You are telling a falsehood; and pray, sir, after we had left the villa, upon what did you employ yourself?"

"Why, my lady, there being nothing to do in the stable, I went up to my own room and busied myself upon a few private matters of my own; there was no harm in that, was there?"

"Not any, if it is the truth. I suspect you are the person whose shouts caused the horses to run away and nearly sacrificed the lives of those gentlemen."

"I cannot see how you can imagine anything of the kind," said Alfred, defiantly.

"I am not asking you for your opinion, Alfred," said her ladyship.

"But I choose to give it. Dick Martingale was a faithful servant of my father, and he was left to my care. Why do boys get upon horses if they don't know how to manage them?" said Alfred.

"Yes, but we did know how to manage them," replied Giles, warmly; "and the horses were tolerably tractable until they were alarmed at the shouts of some miscreant that caused them to start off before we had command over them."

"And it's mighty lucky that it was not some one I know on their backs, or the aristocracy would have lost a brilliant gem."

And Ted Flan, looking at Alfred, gave a very expressive shrug of his shoulders.

"I am determined to sift the matter to the bottom," said Lady St. George, "and for that purpose I shall wait upon the magistrate in the morning."

"Oh, with all my heart, my lady, as far as I am concerned; but after what you have said, and the suspicions you have of me, I shan't stop," said Martingale.

"You shall not leave," said the lady, warmly.

"Who says so?" asked Dick, with a sneer.

"I do."

"You? What have you to do with me? I am not your servant; I belong to him"—and he pointed to Alfred. "I see it all; ever since that affair with the mad girl at the assizes that nice young gentleman and his friend have had a spite against me, and now they're determined upon ruining me; but they

can't do it. Ha, ha! I am independent of them, and you too."

"You are insolent, sir."

"No I am not, I am only standing up for myself, and Dick Martingale always did that, because why?—he had no one else to do it for him. I won't stop another hour in the house."

"And by that," said her ladyship, "I know you to be a guilty man."

"I don't care what you know. I won't stop half-an-hour upon your premises. I dare you to stop me! I'll let you know where to find me, Master Alfred; you won't desert your father's faithful servant, I know."

"Never, Dick."

"I knew it; and as for you,"—addressing Giles and Ted Flan—"I'll put my mark upon you some of these days, and it shan't be a light one."

"Leave the house instantly, fellow, or I'll have you turned out."

And Lady St. George extended her hand to the bell-rope.

"Oh don't trouble yourself, I'm going. I won't forget you, my young swells, depend upon it. That for the lot of you!"

And snapping his fingers defiantly at them, he left the room.

"He has been shamefully used," said Alfred, with a violent burst of passion, "and for a couple of fawning curs!"

"Do you apply the term of cur to me?" said Giles, his temper thoroughly roused.

"Be aisy, Giles! he's thinking of himself, when he was going to knock the little boy down with a cricket-bat. Who is the cur after that?"

Alfred made no reply to this; the veins in his temples seemed as though they would burst.

He made a spring at Ted and Giles.

Hilda, seeing this, sprang between them, but, seizing her by the arm, the maddened boy swung her round, and she fell heavily upon the floor.

"Now who is the cur?" said Giles Evergreen.

And the next moment, Alfred measured his length upon the ground.

The confusion attendant upon this scene brought the servants into the room, and they stood gazing upon it with wonder and amazement.

Lady St. George stood as though she was petrified, Giles had snatched Hilda up in his arms, while Ted Flan stood upon the defensive, Alfred having sprung to his legs.

He stood glaring round at them as though he would have annihilated them.

He placed his hand for a moment to his forehead, upon which a mark was seen gradually swelling.

"It only wanted this to complete the bitter hatred I have always felt for you, and the vengeance I will some day pour upon your head. I shall not rest easy, Giles Evergreen, until I have paid with interest the debt I owe you. After this, your ladyship, I shall decline to remain under the same roof with either yourself or those fellows."

And, so saying, he left the room, and shortly after the villa, in search of the jockey, Dick Martingale.

It was some time before the exertions of those left behind could recover Hilda from the deep swoon she had fallen into, or the terror this scene had occasioned, and the rest of the evening was passed in great anxiety for her recovery.

CHAPTER XVII.

SOFT TOMMY AND SUKE'S VISIT TO LONDON.

THE Jolter family had, during the events we have just narrated, been living their usual quiet life at the farm.

It had taken Tommy and Suke some time to recover from the effects of the dinner party, and whenever the word "soup" was mentioned, poor Tommy felt his mouth as hot as a baker's oven, and the tears came into the eyes of Suke.

"I tell thee, Tommy," she said one day, "f ever I catch that Mister Ted Flan, I'll larrup him to his heart's content."

"Stuff a' nonsense, Suke; he'd larrup a dozen such as thee. Didn't he tell thee it wur the custom o' the country?"

"What, to burn a mortal's throat to cinders? Yah! you won't make I believe that, boy Tommy."

"You be as unbelieving as a—goose," replied Tommy. "They're two of the best fellows living."

"Are they?" retorted Suke. "Yah! you know a great deal about it; didn't he pepper that confounded soup until he made my precious eyes the colour of a carrot? Didn't he?"

"Ha, ha! yes, by gum! not only your precious eyes were that colour, but likewise your precious nose were main red. By gum, Suke! I thought you'd set fire to the table-cloth."

"Did ye? yah! softhead; and what did thee look like? The water ran down thy nose like peas, and thy eyes started out of thy head like boiled gooseberries."

And Suke laughed heartily.

"Did they? but I didn't try to swassinate old Lawyer Tough Mutton. You be a nice one for a small dinner party, I don't think."

"Yah! you are a nice innocent lamb to talk about old Tough Mutton. I arn't got a liquorish tooth, Soft Tommy, and go dipping my fingers into raspberry jam jars and currant jelly pots. I'll mix thee up a pot of summat nice some day, that shall last thee a month o' Sundays, I warrant me; and, what's more, baste thy hide for thee."

And here Suke caught up an old brush, worn to the stump, while Soft Tommy could only defend himself by seizing a large saucepan lid, to act as a shield in the " civil " war that was about to commence.

The appearance of the combatants was ludicrous.

Tommy was dressed as a farmer's boy, in smock frock and leather breeches.

The farmer had had a cart-load of soot in that morning to manure his land with, and Tommy had been assisting at unloading it, therefore, his red head and black face, as he threw himself in an attitude of defence with the saucepan-lid, might have reminded one of the son and heir of the Black Knight with the Woeful Countenance.

Suke had her ordinary coarse farming dress on, a rough sort of apron and pinafore, a large check gown and thick shoes, while her long red hair streamed about in the excitement of the moment, as she raised the old stumped brush to bring it down upon Soft Tommy's head.

These " desperate " combats were of constant occurrence, and were only suspended when the farmer himself appeared on the scene with a double-thonged hunting-whip in his hand, and which he liberally and impartially bestowed upon both of them.

On the present occasion he was too far off to interfere.

"I'll give it thee now, Tommy, to thy heart's content, my lad. I'll make thy head like batter this time."

And Susan made a desperate blow at Tommy, but which the soft one caught upon the shield, cleverly; but in the effort to save his head, he was nearly knocked off his legs.

Recovering himself, he made a dash at Suke with the saucepan-lid, which she seized.

This brought the combat to an end.

The impetus which Tommy gave to his rush sent Suke off her legs into a large tub of hog's-wash that was behind her, Tommy clinging with desperation to the lid.

Had the tub been full the consequences might have been something fatal; but, as it was, Tommy, giving Suke a parting grin, was off.

With great difficulty Suke emerged from her savoury bath, and a pretty figure she cut.

At that moment a loud knocking came at the door.

All the men and girls were at work in the fields, so there was no alternative but for Suke to open it.

She did so, and the person who stood there was no other than our old friend Tough Mutton.

At the appearance of Suke he started back, then burst into a roar of laughter.

"Yah!" yelled Suke, showing her teeth. " What are you laughing at, eh, lawyer?"

" Laughing," said the lawyer, as well as he could speak, " at you, Suke !—pah !" and he held his nose. " You've been in the wash-tub."

" Yah! What if I have, eh?"

" Ha, ha, ha! Nothing particular, only I should advise you to get into another as quickly as possible. You and Tommy have been at some of your larks."

" Have we; and you call this a lark, do you?" said the irate Suke, wringing her fiery locks. " Tommy and I had a set-to; but I'll be even with him for it. Eh, what a mook I be in! If feyther comes it will be a summut worse. If you want he, he'll be in directly. You can go into the parlour, lawyer; you'll find the gooseberry wine and a loomp of cake on sideboard, and you can amuse yourself with them till I coom down. Yah! What a mook I be in!"

And Suke was off, leaving the lawyer to find out the gooseberry wine and the " loomp " of cake by himself.

Knowing pretty well the ways of the farm, Mr. Sheepshanks was not long finding the room, and seating himself, he took out a newspaper, and awaited the farmer's return to his tea.

Half an hour elapsed, when Farmer Jolter made his appearance.

He was followed by Tommy, who had shifted his clothes, and made himself spruce, with the exception that he had not got the soot well out of his skin, and there was no coming to a safe conclusion what the colour of his hair was, red or black.

Then followed Suke, clean as print, with a servant bearing the tray for tea.

Now, Farmer Jolter's tea table was of the old-fashioned style; he had a cold joint, either roast or boiled, on the table, flanked by a foaming Toby Philpot filled with old ale.

Tea and hot cakes made up the rest; and, as the farmer observed—

" The man or woman that couldn't make a good tea upon that might go hang !"

He never allowed business to interfere with his meals.

This the lawyer knew, and therefore wisely kept silence upon the matter that had brought him there until the honest farmer had satisfied the cravings of nature.

" Come, lawyer," said the free-hearted yeoman, " fall to—make yourself at home. Ecod! it be a sight to see thee. How do'ee get on wi' that Weazle?"

" Very well. Excellent beef this.

Thank ye, Suke, I'll take tea; old ale and I never agreed yet."

And the lawyer attacked the beef with an excellent appetite.

"Bravo, lawyer! but you should tackle the old ale; it be splendid stoof; I never brewed better. But do as you like—Liberty Hall here."

"I know, I know; doing well," he replied.

And the same remark might apply to the rest.

Tommy and Suke appeared to have forgotten the battle of Stump and Lid, and after a time the tea things were sent away, and pipes and tobacco placed on the table.

"I know you don't mind me smoking, lawyer."

"Not at all, not at all; don't mind me. My visit is one of a very important nature."

"Oh, well, if that's the case, Tommy and Suke, you can leave the lawyer and I together."

"Not so, because the matter interests them as well."

"Blame me, if I understand you," said the farmer.

"Well, then, now for the object of my visit. I think some years ago you had a brother?"

"What, Tommy Jolter? Of course I had; I never had not no more than one brother, and when old father died he left I more than Tommy, which wasn't fair, because we were of the same flesh and blood; but he was the younger like. Well, what about he?"

"He went abroad, didn't he?" asked the lawyer.

"Of course he did; I made him take his share, and he went off to Australia; oh, a matter of twelve years ago, and I only heard of him twice. Be he coming back?"

"Well, not exactly."

"Well, what be he about?"

"That I can't tell."

Here the honest farmer paused, and laid down his pipe, looking the lawyer full in the face.

"Be—be he dead?" he said, in a low tone.

"Yes, farmer," said the lawyer, taking his hand, "the brother to whom you behaved so kindly has left this world."

The farmer sank back in his seat, deeply affected.

His rough, honest heart keenly felt the pang, and, spite of his rugged nature, the tears rolled down his cheeks.

"Poor brother Tommy!" he said; "I shall never see him more."

This was too much for Tommy and Suke; they blubbered outright, and the comical faces they both made nearly upset the gravity of the tough old lawyer.

Tommy added to the fairness of his complexion by rubbing his face with the cuff of his jacket, while Suke added to the natural ruby of hers by rubbing it with her apron.

The only information we have of it is contained in this paper," said Sheepshanks, "and which I accidentally read this morning. Listen—

"'To the next of kin of Tommy Jolter, who died at Melbourne, in Australia, in the month of August, 1864.—The next of kin, by applying to Messieurs Faithful, Son and Steady, Lincoln's Inn Fields, will hear of something greatly to their advantage.

"Now, Jolter, my friend, you must go to London."

"Not I; never was there in my life," was the reply.

"That matters little; go you must." if only for the sake of your children."

"I am rich enough, and so will they be."

"That I know; but you don't know what your late brother has asked you to do in his will."

"That's quite another affair," said the farmer.

"And take Tommy and Suke with you; leave the farm with your foreman."

"But what can I do with them in London?"

And the farmer looked doubtfully at Tommy and Suke.

"Do with them? I know Faithful, Son and Steady well. I'll give you a letter to them. Then I'll give you another to Mrs. Wilson, Gower Street, where Giles and Ted are living."

"Yes; but, then, only just think of the tricks that may be played upon them," said old Jolter.

Tommy grinned at the thought of meeting his schoolfellows again.

Suke clenched her great, red fist at the thought of again meeting Ted Flan.

"Well," said old Jolter, "I really don't see any harm in it, so next week we'll start."

"Next nonsense; you'll start to-morrow; strike while the iron is hot; why cannot you get ready in an hour?"

"What dost thee say, Suke?"

"Why, I thinks Mr. Sheepshanks be right; if Uncle Tommy be dead and left money, why, I think the sooner the rightful owners have it the better. I ha' been told that lawyers are as slippery as eels."

"Thank ye for the compliment, Miss Suke."

"You be heartily welcome, and many more of the same sort. Yah! I like to take care of my money myself."

"Ha, ha! well done, girl," said her father. "What say you, Tommy, to a visit to Lunnon?"

"Oh, jolly well, feyther. I am told there's plenty of larking there, and fine sights, and I shall see Giles and Ted Flan again."

"Yes, and so shall I," grinned Suke.

"Well, then, it's all settled," said the lawyer; "you'll have an early dinner at my house to-morrow, and then, hey for London; good night," and so saying the good lawyer departed.

The farmer, Suke and Tommy sat for some time after the lawyer had left, immersed in a strange variety of thoughts; in fact, they were indulging in that pleasing amusement of "building castles in the air." At last the farmer laid down his pipe.

"Well, children," said he, "this be a rare piece of news old Tough Mutton has brought us."

"Yes," said Tommy; "I hope Uncle Tommy has left me a lump of money."

"Yah! leave thee money? What should he leave thee money for, I should like to know?" and Suke laughed at the idea.

"Why, warn't he my godfeyther?" answered Tommy.

"Well, what o' that? It be a main deal more likely he'd leave a lot to me; would it be worth anybody's while to leave money to Soft Tommy?"

"You'd best mind who you're calling names, else I'll give thee a dowse of thy red chops."

"Yah! two can play at that game, my lad." So saying she jumped up for the purpose of carrying out her threats.

This roused old Jolter from his train of thought, and seizing an ash stick that was close to his chair, both Tommy and Suke, knowing the potent effects of it, sank back into their seats, and so hostilities were for a time suspended.

"Will thee be quiet?" said the farmer, shaking the stick at them.

"It be all her fault," said Tommy, "she is always trying to be cock of the walk over me. I be your son and heir, and I'm not going to put up with that; I'll go for a soldier first."

"Go for what?" roared the farmer, grasping the stick. "A soger! Ha! ha! why, the lad's mad."

"No, he ain't," sulkily replied Tommy. "You don't think I'm going to spend all my days here, do you? I only hope Uncle Tommy has left me a summut, that's all."

"And if he has, what will thee do with it?"

"That's best known to myself."

And Tommy grinned.

"You'll not leave the plough-tail, my lad, if Uncle Tommy has left thee the crown of England; take my word for that."

"Yah! so you can make up your mind to that, my lad."

And Suke grinned at him.

"I tell thee I won't. Why, there isn't a mortal soul to speak to, except the pigs, and the sheep, and the cocks and hens. I tell thee I won't follow the plough-tail to please anybody. Why, look at Giles Evergreen; everybody took him to be a soft one, but I fancy they found out their mistake; then there is Ted Flan, and——"

Who else Tommy would have mentioned is not known, for, starting up from his chair, Farmer Jolter, grasping the ash stick, made a plunge at Tommy.

But Tommy's agility stood his friend upon that occasion, and, springing nimbly behind Suke's chair, the stick came sharply down upon her unfortunate red head, and down went Suke, chair and all, uttering loud cries of murder; while Tommy made a rush upstairs, and, gaining his room, fastened himself in against any further visitation of the ash stick.

Suke, rising, made the best of her way to the kitchen, where an application of vinegar and brown paper made the wound smart so that she danced about the kitchen as though she had been on hot coals, which made the farm servants indulge in the broadest of broad grins.

A short time after this, the supper being placed on the table, Tommy was called down, peace having been proclaimed, and the father and his hopeful children were again friends.

Jolter, Senior, had been brought up by his father to follow the plough, and perform all the duties of a farm servant. Of the world beyond the market town, which he visited once a week, he knew nothing; all his thoughts were on his stock and crops, the weather, and how prices ruled in that far-off region, Mark Lane; and if ever he felt a disposition to see two places, they were Mark Lane and the Cattle Market.

Very imperfectly educated, he had married, because no farmer ought to be without a wife to look after the pigs, the poultry, and the dairy. Children came into the world and went out of it, without causing any particular surprise. The wife died, and then Jolter wondered what would become of the dairy, the poultry yard, and the piggery. But Suke had been brought up to it by her parents, and so, the gap being filled up, matters went on as usual at the farm; things prospered, and the farmer was wealthy, but that made no difference; and so he went grubbing on the old horse-in-the-mill sort of life.

Books and learning he knew nothing of, and didn't want; he counted them dangerous things, that only led people into mischief, and trouble, and sorrow.

A ploughman who had got a little schooling in the union taught Suke her letters and figures, so that she was enabled to keep the accounts of the farm in pretty good order; and although it might be said that Suke ruled the roast, the farmer admitted no one to be master but himself.

After supper the conversation again turned upon the proposed visit to London.

"You'll pack up all the things in the deal box, Suke," Jolter said; "and don't ye cram too many in, because we ain't going to stay away long."

"How long, feyther?" asked Tommy.

"Well, no longer than we can settle the business in. What the dickens would become of the farm, boy?" It goes confoundedly against the grain going at all, I warrant me."

"Well, but ain't we to see any of the foine sights?"

"Yes, lad; we'll go and see the markets."

"The markets?" said Tommy, in great dismay.

"Yes; the finest sight in all the world. But come, get thee to bed, both of you. You'll start early in the mornng. It's a longish ride to old Tough Mutton's, and you'll put on your market clothes."

"My market clothes?" cried Tommy. "Do you want to send me to London to frighten the people like a scarecrow?"

Here Tommy saw his father's hand gradually moving towards the stick.

"What do you mean, boy? Are you 'shamed of the clothes that get you an honest living? If I thought so, I'd lock thee up until we came back; so thee had best hold thy tongue."

Tommy, though rather soft, took the advice, and said nothing more upon the subject, in case the old farmer might carry his threat into execution, and then he would not see London, or, what he thought most about, his dear old schoolfellows, Giles and Ted Flan.

But Tommy had made up his mind to a little plan of his own, which if old Jolter had for the moment dreamed of, Tommy would have been condemned to the company of the sheep and the pigs, instead of the grand sights of London town.

"THE JOLTERS ON THEIR JOURNEY."

So Tommy betook himself to bed to think and dream of the fun he'd have with his old playmates, whom he loved so dearly.

The next morning they met early, and sat down to a good substantial breakfast, to which all parties did ample justice, and then they proceeded to get ready for the journey.

Old Jolter had dressed himself in his winter market costume, which consisted of a thick woollen great-coat, with pearl buttons, a large felt hat, a red worsted comforter round his neck, thick leathern gaiters, reaching half way up his thighs, and heavy boots.

Jolter, Junior's, costume was a fac-simile of the senior's, with the exception that the covering to his head was a felt cap, which set off the red crop of hair to great advantage, and the cold frosty wind that blew tinged Tommy's nose with a strong dash of vermilion, that gave him an exceedingly healthy appearance.

Suke, like her father, had studied comfort rather than the *beau monde*.

Her shoes and worsted stockings would have successfully resisted any amount of bad weather.

In addition to the linsey wolsey gown she wore, it was covered with such an amplitude of woollen garments, as to forcibly remind the looker-on that she had stepped out of some old Dutch painting; and over all was an enormous grey cloak, which had been handed down on the mother's side for a generation or two, and most decidedly rather of the useful than ornamental class.

To crown the whole, Suke had put on a hat that her mother wore on high days and holidays. It was white, turned up with blue. The red hair and face were in splendid condition, and thus Suke unknowingly carried out the great colours—Red, white and blue.

Old Jolter was delighted at their appearance.

"Blest if thee won't make them stare," said he, "when thee gets to Lunnon, or my name aren't Jack Jolter."

We shall see if the Londoners not only opened their eyes, but likewise their mouths, at beholding the visitors, "fresh from the country."

Into the chaise-cart the trio got, followed by the boy who was to take the vehicle back again to the farm.

The ride to the lawyer's was soon accomplished, for the farmer kept excellent horses.

When they drew up at the house, no surprise was exhibited at the appearance of the old farmer; but the clerks belonging to the establishment could not but express their admiration of the juniors by bursts of suppressed laughter.

They were welcomed by the lawyer, and, in a very short time, were seated at an excellent breakfast, for the early one they had was scarcely thought anything of, after the sharp and bracing ride.

Then they adjourned to the lawyer's sanctum.

"Friend Jolter," said old Tough Mutton, "you have never been in London, eh?"

"No," was the reply, "and don't want to go now; but I'll warrant I'll soon be back."

"Not so soon as you think if you

intend to carry out the business you are going upon ; you'll not return under a——"

"What !" and the farmer stared.

"About a month."

"A month ! What the dickens is to become of the farm ?"

"Oh, that will be all right enough ; it is left in good hands."

Tommy grinned silently at the prospect before him.

Suke stared at the lawyer, and thought he must be mad.

"A month in Lunnon," she said ; "why, it will be downright ruination."

"What dost thee know about it ?" muttered Tommy. "Keep thine own spoon in thine own basin."

"Yah ! shan't," she growled.

"Now, then, in the first place there is the letter to Mrs. Wilson, Gower Street, Bedford Square, London ; there you'll be kindly taken in and done for."

"Little doubt of that, feyther," said Suke, "I've heard of their tricks upon travellers ; but I'll look after the tea and sugar, I promise them."

"And I after the——"

"The jams and jellies, eh, Tommy ?" said the lawyer. "No occasion at all to do that ; you will find everything to your comfort. Well, then, the morning after your arrival you will take that letter to Messrs. Faithful, Son and Steady. I have been in communication with them, and you will find them quite prepared for you."

"No doubt," said Suke.

"Have you provided yourself well with cash ?" asked the lawyer.

"Five pounds like," said Jolter.

"Five fiddlesticks ! that will go in a day."

"If it does, I'll be out of Lunnon in quick sticks," and the farmer buttoned up his pocket as if to defend it against the attack of the enemy.

"Here," said the lawyer, laughing, and opening his cashbox, "you had better have a hundred of me," and he began counting over some notes.

"I'll tell thee what it is, Lawyer Tough Mutton—for that is the name I always call thee by—if you think that you have caught a flat, I think you'll find out your mistake ; and so, before we go any further, put on thy cap, Tommy, and we'll go back to the farm, and Uncle Tommy's next-of-kin may go too," and the indignant farmer buttoned up his coat.

"Nonsense ! don't be a fool, Jolter. It's of no use you're being in London without money."

"Ain't it ?" growled Jolter.

"No ; there's all the expenses attending to prove the will at Doctors' Commons."

"Doctors ! What the dickens do I want with doctors ? I be well enough ; never took a shilling's-worth of physic in all my life, and don't intend to begin now."

"Well, who wants you ? It is not the place you think it is. Listen seriously ; take that money ; when you get to London, you must put Tommy and Suke and yourself into mourning."

"Shan't !"

"What, do you mean that you are going about the streets of London in that fashion ?"

"Yes, and no other."

"Well, then, all I can say is, you will have——"

"What?"

"A nice time of it. There's fifty pounds; yon'll want it, and what you don't spend you can hand back. Here, Tommy, put that sovereign in your pocket; you'll want some sweetstuff."

"I should think so, and blowed if I don't have it, too," and Tommy's mouth watered at the rich treat in store.

"Suke, there is one for you to buy a ribbon, or any fal-de-ral you like."

"Yah, you don't catch me being such a fool, lawyer; and, Tommy, I'll keep yours for you."

"Eh, Suke, I'm not quite so soft as that. Tommy's eyes would be very weak before he saw that again, my girl."

Tommy placed the money carefully away.

The farmer was so bewildered by what was taking place that he paid no attention to what was going on, but kept staring at the notes he held in his hand as though they had dropped from the skies.

"Never travelled by rail, I think, farmer?" said Sheepshanks.

"No, don't like them; I shall go up well enough in the cart."

"What, a hundred miles and more?"

"Yes; Swish-tail can do fifty a day."

"You'll do nothing of the sort. Here, Steelpen," he called out, and one of the clerks entered, a rather dapper young man.

"Yes, sir."

"Put on your great coat, and go to the station with Farmer Jolter and his son and daughter; take three second-class tickets for London; see their luggage in safety, and them, too, and return quickly."

"Yes, sir."

And Steelpen disappeared.

"Now, then, Jolter, when you arrive in London, call a cab."

"A what?"

"A cab."

"A cab? What be that?"

"No matter; you'll see when you get there. And drive to the house I have directed you to."

"Drive! Oh, then, there be a horse in the case?"

"Yes, and an animal of another description," muttered Sheepshanks.

"Then I'll drive myself; I never let anyone handle the reins for me."

"Stuff! Leave it to the man. How do you know where to drive, eh?"

"That's no matter; hanged if any one shall drive me."

"Well, well, that is your own look-out; but you had better be careful."

Steelpen entered at that moment.

"See them safely off. Good bye, good bye, and send you a safe deliverance."

And so saying, Sheepshanks bowed them out of the sanctum, and left them to commence their journey to London.

The chaise cart still stood at the door, and into it they got.

On the first seat sat Jolter, Suke, and Steelpen; behind them Tommy and the farm servant.

Mr. Steelpen was not highly delighted at the position he was placed in.

He was considered in the town and

the environs to be one of the leaders of fashion.

He was studying for the law, and did not depend upon what he did at Lawyer Sheepshanks', having a snug little income of his own.

He was, therefore, well dressed, and sported a small but good assortment of jewellery.

But he also had another amiable weakness.

He had a keen eye to the main chance.

He had heard that Suke Jolter would be very rich.

That was sufficient, and thinking that the colour of her money would tone down the more than roseate hue of her cheeks, he resolved to pay court to her.

Not only did he make up his mind to this, but he set about putting it in execution.

Now there was an addition to the family of the Jolters—the cart was a jolter.

Every time it came to a ruck in the road (and they were not in the best state), the lot appeared as if they were going to pay a visit into the ditches that lined each side of it.

Up they went off their seats, down with a bump they came again.

More than once Suke came heavily into the lap of the future Q.C., nearly smothering him.

There was no harm, then, in the arm of Steelpen gliding gently round the waist of the damsel.

This action, of course, redoubled the natural redness of her face, so that it strongly resembled the sun coming out of a fog.

Tommy, who sat behind, saw all this, and thought that the lawyer's clerk was a leetle too attentive.

He had likewise noticed him laugh at them when they descended at the lawyer's house, and so he determined to revenge himself upon him, and at the same time have some fun with sister Suke.

But how?

Tommy had it.

The top button of Tommy's waistcoat, when he put it on, was missing.

He had, therefore, fastened it with a blanket-pin.

Tommy soon whipped it out, and sat waiting until a jolt occurred.

It was not long first.

Up went the body of the cart, up rose Suke and her gallant; but, as they partly descended, a yell from the latter caused him to fall forward, and nearly drag Suke and himself on to the back of Swish-tail.

"What the murrain be ye about?" shouted the farmer. "Can't thee sit still? Thee'll be into the road, and break thy unlucky neck."

"Well, 'pon my word, Mr. Jolter, there must be a—a—a——"

"What are you ahing about?" said the farmer, surly enough at the journey he was taking, which soured his temper very much.

"Well, sir, you'll excuse me, but—ah—there is—ah—rayther a—ah—sharpish nail, I think, on the—ah—seat."

"Nail be blowed!" said Jolter. "There baint no nails on the seat; what fan-fad wilt thee get on to next? Sit still, and hold tight, there's a precious ugly rut coming. Dang the road! it be as full o' wrinkles as my old grandmother's face. Hold tight!" he roared.

It was too late.

Down went the wheel into the rut, up went Steelpen and Suke; Steelpen went flying out of the cart on Swishtail's back, Suke was pitched upon him; at the same time, the belly-band giving way, the shafts flew up in the air, and Farmer Jolter, Soft Tommy, and the farm-servant, went flying out at the back of the cart, and lay, spread-eagle fashion, in the middle of the road.

Swish-tail, unaccustomed and alarmed at the load on his back, started off into a gallop, frightened by the screams of Suke and the awful groans of Steelpen, who dare not leave go of the collar, to which he clung as the " drowning man clings to the drifting plank," nearly smothered by the weight of Suke and her clothes.

Luckily they were not far off the station, and the officials, alarmed at hearing a horse come clattering up the road, ran out and stopped him and his " double fare" at the station door.

It cost them all the gravity they possessed to refrain from laughing when they lifted the couple off the back of the panting Swish-tail.

The thick coats the farmer and Tommy were enveloped in prevented them receiving any injury.

The farmer was up first, and, staring as if in some dream, started after Swish-tail; Soft Tommy and the boy rose, and a laughable sight they presented.

Both their noses were freely bleeding; Tommy's clenched fist had gone plump into the face of the other, while the sharp elbow of the boy had dug into Tommy's.

" What do ye mean by punching into me in that fashion, eh, Maister Tummas?"

" Why, rip thy old buttons, what dost thee mean by shoving thy elbow into my precious eyes in that fashion, eh, Billy Snivell?"

" Thee punched my nob first," cried the boy.

" Nay, I didn't. Thy elbow dug into my eye fust."

" Well, I didn't whistle to it to do it, did I?"

" I'll whistle thy nose again for thee, Billy, if thee ain't civil. I be thy master," and Tommy pulled up his coatsleeves.

" No, thee ain't; maister be my maister!" and the boy up with his sleeves.

" Now hit me," said Tommy.

" No, you hit I," replied Billy.

" Ah, you're afeard," cried Tommy.

" Oh, yees, I'd like to be afeard of Soft Tommy! Where do they sell pigeons' milk, eh, Tommy?"

" Just at the end of my fist!" cried he.

And at it they went.

The battle was not fated to last long.

The farmer saw that Swish-tail was stopped, and so he turned back to see what damage the box and cart had sustained.

Billy Snivel was the first to catch sight of old Jolter tearing along the road, whip in hand.

The sight was enough for him; he knew what he had to expect, and what sort of *backing* he would get upon the fight and he was off, leaving Tommy master of the field.

Tommy jumped upon the chest, and called out, loudly—

"Come back, you coward! I ain't given yer half enough. Yah! Billy Snivel, you be a nice one."

"Ees, so be you," shouted Tommy's father.

And thwack came the whip upon Tommy's back.

"What do you mean by that?" said Tommy, fiercely, for the moment not seeing his father.

"What, hasn't thee had enough, Tommy, my lad?"

And again the whip was raised.

Tommy was as agile as a sprite, and was soon out of harm's way and making the best use of his legs towards the station.

The farmer now was alone; there lay the cart with the shafts high up in the air, the chest containing the family apparel of the Jolters lying unhurt in the road.

Jack Jolter was somewhat in a fix.

"Billy, my boy, where are you? Come and give us a hand to get this plaguey cart roight again."

Billy was at the station with Swish-tail.

"Tommy, come here, or I'll baste thy hide for thee!" and the farmer looked savagely round.

Tommy was at that moment at a pump in the station-yard trying to restore his face to its natural colour.

At last Swish-tail was brought back, the cart put to its proper position, all made right and tight, the family chest safely stowed away, and in a very short space of time it arrived at the railway station, neither it nor its owners being any the worse for the accident.

When Suke was lifted off the joint backs of Steelpen and Swish-tail, she did not, according to modern custom, go off in a faint, but burst into an immoderate fit of laughter at the sight of her companion in misfortune.

In his descent upon the broad back of Swish-tail, his hat had become jammed over his eyes, so that when placed upon his feet, he appeared as if he had no head on his shoulders, or if he had one it had been transformed to a black one.

It took great exertions to get it off, and when the face was again exposed, it was as pale as that of a corpse, while Suke's, with the exertion she had undergone, was redder than usual.

"I say, Mr. Lawyer's Clerk," said Suke grinning, "did thee ever have such a roll and tumble afore? I thought it it was all over with us."

"Well 'pon my word, Miss Jolter, it was—ah—one of the most—ah—extraordinary falls I—ah—ever had in all my life," and here Steelpen took a long breath. "I thought the game was up."

"Yah! I didn't. I knew I was all right, as long as you held on, and I didn't think that you'd be so green as to let go, and I warn't such a fool as to leave go of you. Na, na, Suke Jolter knows a trick worth two of that."

At this moment, Tommy, with his nose bleeding, rushed into the station-yard, and seeing a pump handy, was quickly at it.

Soon after, the farmer drove in, and the chest having been deposited on the platform, Tommy was placed upon it to keep guard that no one walked off with it, a task which would have been rather difficult to accomplish.

The farmer told Billy to drive the cart and Swish-tail to some stables for a couple of hours' rest, and then start for home.

He then went, accompanied by Suke and Steelpen, into the place to settle the fares, and get a glass of something to recruit his exhausted spirits.

"I say, Soft Tommy," bawled out Billy Snivel, "you have a good berth there. Why, thee looks like a red pole on a dunghill."

"I'll make thy pole red if I come to thee!" cried out Tommy.

"Yah! Can't do it; not in a hundred years!" was the reply.

"Stop till I come back from London, Billy Snivel, and I'll show thee a trick or two."

"Yah! the Lunnoners will show thee more tricks than thee'll loike; pigeons' milk and strap oil be fools to what thee'll get there."

Tommy jumped up at this, but Billy was too quick for him, for he put Swish-tail into a smart trot, and drove out of the railway station, laughing and jeering.

In a few minutes, Jolter, Suke and Steelpen, returned from the pay place.

"I tell thee, Mr. Lawyer's Clerk, it shan't be done. I'll only go third-class —so they calls it. Why, it's a clean waste of money, and I won't do it, and that's flat!"

"But—ah—my dear—ah—sir, Mr. Sheepshanks said that——"

"I don't care a brass varden what old Tough Mutton says. I'll spend my money as I loike."

"Ah, well; you can't help it now, because I've paid second-class."

"Well, then," said Suke, chiming in, "we'll make the lawyer take it off his bill, eh, feyther? Yah! Do you take us for green geese?"

"No, not in the least, but—ah—must carry out my instructions, and ——"

At that moment the bell rang, and in an instant the station swarmed with living beings, who poured out like bees from a hive.

The astonishment of the party completely deprived them of any more talking.

Then came the iron horse, snorting and puffing and screaming, into the station, and dragging after him, with the greatest ease, a number of heavy carriages, and then, to their wonder, it suddenly came to a standstill.

It took some serious expostulation with Jolter, before he could be persuaded to get into the carriage without the family chest, which would have filled it without anything else; but at last all was arranged.

Tommy got a seat opposite Suke, the farmer sitting at the opposite corner.

Mr. Steelpen took his leave, with the understanding that he should call upon them in a few days, as he was coming to London upon business.

The engine made a sudden start, then a sudden stop, which sent Tommy flying into Suke's arms, and the farmer into those of an old lady, a proceeding that brought a tolerable quarrel between all the parties, partially stopped by the train proceeding rapidly towards the great city.

CHAPTER XVIII.

THE JOURNEY TO LONDON.

FOR the first part of the journey but little was said by the occupants of the carriage in which were seated the Jolter family, the surprise at the rapid style of travelling keeping them silent and wonder-stricken.

Tommy and Suke kept snarling at each other at times, varying the amusement by a kick of the shins from Suke, and returned with interest by Tommy.

The old lady into whose arms the farmer had been thrown, kept uttering sundry grunts and growls, occasionally relieving them by repeated applications to a respectable-sized flask.

The farmer held on very tight to the seat, his countenance showing that he felt his present situation anything but an enviable one.

He could not help giving vent to audible groans, shutting his eyes at the same time.

"What be the matter with thee, feyther?" bawled out Suke.

"Matter, my lass!" the farmer ejaculated; "matter enough, I think. I'd give a pound to be behind the plough-tail, or Swish-tail. Oh, Lord! Oh, dear! Where are we going to?" —as the carriages oscillated rather more than usual.

"Going? Why, going to London," said the old lady, taking a pull at her flask and then a pinch of snuff. "First time you have travelled this line, I suppose?"

"First time I have ever been hurried through the air like this, marm, and it will be the last for Jack Jolter, I can tell you."

"First time on a railway? Why where have you lived all your life-time?"

"Lived! why, on the farm, to be sure. Where the dickens should I have lived, eh?"

"Well, I should have thought in New Zealand, or any of the Cannibal Islands. And are those interesting-looking couple your children?" asked the old lady.

"Yes, marm. Why?"

"Why?—bless the man!—why? Because they do you credit. First time on a railway! Ah, then an accident would be a novelty to you."

"An accident! You don't mean to say that any accidents happen, do you? Oh, Lord! I wish my boots had been burnt before I trusted my precious carcase in these infernal boxes."

"Accidents, why they're as plentiful as gooseberries, only not quite so cheap."

"Here! hi!. holloa! stop! I'll get out!" roared the farmer, thrusting his head out of the window, Tommy and Suke doing the same at the other side, and shouting out at the top of their voices.

This set the old lady and the other passengers laughing.

"Don't make that noise, my man; they can't stop, for they can't hear you; and if they did they wouldn't stop. We shall soon be past the place where they shunt the coal waggons, and, perhaps, they have not left more than three or four of them on the line and in the way."

"Well, and what then?" gasped the farmer.

"What then? Why—bless the man !—why, then it is to be hoped you have made your will."

Here the engine gave a most unearthly scream, which so alarmed Tommy and Suke, that they began to scream too.

"Bless my soul !" ejaculated the old lady, "that sounds as if there was something wrong !"

At this they redoubled their cries.

"Don't make that unearthly noise," she said; "it will do you no good, and if a smash should come, it's as well to be prepared."

And here the good old soul finished the contents of her flask.

"Ha, it's all right, and we have just escaped going to another place by a shaving. It's marvellous !"

And so it really appeared, for the train went rushing between two long lines of heavily-laden coal trucks with only a trifling space between them.

The farmer shut his eyes, thinking his last hour had come.

"Good-bye, Tommy; good-bye, Suke ; it be all over."

"Good-bye, feyther," said Tommy and Suke together, blubbering and howling.

The next moment he opened his eyes, and then they were rushing through a high embankment; then, an instant after, they were involved in total darkness, except the occasional flashings from the red lights.

When they emerged from the tunnel they stared at one another in wonder and dismay.

"Eh, but this is wonderful !" said the farmer.

"Beats cock-fighting, eh, feyther," cried Suke.

"Eh, my lass, but thee beest right."

"Well, you won't be long now," said the cheerful old lady.

"Glad of it, marm," was the reply.

Here the train suddenly slackened its speed.

"What's the matter now?" said she. "Why, bless us and save us !"

"Wha—wha—what now ! What now ?"

"Well, I declare there's a fog before us as thick as a dozen blankets !"

Then a loud report was heard.

The Jolter family uttered dismal groans.

"Ah, there go the fog signals."

Bang ! bang ! bang !

And the train moved slowly through a dense fog, that hid every surrounding object from the sight.

Then a rushing sound was heard, and the flashing of lights told them a train was dashing past them.

And so on then they went slowly, until they at last entered the terminus of the railway; but all they could see was a great rush to and fro of a number of persons, a great number of gas lamps burning, bells ringing, men shouting, trunks rattling to and fro.

And then the train came to a dead stop.

A London fog is bad enough at all times for its inhabitants; even they get lost in it, and find themselves confused and bewildered.

How, then, did the Jolter family like it?

They sat still in the carriage, until a rough voice asked them the question—

If they were going to stop there all night?

Frightened at this, Tommy jumped out, only to find himself falling over a lot of luggage, and floundering amongst it.

Suke fared no better, and followed Tommy's example; while the farmer, plunging forward with his great, bulky frame, ran against a porter, and the pair went rolling over the great family chest.

Mutual recrimination, nearly ending in blows, ensued; but at last a cab was procured, the address given, and then slowly through the fog-darkened street it took its way.

Bewildered by the scene, frightened at the shouting, and almost doubting whether they were living or not, they at last arrived at their destination—at the house in which were residing Giles Evergreen and Ted Flan.

When the cab drew up at the door, Mrs. Wilson, accompanied by Susan Flipper, was in attendance to receive them.

The surprise of the mistress and the maid were equally great at the sight of the parties getting out of the cab.

Lawyer Sheepshanks had, in writing to Mrs. Wilson, merely intimated that a "gentleman" with his son and daughter, were coming up to London upon a matter of importance.

Imagine the good lady's surprise when the great head, followed by the massive frame of the farmer, got out of the cab; but, when Tommy and Suke followed, and stood in the passage, while the cab-driver and the servant were hauling the great chest in, they looked at one another in astonishment and dismay.

"Ain't there some mistake here, mum?"

"Why, really, Susan, I think that there is."

"Not no mistake, marm," said cabby, wiping the perspiration from his face, and looking at the number on the door. "It's number—"

"Yes, yes, that's right," nervously answered the lady.

"What on earth's the matter?" said Suke, her face reddening, and, between Susan and herself signals of defiance were already flashing forth. "P'r'aps we aren't good enough for this jimcrack place, eh, feyther?"

"Well, marm, if you don't settle with me," chimed in cabby, "I shall charge you for waiting."

"How much do thee want, my lad?" said Jolter.

"Well, three bob."

"Eh, what be that, eh, Tommy? Thee hast been to school and ought to know."

"Blest if I know, feyther," was the reply.

"Then thee beest an ass, my boy."

"Well, blest if this ain't ignorance with a wengeance," said cabby. "Three shillings, then; that's English, guv'nor."

" Yes, but you don't come any tricks upon travellers with me, my boy."

" Yah," said Suke, " what do you take us for?"

" Blest if I know," replied cabby, looking from one to the other.

" Why, my lad, we worn't five minutes in thy rickety affair. Thee'll not see three shillings of my money."

" No, my lad," chimed in Suke. " We come up frae the country, where fools and their money aren't easily parted. Don't thee be such a born fool, feyther, as to pay three shillings."

" I should think not; but he shall have three shillings'-worth of this fist."

And the farmer, pulling up his sleeve, showed a fist quite capable of felling half-a-dozen cabmen.

Mrs. Wilson, who, during this had been looking from one to the other, and scarcely able to make out what it was all about, here interposed.

" My good sir," said she, to Jolter, " are you the gentleman——"

" No, I am not; I never was a gentleman in all my life; and, what's more, I don't want to be one. I am plain Jack Jolter, farmer and grazier, pay my way like an honest man, and owing no man the valley of a brass varden."

" Well, I mean," said the lady, " are you the person——"

" Of course I am. I am——"

" I mean are you the party that Lawyer Sheepshanks wrote to me about?"

" Yah, of course we are. You might have known that if you'd kept your eyes open."

" Well, missus, if I'd stand that!" broke in Susan.

" Yah! Don't you interfere, Miss Fal-de-ral, with your jimcrack ribbons. Keep thy spoon for thy own basin."

" Thee hold thy tongue, sister Suke. Let the young woman have her say," cried Soft Tommy.

" Yah, hold thy tongue, Tommy, or I'll give thee a clout of thy head that shall make thy eyes dance for a month."

" Two can play at that game, Suke. Hast thee forgotten hog's-wash? Thee took thy pigs to a fine market, then."

Here a second battle-royal would have taken place, but the farmer, seizing them both by the back of their necks, held them as though they had been straws.

" If thee ain't quiet, ye cantankerous varmints, I'll bang thy heads together! What, ye won't, won't ye?"

And he shook them as though they had been a couple of rats.

Cabby grinned, and whispered to Susan that it " was worth half a fare to see this."

" Leave me to settle with the cabman, and pray walk into this room."

And Mrs. Wilson threw open the door of an elegantly furnished apartment.

" I perceive there is a slight mistake."

" No, no; there bain't no mistake. I don't pay three shillings upon any such game as that."

" What do you mean?" said cabby. " Why, here's a chest as big as the Great Heastern. Well, then there's yourself, like two single coves rolled into one; then there's the two young 'uns, and then—and then, there's getting through the fog, and that 'ere ought to be hextra; and then there's ——"

What else in the shape of extras might have been brought forward by cabby, it is difficult to imagine, but it was put a stop to by the servant taking him outside and settling with him.

Susan and Mrs. Wilson showed the party into the room, and begged them to sit down.

Tommy and Suke did so, and the farmer followed their example, but unfortunately he selected a chair that was more fit to look at than to bear his weight.

Annoyed and vexed at all that had occurred, he flung himself into the poor, fragile-looking thing, and the next moment was floundering on the floor.

Tommy roared with delight at this, while Suke's face was a capital illustration of *grin*-age, Mrs. Wilson and the Flipper staring from one to the other.

"I hope you have not hurt yourself," said the polite landlady.

"Well, no, marm," said Jolter, scrambling up from the ruins; "but I don't think them 'ere things was ever made to *sit* upon. I feel shaken a bit."

Here the farmer landed himself in a chair capable of bearing him, and a few minutes after a tray with wine, brandy, and cake was placed upon the table.

The farmer took a drop of brandy, while Suke and Tommy made an onslaught upon the wine and cake, and so zealous were they in their exertions of the cause, that Susan kept twitching her mistress's apron.

"They must have 'scaped from the gardens in the park, missus," she whispered.

"Won't thee have a drop thyself, marm?" asked the farmer.

"No, I thank you, sir," was the rather curt reply.

"Then, by your leave, marm, I will; for you'll excuse me, but your glasses ain't over and above big ones."

"P'r'aps you'd like a pint pot, sir," said Susan, and she made them a mock curtsey.

"Ha, ha, ha!" roared Tommy, "but that be a good 'un! Why, thee wouldn't stifle feyther off if ye brought him a quart pot, would she, feyther?"

"And you say, sir, that Mr. Sheepshanks——"

"Yes, marm; but we knows him in our parts better by the name of 'Tough-Mutton.' Well, you see, my brother Tommy Jolter, he was godfeyther to Tommy, there," and he pointed to Tommy, whose face was nearly purple.

He had put rather a large piece of sponge cake into his mouth, and in making its way down his throat, there the cake stuck.

"Yah! yer glutton! Yer always at these plaguey tricks. Some of these days ye'll choke!" shouted Suke.

And with that, seizing the unlucky Tommy by the collar, she gave him one or two such blows in the back, as not only dislodged the cake, but almost dislocated Tommy's spine, for which she was rewarded with a kick, while the tears descended down his cheeks.

"Wilt thee be quiet?" roared the farmer. "Please, ma'am, move those things, or thee'll have none left."

And the farmer, extending his broad

fist to the decanter, was about helping himself.

But Susan Flipper was a trifle too quick for him, for, in an instant, the tray and its contents were whipped off the table, and had disappeared from the room.

The farmer looked after Susan for a minute.

"Well, you see, marm, to go on with my story :—My brother Tommy dies over in Horsestraylyher, and leaves me next of skin."

"Of kin, I presume?" said Mrs. Wilson.

"You know best, marm. I s'pose it was next of skin, because we were own flesh and blood. Well, you see, we be come up to Lunnon, very much against the grain. Only I wants to see Mark Lane to look after the cash; and there's Tough Mutton's letter, and p'r'aps that will settle the affair. Ah, I knows this, that I wants my pipe most infarnally."

"Indeed, I hardly know," said Mrs. Wilson, opening the letter; "but I'll see."

And she hastily scanned the letter, which ran thus :—

"MADAM,—You will find the Jolter family perhaps the greatest originals in the kingdom. If you are fond of the eccentricities of human nature, you will be delighted with them. I very much question if the British Museum has anything like such curiosities. You told me once you were fond of the varieties in human nature; I think you have got them at last.

"Yours truly,
"TIMOTHY SHEEPSHANKS.

"P. S.—I am answerable to you for the bill of costs."

"Ha, ha!" cheerily laughed the lady. "Like my old friend, Sheepshanks."

"He's not playing fun with us, is he, marm?" asked Jolter.

"Oh, dear, no; merely explaining one or two little matters. Well, now, I think I'll place young Mr. Jolter under ——"

"Yah! call him Soft Tommy; that's the name he's best knowed by."

And Suke grinned.

"Under the care of my man-servant, Jones; and as for Miss Jolter——"

"You call her Suke Carrots; that's the name she goes by in our parts," grinned Tommy.

"And as for you, Mr. Jolter," said the lady, not heeding the interruption, "I think Jones must keep his eye upon you."

"With all my heart, marm; I have little doubt but that we shall jog along together. I'm a plain man in my way, and only want plain, straightfor'ard dealing, so I daresay Jones and Jolter will agree very well together."

"I have no doubt of it," replied the lady. "Will you excuse me for a moment?"

And Mrs. Wilson rose up to leave the room.

"But I say, marm," cried Tommy, "begging your pardon, where be my two schoolfellows, Giles Evergreen and Ted O'Flan?—I do so long to shake them by the hands."

And Tommy's little eyes glistened again at the thought of it.

"Why, my dear boy, do you know those two noble boys?"

"Do I know them?"

And he went up to her and took her hand.

"Why, didn't they tell yer? They

saved my life more than once—once when I should have been roasted like an innocent lamb, and once when I should have been tossed by a mad bull. I may be Soft Tommy in the head, but I'll never be bad Tommy in the heart. Tommy Jolter won't forget that, if he lives for a thousand years."

"I believe not, my boy; you are a rough diamond, and I honour your sentiments. They have been on a visit to Lady St. George at Richmond, but I expect them to return to-morrow. I will be back in a few minutes. Jones," she said to the man-servant, who appeared at the door, "show Mr. Jolter and his son to the room I spoke to you about."

"Yes, madam. This way. Had you not better take off your great coats?"

With the farmer that was easy enough, for his coat was large, and came off easily, but with Tommy it was very different.

Tommy had, with great difficulty, got into his, and it was always with greater difficulty that he got out of it.

Without assistance it was impossible for him to do so.

"Here, Suke, lay hold of one arm, and you lay hold of the other, and then I think you'll get a hedgehog out of his skin as easy."

Both Suke and Jones laid hold of Tommy's arms, and pulled for dear life.

The good living at the farm since he had left Dr. Birchenough's school had rather swelled the lad out.

It cost him some muscular exertion to force himself into it, and the united pulling and hauling of Suke and the man Jones, seemed to have but little effect.

The farmer enjoyed it hugely, and roared again with laughter, as he sat close and opposite to him.

"Pull harder!" he cried out, "and you'll do it at last."

It was done at last.

Suddenly Suke and Jones went reeling away with a sleeve of the coat in each hand, and Tommy shot forward, head first, like a catapult, into old Jolter's stomach, and away they went flying on to the floor together, amidst the unrestrained laughter of Mrs. Wilson and Susan, who had just entered the room.

The farmer, who thought Tommy had done this on purpose, was pummelling Tommy, who was roaring out at the top of his voice, while Suke, who had partly risen with one sleeve in her hand, was striving to regain her legs.

And so for the present we leave them to recover from their disasters.

CHAPTER XIX.

A SLIGHT INSIGHT INTO A MYSTERY.

WHEN Alfred Ravensborne rushed from the villa on the night he showed his deadly animosity, and fierce, ungovernable temper in the drawing room to-

"TOMMY JOLTER BECOMES DUKE OF CRABS."

wards Giles Evergreen and Ted Flan, he scarcely knew which way to turn his steps.

He stopped for a moment in his mad career, and hastened to the stables, in hopes of finding Mr. Richard Martingale.

He soon reached them, and, looking up at the window of the room in which that worthy resided, found all was in darkness.

" Why, the fellow can scarcely have gone away so soon," he muttered. " If he has done so, he must have anticipated all this, and made a clean run of it. He is a clever fellow, but I think he will meet with one as sharp."

And looking up at the darkened window, he listened.

Not a sound was to be heard.

Or any person seen moving about.

Then, opening the stable-door, he made for the stairs leading to the jockey's chamber.

He knocked firmly at the door.

No answer.

" Dick, Dick Martingale," he called ; " don't be sulky. Answer me, Alfred Ravensborne. Curse the fellow, he is doing this to annoy me."

And, in his rage, seizing the handle of the door, and turning it, it flew open.

All was in darkness, except a faint light from the moon, that beamed slightly glancing across the fire-place, showing Alfred that the means for procuring a light were there.

" Perhaps I may find something he has left behind him that may tend to throw a light upon the dark mysteries that he is always hinting about, and connected with my father's earlier life and Evergreen ; there can be no harm in looking."

And he seized the match-box.

A light gleamed in the room.

" I may be observed," he muttered.

And the next moment he had closed the shutters ; then he shut the door and, throwing himself into a chair, he looked round the place.

Everything appeared in the same state as when he was last in it.

" The fellow's bolted ; scared out of his wits by that woman's threats. My temples ache most confoundedly, ha, ha !"

And his bitter laugh was that of a demon's, and well it might.

" It's Giles Evergreen's handy work. Ah ! my fine fellow, I'll be even scores upon the wicket with you before long. Curses on this infernal Dick, where has he got to ?"

And he sprang up, and taking the light, approached the bed, and looked carefully round it.

" Master Dick is too cunning to leave anything behind him, that is pretty certain. What the deuce is that ?"

And so saying, he laid hold of a piece of red tape that hung dangling from underneath the pillow, and pulled from beneath it some four or five papers tied tightly together.

" Some of the fellow's bills, I suppose ; or, better, perhaps his love letters ; they would be worth looking at."

With this he resumed his seat by the table, placing a light upon it.

Scarcely had he untied them, and taken up one, than he started from his seat.

" In the name of all that is good, what is this ? My father's handwriting ! Ah ! here is some of the mystery."

He read the superscription " Draft of letters from A. R. to G. E."

" A. R., that stands for Alfred Ravensborne ; and G. E., that stands for—ah—joy—joy ! I have it—Giles Evergreen."

He opened it hastily, and read in low, agitated tones, as follows :—

" You hold in your hands not only my life, but my fame. I do not ask you to spare either the one or the other, because whichever way it goes your escutcheon will be dimmed. So far it may serve to check you— if anything can check the hatred we have felt for each other from our boyish days up to the present time. Had fate not cast us together, our lives might have been lives of honourable rivalry, laudable ambition, and fame, gloriously and fairly won ; but, as it turned out, the rivalry gave birth to hate, the ambition (on my part) to strike you from my path at any or every risk, and the fame—ha ! ha !—the fame of a——Fiends of despair ! I cannot, will not write the name !

" When you receive this I shall have left the land—the shores of England for ever ; therefore, whatever you do will be futile ; for, hidden under an assumed name, I shall defy you and your revenge if you choose to exercise it. May my curse, and that of my descendants cling to you and yours.

"A. R."

When Alfred had finished reading the paper, he sat gazing at it as though he had been transformed into a statue.

At last he lifted up his head, and the sickly light that burned in the room showed a face paler than marble— colourless as the dead.

" What can this mean ?" he said in hollow tones. " What curse is this hanging over our heads ?—hatred in boyish days, and hatred to Giles Evergreen !"

And he sprang up, clutching his hand uplifted in the air, as though to draw down that curse from above.

He took up another of the papers, and opening it, an enclosure fell out.

He cast his eyes upon the portion he held in his hand, and read :—

" From J. S. to A. R.

" Having received from you the money— a one thousand pound note—I redeem my promise by sending you the paper in your handwriting. I should advise you to destroy it, before the event comes off, in case of accidents, otherwise, it might place certain necks in jeopardy.

" Yours,

" J. S."

The shadows darkened still deeper on Alfred's brow ; but he bent his mind resolutely to the task, and read as follows :—

" There would be no chance of making the a—— safe ; that game must rest with the boy ; he is weak and vain—very accessible points, but as cunning as Lucifer, and as wily as the oldest fox that ever run to earth. If you can make all safe, I'll pay the thousand instanter. The cards have turned up trumps. I am strong on the wing, and shan't mind losing a feather. I send this because it won't do to be seen together.

" A. R."

" More villany, more crime," muttered the boy. " Shall I go on with the task ? Yes ; for that accursed fellow's father is at the bottom of all this, and I'll see it to the end or may ——"

He stopped and listened.

" Was not that a footstep ? No ; these infernal papers have made a fool of me. I'll look at another and then ——"

He took up the one nearest him, and opening it, read thus (the handwriting was a female's):—

"We part on this side the world of eternity for ever; there is nothing to live for. The darkness of the grave will be light compared to this world; and eternity a bliss, because sorrow ends, and joy begins. Wronged, deceived, betrayed by you, I leave you my greatest curse—my blessing. The hour of midnight will send its hoarse tones over the dark, flowing, silent river—and my grave! Farewell!"

"Some poor wretch!" he muttered, and he fastened them together and sat deeply immersed in reflection npon the nature and character of what he had been reading.

The papers that had so mysteriously come under his notice were a portion of those Dick Martingale had stolen from the "chamber of the dead," when he and Dark Davy paid a visit to it on the night when the "angel of death" so suddenly appeared at the mansion of the Honourable Alfred Ravensborne, and bore away its master.

They were not the important ones sealed up, and which the jockey had thrust into his vest.

No, no; he had deposited those in a place of safety, so that they never were absent from him day or dight.

He had been perusing them the night before, and the light suddenly going out he had thrust them under the pillow; the occurrences of the day had driven them from his memory, and so Alfred had, in finding them, got a little insight into a great mystery.

"It's no use thinking any longer about it, I must find Dark Davy, and ask him; at least, I've got a slight clue to go upon. These papers are invaluable."

"I know they are," said a voice, "and I don't intend to part with them."

And they were snatched out of Alfred's hand.

It was Dick Martingale, who had stealthily entered the room just in the nick of time.

Alfred Ravensborne, staggered at the suddenness of the affair, could just see through the dimness of the light who his visitor was.

An instant more he had flung himself upon him.

And a deadly struggle commenced.

"Give me up those papers, Dick; they belong to me," said Alfred, hoarsely.

"Not they, my young 'un; they belong to me. Let me pass!"

"How, villain!" replied the other, flinging him off and standing with his back to the door. "You shall only pass over my dead body."

"And that I'll do rather than part with these. Give way, you fool!" said Dick, savagely.

"Scum, you frighten not me!"

And with a spring, Alfred seized the poker from the fire-place.

"I'll brain you if you attempt to pass without restoring me the papers."

"Indeed! We'll soon see about that."

At this instant loud shouts were heard resounding through the grounds, and the ringing of an alarm bell.

They were caused by a half-muddled groom, who had fallen asleep.

Hearing the noise overhead, he rang the alarm bell, and rushing out, shouted, in his half-dozy state—

"Thieves ! fire ! and murder !"

Not only the servants and the noble inmates of the villa rushed out at hearing the cries, but the people living around, and so in a short time the usually quiet town of Richmond was in a state of alarm and excitement from one end of it to the other.

"You hear what you have done ?" savagely shouted Dick.

"No matter ; give me the papers !" was the reply, and a blow at him.

The next instant they were locked in a deadly struggle.

The frail door they were hurled against gave way, and with a crash they rolled down the stairs into the stable.

Dick was uppermost in the fall, and feeling the grasp of Alfred had relaxed, he was up and off with the fleetness of a deer, and over the low river wall and safe from pursuit.

When Giles Evergreen, Ted Flan, and the servants entered the stables, they were alarmed by the terrific plunging and snorting of the frightened animals.

One horse in particular was kicking and plunging within a couple of yards of Alfred's head, and had he fallen but a little nearer, there would have been an end to all his hates and jealousies.

In an instant Giles and Ted saw this, and he was soon out of harm's way between them.

He was perfectly unconscious, and so was at once carefully removed to the villa.

Great was the consternation and surprise at this affair.

Our old friend, the doctor, was speedily called in, and, upon a close examination, it was discovered that Alfred Ravensborne was labouring under a severe concussion of the brain, caused by a blow.

The greatest quiet was to be observed during the night.

He was carefully and kindly watched by his schoolfellows Giles and Ted, but he remained alike insensible to joy or sorrow, to their regret or their kindness.

The slumber of the dead seemed to have fallen upon him ; not a sigh escaped him, and so the long, dreary hours of the night passed away.

CHAPTER XX.

A VISIT TO TOWN.

THE morning after these events occurred, the Lady St. George, Giles, Ted, and Miss Hilda, met at the breakfast table, and after talking over the events of the preceding night, the plans for the future were determined upon.

"It was my intention," the lady said, "to have had the pleasure of your company a few days longer at the villa, and then to have gone to town with you for the season, but for the present the plan must be abandoned. It is, therefore, my intention to send you up to town to-day in the carriage."

"But cannot we remain here and watch over the fate of Alfred?" said Giles. "I can assure your ladyship that we feel a deep sympathy for him."

"Giles spakes my sentiments," said Ted. "We might be of some assisttance."

"You have both of you noble, forgiving dispositions, but it is better that you should leave. Should he recover consciousness—of which there are very grave doubts—the sight of you may cause a relapse."

"I am sure we never gave him cause," said Ted, "and in spite of all his insults and the et ceteras, I'll hold out my hand to him and forget and forgive."

"And so would I, cheerfully and willingly," said Giles. "Has your ladyship any clue how this sad affair occurred?"

"No. I have questioned the groom, who was asleep in the stable at the time, if he could recognise the voices of the persons who were quarrelling in the room; but he says he was so frightened that he should never be able to do so. There is a mystery about it I should like to see cleared up very much."

"I don't think robbery was intended," said Ted, "bekase there was nothing to take. It must have been an attempt at murder, for at the foot of the stairs there was an illigant bit of iron, called a poker, lying there. A small crack from that would confuse a man's ideas in a most extraordinary manner."

"The blow on the head was not caused by that, so said the doctor. I cannot divine the cause," said Giles. "Can anybody tell me if that amiable gentleman, Mr. Martingale, has been seen about?"

"I have made inquiries myself about him, but understand he left the town," said Lady St. George.

"Ah, then, joy go with him. It's a lucky place that will have the benefit of his countenance," remarked Ted Flan.

At that moment the doctor made his appearance; he was happy to say that his patient was wonderfully better, and in a few days he would be, if things went on improving, convalescent.

This news imparted a general joy to all.

"But," said the doctor, "any sudden shock would be fatal."

"All of which shall be avoided," said Lady St. George.

She then retired with the doctor to visit Alfred; upon her return the carriage was in readiness, and, after taking a farewell of the ladies, Giles Evergreen and Ted Flan were driving rapidly back to London, discussing the various stray things which had taken place at the charming villa at Richmond.

On the night the Jolters arrived at Mrs. Wilson's, after they had dined with the worthy hostess and old Walmisley, it was arranged that Suke and Tommy should see many of the sights of London under the fostering care of Old Jones, the man-servant, while the farmer was to be handed over to the protection of Walmisley, who would show him to the lawyer's in Lincoln's Inn Fields, and to any other place he might like to go to.

"And I hope you will make yourself at home in my house, Mr. Jolter, as well as the young lady and gentleman, as long as you stay in London."

"Ees," replied Tommy, "I knows how to make myself at home; and, ecod! if you make such jolly jam puddings as you've made to-day, I shan't want to leave for a long time."

"Yah!" snarled out Suke, • "yer always thinking of yer stummack. I say, marm, take care to lock up the cupboard, for if Tommy gets in I wouldn't give much for the jam or the jelly either."

"Ah, you're a nice couple; you plague my life out of me! Blest if I know what is to be done with you!" and the farmer looked puzzled.

"I should think a school——" said Mrs. Wilson.

"Yah! school be bothered! You don't catch I at school. I knows enough of larning; and I knows how to brew and bake, to mend and make, look arter the pigs and the poultry, and, what's more, I knows how to sell 'em, and blest if any on you here can beat me at that!" and Suke gave a triumphant grin at the whole party.

"That's all very proper; but, then, my dear——"

"Na, na, I doesn't want any flummery; I won't go to school, that's flat! Why, feyther would be in the bankrupt's list in less than a month if I warn't in the farm. What sayest thee, eh, feyther?"

"Say? Why, thee sayest right, gal. Thee be'est my right hand; thee art worth thy weight in gold and diamonds, so we'll let the matter rest until this plaguey law business be settled, and then we'll see. Let me

get over that and I'll see if they get me into the next-of-skin line again."

"I should think not, feyther," said Suke.

"Yah! A great deal you knows about it," said Tommy. "If thy skin had a good tanning it would do thee a main sight of good."

"Yah! But thee can't do it, Soft Tommy. I can give it thee any day," and Suke made a spring at Tommy.

"That's the game they are always carrying on, marm, and the only thing to stop it I've left at home," and the farmer felt about the side of his chair in vain for the chastiser. "That, and another thing, I miss most confoundedly."

"And what is that?"

"My pipe. All this mortal day I haven't had one, and that would have tried the patience of Job."

"No doubt; but that difficulty we can easily get over. Mr. Walmisley will conduct you to a comfortable room where you and himself can enjoy yourselves, eh, Mr. Walmisley?"

"Certainly, madam," was the reply.

"Well, then, that's jolly," said Jolter, jumping up; "and I think we shall get over next-of-skin after all. I am your humble sarvant, sir."

And the pair left the room.

"Yah! I shall go along with feyther," and Suke rose.

"Not so, my dear. Flipper is going out, and perhaps you would like to see some of the shops?"

"Yah! That I should," grinned Suke.

"And I'll go with them," said Tommy.

"No, my dear. Jones is going out a short distance and will take you."

"Yah! I like that better than going along with she," and Tommy grinned defiance at Suke.

"Yah! Wouldn't be seen among pigs with thee, Soft Tommy," said Suke, leaving the room.

Now, when the accident happened to Tommy, namely, the sleeves parting company with the body of the coat, the family chest was rummaged over for the purpose of finding another covering for the lad, but nothing could be found except a very clean smock-frock.

Suke had, with her usual spite against the soft one, left his best clothes behind, so that the lad had to put that on or sit in his shirt-sleeves, the farmer declaring that there was no dress equal to a clean, honest smock-frock; and so Tommy sat down to dinner in it, and in it went out with Jones.

Suke again enveloped herself in the grey cloak, and, much to Susan's disgust, could not be persuaded to leave it at home.

"I'll lend you one of mine, miss," said Flipper, "almost a new fashion."

"Yah! Don't care about fashion, Nipper," was the reply.

"My name is Flipper, miss," said the indignant Susan.

"I call thee Nipper, because it wor the name of one of our dogs, and a rum one he was. Eh, if he once got hold o' thee, he'd make his teeth meet."

And Suke grinned.

"Indeed!" replied the other. "I'm not a dog, although some servants are treated worser. You make your teeth meet pretty well."

"Yah, do I? Don't thee sarce me, or I'll make something else meet."

And Suke's face flamed up to a high crimson pitch.

"What will you make meet? Upon my word, I should like to see it!"

And Flipper looked defiance to the teeth.

"Yah, no, you wouldn't. I'll make thy chops and my hand meet, if you sarce me. Drive me gently, my lass, and I'll go quietly; but if you use the whip, I'll be like Swishtail."

"Indeed! Who was Swishtail? Some country bumpkin, I suppose," sneered Flipper.

"Yah, yer clever; it was our horse. If you laid whip on him, he kicked clean over the traces. If I do it, Nipper, ——"

And Suke's fist instinctively doubled.

Flipper, like a prudent general, seeing she was not only overmatched, but overweighted, retreated.

"Lor' bless me, miss," she said, with a well-affected surprise, "how hasty you are! I didn't mean to offend you —nothing was more opposite to my thoughts."

"Yah! Well, p'r'aps you didn't; but I doesn't stand it with anyone. I haven't been used to it. Master Billy Snivel, one of our plough-boys, tried it on once with I, and I gave him such a drubbing that he couldn't eat his dinner for a week; and two good things turned out of it—we saved some pounds of bacon, and he larnt manners."

"Indeed! Well, miss, are you ready?"

"Yah! I have been only waiting for my betters."

And Suke grinned in Flipper's face.

And, so saying, they left the house, Susan Flipper mentally vowing she'd serve her out yet.

"I'll be even with you," she muttered. "I'll put cook upon you some day; she's a good hand at basting. I wouldn't have such a face for no end of money. What is the world coming to?"

Jones, with his charge, was soon in that busy, ever-thronging, ever-bustling street of London, named after the classical spot on the banks of the Isis.

The fog had cleared away, and all the shops were brilliant in gas and glitter, striving to make up for the fog and failure of trade.

Had there been a shower of larks, Tommy would have caught sufficient to have lasted him a long time.

His mouth was stretched to its greatest longitude, while his eyes seemed starting from their sockets; his cap seemed at times as if it were dancing, and about to leave his head, for his red hair stuck up with wonder and amazement.

Old Jones was delighted to witness this wonder and astonishment, as were many of the spectators.

"I say, Maister Jones, be all them things real?" said Tommy, pointing to one of those magnificent shawl shops.

The shawls, being reflected in the dazzling mirrors, they seemed doubled and doubled again.

"Real! Yes, my lad; there are thousands more like them."

"Come, I say, don't you come Ted Flan over I," said Tommy.

"What, do you know that young gentleman, and——"

"Giles Evergreen? I should think I did! Didn't we go to Birchenough's together? I only wish they were here."

"So do I," said Jones. "But come along, or we shall have a crowd round us."

For Tommy had become so excited at the sight of the shops that he began dancing like a wild Indian; then, rushing up to the looking-glasses, grinning and bowing at his own shadow, until a crowd had got round him and roared with laughter.

This pleased Tommy, and he roared with them, until Jones, finding the lark becoming serious, dragged him from the spot.

Mr. Jones had been sent by his mistress to procure some lobsters for supper, and after, by dint of great exertion, he had extricated himself and Tommy from the crowd, he proceeded to the shop to effect his purpose.

Now lobsters and crabs were quite a novelty to Tommy, and there being a basket of the latter unboiled close at hand, Tommy was wonderfully struck by the peculiar manner in which they opened and shut their claws.

The attention of Jones being directed entirely to his purchase, Tommy was thus enabled to have all the fun to himself. Attracted by the manner in which one very venerable gentleman opened his claws, Tommy popped his finger in; the next moment the crab had closed his claw upon it with such a grip as made Tommy yell, and, frightened out of his wits, he ran out of the shop with the crab clinging to him.

The man behind the counter, seeing all this, and not knowing that he had come in with the servant, thought Tommy had walked into the shop with the intention of stealing the crab.

Seeing Tommy run out of the shop with it, he raised the cry " Stop thief !" and, rushing out, gave chase.

The cry became general, and poor Tommy, alarmed at it, dashed down the first street, with the crab sticking to his hand, and a mob of persons close at his heels.

The chase after Tommy Jolter had now commenced in earnest, and right well and gallantly did Tommy hold on his way.

The crab, the innocent cause of this, still held on to Tommy's fingers, giving it every now and then an extra pinch that made Tommy yell again.

The scene was a very excitiing one, as, by this time, several policemen had joined in the chase.

But they were distanced, in consequence of the weight of their clothing, by the shopman, who, being an amateur pedestrian and runner, felt his credit in that particular science was very much at stake.

In the rear was our old friend Jones, who followed up Tommy with all the zeal of an attached friend.

The tail of this exciting chase was brought up by an extraordinary number of men—the butcher, the baker, and the crossing - sweeper with his old stump broom — women, and even children, for when was there a London mob ever complete without the two latter?

Down Portland Place, and that in the centre, did Tommy race at a speed seldom seen.

Coming out into the New Road, he dashed through the park-gates, the gate-keeper making a desperate grab at him, but missing, rolled over into the road.

The inner circle gates having been closed, Tommy suddenly found his progress barred.

Yes, but only for a moment, for, before his pursuers had got through the gates, Tommy, with his tenacious friend, was over the palings, but in doing so he missed his footing, and came down with all his force apon the crab, crushing him all to pulp.

By this lucky affair (for Tommy) the claws relaxed their tenacity, and the finger of Tommy, though swollen and bleeding, was free.

Tommy heard the shouts and inquiries, and for a time lay hid to recover his breath.

"There he goes," said a boy. " Look, guv'nor "—to a policeman—" flying like mad over the circle."

And he pointed up the road.

There was a something seen in the distance, in the road, remarkably like the phantom figure of Tommy.

Again was the hue-and-cry raised, and off the whole body started, round the circle, except poor old Jones, who, exhausted by the long run and his fright at what had taken place, leaned against the palings, puffing and panting for breath.

Again the cries were heard in the distance of the pursuing party returning, but still Tommy kept himself well concealed and snug in the grass he had fallen into, every now and then sucking his poor maimed finger, which caused him great pain.

At last the party returned, consisting of a couple of the force, the shopman, and one or two others.

"Well, old gentleman," said one of the force, to Jones, "seen or heard anything of the thief, eh?"

"Thief! He is no thief! It's his curiosity brought him into this scrape," answered Jones, indignantly.

"Oh, that's the new term for stealing crabs, is it? I'll trouble you to walk with me to the station, and give an account of yourself; you was in it. What's your name, eh?"

"Jones," was the reply.

"Ah, that's quite enough. Pity you didn't say it was Smith."

Here the whole party burst into a laugh.

"What are you laughing at? I tell you I am butler to Mrs. Wilson, of Gower Street, and I came out with that lad—who is on a visit—to order some lobsters, and——"

"He caught a crab," grinned the policeman.

"Na, he didn't," said a voice. "The varmint caught me."

"Oh, Lord, what's that," murmured Jones.

"Why, it be I—Tommy Jolter. Here's the plaguey thing."

And Tommy handed over the mutilated cause of all his troubles.

"Why, it's the boy that's given us such an infernal chase. I know him. I've had him more than once afore."

"No, you haven't," said Tommy, climbing up the palings. "Don't thee tell lies. Here, give I a hand, Maister Jones. Blowed if Tommy Jolter was ever a thief."

Tommy, therefore, was soon amongst them, but no sooner had his feet touched the ground, than he was collared on each side by a policeman.

"What be that for?" shouted Tommy, beginning to kick and plunge about.

"What's it for? Why, you don't give us such a spin again. Here, come along. We shall soon know all about you."

By this time a crowd had again assembled, and so round the park, into Albany Street Station, followed by a crowd of boys, shouting, "Who boned the crab?" was Soft Tommy Jolter led, threatened by the two tall policemen that if he didn't go quietly they would clap the handcuffs on him, while another of them politely intimated to old Jones that he must make one of the party, for he had long had his eyes upon him, but he didn't know that lobsters was his game, although it was all fish that came to his net; and so, with many pleasant witticisms, they at last reached the station-house.

Tommy cut rather a comical figure when he was placed before the inspector. In the first place he had lost his cap; his smock-frock was torn and daubed with mud from his fall in the grass; his face had some patches upon it, with occasional streaks and marks of blood, caused by his rubbing it with his bleeding finger; while, partly with fright and the violent exercise he had taken, his red hair stood up like a well-grown crop of carrots.

The inspector could not refrain from

smiling at the figure standing before him.

"What's your name.!" asked he.

"Tommy Jolter, son and heir to Jack Jolter, next-of-skin——"

"Come, come, this is no place for fun, my lad," he said, sternly, "and so you'll find."

"What has he been doing?" he asked the constable.

"Stealing a crab, sir, from the shop of——"

"It's a lie. I sees the plaguey thing open its—what-do-ye-call-ums, and I popped my finger in, and blest if it didn't bite 'un right through to the bone. Just you look here, maister."

And Tommy held out his finger.

"First time I ever saw a varmint like that; blest if his teeth ain't sharper than a weasel or a badger."

And here Tommy took a good suck at it.

The action was so extremely farcical that the whole place rang with laughter.

"Yah, you may laugh. I wish it had got hold of thy nose; the grin would ha' been on the wrong side of thy chops."

He said this to one of the men who had rather a large one.

At that moment the master of the shop entered the place.

"There is little doubt," he said, addressing the inspector, "but this is entirely a mistake. A gentleman who was in my shop observed it all; and I am the more confirmed in it, because the mistress of Mr. Jones here is one of my best customers; it is not likely that the lad there would steal."

"Yah, steal! What, I? Tommy Jolter, fresh from the country, steal such a cantankerous varmint as that? Why it's the first time I ever clapped eyes on such a sprawling what-do-ye-call-'em in all my days. I steal? Ha, ha! by gums, that's a good 'un. I only wish feyther were here, he'd leather the whole lot on you round, let alone what sister Suke would do."

During this the inspector had held a conversation with Jones, and the result was, that a cab was sent for, and Tommy set at liberty.

"But what made you run, my lad?" said the inspector.

"Yah, what made me run? Why, then, that plaguey thing got hold of my finger. Don't you see, I wanted to run from it, but, bless you, it held on just the same as my terrier holds on to a rat. Why, bless your heart, I didn't know what I was doing."

Here the laughter broke out again, as the cab was announced.

"There, take him home safely, Mr. Jones," said the inspector, smiling.

"Yes, and blest if you catch Tommy Jolter putting his finger into anyone's mouth again. Eh, but he did bite main hard."

"Yes, and you ran main hard," said a policeman.

"Yah, you're right. I only wish I had you down in our parts; I'd give thee such a winder across country as would make thy face the colour of thy coat."

And with that, Tommy entered the cab with Jones and one of the force, while a few anxious boys round the door saluted him by the style and title of the "Duke of Crabs."

During this adventure of Soft Tommy, Susan Flipper and Suke Jolter had wandered into Tottenham Court Road.

There everything so astonished the latter that she stood like Tommy had done, spell-bound, staring in at the shop doors and the windows.

Then the number of the vehicles, the rapidity with which they travelled, the crush and the crowd of persons jostling and pushing one against the other, caused her to stand and stare with such a wonderful expression of face, as to draw down upon her the same sort of attention that had been paid to Tommy.

Wandering on, Suke had her attention drawn by Susan Flipper to one of those stalls that rejoice in combining more than one line of business, and which was the property of an old woman not blest with the best of tempers.

A delicate assortment of red herrings, flanked by a blooming display of turnip-radishes, in close contiguity with the largest of "native oysters."

At this "freehold" and its tempting display, Suke stood for a moment looking at the oysters—things she had never before seen.

"What do you call them 'ere things!" asked Suke, of the proprietor.

Now, the trade having been very bad all the day, the old lady's temper might be justly termed of the most "powerful vinegar" description.

"We call them golden pippins," replied the old crone, taking the pipe out of her mouth and looking at Suke.

"Yah, what funny things! How do you eat them?" asked Suke, innocently.

"How do you ate them? Ha, ha! well, if that ain't good! Here, Nancy," calling to a woman who sat next to her, "here's the lord mayor's eldest daughter asking how you ate oysters!"

"Why, they are generally fried with onions until they're quite soft; then sarved up with mashed turnips, and ——"

"What you've plenty of, my beauty," chimed in the old woman.

"Yah! what's that?"

"Sauce, my chicken!"

"Sarce! Don't you sarce me!" Suke said.

The blood of the Jolters was rising rapidly to fever heat.

"I asked you how they ate them."

"And you have been told, my lambkin."

By this time a crowd had gathered round the stall, which rather alarmed the nerves of Susan Flipper.

"Let us get out of this, miss," she whispered.

"Shan't! She told me they was golden pippins; as if I didn't know!"

"Then, if you knowed, what did you ax for, eh, my bunch of carrots?"

At this unfortunate allusion to the colour of Suke's locks, she was springing upon her, Susan holding her back by the cloak, when a drunken man came reeling along, and, forcing his way through the crowd, and before he could be prevented, he went head over heels over the stall, old woman, and "golden pippins," etc., into the road.

The screams of the woman, the shouts and laughter of the mob, and the confusion attendant upon dragging them out of the road, enabled Susan to get Suke Jolter out of the crowd and, turning rapidly down a street, got away from what would have been otherwise an awkward affair; as it was, a policeman who had witnessed the affair from the corner public-house, settled the whole affair by taking the man into custody.

There was a good deal of difficulty in getting Suke to consent in leaving the spot.

The obstinate, self-willed girl would have stayed and " seen it out," as she expressed it.

They arrived at the door of Mrs. Wilson's house just as the cab containing Tommy, the butler, and the policeman, pulled up.

The latter party, having been satisfied that all was correct, departed.

It was arranged that the matter should be kept concealed from old Jolter; and Tommy, having had something placed upon his finger, and a decent quantity of jam tart for his supper, was placed under the care of the faithful Jones, and conveyed to his bedchamber.

A few hours after, the whole household were aroused by a tremendous crash, and loud cries of murder and fire !

Out rushed the farmer with the tongs.

Mrs. Wilson, in a peculiar nightcap, protruded her head from her bedroom.

Flipper stood at the top of the stairs, screaming, while Suke, with her red head, was shouting out.

The whole household were in a state of the greatest confusion.

What was it ?

The noise proceeded from Tommy's room.

It appeared that the old fit of walking in his sleep occasioned this uproar. Tommy had tumbled over the wash-hand-stand and caused this commotion. Again, after a short interval, all was quiet, and when Flipper rejoined her mistress she related what had occurred, which occasioned that good lady to lift up her hands in astonishment, and breathe a silent wish that the Lawyer " Tough Mutton," as he was called, would have kept such " tender lambs " in his own " fold."

" We must always make the best of a bad bargain," said her mistress.

" Very true, mum; but there are some bargains so bad that you can't make anything out of them; and, with all due submission, this Jolter family appear to be one of the worst of bargains."

" We must do the best we can, now we have got them," was the reply.

" Yes, mum; that was what mother said when she had eight of us laid down with the measles, and father had swallowed a tenpenny nail."

" Bless me, girl, what a misfortune ! What did your mother do ?"

" Made the best of a bad bargain, mum. Good night."

CHAPTER XXI.

THE ZOOLOGICAL GARDENS.

THE next morning it was decided at the breakfast table that Farmer Jolter and Mr. Walmisley should proceed together to the lawyer's in Lincoln's Inn Fields, while Tommy, attired in a new suit of clothes, should visit the celebrated Zoological Gardens, in Regent's Park.

"I shall take the young people myself," said the worthy lady, "because then I shall be certain they will not get into mischief."

"Well, madam," replied Jolter, "it be very kind of you; but Lor' bless yer, they know all about gardens. What's the name on 'em?"

"Zoological," was the reply.

The farmer stared at Tommy, and Tommy stared at Suke, while Suke looked flushed at Mrs. Wilson, thinking she was playing some fun with her.

The girl had always been of a strange suspicious disposition, which had been very much increased by her taking her mother's place in the farm; and the affair of the night previous at the oyster stall had rather added than diminished the feeling.

"What do they grow in the gardens, marm?" at length asked Suke.

Mrs. Wilson looked at Mr. Walmisley with great surprise.

"Grow, my dear; what do you mean?"

"Yah! What do I mean? What's a garden for but to grow things in?"

"But this is a collection of wild animals, my dear."

"Eh, feyther," said Tommy, "things have come to a fine pass when they can grow them. I ha' heard of this place afore. One of our boys told us he had been there, and he said there was a jolly lot of monkeys. I saw a monkey once, and——"

"Yah! When you looked in the glass, Tommy," said Suke.

"Ees, and you were looking in at the same time, and blest if there weren't a couple," was the reply.

Mrs. Wilson inwardly thought the truth was spoken on both sides.

"Well, marm," said the farmer, "I leave it all to you. This gentleman," —pointing to Walmisley—"is main kind, and says he will see me to the lawyer's respecting the next-of-skin, and——"

"Which I hope you will find turn out to your advantage," said Mrs. Wilson.

"If I don't, there'll be a bit of a row between old Tough Mutton and myself. Danged if I don't hide 'un, if he sent I upon a wild-goose chase, I can tell 'un."

"Well, I don't think that is at all likely, Mr. Jolter."

"I hope not, marm. I'll make his hide smoke for it, if it costs I a hundred pounds!"

"Well, come, I think it's time we started for the lawyer's," said Mr. Walmisley.

"MONKEY TRICKS."

"With all my heart, sir."

And so saying, Jolter, rising from his seat, was about following him from the room, when he turned round to Mrs. Wilson.

"You mun keep a sharp eye and a tight rein on that couple, marm. Sights are things they arn't seen much of, and they'll be apt to run wild. I merely gives you a bit of advice upon the matter, that's all."

And so saying, he left the room, and shortly after, the house, with the old stockbroker.

The transformation effected in the outward appearance of Soft Tommy was something extraordinary.

Dressed in a neat suit of clothes —black jacket, light waistcoat, ditto trousers, and a smart cap on his head, Tommy would scarcely have been recognised as the boy racing up Portland Place the night before.

Suke had made some great alterations in her toilette.

She had discarded the cloak, and substituted a flaming red shawl, belonging to her mother, and only used on grand occasions.

Mrs. Wilson had made her a present of a round velvet hat with a feather in it; and so, on this, their first visit to one of the "sights of London," their appearance was somewhat passable.

Having some calls to make upon the tradesmen and other little matters to attend to, it was not Mrs. Wilson's intention to be at the gardens before noon; so, after an early luncheon had been partaken of, at which Tommy and Suke played conspicuous parts, the carriage started with them — Mrs.

Wilson and Suke inside, while Tommy would have his seat alongside the coachman.

Half-an-hour had scarcely passed when a carriage drove up to the door, containing Giles Evergreen and Ted Flan.

The Lady St. George had thought it best that they should leave the villa at Richmond during the severe illness of Alfred Ravensborne, who was at the time of their departure lying in a very critical state.

Leaving the carriage at the door, Giles and Ted entered the house, respectfully welcomed by both the butler, Jones, and Susan Flipper.

The former, having placed refreshments on the table, Susan was desired to wait.

"Any news, Susan," asked Giles, "during our absence?"

"News, sir? Why, it's been wonderful," was the reply.

"Are the spirits up or down, Susan?" said Ted Flan. "And have you heard anything of my grandmother? — rest her!"

"The old lady has been remarkably quiet, sir; but if we have lost it in one way, we have it in another."

"How is that?"

And Giles looked curiously at Ted.

"Well, sir, do you know anything of a family called the Jolters?"

"What!" said Ted, springing from his chair. "The Jolters! — What Tommy and Suke! Know them, by the powers! Do I know myself? What's the matter with them?"

"Oh, goodness knows! All I know they are up in London."

"Oh, by the piper of Howth, and

that's no swearing, then there's a budget of fun in store for us. Go on, Susan."

"Well, sir, they came to town, a few nights since, to look after a relative they've lost."

"Oh I'd like to look after one of that family. And what's his name?"

"Well, it's hard to speak it. I've often seen it in the papers, and its rather a numerous family."

"Well, and what is their name?" said Giles, impatiently.

"Next of Skin, sir."

"Ha, ha, ha!" shouted the boys.

"Oh, by the powers, who told you that, Susan?"

"The old farmer said he had come up to London to look after him, and Tommy told me the same, and Miss Suke—she's a beauty—told me as much. We've had a fine time with them, I can tell you."

"What's been the matter?"

"The matter?"

And Susan twirled her apron very nervously.

"I never had strong nerves at the best of times, but that girl Jolter will drive all of them from me."

"Oh, the beauties, where are they?" asked Ted.

"Where? They've gone with the missus in the carriage to the gardens, where the wonders of nature are preserved, and a nice lot they are to preserve."

"But where do you mane?" said Ted.

"I mean up in the park, sir—the Zoo-o-logical. I went there once on Easter Monday, and came away perfectly astonished."

"But have they gone there—and how long is it since they started?" asked Giles.

"Well, sir, they are gone there, and they started about an hour ago."

"Then, we'll just be after them for the glory of ould Ireland! We have one call to make, Giles, and then hurroo for the recreations of the Jolter family."

"Right, Ted. It is a long time since we saw Soft Tommy and dear sister Suke, and so suppose we take a stroll to the gardens, and pay our respects to them?"

"And the grate wondhers of natural historic history," and in a few minutes they were again seated in the carriage, and on their way to Regent's Park.

There was nothing of any speciality to notice in the ride of Tommy and Suke Jolter to the great Zoological Gardens of England.

Once, Tommy nearly fell off the box, and, in laying hold of the rein to save himself, suddenly caused the horses to swerve and turn over a wandering china or delf shop. At the moment this occurred the man proprietor was jingling a basin and plate together, and, in a loud voice, telling the British public—

"That this ware was none of your whereabouts, but warranted to last for ever."

In one instant, like the ancient basket of glass, the hopes of the "visionary" were dashed to the ground.

The pole of the carriage catching the wheel of the shallow, sent it reeling into the centre of the road, while, sounding forth his "cymbalic wonders," the proprietor lay embedded in the glorious ruins.

After a parley, in which Tommy and Suke indulged in loud peals of laughter, much to the indignation of the "bankrupt proprietor," Mrs. Wilson gave her card to the man and the policeman, they again resumed their journey, and at last arrived, without any further mischance, at the celebrated gardens.

During the ride of Giles and Ted they concerted a plan to have their fun with the Jolters without being recognised.

They, therefore, left the carriage at the house of the Lady St. George, and resolved to walk to the gardens.

On their way thither they went into a cap shop and purchased two caps having furry pieces hanging down to protect the ears, and, directing the man where their hats were to be sent to, started off laughing heartily at the great fun they should have with Soft Tommy and his sister Suke.

It is scarcely possible to find in London a more delightful and instructive lounge than the gardens we are now conducting our readers to—the young, the old, the cheerful, the melancholy, the ignorant and the learned, all find enjoyment and instruction in this delightful spot.

There is wonder and amazement at the great works and organisation of our Maker even to those who have been in some degree accustomed to them. What, then, must be the feeling of awe and astonishment of those who see them for the first time?

In consequence of the delay occasioned by the accident to the peripatetic vendor of delf, the Jolter party were a considerable time in arriving at the gardens, and so by the time they had reached them, Giles and Ted had been enabled to take a slight glance round the place, which filled them with feelings that their intelligent minds would have found it rather difficult to describe.

At last, while standing watching the antics of the bear, they discovered the party approaching.

Mrs. Wilson had one of them on each side of her; and it was easy, at a glance, to discover that the good lady was greatly perplexed.

Every eye appeared to be fixed upon them, and the quaint appearance of Tommy and Suke seemed to cause as much sensation as the animals themselves.

Tommy and Suke, though rather wonder-stricken at all they saw, yet returned stare for stare.

Hostilities commenced first on the part of Suke and a bystander, an elderly female, who seemed to have under her charge a large family of very small children.

One of the juveniles, with a diverting simplicity, anxious to get a nearer sight of some object, for the gardens were very much crowded, pushed against Suke, at the same time jumping heavily upon her toes.

" Yah fule ! where are you jumping ?" cried the irritable young lady. " Don't ye know manners ?" and with that she sent him a drive that set him roaring.

This, of course, brought down upon her the indignation of the woman.

" Pray, miss, what did you do that

for? Keep your 'ands off my property, or you'll get as good as you send!"

"Yah! who are you? Tell him not to smash in my toes!"

"Put your toes in your pocket, Redhead," replied the woman.

At this fatal (at all times) allusion to Suke's head, a rather large parasol that the young lady carried was raised, and a right battle royal would have commenced, but Mrs. Wilson caught her arm, and so kept peace.

"My dear young lady, you really must not do these sort of things," whispered Mrs. Wilson.

"Yah! mustn't I though? Am I to have my toes smashed, and then be called Redhead for nothing at all? You said we were coming to see the wild beasts, and I think we've got among 'em, eh, Tommy?"

"Ees, I think you be right, Suke; but I never heard they let them loose."

At that moment a noise was heard resembling the growl of an angry bear close behind them, and a consternation seemed to seize upon the whole party, and they ran helter skelter in all directions, thinking that some mischief was brewing.

Out of the group there were only two lads who seemed to stand quietly gazing on, and not at all alarmed at the noise that had scattered the group so unceremoniously.

"What be those tall things with great lumps on their backs, and people riding on 'em, eh?" asked Tommy.

"Dromedaries, my dear," replied the lady, their guide.

"Can't I have a ride like the rest on 'em, eh?"

"Yah! you'll break your unlucky neck," said Suke.

"Ees, and that would bring the tears in your eyes, wouldn't it? You'd come in for all the brass, eh, Suke?"

But Mrs. Wilson declined to let Tommy have his wish, fearful that some accident would happen to him.

Thinking the sight of the elephants would please them, she directed their steps to the house in which they were kept.

It happened when they entered the place it was comparatively deserted.

Everybody who has seen these sagacious animals is pleased to witness the graceful manner in which they wave their trunks to and fro, rewarded very often with a cake or a biscuit.

Not so with Suke.

When the tractable animal put forth his trunk, nearly in that young lady's face, she rewarded him with a smart tap from the parasol, that caused the ponderous beast to utter a peculiar kind of noise.

Before Mrs. Wilson could pull her out of the way, the elephant had his trunk round the parasol, and Suke, holding on with both hands, screaming, was being lifted as easy as a feather from the ground, when Tommy, seeing the trouble she was in, laid hold of her by the legs, and the pair were being gradually raised in the air, shouting, screaming and kicking, amid the laughter of some and the fright of others, when the keeper rushed to their assistance; shouting to Suke to let go the parasol, which she very soon did, he caught them safely in his arms.

The instant after the parasol was a

perfect wreck under the ponderous feet of the beast.

"What have you been about, miss, with the beast?" said the keeper.

"Yah! what has the beast been about with me?" screamed Suke. "What right had he to poke that in my face for, eh?"

"It was only his fun, miss."

"Yah! let him keep his fun to himself; he's broken mother's parasol, and he shall pay for that. Yah! ye ugly black varmint! I only wish I'd had one of our pitchforks, I'd teach thee a lesson. Pay me for mother's parasol."

"Stuff and nonsense! You mustn't make this noise here," said the keeper.

"My dear child!" said Mrs. Wilson, who had just recovered; for when the good old lady saw Tommy and Suke dangling in the air on the elephant's trunk, she thought that it was all over, and then she suddenly fell back in the arms of a bystander.

This was an unfortunate thing for the good lady, for an hour after, when requiring her portemonnaie, it was not to be found.

The "gentleman" who had so sedulously and kindly attended to the distressed lady, had, by a close study of "human nature," been able perfectly to understand the sort of persons who required his assistance, and well knew the precise moment when he could "advantageously" tender it for the benefit of—himself.

Suke looked round to find someone to wreak her vengeance upon.

Unfortunately, Tommy stood in the way, and, in addition to that, was grinning at the idea of the elephant paying for mother's parasol.

Suke flew at Tommy; but he, like a prudent general, fled from the spot, followed by his sister, Mrs. Wilson, and a crowd of persons, amid roars of laughter.

CHAPTER XXII.

TOMMY AND SUKE AMONG THE MONKEYS.

MRS. WILSON, as soon as she had got herself and her "interesting charges" free from the mob, made up her mind to get home as soon as possible.

Acting up to her favourite maxim of "making the best of a bad bargain," she commiserated with both of them upon the unfortunate affair that had taken place in the "house of elephants."

"I am glad that it is no worse, my dears," said the worthy lady.

"Yah!" said the now really irritable Suke, "I don't see what there is to be glad about. The great black monster! I'll make him pay for it."

"It be all your own fault, Suke," said Tommy, as he stood at a distance. "What the dickens made you strike the animal for? Ecod! if he'd a swallowed you, he'd had a nice cantankerous morsel to feed on!"

"Yah! would he? You'd better look

out; if I catch you, I'll warm your new jacket for you!"

"Will you? That head of yours would have warmed the elephant's gullet if you'd stuck in it, and set un' on fire."

Suke made a rush at him.

Mrs. Wilson seized tight hold of Suke, and that instant Giles and Ted, who witnessed the whole affair, approached.

They had tied up the covering of their ears, and were in a moment recognised.

It is impossible to describe the antics and wild joy of Tommy when he saw them; he shook them by the hands as though he would have dislocated their bones.

He danced round them with all the frenzy of a wild Indian, and, in fact, so exuberant was he in his joy, that a crowd would soon have gathered round them, but that Giles and Ted laid hold of him, and by sheer strength kept him quiet.

"Eh! Dear, blessed heart, how glad I be to see thee, lads! I be better pleased to see thee, Giles Evergreen and Ted Flan, than if old Next-of-Skin left I five hundred pounds. Feyther be in Lunnon town, and there stands Suke, and—oh dear! oh dear!—this be a grand day for Tommy Jolter."

"I am sure I am happy to see you, Tommy, as well as your sister and Mrs. Wilson, and shall be glad also to see your father."

And Giles Evergreen approached to pay his respects to Mrs. Wilson and Suke.

The former was heartily glad to see them, but Suke hung back, and when Giles held out his hand, she refused to take it.

"And, pray, what is the matter with Miss Suke?" said Ted Flan, approaching with Tommy.

"Yah! You had better keep away. I arn't forgotten your tricks at old Lawyer Tough Mutton's, I can tell you."

"Tricks? By the powers, you must be draming, Miss Jolter. He must be a bold specimen of humanity who would play tricks with you, on the honour of an Irish gintleman."

"Yah! that'll do. I didn't come here to listen to any of your palaver, Mr. Ted O'Flan. I know you," said Suke.

"Do you? Then I hope you are proud of the acquaintance," and Ted grinned. "But joking apart, I'll be happy to show you the wonders of this wonderful place."

"Will you though? Well, that's kind; but you won't fun us, will you?" said Suke, a little mollified.

"Fun you! Upon my word I'd like to catch myself at it. Giles will take care of Tommy, while I'll be as proud as a paycock in attending upon you and Mrs. Wilson," and Ted winked at Giles which was a signal that fun was in store, and he must be on the alert for it.

So saying, Ted took an arm of each of the ladies.

"If ever there was a happy man, that blissful mortal am I."

"Ah, ah! Ted, what a rattle you are. Where shall we commence?" said Giles.

"What say you to the parrots, ladies?" was the reply.

"Oh, the parrots, by all means," said Mrs. Wilson.

They entered the parrot-house at a moment when the screaming and chattering was at its height.

"Do you see that old gentleman there?" said Ted, pointing to a venerable-looking bird.

"Yah! What covered with feathers, and——"

"Whist! Don't say feathers, or you'll insult him. It's a wig he puts on hen he attends a trial. He's the lord chief justice of the place."

"Yah! What do you mean, Mr. O'Flan?" said Suke.

"Flan, my darling; lineally and truly descended from the Fin-Flan-MacHowlagain, the first King of Ireland, who was lawfully married to the Queen of the Canary Islands—and a lovely bird she was—and the notes she brought him were all of her own making."

"And what's the old judge about now?" asked Suke.

"Well, you see that old general in red?" said Ted, pointing to a magnificent bird.

"Yah! He be mighty fine."

"Fine feathers make fine birds, my darling; but, there, on the other side, you see that little creature dressed all in green?"

"Well, what o' she, eh?"

"A great deal, as you shall hear. The ould gineral there is a gay deceiver."

"What's that?" asked Suke.

"Well, he went a-courting Miss Green, an unsuspecting young lady just come up from the country, and pretended such violent love and affection for her that he said his heart was burnt up to a red-hot cinder."

"Yah! she was as green as grass to take in all that," and Suke grinned. "Catch any one flaming me in that way."

"By the powers they must get up a trifle before daylight to do that," and Ted grinned, as he caught Mrs. Wilson smiling at him.

The good old lady saw the drift of Ted Flan's fun; but she resolved not to interfere, so long as that fun was harmless.

"Well, go on," said Suke, impatiently.

"Well, you see, things went on as smooth as water in a basin, when all at once the gay deceiver cast his wicked old eyes on Miss Yellow Plume, the one perched there," and Ted pointed out an old yellow bird.

"Yah! what that old thing?" and Suke elevated her nose.

"Whist, my darling; she'd got lots o' money, and that covers a hape of deficiencies. Would you belave that human nature is so base? Directly the old sinner heard of that, he bowls away from pretty Miss Green, and got married to old Yellow Plume."

"Yah! if any man sarved me such a trick I'd tear his eyes out," and Suke, by an energetic action of her nails, showed she was quite prepared to carry her threat into execution.

"Well, and what in the name of wonder are they at now?"

"Trying the ould General Fitz-foodle

for a clean breach of promise of marriage."

At that time there was an unusual quiet reigning in the house.

"The old sinner, I'd——"

"Whist, my darling; the judge is busy thinking of what Serjeant Macaw has been saying upon a point of law."

"La, how do you know all that?" and Suke cast a very suspicious glance at him.

"Well, you see, it may appear very astonishing, but I had an uncle who had a first cousin, who was a mighty traveller, and he once travelled into a forest that was full of parrots, and the head man who had the charge of them taught him the language."

"Yah! stuff—nonsense; it won't do. Arn't he bamboozling me, marm?"

Before Mrs. Wilson could reply, there arose such a screaming and fluttering of wings and agitation among all the birds enough to deprive anybody of their sense of hearing.

Suke was astounded.

"The jury have found him guilty, with a thousand pounds damages," said Ted.

But, above all the din, was heard the shrill cries of the human voice; and so, excited by curiosity, they made their way to the spot from whence they proceeded.

There they found Tommy had, with his usual luck, got himself into a scrape.

While Giles's attention was directed to some other object, Tommy took the opportunity of giving a respectable old gentleman parrot a flip on the beak with his fingers.

But the wily old bird was too much for Tommy, and while supposed to be fast asleep was in fact wide awake.

In an instant he had made his beak, *à la* crab, meet in Tommy's finger.

The rest of his tribe screamed out screams of joy at this; and so, what with Tommy's yells, the noise of the birds, and the laughter of the people at Tommy's frantic antics, the place was in a complete uproar.

At last, by the aid of the keeper, the bird was released from Tommy's finger, and then tying it round with a pocket handkerchief, the whole party hurried from the parrot-house.

"What made you irritate the bird for, eh, Tommy?" asked Giles.

"Why, I thought the old gentleman was asleep, and that I'd just stir 'un up. Bother him! he's given I a rare nip."

"It's what you must expect if you tease and annoy them; they have their feelings, Tommy, as well as us. You had better be careful for the future."

"Yah! it sarves Tommy right. If he sarved I so I'd wring his plaguey old neck; but I am glad he sarved Tommy out," said Suke.

"Och, murder! remimber the elephant and his trunk, Suke," said Ted.

"Yah! I'd trunk him if I had a good stick and our old bull-dog. Eh, dear me! what be that great varmint atop of the pole?"

"Why, the polar bear," said Giles.

And so they approached the splendid animal to get a nearer view of him.

Tommy, in spite of all Giles could do, would push in the front, and in so doing was nearly pitched over into the bear pit.

But Giles and Ted, catching him luckily by the leg, saved him from a hug that would have made his bones ache.

The bear, seeing what was likely to happen, hurried down the pole in his anxiety to give his new and unexpected visitor a fitting reception and a loving embrace.

He sat upon his haunches, and uttering a loud growl of welcome, opened his jaws, while his eyes glistening like fire, bespoke the cordiality with which Soft Tommy would have been received in Bruin's arms.

Here the old adage of the cup and the lip was verified : all that Bruin got was Tommy's new cap, which fell down the pit, and was caught in his paws, and who quickly showed his rage and disappointment that Tommy's head was not in it by tearing it into a hundred pieces.

When Tommy was again safely placed on his feet, his scared look, and the bristly appearance of his red hair so tickled the humour of the crowd that they treated him to three loud huzzas, which was still further heightened by Suke making a number of wry faces at them.

Giles quickly dragged him from the spot and away from the crowd, while Ted did the same for Suke, with great difficulty.

Mrs. Wilson, who had been an alarmed spectator of all these little accidents, now thought it time to interfere.

"I think now we'll find the carriage, and get home," the lady said.

"Na, na," said Tommy, in spite of his fright; I won't go home until I have seen the monkeys."

"Tommy be a great fool, but there he be right," chimed in Suke. "And I want to see them—and I will, that's flat."

"But, my dear, I think——"

"Yah! I don't care what you think; my mind is made up—I don't go home until I have seen the monkeys!"

"Sister Suke be right; why, they be the finest things in the world, be monkeys. They be main scarce though."

"There I differ from you, Tommy," said Giles. "The world is full of them."

"But, my dears," said Mrs. Wilson, angrily, "your father placed you under my care, and I must insist that you leave the place with me."

"Yah! you may do what you like, and insist as much as you like, but you won't make me budge an inch till I see the monkeys and their tricks."

And Suke looked daggers at the lady.

"Besides, feyther baint here, and you know when the old dog's fast asleep the rats can nibble the cheese!" and Tommy, in spite of his fright, laughed.

"You be right, Tommy : old un be gone to look after Next-of-Skin, and the young uns mean to have their fun out."

"Well, then, I'll have nothing to do with it," replied Mrs. Wilson.

"Well, who axed you?" said Suke. "You'll be paid for all you do, and that's all you want, I suppose. Which be the way to the monkey-house, my man?" she said, to a passer-by.

"Well, that's a good un," said the

man; "as if you didn't know. Why, arn't you just come from it?"

And he walked on.

Giles and Ted smiled at this.

"Leave Tommy and Suke with us, madam, and let their wish be gratified. We'll do all we can to keep them from harm."

"Do as you think proper; you will find me in the carriage at the Primrose Hill gate; but it's the last time I shall subject myself to such an exhibition as this, depend upon it."

And the indignant lady walked off to the carriage that was in waiting for her.

"Yah! who cares for her?" said Suke. "We be our own maister and missus, eh, my lad, Tommy?"

"I should think so, Suke. What's the use of going out for a day's pleasure, if you don't enjoy yourselves? Why, the monkeys be worth all the money. Lor', I saw one at market one day, with a man and a organ, and blowed if ever I seed such tricks."

"Not even your own, eh, Tommy?" said Giles.

"Na, na, blowed if I can climb a rope, and hang on with one leg, like that one I saw."

"Did you ever try, Tommy?" asked Ted.

"Na, never had the chance," was the reply.

"Then you don't know what you can do."

And Ted laughed.

"I know I am monkey enough," said Tommy, "but I can't do that. I'd come down on my head, and hurt myself."

"Not you; it's the safest part you could fall on," said Giles.

They had by this time reached the monkey-house, and without any more words they entered the building.

Perhaps in this splendid collection of natural history there is no place more extensively patronized than the building which contains this truly "comical family."

To say that all the party were astonished would be to use a mild phrase— they literally brimmed over with enjoyment.

Giles and Ted had very often seen and read much of these extraordinary fac-similes of the human race, but here they were greatly astonished at what they saw.

The amazement of Tommy and Suke was ludicrous to behold, and more than once the former had to be restrained from putting his fingers through the wires to get hold of their paws.

"By the powers!" whispered Ted to him, "you must not show any brotherly love to them, Tommy, if you don't want to lose a finger."

"Ha, ha, ha!" roared Tommy. "Look at that funny little fellow; he bangs all I ever saw. Why, he's got a book and pencil, and is making up his accounts for his board and lodgings. Give us thy fist, little un."

"He be as like old Tough Mutton as two peas," said Suke. "Eh, dear! look at that one hanging down by his leg. Why, Tommy, thee'd never do that, my lad."

"I mean to have a try in the old barn, some day, Suke."

"Yah! I'd like to see thee do it."

"Well, so thee shall, if thee'll open thy eyes. Stick to un, little un; don't thee let **thy** book go. Give it the big un, my lad !"

This was shouted out by Tommy in consequence of a bigger monkey (the way of the world) attacking the smaller one, and trying to wrest the book and the pencil from him. The little one held on bravely for his rights, and the jabbering and row running among the " happy family" ended in a general *mêlée*, much to the delight of the frequenters of the monkey-house.

Tommy roared with delight.

Suke grinned and danced about.

Giles and Ted, boy like, enjoyed the fun.

Now it happened that Tommy and Suke stood with their backs to the cage in which two long-armed baboons were residing.

For a long time these " intelligent" animals had quietly and intently been viewing the very red heads of both Tommy and Suke.

The sight seemed not only to astonish them, but in a great measure to puzzle them as well. They had never seen any of their race like it before.

They stared with all their eyes at the great phenomena; they scratched their heads as if to rouse up a dormant memory, and held communion together in a language peculiarly their own.

So great and absorbing was the conversation, that they, unlike the world in general, paid no attention to the war in the next house, but, like prudent people, held a strict neutrality—" They looked and wondered, wondered and looked."

In the midst of the paroxysms of laughter which Tommy and Suke indulged in, they flung their heads back very close to their cage. This they repeated more than once, and during one of those visitations the strings of Suke's bonnet broke, and it fell to the ground.

Of this she took no notice, so absorbed was she by the sight before her.

Again, in the midst of a peal of laughter, their two flaming heads went close to the cage.

Then, like a dart from a bow, out came the long arms of the hitherto silent baboons, and fastened upon them.

The male baboon held in his bony fingers, as though they were in a vice, one of Suke's flowing, fiery tresses.

The lady baboon showed an intense affection for Tommy's scalp, and, Indian like, had got a firm grip upon it.

At this sight, all attention was directed to this unfortunate pair, who were kicking, shouting, and plunging, but all to no purpose.

The uproar was at its height.

Giles and Ted laid hold of Tommy's legs, almost convulsed with laughter, and pulled for dear life; but the more they pulled, the fiercer the baboon chattered, and the stronger he held on.

Others laid hold of Suke, but with no better success, while the whole building rang with shouts of laughter, which, in spite of the position of the individuals, could not be repressed.

At last, one of the keepers opening the door of the cage, the animals gave a desperate tug.

Away came all the hair from Tommy's crown, leaving him quite bald on that part.

At the same moment a large quantity flew from Suke's head, and the next moment the baboons were at the top of their cage on their trapeze, minutely examining it, and tasting what it was like ; and, judging from their exultant ejaculations, it appeared to be extremely palatable and savoury.

Tommy and his sister, furious, wild, and frightened out of their wits, directly they felt themselves at liberty, plunged into the crowd.

Then getting jammed all together, the scene was one of the greatest confusion, when suddenly the scream of an enraged monkey (or Ted Flan), as if he had got loose among them, struck such a panic to their minds, that a general rush was made to the doors.

Luckily, they were swing ones, and gave easily, and out rushed the mob into the open air without injury, the cry pursuing them to the very doors.

Through the gardens they went, helter-skelter, under the impression that the great baboon had got loose and was after them.

But there were none so fleet in that race as poor Tommy, with his bald crown, and Sister Suke, minus a great portion of her hair.

Away they ran, and the report having got wind that an animal was loose, led to a general rush into all the closed collections such as had never been seen before.

The gardens, in a few minutes, were quite deserted, to the astonishment of the officials, who, however, with their tact and coolness, soon succeeded in calming the fears of the multitude.

Giles and Ted rushed out with the rest, laughing until the tears ran down their cheeks, and looked eagerly around for Tommy and Suke, but in vain ; they were nowhere to be seen.

A strict search, however, being made, they were at last discovered hid under a lot of hay in one of the empty deer stalls.

It required not only persuasion, but likewise threats to get them from their hiding-place.

When they emerged from their hiding-place there was a general shout from the lowest portion of the persons then present.

In all crowds, especially an English one, there is always a number of persons, who, regardless of the feelings of others, will carry out their own ideas and propensity for larking, and it will and has occurred in our places of recreation and amusement, spite of well-ordered regulations to prevent it.

On this occasion there had congregated together in the gardens some half-dozen fellows who seemed desperately inclined to make more fun out of Tommy and his sister than they had any right to do.

This was observed by Giles and Ted Flan, and to avoid it they proceeded to leave the gardens, and, on finding Mrs. Wilson's carriage, proceed home.

Certainly the appearance of the Jolters was calculated to produce fun and amusement.

Tommy, as we have said before, had lost a considerable portion of hair from the crown of his head, and the nails of the baboon having inserted themselves tolerably deep in the flesh, the blood was flowing pretty freely down his face.

In his struggles his new jacket had

one sleeve torn off, and, take him all together, he appeared as if he had been engaged in a desperate encounter, and had not by any means got the best of it.

Suke's naturally bad and irritable temper was not upon this occasion by any means improved, and her face presenting an appearance very similar to her brother's, raised from the persons we have just spoken of derisive shouts of laughter.

That feeling, of course, could not be prevented, and so Giles and Ted hurried them along in the direction of the gate where the carriage was in waiting.

But while hurrying along two of the fellows who were following, shouting and laughing, laid hold of Tommy by the hair in imitation of his brother brute, the baboon, while the other took the same liberty with the " gentle " Suke.

The latter, turning suddenly round, dealt him such a blow as caused him to reel, while the blood of Giles being throughly roused by this unprovoked insult, he seized the other fellow by the collar and flung him off, thus releasing Soft Tommy from his clutches.

In an instant they were set upon by the rest of the gang, and evidently for the purpose of a little plunder as well as larking.

For the moment the party were placed in peril—two ruffians had attacked each of them ; but the bravery of the boys kept them off and well at bay.

Suke kept her name well up, but Tommy was laid hold of by a couple of fellows, and was getting very much the worst of it, when suddenly the ruffians were struck down.

This turned the tide of affairs, and the approach of the police caused them speedily to run for it.

Giles looked up, and in an instant his hand was held out.

" What, Norman Campbell, is that you, old schoolfellow, come to the rescue ?"

" Eh, mon," said Norman, grasping his hand, and that of Ted. " Ye ken a Scotchman never deserted a friend in the hour of need ; how's a' wi' ye ? Ye look brawly."

" Thank you, Norman, we are quite well," said Giles, " and glad to meet you again."

" And I'm as plased to see you as if you were my own brother, who is dead, only you see I never had one," and Ted grinned.

During this, Suke had been getting poor Tommy a little to rights, although she herself had been terribly alarmed.

" Come along," said Giles ; " let us find the carriage or get a cab ; the mob will collect round us again ; I think we've had enough of the Zoological Gardens."

" I think so too," said Tommy, shaking from head to foot, for the baboon's claws had inserted themselves rather deeply in Tommy's caput, and it smarted terribly.

" You'll never catch me looking at a monkey again," said Suke. " Nasty, spiteful things ; I thought my head was being pulled off my shoulders. Yah, let's get out of the place ; supposing they got loose."

The clock striking at that moment,

suggested an idea to Ted Flan that he thought would hurry their movements.

"By the powers, we'd better make haste out of this; it's the time when the lions and tigers come out for their promenade," said Ted, winking at Giles and Norman.

"Yah, what's that?" inquired Suke.

"What's that, you say; well, it's neither more nor less than taking the fresh air."

"Yah, you don't mean to say that they walk out?" said Tommy and Suke in the same breath.

"That's my maning," replied Ted, and——"

But before he could say any more, Tommy and his sister were rushing to the gate with all their speed, followed by the three lads.

Through the gate they dashed, much to the astonishment of the men at them, who, for the moment, were fearful that something had gone wrong in the gardens.

When Giles, Ted and Norman came up to them, they looked round for Mrs. Wilson's carriage; but the good lady had had her equanimity so dreadfully disturbed, that she had driven home, leaving Giles and Ted to take care of the Jolters.

A cab was soon procured, into which they all got but Ted, who mounted the box, saying that he did it to "kape the road clear."

The vehicle soon arrived in Gower Street, and the door being opened by Susan Flipper, she gave a spasmodic scream when Tommy and Suke landed safely in the hall.

"Great Evens and all look down upon us! Where have you been?" she said, in accents of surprise.

"Yah! don't stand jabbering there. Where's feyther, eh?" said Suke.

"Not come home," said Susan, curtly.

"Then, Tommy, we'll have time to put ourselves to rights afore he does come."

And away Suke rushed upstairs.

At that moment Mrs. Wilson made her appearance, having regained her usual good temper.

"Are you much hurt, my dear?" she inquired of Tommy.

"I feel main sore on the poll," replied Tommy. "Danged if it don't twitch and burn as though somebody were running hot pins and needles in it. I say, Giles, the top bain't off, be it?"

"No," said Giles; "but it looks very bad."

"Ees, and I feel very bad—sickish, like, and as if I was going to——"

Here poor Tommy fainted right off, to the great consternation of all of them; while Giles and Ted laid him on a sofa, Norman rushed out for a doctor, when the violent ringing of the bell caused Susan to rush upstairs at the risk of breaking her neck.

By the time the medical gentleman had arrived Tommy had partly recovered, having been well sprinkled with water, and made to sneeze, at the risk of shaking his head off, by Susan's application of burnt brown paper applied to the nostrils.

But matters wore a more alarming aspect, when Tommy, starting up, rushed frantically about the room, shouting for them to keep the monkey off.

"Take your paws off I!" he shouted.

"A BED-ROOM SQUABBLE."

"Here, feyther, give I the pitchfork and see if I don't give 'un as good as 'un sends. Giles! Ted! lay hold of the monkey, he be a-tearing my precious eyes out!"

And he clung to them with all the intensity of insanity.

In vain they tried to calm him. When the doctor arrived, Tommy was shaking in all the dread symptoms of delirium.

Upon the case being stated to the surgeon, he advised him to be carried up to bed immediately, while Susan was dispatched for a hair-dresser.

In less than ten minutes Tommy Jolter was in bed, partly insensible.

The doctor then applied chloroform very slightly, and while under its soothing influence his head was cleanly and smoothly shaved, a large poultice, completely covering it, placed upon it; and then, a composing draught having been administered, Tommy fell in a still, deep slumber, though he kept occasionally dreaming that he was in a "wilderness of monkeys," and that they were all grinning and tearing at him.

Giles having introduced Norman Campbell to Mrs. Wilson, the three agreed to sit and watch over Tommy, and have a little converse with each other.

"Well, ye see," said Norman in reply to Giles, "I have somewhat altered my opinions, since I set out on my lang journey from the worthy Doctor's, and I just thought that I had treated baith of you once wrang; but, you see, we Scots don't jump to conclusions in a hurry; we hae sense enow to confess when we are in the wrang, and I can truly say upon ma conscience, and with my whole heart, that I respect and esteem you baith."

And the frank Scot held out a hand to each.

Giles and Ted grasped them warmly.

"By the powers, I always said you were a credit to the Land of the Heather, and if it came to my turn to be born again, I'd choose Scotland, just by way of a change, Giles."

"I suppose you're tired of your own quiet place, eh, Ted?" and Giles smiled.

"Ah, weel, I have heard my father say 'bluid is unco' thicker than water,' but the bluid of the Scot is as warm to his native land and his friend as any in the warld, and into all the canny nooks and corners of the great globe the Scotchman has carried his courage, his learning, and his perseverance, and left behind him a proud name; eh, sirs, what do you think of that?"

"Think?—that you have gallantly spoken the truth, Norman, and we honour you and your noble country."

"Thank ye, Giles, and you, Ted, and when you want a friend call upon Norman Campbell, and if he is within hearing, he'll soon be at your elbow."

Here the conversation was interrupted by the door of the room flying open, and in bounced Suke, followed by Flipper.

The trio started up, and placed themselves before the bed, the doctor having left strict injunctions that quiet should be observed.

"What have you done with Tommy?" she asked.

"Don't spake so loud, Miss Jolter. Your brother is very ill," said Ted.

"Yah! I daresay he is, and it's all

through you, I firmly believe. You can't deceive I, Mr. Flam. I can look as clean through a milestone as you can. Yah! you're a nice boy. I arn't forgotten the soup yet."

"But don't make such a noise, Miss Jolter," said Giles.

"Shall. Where's Tommy?"

"In bed."

"Yah! In bed! What for?"

"Very ill. Had his head shaved."

"Yah! What for? He hadn't got any hair left. Your brother monkey took care of that," and Suke gave one of her choicest grins. "Let me see 'un."

"No," said Giles, firmly. "You must not."

"What! Must not see my own brother Tommy? Why, the world's at an end."

"I think it is," murmured Flipper.

"Yah! If you don't let I pass, I'll give thee some marks that shall last thee some time, I'll warrant me."

And Suke pulled up her sleeves to prepare for action.

"Now, Miss Jolter——" said Ted Flan.

"Don't thee Jolter I. I tell thee, let me get to Tommy."

"We can't," said the three, firmly.

"I'll soon see about that. Thee hadst best look out for squalls."

And so saying, she made a rush at them.

Giles seized her tightly by the arms, while she began to kick and was about to give them what she warned them to look out for—squalls—when Ted Flan, catching up a towel, effectually gagged her.

Then, Flipper, with excellent presence of mind, and great dexterity, caught Suke's legs, and Norman helping Giles, she was carried comfortably out of the room just as Tommy began to show great restlessness.

Carried into another room, she was quietly placed in a seat.

Giles, Ted, and Norman, then released her.

We have before noticed Suke's complexion, but her pent-up anger and rage had thrown an additional glow upon its natural fiery colour as she glared round from one to the other.

Flipper, perceiving this, quickly beat a retreat to acquaint her mistress.

"You see, Miss Jolter," said Giles, we——"

What Giles was about to say, was effectually cut short by Suke seizing the poker.

The next moment she found herself alone, and fastened in, Ted having dexterously turned the key in the lock.

"Miss Jolter, my darlin'," said Ted, through the keyhole, "will you listen to me?"

Whack went the poker, and smash went the looking-glass.

"Och, murder, Giles! the looking-glass has gone to smithereens."

"Miss Jolter," said Giles.

Whack came the poker against the door.

"Wood and iron claiming acquaintance," said Ted, with a grin. "Don't be a fool, my angel."

"Yah! I'll tell thee who is the fool when I get out. Open the door, and let I go to Tommy."

"No; it is against the orders of the doctor," said Giles.

"Yah! old Nick take the doctor. If thee don't let I loose I'll joomp out of the window!"

At that moment Mrs. Wilson, who had been informed of all that was going on, and had called in a gentleman in blue, made her appearance just as Suke uttered her threat.

The policeman opened the door, and Suke, flying out with the poker, was caught by him, while at the same moment Tommy, who had been alarmed at the noise, jumped out of bed and ran out of the room, fancying the baboon was after him again, and there he stood at the door, with the poultice half off his poor bare poll, exhibiting such a ludicrous picture of fright that the gravity of the situation was entirely upset.

CHAPTER XXIII.

A DARK NIGHT'S WORK.

UPON the night that the deadly struggle occured between Alfred Ravensborne and Dick the jockey, the latter fearing that he had killed his master, fled from the stable, and, gaining the High Street, turned swiftly down a lane, and passed over the bridge to the other side of the river.

Here he paused, and listened intently, for he had fancied more than once during his flight that he was being pursued.

Casting his eyes over the river, he saw lights flashing about in the villa, and could plainly see the shadows of persons hurrying to and fro.

"The young 'un is killed, I fear," he muttered, between his close-set teeth; "it was an infernal fall for both of us. Well, p'r'aps, take it altogether, it's lucky he was the underneath one; but I feel cursedly shaken myself. Ah! there go the lights again; the young one must be bad for all that bother. What's to be done, eh?"

And he stood reflecting for a moment.

"I have it; they none of them know that I was there, and so I'll go back, and see what information I can gain. All this is owing to that Giles Evergreen."

And he ground his teeth with rage.

"Here goes," he said.

And, buttoning up his coat, he passed again rapidly over the bridge, and entered the public-house that stood at the corner.

Scarcely had he entered the place, when one of the servants at the villa passed on hurriedly.

"Hulloa! what's that you, Dick?" he said. "Pretty goings on up at the willer, old fellow."

"Indeed," said the jockey; "what's the matter now?"

"Murder, robbery, and arson!" replied the footman.

"Eh, what do you mean?" and Dick

assumed his usual coolness of demeanour.

"Murder! who is murdered?"

"Why, the young one" (be it known the footman, a young hand, had a very powerful imagination); "dead with fractured skull; there must have been at least half-a-dozen of them in it."

"Half-a-dozen what?" said Dick, with a sneer.

"Thieves, robbers! I saw three of them rush from the place; I seized two of them, and shouted loudly for help, but they tripped me up, and got away."

"Did they?" and Dick stared at him, almost doubting whether he was asleep or awake. "What sort of men were they?"

"Sort of men—why, I should think they were—ah! let me see. Why, you see, it was dark, and——"

"Dark! why the moon was shining, and——"

"Ah, yes, that's all very well; but, at the time that I laid hold of them, the moon went behind a dark cloud, and shut them all out. They were both very tall men."

"Did you see their faces?"

"No; that was not very likely when they wore large, black masks; and such knives in their hands, it makes my blood run cold to think of it. I'll take two pen'orth more."

"I daresay your blood did run cold; but what about Master Alfred?"

"What about him? He was picked up by that daring young blade, Evergreen, and his friend, the Irishman. No doubt he was set upon in the grounds, robbed, half-murdered, and then carried to the stable to linger out his miserable existence."

"And you say he is dead?"

"No; they say so."

"They! Who the devil do you mean?"

"Why, the doctor, and my lady and all of them; but the worst part of the story is to come."

"Indeed."

"Yes; it's awful."

"Is it? Let's have it."

"Well, would you believe it?"

"Well, scarcely."

"They tried to set fire to the stables, and so burn the body; it was burning in your room."

"In my room?"

"Yes; and if it hadn't have been for my presence of mind, the whole place, willer, and missus and servants, would have perished in the uniwersal conflaberation."

"Ha, ha, ha! you make me laugh," said Dick.

"Well, it's no laughing matter; and —oh! I say, I'd nearly forgot."

"Forgot what?"

"Why, my lady, directly she saw it all, asked for——"

"Whom?"

"You. 'Where's the groom—Martingale?' she said."

"Asked for me?"

And Dick's face turned pale.

"Yes. 'Where is the groom—Martingale?' was the question."

"'Left some hours since, my lady,' answered one of the men; and so you had, you know."

"Of course; I had been looking after another place, and I am in great hopes I shan't be long in getting one. But all this is a great mystery to me."

And Dick looked the man full in the face.

"And so it is to everybody else. But, however, I must be off. It will be rather an awkward affair if the young one is dead. I shouldn't like to stand in the chap's shoes; should you, Dick, eh?"

"No; I shouldn't be surprised if that *popular* young gentleman, Giles Evergreen, isn't at the bottom of it," replied he, after a pause.

"You don't say so, Dick?" And the man opened his eyes as if a new light had struck in upon him. "Why, now I come to think of it, they had a bit of a row in the drawing-room together.

"A bit of a row! Why, it's plain enough. They always hated one another at school. Well, then, can't you see that that fellow Evergreen has crept into the good graces of Lady St. George and Miss Hilda, and so sent Master Alfred to the rightabout?"

"Well, I think you have hit the right nail on the head, and so I shall tell them when I get home."

"Mind, I only guess at it, so it will be just as well to keep my name out of the affair—you understand me?"

"Oh, yes," replied the other, with a knowing wink. "Good-night."

And so saying, the man hastened from the house.

Dick chuckled within himself at the ruse he had played off upon the servant.

The next moment he began to reflect what had best be done as far as regarded himself.

"I'll make for London," muttered he.

"The distance is not great. I'll find out Dark Davy, and consult him upon the matter. Aye, aye; I think that is the best thing to be done. I am too late for a train, and so I'll walk it."

Ordering a small flask to be filled with spirit, Dick Martingale buttoned up his coat, and was about starting on his journey, when he perceived the same man-servant running towards the house at great speed.

Fancying that this sudden return was in some manner connected with himself, he quickly withdrew into a dark recess which stood close to the door.

Here he could see and listen to anything which might occur relating to himself.

"Where is Dick Martingale?" asked the servant.

"Gone," was the curt reply.

"Gone—where?"

"How should I know, James? What's up?"

"A lot, I think. I happened to mention his name to my lady, and she bade me instantly find him, and bring him to the willer."

"Ah, the 'willer' as you call it has been talked about all day, all through the town."

"But where is he gone?" asked the man.

"To Halifax, for what I know," grinned the landlord. "How is young Ravensborne, eh?"

"As queer as he can be; hasn't got any sense or motion; barely lives, the doctors say. If they could only restore him to his blessed faculties, he might be able to say who the murderous assassin was; however, off I am."

And away he sped back to the villa.

"So, so," muttered Dick, when he had watched him disappear, "the scent grows rather warm, and the sooner I am in London the better. He'll be able to say who it was—aye, aye! he may, but then they will have to find him."

And so saying, he stealthily crept from his hiding-place, and was soon walking at a rapid pace towards London.

We leave him for the present on his journey, and return to the Jolter family.

The sight and determined bearing of the policeman for the moment tamed the young vixen, Suke, but she kept casting looks of grim defiance at Giles and Ted.

"Now, Miss Jolter, what is the reason of all this disturbance in my establishment?" asked Mrs. Wilson.

"Yah! what be the reason? You know well enough; and if not, ask that boy, the wild Irish one and his companion; it be all through them."

And Suke looked as if she was going to make a dash at them.

"Keep off, you cantankerous warmint!" shouted Tommy. "It be all through you and the monkey at the 'Logical Gardens that I got my head shaved, and this puddin' stuck on it; but I don't care so much so that old baboon had a grip at thine, and gotten his fingers burnt for it."

Then Tommy was led into his room by his companions, while Mrs. Wilson went into that of Suke.

The sight that met the astonished lady's eyes was a most extraordinary one; the chairs and tables were all overturned, and the looking-glass that stood upon a dressing table was broken into fragments.

Such a scene of wreck the good old lady had not in the course of her life ever witnessed before.

"Well, Miss Jolter, upon my word this is the most extraordinary behaviour that ever——"

"Yah, shut up! I don't want any palavering. Well, what are you staring at, like a couple of sucking calves at a gate, eh?" she said, turning upon the policeman and Flipper.

Here Mrs. Wilson, slipping a piece of coin into the hand of the officer, whispered to him to go below, the man almost choking with suppressed laughter.

"A month would be of great service to her," he muttered, as he went downstairs.

"Well, what are you and that gawkey stopping for, eh?"

And Suke pointed to Flipper.

At this, Flipper's patience deserted her.

"I'll tell you what it is, you country gowk, I won't put up with any more of your nonsense; no, not for the best place in the world."

"Yah, who cares for you or your place? Troop your baggage, or I'll serve thee as I served the looking-glass."

"Now, Miss Jolter," expostulated Mrs. Wilson.

"Yah, don't *Miss* me; my name be plain Suke Jolter, and so was my honest mother's afore me. Don't come any of your fal-de-ral London gibberish over I, it won't do. Yah, you think you've got a green gooseberry to deal with, do you?"

And so saying, Suke jumped on the bed and sat with her red arms folded, grinning at them.

At this Mrs. Wilson's temper bristled up.

"Once for all, Miss Jolter," she said.

"Yah! I tell thee I 'on't be called Miss, I'll be called plain Suke."

"Well, then, plain Suke, I won't have this rioting in my house, and if you can't behave yourself in a proper manner, you may leave, and the sooner the better."

"So I say, mum, and a good riddance of——"

"Be quiet, Susan; I am the mistress here," said Mrs. Wilson.

"I know you are, mum, and as sich I leave you to all its benefits; but mind she don't set fire to the house with that light atop of her head," and Susan sarcastically pointed to Suke and her fiery tresses.

"You'd best keep your tongue quiet, Miss Mops and Brooms, or I'll make thee," said Suke.

"Keep quiet for you, indeed! the idea!"

"Susan, will you hold your tongue?"

"No, mum, I will not. Mops and brooms! what does she mean by that? I may be a sarvant girl, but I've got my feelings as well as the finest lady in all the land, the 'evens be praised."

"Well, well, Susan."

"No, no, it's not well, mum; I've been a good and faithful sarvant to you for years, but rather than be called Mops and Brooms, I'll brush, and there's an end of it," and Susan lifted the corner of her apron to her eyes.

"There, Miss Jolter, you see what you have done," said Mrs. Wilson.

"Yah! I arn't done anything; she ain't crying, she's gammoning; I've seen lots of it at the farm."

And Suke grinned.

"Yes, with your relations, the pigs," was Flipper's retort.

This was enough.

Down jumped Suke, and away ran Flipper, while Mrs. Wilson sent forth a piercing scream that brought the boys out of their room.

Now, our friend the policeman had been taking a glass of treble X with Butler Jones, and was upon the point of leaving the house; hearing the scream, he rushed up stairs, but was met by the flying Flipper, hotly chased by the fiery Suke, the rear being brought up by Giles, Ted, Norman, and Tommy, the whole closed in by the alarmed landlady, who stood on the top.

The gallant policeman held out his arms to catch the fugitives, forgetful of the risk and danger he might bring upon himself; into them fled Flipper and Suke, and down half-a-dozen stairs they rolled at the moment Jones had opened the door to a knock, admitting Farmer Jolter and the stock broker, while the boys stood half way down the stairs, roaring at the fun.

The farmer seeing, as he thought, Suke and the girl in danger, laid hold of them and pulled them on their legs; but no sooner had the "gallant blue" gained his, than Jolter seized him by the collar and shook him like a rat.

"Fire zeize thee! what be thee at with the women, eh?" roared Jolter.

"Take your hands off me," gasped

the policeman; "don't obstruct me in the execution of my duty."

"Who wants to obstruct or construct thee in thy duty? But what art thee touzelling the gals for, eh? Send for a constable, I'll give thee in charge."

"No, no," called out Mrs. Wilson, in a loud voice; "it's all right, Mr. Jolter."

"Oh, is it, marm? Well, it's the first time I've seen it all right in that fashion." So saying, he let go the policeman, then seizing Suke by the arm, he asked, "What's thee been doing, eh, Suke?"

"Yah! nothing, feyther," replied Suke.

"Oh! miss," said Flipper.

"Susan Flipper," interrupted Mrs. Wilson, sternly, "go below directly."

"Certainly, mum; talk of 'mancipating the black niggers, why don't they think of the white ones, the poor sarvant girls?" and Susan, turning up her nose at Suke, went below.

"I will explain it all, Mr. Jolter— Walmisley and the rest, pray retire— it's all a mistake, and can be easily cleared up."

"Oh! wi' all my heart, marm. Heart alive, Tommy, what have you been doing to your head? Where bee'st thy hair, lad?"

"Monkey got part, and barber the rest, feyther," replied Tommy; "thee'll have to buy me a wig."

"Thee can'st buy that thyself, my lad; uncle left thee plenty of money."

"What dost thee say, feyther?"

"Come in here, all of you, and I'll tell thee," and, so saying, they went into an adjoining room, followed by Mrs. Wilson, who had placed the shaken policeman in the safe custody of the butler to cure all his wounds, outwardly and inwardly.

"Well, Mr. Jolter," said Mrs. Wilson, when they were all seated, "and, pray, how have you got on today?"

"Well, marm, the goings on of today have been wonderful loike," was the reply.

"Yes, I think they have, indeed," said the lady, with a significant look at Tommy and Suke. "Have you seen the lawyers?"

"Ees, there's no mistake about that; they arn't such fools to be out of the way when the pudding is on the table, and there's plenty of plums in it," and the farmer had a grin at his joke, in which Suke joined.

"Well, and what is the result?"

"Well, it arn't a bad 'un, if all turns out well; but we has a curious old saying down at the farm, about not counting chickens afore they're out o' the shell, arn't we, Suke?"

"Yes; and it be a downright good 'un," said the young lady.

"Well, you see, marm, to cut the matter short, for I'm main hungry and tired, and, I may say, frightened!"

"Frightened!"

"Ees. Arn't the sights of Lunnon enough to frighten any one? Why, in the whole course of my life, I never saw such riding and driving; why, they'd think no more of driving over a body than I should over a dead cat, and danged if they don't do it in a curious fashion; they run you down and knock the wind out of your carcase, and call out, 'Why don't you get out of the way, stoopid?'"

"Well, but about the lawyers," for the old lady was all anxiety to hear the news.

"Ah! well, that's all right; Faithful, Son, and Steady, be right down good men for lawyers, and, I dare say, there's lots like them; old Tough Mutton, for instance, and——"

"But about the money, feyther?" said Suke.

"Suke wants to finger it, feyther," called out Tommy.

"It's more than thee'll do, pudding head," was Suke's reply.

"There thee's wrong, lass; Tommy can buy thy feyther out stock and fluke," he replied.

"Yah! thee's talking nonsense."

"It's all in black and white. Why, thy uncle Tommy Jolter knew how many beans made five when he went a digging to Horsestrayliar, I warrant me."

"Yah! digging's the same everywhere."

"There thee beest in the wrong; down in our parts we dig up taters, carrots, and sich like things, but where uncle went to, why, lumps o' gold's as common as turnips. Eh, I wish I'd gone wi' Tommy; why, he's left——"

"Yah! what?"

"Lumps!"

"Lamps of what? You've been tackling the old yale, feyther, and it's made thee nappy," said Suke.

"I'll tackle thee, if thee dost sarce I, my lass."

"Sarce, she's full of sarce, feyther," said Tommy.

"Hold thy tongue, Tommy, or thee'll be painted with the same brush. Well, then, Uncle Tommy went up to the diggin's, and made money as fast as I seen thy mother make rolls and turnovers; and when he'd made enough, he went back to yon place, and sent it over to Bank of England. The old gentleman there," pointing to Walmisley, "showed I the place, and told I it belonged to an 'old lady' with a darned long stocking, in Thread-my-needle Street, and I went there and axed to see her to know if all was right, and a man big as thy feyther said she'd gone out to tea, and I'd better call again to-morrow; and so I mean, I can tell thee."

Here the farmer paused, and Jones entering with some refreshment, took a jug of ale to him, and then announced that dinner would be on the table very shortly.

Old Jolter having affectionately lightened the jug, resumed his story.

"Well, the upshot of it was that Uncle Tommy intended coming home, but he fell sick and made his will, leaving all his money to his next-of-skin; that means old Jolter, Tommy, and Suke, we be the three next of-skins—and then the lawyers put it in the papers, and old Tough Mutton (leave him alone) found it out, and—phew—it takes away my breath to tell the rest."

"Yah! out wi' it, and then get thy breath, feyther. He left I a lot, I know," said Suke.

"Not a brass varden."

"Then what's the use of being next-of-skin? Then he left it thee."

"He left I five thousand pounds, like a good brother."

"Yah ! is that all he died worth?" asked Suke.

"Na, my lass, put forty and five to that, cast it up, and what do you make on it ?"

"Why, that make fifty thoosand pounds, feyther. Where be the rest going ?"

"It do all belong to Tommy, there."

"What !" said Suke, with a scream, "Soft Tommy worth forty-five thousand pounds !"

"Every varden, and p'r'aps more."

Tommy, who had been sitting with Giles, Ted, and Norman, with his mouth wide open, no sooner heard this than off went the pudding from his head into Suke's face, and he sprang into the middle of the room, and began shouting and dancing as if he were mad.

"Forty-five thousand pounds !" he shouted ; " I'll be a dook, hurrah ! I'll marry a duchess, hurrah ! I'll give all the boys at the old school as much bacon and cabbage as they can cram and stoof, hurrah ! I'll build up old school again, and we'll all go back, Giles, Ted and Norman, and all—and—Ha ! ha ! ha ! dang it, we'll burn it down again, just for the fun of the thing, and to make the brass fly, hurrah ! hurrah ! hurrah !"

And here he became so exhausted, that the poor excited boy would have fallen had not Giles and Ted caught him in their arms.

He soon recovered and then he ran up to his father.

"Feyther, thee'll have a lot of it ;"

and, throwing his arms round Suke's neck—

"Suke, I'll make thee a lady !" he said, kissing her.

"Yah ! nobody can do that, Tommy. I wish thee joy, my lad, and I hope thee'll buy a monkey," said Suke, with a grin.

"I'll buy thee a husband, Suke, and that will be the same thing. Giles Evergreen, thee saved my life twice, and I'll give thee half ; and Ted, I'll give——"

"Whist, Tommy, my honey ; I'll give you something first." And with that he clapped the poultice on Tommy's head. "Suppose the old lady should bolt, eh, and forget to leave her stocking behind her ? I've heard she is of a very changeable character. I say, Norman, what do you do when you lay hold of a thistle ?"

"We grasp it tight, my mon," was the reply.

"Then by the powers, you do the likes with your money, Tommy, when you get it, and I hope your shiners won't be like one of my countrymen's."

"What was that, Ted ?" asked Giles.

"Moon-shiners, my honey," was the reply.

Here dinner was announced, and away went the whole party, full of fun and lightheartedness, to enjoy it.

The evening was passed in mirth and glee at the day's adventures, those of Tommy being at the head of the poll.

*   *   *   *   *

We left Dick Martingale hastening on the road to London, and the feelings of the crafty and subtle fellow were not of the most enviable description.

He had, like a great many others, over-reached himself, and by his endeavouring to grasp too much, he stood a fair chance of losing all.

"Well, it goes against the grain, but I must see Dark Davy, and take him into my confidence. All my own fault at leaving those papers under the pillow in my room. Ah, but he didn't get the right ones. And then how the young imp fought! Aye, aye; the old blood—the old blood! But then suppose he should die and have made a clean breast of it! Why, then, Dick Martingale, you'll pay a visit to a spot a long way off, and not at your own expense."

At this moment he had arrived at one of the old inns on the road, where the market gardeners stop on their way to the great Covent Garden Market to take rest for their horses and refreshment for themselves.

Into this place, therefore, Dick walked, and going into a room that was both kitchen and parlour, found it so full that he barely got a seat.

The men assembled there were not only discussing their breakfasts, but were whiling away the time by playing cards.

Dick called for breakfast, and while partaking of it, narrowly scanned the men assembled in the room, but more particularly the little knot that sat near him.

"I think I can make something out of this lot," he muttered, "and I may as well earn a trifle as be idle."

The party were playing their game unskilfully, a fact that did not escape his keen penetration.

At last one of the party, in a rage, threw up his cards.

"I'll take his place, if you like," said Dick, "just for a game or two."

"With all our hearts," was the reply, and Dick rising, changed seats with the late player, which placed him close to the door.

Game after game was played, heavy betting went on, and Dick was pulling in the money heavily, and the excitement was at its greatest height, this being the last game, it wanting only a short time to daylight, and the green men must make the best of their way to the market.

Suddenly a countryman called out—

"I say, guvnors, that man be a magicianer; blessed if one of the cards baint flown up his sleeve."

Up sprang Dick; the potman stood in the way; but in an instant he went flying into the bar, and the jockey the next moment was in the road, and racing up it with the speed of lightning.

There was a rush to the door, amid loud shouts and execrations, and a mad gallop up the road; but Dick could have run any of them for their lives, and given them a trifle in advance.

It was to no purpose they ran or roared, they were compelled to proceed to market, inwardly growling and confessing that they had been sold before their goods—a just punishment upon them for indulging in such a pernicious habit.

The men galloped their horses and vehicles furiously up the road, but all in vain. Dick had managed to conceal himself in a thick hedge, and quietly laughed as they rushed past him with heavy hearts and lightened pockets, hurling fierce denunciations of their wrath upon his crafty head.

A short time he allowed to pass, and then he sprang again into the road.

All was silent, and he resumed his journey.

He had not, however, proceeded far, when a light cart overtook him.

"Hulloa, my lad, are you bound for town?" was the question asked by the driver.

"Yes, I am," was the prompt reply.

"What will you stand for a ride, eh?"

"Half-a-crown, and a drink whenever you like," said Dick.

"You're my man; jump up; I should like to pick up half-a-dozen more like you."

Dick was soon up, and alongside the driver, a butcher lad, bound to Newgate Market, and off they started.

In a very few minutes Martingale could tell what sort of an animal he was seated behind. At the rattling pace the beautiful creature, so full of bone, blood and muscle—for when did you ever see a butcher behind a bad horse?—was going, they would soon outstrip the gentlemen who were so anxious to see him.

"I say, pull up here, and let's have something," said Dick.

"With all my heart," was the reply.

And so saying, he stopped at a public-house, and here, in order to delay the time, they rather copiously indulged.

Soon they were off again and at an increased speed, because the butcher wanted to make up the lost time; and so fleetly did the seventh descendant of a Derby winner rattle on his way, that Dick soon discerned the carts of his friends in the distance.

"Curse the fellow, how he goes," he muttered. "I'd give him breath, if I were you," said he to his companion.

"Stuff, my lad," said the butcher; "that's nothing to what he can do; you'll see how I'll put him past that lot of carts."

"Mind what you're about," said Dick.

The butcher was a boy not more than sixteen, and he saw with great anxiety that the day was fast breaking.

"Mind what?" said the boy, with a curl of his lip. "Why, I'd drive him fast asleep. Why, you ain't frightened, are yer?"

If the boy had only known that the half boy, half man, that sat beside him, had won a Derby!

"Frightened! well, not exactly," was the reply.

"Then, we'll soon cut the cabbages," said the boy, with a grin.

Dick pulled his hat down over his eyes, and trusted to the speed of the horse and luck to carry him through.

With that peculiar sound they know how to convey to their high mettled steeds, the little Beauty seemed as though it would fly out of the harness, and, like a flash of lightning, it went dashing past the gardeners' carts.

The driver of the leading one, hearing the rushing of the trap behind him, looked round.

In an instant he recognised Dick.

He made a blow at him with his whip.

But falling short, he cried out—

"There he goes! there he goes!" at which they raised a shout.

The butcher, taking it for a challenge, sent forth a shout of defiance, which Dick encouraged by giving another, which, if possible, increased the speed of the horse.

Now it so happened that the first cart had not only a light load of cabbages, but a fast bit of blood in the shaft; so, giving his horse the reins, he started off in hot pursuit of the "magicianer," up whose sleeve the card flew, followed by all the others at a furious gallop.

The morning now having fairly broken, the world seemed suddenly to have sprung into life and animation.

As they came rushing along, the people going to their work gave them a rattling cheer that roused the poor drowsy policemen and the heavy sleeping cabmen, who greeted them with a husky sort of foggy "view halloa!" at this race between "Beef and Greens."

Well and gallantly did the butcher's "Beauty" carry out his noble blood and pedigree, and gamely did the gardener's "Bloomer" struggle after him; the latter kept losing weight by the cabbages every now and then flying right and left among the astonished bystanders.

There was no chance of the latter catching the former, so just as he was nearing Hyde Park Corner, the butcher being "lost to sight yet to memory dear," the gardener began to pull in, when down with a crash came cart, cabbages and grower; the linch-pin, unused to such extraordinary treatment, fell quietly into the road, the vehicle rapidly following its example, while the Bloomer, released, went after the Beauty at a slapping pace.

When Dick had arrived in Trafalgar Square, he asked the boy to stop.

Pleased with the little fellow's skill in handling the reins, he gave him a crown piece, and, thanking him, walked off.

"I say, guv'nor, if you do it like this, give us a call every morning, will yer?"

And off he drove.

Feeling somewhat relieved at having escaped from his pursuers, but likewise feeling that he was, from the excitement and the drink he had taken, anything but right, he made up his mind for a short stroll, and thought Covent Garden was the place for it, forgetting that it was the destination of his friends the "vegetarians;" but before doing so, he walked into a coffee-house, both for rest and refreshment, for the excitement he had undergone for the last twenty-four hours had somewhat exhausted both mind and body.

It happened on that morning, the one after Tommy's adventures, that Giles, Ted, and Norman had determined to visit the market in order to purchase some flowers to present to Mrs. Wilson, who was remarkably fond of them.

They were early risers, a blessing so conducive to the health of all, but which so few practise, and so between five and six o'clock, with the ruddy glow of health upon their handsome cheeks, their lithe a d well-developed forms rendered more so by the proper use of the manly exercises, added to the style, dress, and deportment of gentlemen, off they started.

Having ascertained from James the night before the way to it from Gower Street, it was easily found by them.

At the sight of this splendid depôt of choice fruit and flowers, they were both surprised and delighted, but out of the happy trio, none more so than Ted, who, at the scene of bustle and excitement going on, determined to have some fun.

"Would you want a basket, your lordship's highness?" said an old woman to him.

"An' what would I be doing with a basket, mother?" replied Ted, in his broadest brogue.

"Och, but the Heavens be your bed, but you come from the blessed land—it wouldn't hurt my mouth, or give me the slightest toothache, to drink your health this blessed morning, cushla. I can see by the eye that you've got the rale Irish blood in yer, and that you wouldn't hould out your hand but there be a summat in it."

Here Ted put his hand in his pocket.

"Here, Biddy—Molly—come hither, avourneen, did you ever see such jims of the say? Oh, I'd been prouder than the Queen of Chanay to have been their mother or their aunt, or even their uncle, for the matter of that. Talk of a flower-show, we've got it this morning, anyhow!"

Here the crowd of porters round them became so pressing that Ted thought a little of his ventriloquial powers might be of service; he therefore threw his voice a little before him—

"Basket! basket! basket!"

"Here, here, here, your honour!"

And away rushed a dozen of them to the spot, stumbling over each other and falling in their anxiety to reach the spot; but greater surprise was caused among the anxious basket men and women when they were told that no one called them.

"Sure you are larking with us," said one of them to a stout, red-faced old gentleman, who was trying to cheapen a lot of capsicums, "and you ought to know better than to do so to poor honest men who are trying to get a living. Let us give him a groan, my boys."

At this the face of the gentleman became the colour of the article he was buying.

"I tell you, you vagabonds, I didn't call you," said the angry gentleman.

"Ah, by the powers, that is his very voice!"

"I'd swear to it," answered another.

"Here, beadle! police! I'll give the lot of you in custody if you molest me, you shirtless vagabonds!"

"Shirts! By the powers, when you next call for a basket may it be one to carry you to the bone-house. Bad luck to you!"

And the men walked away.

And then the boys, enjoying the joke, made the best of their way to another part of the market.

A few minutes after, while they were purchasing some flowers, Giles felt a hand placed upon his shoulder.

Turning angrily round, he saw standing close to him his old enemy, Dick Martingale.

The fellow had been indulging in more drink, and his countenance plainly

"THE FLIGHT OF FLIPPER."

showed that he was reckless and bent upon mischief.

Giles shook the villain's hand off his shoulder.

"How dare you, contemptible scoundrel, place your hands upon my person?" he indignantly asked.

"Had you done that to me, my mon, I hae made ye kiss your mither earth," said Norman; and the brave Scotch lad buttoned up his coat and advanced towards him.

"Don't you interfere between me and this chap," said the ruffian. "I came to London to look after you, and I am very glad I've found you."

"Are you, my fine fellow?" said a rough voice, "and I am glad I've found you," and a brown, brawny hand laid hold of him firmly by the collar. "Here Dick, Tom, Bill, I found the magicianer."

He had fallen into the hands of one of the men he had cheated at cards.

In a moment he was surrounded by the rest.

He made a blow at the man who held him, but his arms were caught and held down tightly by his side.

The next moment a stinging lash from a heavy whip rang upon his back —another, another, and another followed in quick succession.

Giles, Ted, and Norman looked on with the greatest astonishment at this strange scene.

"You are a nice lot, four to one upon a man. Suppose I have done wrong, are you going to murder me, eh?" and Dick glared savagely round.

"Wilt thee give back the money thee robbed us of?" said one of the men.

"Put him under the pump!" shouted the others.

Matters looked fearfully serious for Dick Martingale.

At this moment a couple of policemen came up and rescued the jockey out of the hands of his rough assailants.

After hearing the case pro and con, they looked at each other as if uncertain what to do.

The doubt they felt with regard to the case was cut short by Dick himself.

"I'll walk with you myself to the station-house and answer any charge these drunken fellows may have to make against me," said Dick, with an air of injured innocence.

"Ah, that's right, my lad, that's the way to meet it," said the policeman. "Come along, there's not a man of them sober."

"They had no right to assault me in any case," boldly blustered Dick, "and I'll make them smart for it, as well as some others I know something about."

And he gave Giles and his companions, who were looking on at this strange scene, a look of peculiar meaning.

Giles returned it with one of the most supreme contempt.

Away went the whole party, Dick leading the way with a guard of honour (blues) on each side, followed by two of the men who had assailed him.

The rest had slunk away to their respective waggons and carts, thinking a certain business better than any uncertain decision of a police-court.

The charge against Dick having been

duly made and entered, and a counter-charge made by Dick for an aggravated assault, they then all made their way over to the police-court.

Following the crowd, and anxious to see the result of the matter, Giles, Ted, and Norman passed into the court with the rest of the motley group.

CHAPTER XXIV.

JUSTICE DEFEATED.

No sooner was Dick placed at the bar than a man rose up at the attorney's table and shook hands with him.

That man was Dark Davy.

"What's all this about, eh, Martingale? Didn't expect to see you here."

And Dark Davy looked searchingly at him.

"I daresay not, any more than I expected to see you. What do you do here?"

"A little business."

"Anything serious?"

"You'll soon hear and judge for yourself. I shall watch the case for you."

"Just as you like. I'm rather muddled myself and might mull it."

"Right; a man that is his own lawyer——"

Dark Davy's remark was cut short by the clerk asking who charged the prisoner, and an answer having been given, Dark Davy rose and said "he had the honour to appear for the person placed at the bar."

Now, when the first witness (the market gardener who came to grief in the chase) entered the witness-box, Dark Davy saw his way clear.

He had been indulging rather freely in a drink compounded of beer and old Tom, and that, in conjunction with the loss of his money, the unlucky tumble from his cart, and the worry and vexation all mingled together, he was anything but clear-headed.

His evidence was incoherent and incomprehensible; it puzzled the magistrate and the officials, and when Dark Davy, recalling to the unfortunate man's memory, more than once, that he was upon his oath, and warning him to be careful, or he might find himself at the bar of the Old Bailey upon a charge of conspiracy, he fairly broke down.

"The witness is not sober," said the magistrate, "and not a word he says is to be believed. Let him leave the court."

"Not so; with your worship's permission, I have a serious charge of assault against him," said Dark Davy.

"Oh, very well; any other witness?"

"Yes, your worship," said the inspector.

And the other market gardener stepped into the box.

If anything he was worse than the preceding one, and was in such a confused state of mind that the magistrate indignantly dismissed the case, and Mr. Richard Martingale was free.

"Now, then, comes my turn," whispered he to Dark Davy.

Finally, the charge of assault was substantially proved against them, and the magistrate severely lectured them.

Then, with an air of great magnanimity, Mr. Davy interposed.

His client had no vindictive motive.

His character having been fully vindicated, he should feel satisfied by their confessing they were wrong in their conduct and in the charge brought against him, and contributing a sovereign each to the box for the relief of necessitous cases.

The magistrate assented to this humane view of the case.

The two men looked at each other with such puzzled expressions of countenance, as if asking each other if the whole affair was real or not, that it caused a general titter throughout the court.

However, there was no alternative, so, with the greatest reluctance and hesitation, they "confessed themselves in the wrong," begged pardon, and, putting down a sovereign each towards the poor-box, were duly cautioned how they made such mistakes again, and left the court, only to receive outside a complete ovation of jeers and mock congratulations from their friends and acquaintances.

"We will not leave the court directly, Ted and Norman," whispered Giles. "I do not want to come into collision with that fellow, Martingale."

"By the cross of St. Andrew, the deil a bit am I afraid of him; and if he comes any tricks upon me, I'd give him a touch of a Scotch fist that should make his lug ding for a week," said Norman.

"Afraid!" said Ted; "that's a word not in our dictionary. But Giles is right; in this case discretion is the better part of valour."

In a short time after this the court was cleared, and the three friends walked out and again went into the market.

During this time, Dick and Dark Davy held a brief consultation.

"Giles Evergreen and his friend are in the court. Let him be followed; I want to know where he is to be found."

"Right."

They had now emerged from the court, and walked gently up the street, followed by a singular, shabby-looking individual, with a peculiar shambling gait.

Stopping at the entrance of a court that commanded a view of the police-office, they stood intently watching it.

"Who is that fellow?" said Dick to Davy.

"He is called 'Shambling Jack,' the very man we want. Here, Jack, do you see those three lads?"

"What, them 'ere?" the man replied in guttural tones, composed of spirit, fog and tobacco. "Yes, I sees them."

"Follow them and tell me where they go to. You'll see me at the 'Den' to-night."

And he slipped half-a-crown in his hand.

"Ha, ha! never fear me, they won't 'scape Shambling Jack arter this," grinning at the silver coin. "It's a pleasure to work for you, you always pays well."

And away he shambled off after the three lads, like a spirit of evil and darkness.

"They'll be all right, he'll never leave them; we shall have a good account of them," remarked Davy.

"Is he to be trusted? He looks as if a shilling would buy him to any side," said Dick.

"So it would; but I have a stronger hold upon him than money."

"What is that?"

"Fear. I have him under this."

And Davy held out his thumb.

"Ah, I see, that's better than gold."

"A thousand times. But come, let us go to my rooms; they are not far off."

Hailing a cab and giving directions, Dark Davy and his client were driven rapidly to the chambers of the former, and while doing so, we again join Giles and his companions.

They felt a pleasing sensation at leaving the close court, and exchanging its foul atmosphere for the cool shade of the central avenue of the market; they seemed to throw off a great weight and oppression at being again in the glorious free air, and were all in high spirits, especially Ted Flan, who was ripe and ready for any fun.

It was not long before an opportunity occurred for him to indulge his humour.

Looking in at one of the windows, loaded with, perhaps, some of the most magnificent fruit that eyes ever beheld, stood a sweep, with his bag on his shoulder, and evidently tolerably full; against him stood, strange to say, a man of the very opposite colour, a baker carrying a bag of flour.

There was evidently some little contention between them, and the three boys drew near to listen.

The sweep, in pushing in to look at the fruit, had left some of his colour and calling upon the sleeve of the baker, which seemed to rouse his ire.

"I say, darkey," said the baker, "mind where you're pushing."

"Hulloa, my flower, what's the matter?" was the reply. "Is it down again to even money?"

"Well, not exactly; but we don't know what may be down in the course of a day."

And he began to brush off the soot from his shirt-sleeve.

"Sorry I've sp'ilt your Sunday-going shirt. What will Maria Louisa say?"

And the sweep grinned, and showed his teeth like a set of pearls.

"What's Maria Louisa to you?" said the baker, getting awfully crusty.

"Come, move on there," said one of the beadles.

"All right, guv'nor. I'll move off as quick as a cove bolting the moon because his landlord won't take a double rent. Well, dead 'un, good-bye. Give my compliments to Maria, and say I can't take Sowshong with her until six on Sunday, because I'm churchwarden to a charity sermon, for the benefit of the Full Weight Society."

The bystanders burst into a roar of laughter as the sweep moved off.

"Go on, Chummy!" cried out a voice.

Master Ted was at it.

"Well, what do yer want with Chummy, eh, bones and alum?" said the sweep, going up to the baker.

" I didn't call yer," said the baker.

" Yes, yer did," said a voice, tipped with a slight Irish brogue.

" Come, move out of this and settle it outside," said the beadle.

And accordingly the baker and the sweep moved off, wrangling with each other, and followed by Giles, Ted, and Norman.

" I say you did, Pepper's ghost !" said the sweep.

" I say I didn't, Chimney," retorted the baker.

" I say you did !" shouted a voice.

" Now, then," said the sweep.

" Now, then," said the baker.

" Got any bones in that bag ?"

And the sweep pointed to the small bag of flour the baker had in his hand.

" How are you off for spoons in yours, eh, Chummy ?" was the reply.

" Well, that arn't so bad. I'll just feel. P'r'aps one got in by mistake. Sarvent gals are so werry careless, arn't they ?"

And the sweep, dipping his hand in his bag, pretended to feel for one.

" Well, there is a summat."

At this moment, who should join the three boys but Farmer Jolter, Tommy and Suke.

They had come out to see the market.

" Well, why don't you give it us ?" said a voice behind the baker. " Out with the spoon."

" There it is, ' Flower of the Walley,' " grinned the sweep.

And away flew a handful of soot into the baker's face, but the greater portion flew into Tommy's, who stood behind, and who, in starting back, lost his hat and red night-cap, which old Jolter had put on him to keep his head warm.

A roar of laughter burst from the crowd at Tommy's bald pate.

This was enough ; the first shot, and a black one it was, had been fired, and the battle began—black and white, like a game at chess, were hard at it.

Flour covered the sweep, while the soot had almost converted the baker into a piebald nigger.

Giles, Ted, Norman, and the crowd, enjoyed the fun, while old Jolter, Tommy, and darling Suke were covered with the contents of the sweep's bag.

But it was not fated to be kept to the two.

Decayed cabbages and stale turnips began to fly about, and the battle became general.

Farmer Jolter received a turnip in his eye, and returned the compliment by knocking an Irish porter into an empty basket, where he lay jammed and nearly choking.

Giles, Ted, and Norman dragged Tommy and Suke out of the crush, and succeeded in capturing old Jolter, and they all got safely out of the crowd, when a strong body of police rushed among them ; but the blood of the sweep was up, and he laid about him vigorously with his soot-bag, until the blues were turned into blacks.

The baker fought like a well-bred one, and the fight had become so general that it was not very easy to subdue it.

Giles and his party had got into a couple of cabs, and the last they saw of it was the sweep tied down on a stretcher, covered with soot and flour, singing, " Britons never will be slaves," followed by the baker on a stretcher, with his colour sable from head to foot ; a dozen others followed in custody, and such was the crowd that had congregated and swelled as it passed along, that Bow Street was, for a time totally impassable.

When the cab containing Giles, Ted, Tommy and Suke drove off, a man with a shambling run followed it, keeping within a respectable distance from it.

Shambling Jack knew his business, for he had practised it for many years and was the first of his class in London ; originally, he had been brought up to the law, but with a perverted taste, he had chosen the dark side of it, and instead of becoming an ornament to a great profession, he became a blot, a stain, and a disgrace to it ; down he went like an ærolite from the skies until he became a touter and hanger-on at a police-court, open to do any job however dirty or bad.

Such was Shambling Jack.

When the cab stopped Jack stood at some little distance off, and when they had driven off he walked past the house whistling, and looking up at the door, as though by accident, he had the name and number in an instant.

When he had got some distance, he took out a stump piece of pencil and a greasy, worn-out memorandum-book, and wrote :——

" Mrs. Wilson, No. —, Gower Street, Russell Square."

" Ha, ha, ha! I've got it ; thought I should have lost them in that row. Dark Davy wouldn't have been pleased ; mustn't offend old Davy, because he could put the screw on me. Wonder what he is going to do with those lads? No good ; fine lads. Ah! I remember once when I was a lad like them, and ——What are you talking about, you fool? You will be heaping coals of fire upon your own head."

He glanced at a bill stuck upon a wall.

" Humph! ' Never too Late to Mend.' Hem! thought of mending, turning over a new leaf ; almost time ; the old book is nearly worn out. Ah! we shall see."

All this Shambling Jack muttered to himself on the way to Dark Davy's den.

CHAPTER XXV.

DARK DAVY AND THE DETECTIVE.

THE den of Mr. Davy Close, one of Her Majesty's attornies-at-law, was situated in that well-known inn called Clifford's.

It was placed in a very dark corner of the ancient inn ; the stairs leading to it were very old, very narrow, and very gloomy.

A faint, musty smell pervaded it, and the person who ventured up the stairs felt an indescribable sensation of gladness when he came down them again.

The den had two cages, or rooms; the outer one was intended for a clerk or unfortunate boy that had been trapped out of some charity school, and condemned to undergo penance by sitting all day long counting the sparrows on the old black trees, and wondering what they were talking about.

No clerk had ever been known to serve Mr. Davy Close; he transacted all his business himself.

Most of his clients called upon him at night, because he was always in the City in the day.

He had lived in the chambers (the den he called them) as long as the porter could remember, and, by referring to the books, it was found that Mr. Davy Close had lived in the said den more than forty-and-four years.

In the inner room, well and comfortably furnished, sat Dark Davy the lawyer, and Richard Martingale, the jockey.

On a table before them were the skeleton remains of a fowl, a loaf of bread, and two bottles, one containing brandy, the other sherry.

Dick had made an excellent meal, and, compounding a glass of brandy and water, had thrown himself back in his chair in a "brown study."

"Well, what you have told me convinces me that you are a very clever man, Dick Martingale."

And the lawyer looked keenly at him from under his grey shaggy eyebrows.

"You think so, do you, Mr. Davy?" was the reply. "I haven't played my cards well lately, though."

"Well, no; you see, a good player ought to be cool, and never under any circumstances for one instant lose his temper. Directly you do that, your adversary will most certainly be the winner."

"As you see, we are not blessed in the same way as you are. I suppose, now, if you were surrounded by fire, you'd keep cool?"

And Dick smiled.

"As a cucumber. Don't you see that would be my only chance of escape. You lost your temper with the young one, and he'll have the best of it."

"Will he?"

"Yes."

"That's to be seen."

"Yes; and here we have the first glimpse of it."

And taking up a paper, he read as follows:—

"Daring Outrage.—A daring assault was committed upon the person of the Honourable Alfred Ravensborne, at the villa of the Lady St. George, at Richmond. The young gentleman lies in an unconscious state at present. The police have a clue to the offender, who it is to be hoped, will soon be in the hands of justice."

"That's pleasant, ain't it?"

"Who for?"

"You."

"Me! what's it to do with me?"

"Everything. You are the offender pointed at. You left the service abruptly; that little card affair will soon be known, and the detectives will be upon your track, and should the boy recover his senses, and mention your name, why then——"

"What then?" said Dick, nervously.

"Why, then, the game will be up."

"What do you advise?"

"Go back instanter; I will follow. You haven't a minute to lose. Walk about the town; go to the villa, ask after his health, disarm suspicion, and ——there, there, down with your brandy and water. Hush!"

Here Dark Davy started up and listened.

"All right, it's Shambling Jack."

"Ah, Giles Evergreen——"

"Must be left alone for the present."

Here a peculiar whistle sounded through the keyhole of the outer door.

"Come in, Jack," said Davy.

The next moment the door was opened, and Jack shambled into the room.

"Well, Jack, all right?"

"Yes."

"You never fail."

"Never."

"Where is it?"

"There."

And he placed a piece of dirty paper on the table.

"Humph!" after reading it; "saw them safe there?"

"Safe."

"Go and get a cab round at the other entrance in Fetter Lane."

"Yes."

"A four-wheeler."

"Good."

And away shambled Jack.

"Now listen. Attend to what I have said; I will be down at Richmond in less than two hours."

"But——"

"No buts, but be off; quick! follow me."

And so saying, they left the den.

They were soon out at the other gate; there stood Shambling Jack and the cab.

"In, quick. Good-bye. Waterloo station; drive on; in an hour come to me at——" he whispered the name of the place."

"Right! I'll be there to the minute."

And away went Shambling Jack.

Pondering upon what had occurred and muttering to himself, Dark Davy walked slowly back to the den.

"I don't want any detective visiting my place," he said, "and asking questions, and perhaps searching, which would not be pleasant. That fellow, Dick Martingale, is drawing a net round him, which, if it once entangles him, he won't find it easy to break through. Only let me get hold of this secret, and he may go to the——"

He was suddenly roused from his musings by a tap on the shoulder, which caused him to start round violently.

A person dressed in black, with a white neckcloth on, a clerical style of hat, and a prim-looking umbrella, stood before him.

"Mr. Davy Close, I think?" said the person.

"Yes; at your service."

"You are the gentleman who defended a man at the Bow Street Police

Court to-day, upon a case of card-sharping."

And the man who addressed him looked very keenly at him.

"Hulloa," thought Davy, "the game has commenced already, has it? Yes, I am that person."

"Ha, humph; I think he was very hardly treated."

"Do you?"

"Yes; I am rather interested in that young man."

"Are you, indeed?"

"Yes; let me see, his name is——"

"Dick Martingale," was Davy's quick reply.

"Ah, yes, that is the name. I see these are your chambers," and the man pointed with his umbrella to the name. "Mr. D. Close, solicitor. Is he within?" and he moved forward to the door.

But Davy was too quick for him, and stood before him in an instant.

"Oh, dear, no, he is not within, nor will you go within," said David, dryly. "Pray what may be your business with him?"

"Oh, that's my business," was the reply; "something for his good."

"Oh, yes, I dare say it is something for his good," and Davy gave a short, dry laugh so peculiar to himself. "Oh, yes, very much for his good; oh, ha, ha, ha! very much for his good."

"How do you know to the contrary?"

"How do I know? Why, we all know that when a detective makes affectionate inquiries after anyone, it must be for their good, of course, and very much obliged they ought to be to you for it."

"You know me, then?" said the person.

"I have known Mr. Grey, of the D. M. P., for the last ten years, and could tell him under any disguise."

"I believe you could, Davy, and so, therefore concealment is no longer needed," said the detective, for so he was.

"Certainly not, certainly not; nor need there be any between us, eh?"

"Certainly not. A glass of wine, Davy?"

"Not a drop; got a heavy case on at the Mansion House."

"Always full of business."

"Always," and Davy gleefully rubbed his hands together, "something always turning up in the world, eh? But you were asking after my client, Mr. Richard Martingale?"

"Yes."

"What's up with him?"

"You've heard of that little affair at Richmond, at Lady St. George's?"

"Oh, yes, it's in the papers. What has that to do with Martingale?"

"Why, he is the party suspected."

"Ha, ha, ha! well, that is rich; why, he was the very man that had the greatest interest in the life and welfare of that 'young sprig of nobility;' besides, no sooner did he hear of it than he was off to Richmond as fast as the train could carry him."

"Oh, then he has gone back?"

"Gone back, of course he has! I never saw a man so much cut up when he heard the news—jumped into a Hansom and drove off at such a pace—I only hope no accident will happen, and by this time he is at the bedside of the poor young gentleman."

"Why, then," said the detective, "it's a flam after all."

"Ha! ha! ha! And a very nice one of the sort."

And Davy grinned maliciously at him.

"Well, good day, Mr. Close; I shall give up this affair, losing my time in this wild-goose chase. Good day."

And the subtle inspector and detective walked off in a towering passion, while Davy, chuckling within himself, went up to his den.

"Indeed, Mr. Dark Davy, you think you have put me off the scent, do you? Gone to Richmond—humph! Well, it's a fine day, and so I'll have a run down to Richmond myself."

And away went Mr. Grey, at a smart pace, towards the Waterloo station.

"We've had our eyes a long time upon you, Mr. Davy, but you haven't got the length of your tether yet."

"So, so," muttered Dark Davy, "I think I've settled the affair for you, Mr. Pry. Wanted to peep into my den, did you? Oh, no, thank ye; many little things in there that I don't want anybody but myself to look at. I'll go down to the villa—send in my card—transacted business for the father. Humph! good! Offer my services to trace out this diabolical outrage, and ——humph! Mrs. Wilson, No. —, Gower Street"—taking up a dirty piece of paper. "Ah! Giles Evergreen—strange affair—no matter—money at the bottom—keep it dark, Davy, keep it dark."

And then, double-locking the door, Mr. Davy Close walked slowly down the stairs, immersed in deep thought at the events that had occurred during the earlier part of the day.

CHAPTER XXVI.

DARK DAVY ON THE TRACK.

WHILE Dark Davy was taking a cursory glance at the outside of the house in Gower Street, the inmates were recruiting themselves from the fatigues of the morning.

The Jolter family had met within the last few days with so many mishaps, that they thought a little rest very advisable; they, therefore, resolved to remain in for the remainder of the day, old Jolter enjoying his pipe and tankard in company with the stock broker, while Tommy, acting under the orders of the doctor, was condemned to have his poor, monkey-torn head encased in another powerful pudding to keep down the inflammation; Suke, having received from her father sundry documents from the farm, had set herself to work to see if the milk, the butter, the cheese, and the eggs had been truly and duly accounted for; in fact, the hieroglyphic characters in which the said accounts were written could only have been interpreted by Suke Jolter herself.

Mrs. Wilson and Flipper were busy in looking over and arranging all the household affairs, so that Giles, Ted, and Norman were left to themselves.

"I propose, Ted," said Giles, "that we take a run down to Richmond by the rail, see Lady St. George, and inquire how Alfred Ravensborne is getting on."

"The very thing my own swate thoughts were bent upon," was the answer. "What say you, Norman?"

"Weel, I'm thinking I'll mak' ane o' sic a pleasant party. Ye'll ken that the vacation is on, and the learned professors gone into the country for their holidays, and so with your permission, I'll just mak' ane o' the party."

No sooner said than done, and in less than ten minutes they sallied from the house, arm-in-arm, and that with such impetuosity, as nearly to upset into the kennel a dark-looking man, who was very intently looking up at it.

Walking rapidly down to the Waterloo Station, and laughing heartily as they passed Covent Garden at the fun they had witnessed in the morning between the sweep and the baker, they crossed the bridge to the terminus, and were speedily ensconced in a first-class carriage.

Hardly had they taken their seats, when the one in the centre was occupied by a person who immediately pulled out a *Times* newspaper, which completely enveloped his face, and with the con-tents of which he appeared to be deeply interested.

It so happened that he sat in close contiguity to Ted Flan and Giles, so that almost every word they said he could hear; but to that and everything around he appeared not to pay the slightest attention.

"I hope, Ted, we shall find Alfred restored to consciousness when we reach the villa," said Giles. "It is a most mysterious affair."

"Mysterious! By the powers, it bangs 'Banagher,' and that took a great dale of bating. I may be wrong, but if that jontleman, Mister Richard Martingale, ain't at the bottom of it, there's no power in pase or virtue in buttermilk, what think you, Giles?"

"My opinion entirely coincides with your own, and yet Alfred has always manfully stood up in defence of the fellow. Do you remember the night in the drawing-room?"

"Remember? Will I ever forget it, or do I think Alfred ever will? Och! he's a darling. I'd like to have a large family like him, but it would be on the prairie, where there's plenty of room."

"Our visit must be a short one, Ted," replied Giles, "and some inquiry must be made about that fellow Martingale."

"I'll wander about the town, and wait for you until you return," said Norman.

"You'll do no such thing, Norman Campbell. You'll be just as welcome at the villa as ourselves."

"Weel, then, I've got a proposal to make to you," said Norman.

"By the powers, out with it."

" Weel, then, the tide will suit in the evening, and we'll just have a boat and row up; there's a friend of mine been rowing a party down here to-day and he'll be going back by himself, and so, if we join him, we can just make a nice four, eh, ma' lads? What say ye to that?"

" Say, Scotland for ever!" laughed Giles.

" What sort of a countryman is your friend?" asked Ted.

" I canna exactly tell what sort he is, but he comes from Wales, and I have a verra strong presumption that he is a Welsh boy."

" Hurrah for the four corners of the globe, wherever the fifth may be! Did you ever hear the likes of that, Giles? The four saints of the world all rowing in the same boat. Oh, it's mighty."

" What's amiss with it, mon?"

" Amiss? By the piper of Tim McCoul, who made the rocks and mountains dance, it's the most wonderful wonder. Ain't there Saint George in the nate person of Giles? Ain't there Saint Andrew in your own swate self, and Saint David in the person of your friend, the Welsh boy? And don't I represent in my immaculate person Saint Patrick, who banished

" 'All the frogs and sich like watery
        varmint,
   And sent them off to dance a jig
   With the famous great say-sarpint.'

Oh, with that nice little lot, we'll——"

Ted's rollicking humour was put an end to by the train stopping at Richmond.

Jumping lightly out of the carriage, they walked rapidly towards the villa near the hill.

No sooner were they out of sight than down went the paper from the face of the man, disclosing the sinister features of Dark Davy.

Chuckling to himself as he descended from the carriage, he walked slowly out of the station.

" An inquiry must be made about that fellow, Martingale. Must there? Humph! we shall see. I wonder where he has got to? At any more of his card tricks? Let me see my scheme of operations—to call first at the villa, and then after that shape my plan of action. Perhaps I shall hear something respecting Martingale there; but I won't call for at least an hour. No, no, take it coolly, Davy, and keep it dark."

And, so saying, he entered a tavern in order to rest and think.

When the boys reached the villa they found almost the stillness of death reigning in the place.

Their inquiry of the servant as to the health of Alfred Ravensborne was answered by a very ominous shake of the head.

They were speedily ushered into the presence of Lady St. George and Hilda, who received them with the greatest cordiality and joy, tempered by saddened smiles at the critical state that Alfred Ravensborne then lay in, hovering, as it were, between life and death.

" He has had no return to consciousness since you left, my dear boys. A consultation is now being held with the most eminent men of science from town, and we are waiting in fear and trembling the result."

"Have you gained any clue to the perpetrator of this outrage, madam?" asked Giles.

"There is one person we strongly suspect."

"Martingale, the groom, or I am not the son of my maternal parient!" said Ted.

"You are not far off, Mr. Flan," was the lady's answer; "and a little circumstance which happened—since your departure yesterday morning—has made me consult my solicitor, and by his advice I have caused a search to be made for the groom."

"We met him in Covent Garden only a few hours ago," said Giles.

"Indeed! Under what circumstances?"

Giles related them.

"But the little circumstance, **my** lady?" said the impatient Ted.

"After you had left the villa, **a** reaction set in, and Alfred was very restless and violent, gnashing his teeth, muttering in a strange incoherent manner, and wildly tossing his tightly-clenched hands about, as if engaged in a fierce and deadly struggle with some person."

"Did he mention any name?" asked Giles.

"We could not distinctly hear what he said. His violence was so great that it became necessary to call in the servants and hold him down. To that after a short interval, succeeded a stupor so intense that we all thought that life had departed from him."

"Poor Alfred! Spite of all his unkindness to me, I deeply feel for his sufferings," said Giles, struggling with his feelings, "for after all, he was our schoolfellow, eh, Ted?"

And a manly tear stood in his eye.

"He was, Giles, he was," replied Ted, pressing his hand; "and whatever may be his faults or the troubles of learning, it's not aisy to forget the ould school, and its many, many dear hours of sunshine. By the powers! I'll catch myself blubbering like Biddy McGrowl, when the string parted from the pig's leg, and he parted from her."

"I can only say for mysel', a puir, simple Scotch laddie, that if I knew the scoundrel that had done it, I'd mak' him feel what good honest porridge had done for me first. Ye'll excuse me, my leddy, but we Scotch boys maun out wi' the truth when it's glib on the tongue."

"All your sentiments do honour to you; but you must be fatigued. Let me——"

And the lady rose.

"Let us have the little circumstance first, my lady," said Ted.

"While in that torpor," resumed Lady St. George, "I raised his right hand, which, up to that moment, had remained desperately clenched, when suddenly it opened, and a button, attached to a small remnant of cloth, fell into my hand."

Here the excited boys started to their feet.

"I took no notice of the article at that moment, but on retiring from the room I attentively examined it."

"It is as plain as a pike-staff," muttered Ted.

"No," said her ladyship, "the button had a crest stamped on it."

"A crest!" re-echoed the boys.

"Yes; the crest belonging to the unfortunate boy's father, attached to a small piece of cloth belonging to the family livery."

"Och! murder!" said Ted, springing up. "It's becoming as plain as the pimple on Darby Murphy's nose! That must have belonged to——"

"His assailant," said Giles, firmly.

"No doubt," replied Lady St. George; "and the only person wearing that livery in my establishment was the groom, Richard Martingale."

"Och! The murder," said Ted, jumping up, "is like the cat—out of the bag. I'd like to see it, my lady."

"You cannot; it is in the hands of my lawyer."

"Ah, then, it's safe enough," said Ted; "it's seldom they get anything out of their hands when once it gets in."

At that moment the door was opened, and the surgeon who had been specially summoned from London, entered the room.

"Well, Sir William," said Lady St. George, in anxious tones, "is there any hope?"

"A glimpse. The operation I have performed has materially assisted the patient, so much so, that he has spoken one name intelligibly, but it was in a tone of the deepest anger, leading me to suppose that it must be the name of his brutal assailant."

At this the whole of the parties assembled in the room stood up, breathless with excitement.

"And that name was——"

"Giles Evergreen!" was the reply.

"Mine!" said the astonished Giles.

"Are you Giles Evergreen?" said the surgeon, bending on him a look of deep scrutiny. "I have heard much of you."

"But nothing to my disgrace or discredit!" said our hero, proudly.

"It's a big bating I'll give the spalpeen that says so!"

And Ted Flan was so indignant at the bare idea, that he partly pulled off his jacket, forgetting where he was for the moment.

"I beg your pardon; I forgot we were in the presence of the lords of creation—the ladies."

Sir William smiled gravely.

"No, certainly not. I read; and have never forgotten that noble bravery of yours at the railway station in rescuing my dear little favourite, Miss Hilda, from a painful death—and I see she has not forgotten it."

Hilda had one of her hands on Giles's shoulder, while the other was clasped in his.

"But, at all events, your name was mentioned. I shall run down again to-morrow, Lady St. George, when my hope is my patient will be a little more sensible."

With that he took his leave of the parties.

Scarcely had he left the house when the servant entered bearing a card, which he handed to his mistress.

"Mr. David Close, solicitor," said the lady, reading. "I really do not know him."

"He wishes to see you, my lady."

"Perhaps he may come to throw some light upon the late events," suggested Giles.

"A SPY, SIR. LEAVE THE ROOM," SAID GILES."

No. 14.

" You are right, Mr. Evergreen. At all events," said that lady smiling, " we have three brave champions to protect us. Admit him."

Giles, Norman, and Hilda began looking over a book of very rare engravings, while Ted sat down on the sofa, and engaged himself with a book.

CHAPTER XXVII.

DISCOMFITURE OF DARK DAVY.

DARK DAVY entered the room, almost dislocating his neck by a rapid succession of bows. He bowed to the lady of the house, who slightly curtsied in return; he bowed to Giles, Norman, and Hilda unnoticed; and he bowed to Ted Flan, who gave him a slight one in return, and a stare that made Dark Davy's eyes blink.

" Your business with me, sir?" said Lady St. George. " I have not the pleasure of knowing you."

" You're quite right, my lady; hem! that pleasure is to come, and——"

" Sir."

" On *my* part, I mean; I had the pleasure of serving your late relative, the Honourable Plantagenet Montmorency Ravensborne, in many very *delicate* matters."

And here he looked very significantly at her ladyship.

" Well, sir, what of that? All claims against his estate have been paid."

" Yes, yes, just so, just so; but there is a claim greater than money can pay —I mean gratitude."

And here Davy the Dark made another bow.

" Gratitude! I am at a loss to under-stand your meaning. Be brief with it; my time is valuable and, and——"

" Just so, my lady, just so; time is valuable to all of us. Well, my lady, I have heard of the outrage committed upon his son, the Honourable Alfred Ravensborne, and I thought my poor services might be useful in searching and finding out the party."

At the first sound of Davy the Dark's voice, Ted fixed all his attention upon him, striving to remember where and when he had seen him before.

It did not take long for the sharp, bright intellect of the Irish boy to settle the point. It soon flashed across him, and so, while Dark Davy was offering his services, he rose silently, and, joining Giles, whispered his suspicions to him.

" May I ask your ladyship, if any suspicions attach themselves to any one?" asked Davy.

" Yes, they do," replied the lady, sternly.

" Ah! yes; while I was having my luncheon, I think I heard the name mentioned. It was that of one Dick Martingale, a discharged groom. Martingale! Martingale! I—I think I have *some* recollection of the name."

"Well, I *think* you must have," said Giles, sternly advancing, "since a few hours ago you were defending the villain at a police-court upon a charge of swindling at cards."

Had the roof opened over his head, or the ground beneath his feet, with all his daring coolness and effrontery, Mr. Davy Close could not have felt more astounded when the voice of Giles sounded in his ears, and he saw his denouncer standing with a smile of contempt upon his handsome countenance.

Lady St. George and her daughter stood looking from one to the other with wonder and amazement.

At length Dark Davy found his tongue and his daring assurance.

"Upon my word, young gentleman, you must be mistaken," he stammered out.

"Not a bit of it, my fine fellow; you're bowled out, like Mike Daly was at cricket. I saw you in the court myself, defending the gentleman (*you know nothing about*). Och, murder!—and if you want another witness, Mr. Norman Campbell."

"There's nae doubt but you are the vera mon. I took unco notice of you, for I thought you'd got the face of auld Clootie himsel—save us."

"Well, gentlemen, when you have done bantering me, we'll proceed to business," and Davy gave his peculiar low laugh and rubbed his hands jocularly.

"Oh, yes," replied Giles, coolly, "with this lady's permission we will proceed to business."

"Ah, ah, that is right; that is right. May I be permitted to—" and he placed his hand upon a chair, and drew it towards him.

"To sit down! Certainly not," replied Giles; "you have dared to intrude yourself here, sir, in the detestable character of——"

"What, sir, what, sir?"

"A spy, sir! Leave the room. Are you satisfied?"

"No, sir; no, sir. What else, what else? You see, madam, I take these paltry accusations coolly," and Dark Davy smiled.

"And do you know what else you had better take, my darlin'?"

"No; what?" and he sneered at Ted.

"Take yourself off; there are two mighty convanient places here for curs."

"Curs! Mind what you say."

"Oh, botherashun, you won't frighten me. I said curs. There's a horse-pond first, and a mighty fine river to rinse your carcase in."

"But, my lady, do you think or believe——"

"Every word these young gentlemen have uttered; and I must request you will leave quietly before the servants eject you from the house. Begone!"

"Certainly; but before I leave permit me to say there have been many cases of mistaken identity, and in this case——"

"There is none," said Giles, and he pointed to the door.

"Ha, ha! well there is no convincing you, and so——"

The door at that moment opened and a couple of servants appeared at it; Davy glanced at them.

"And so I take my leave. I am

under a very deep obligation to both of you," addressing Giles and Ted; "will you favour me with your names?"

"Giles Evergreen," was the reply, accompanied by a mocking laugh and bows.

"And yours?"

"Oh, Ted Flan! any blaggard can spell that without spectacles. Shall I write it down for you, my darlin'?"

"Oh, dear, no, I shall remember them, fear me not; mistakes will occur to all of us, and you have——"

"What, sir?" said Giles, sternly.

"Made one, that's all," and with a look of deep and bitter malignity Dark Davy slowly passed from the room, and then receiving a polite intimation that upon his next visit he would be handed over to the police, he left the house, the rage of a thousand fiends waging war in his disappointed heart and mind.

"Curse those boys! I'll ruin them if I swing for it! Silence, Davy, keep that dark; if I could only find that Dick Martingale. I don't believe the fellow ever came down here; frightened, I suppose. Ah! well, fright's a thing I never knew yet. I'll just go back to the inn and have a chop and a strong glass of grog; for in spite of my pluck, my nerves feel shaky. Ah! here I am."

So saying, he entered the room he had only a short time previously left, and seating himself, gave his orders. Then taking up the paper, he looked round and perceived that he was not alone. In a corner of the room lay a man huddled up and fast asleep, his face buried in his hands.

He was rather respectably dressed, though his coat appeared to have suffered in some affray, for here and there it was patched with mud, and in one or two places torn as if in a struggle.

Dark Davy just glanced at him, and finding the man quiet he ate his chop, and then turning his back to the sleeper, fell into a deep study, now and then taking a sip at his spirits and water and trying to fix his attention upon the newspaper.

"Pah, it's no use attempting to read the paper; everything seems to be headed 'police' and 'assizes,'" and so saying, he threw it down.

"If I were only in London, I could get three or four desperate devils to join me in the plan. I dare say there are plenty of that sort here, if one only knew where to find them; if I had only Dick Martingale here, he could get a lot, no doubt; but, as it is, the best job to settle those boys at once must be given up."

Here his cogitations were interrupted by the heavy breathing of the sleeping man; so loud and heavy was it that it ruffled even the coolness and equanimity of Dark Davy. Rising and going up to the man, he shook him roughly.

"Holloa there, you sir, don't make that infernal noise, d'ye hear?" and then another shake.

In an instant the man was on his feet looking savagely upon the one who had disturbed his slumbers; his desperate rush upon the man was suddenly stayed.

"Wh a, Dark Davy, by all that's infernal!"

"Dick Martingale, by all that's lucky!" burst from the lips of Davy.

"Ha, ha! I was dreaming of you,

and here you are," said Dick, sinking into a chair.

"Yes, here I am."

And Dark Davy resumed his seat.

"Didn't I tell you that I was coming down after you? You haven't been up yonder."

And he pointed in the direction of the villa.

"I should think not. How I got here I don't know. Look at this."

And Dick pointed to a black mark on his forehead, then to his eye, that was swollen and black.

"I don't think these ugly marks would be any recommendation."

"Why, no; what row have you got into, and how come you to get the worst of it, eh?"

"Well, I think somebody else has got a trifle the worst of it."

And Dick, raising Dark Davy's glass, emptied it of its contents at one gulp.

"And now you have got the worst of it."

"Not at all; there's plenty more where that came from."

And so saying, Davy rang the bell, and, ordering more, he waited until the waiter appeared with it.

He gave him to understand that for a short space they wished to have the room to themselves, and enforced his wish by locking the door the moment that functionary had quitted the room.

"Now, Dick, out with your news first, then I'll to mine, and good it is," and Dark Davy pushed the glass towards him.

Dick Martingale took it up and drank heartily.

"Well, you see, when I left you and got into the train, what with one thing and another, I felt savage with all the world, myself included, and, having provided myself with a flask, I kept drink, drink, until, I suppose, instead of coming down here, I found myself out at Kew, and so I went staggering on until I found myself in a field, and down I went, and was fast asleep in a few minutes.

"Well, when I woke, I found that the nap had lasted a couple of hours; but up I got all right, into the road I was again, and making the best of my way up Kew Lane until I came to a public-house, there I stopped and called for a nip of brandy. The words were scarcely out of my mouth when out rushed the four men that I had met in the morning."

"The deuce! the men that lost at cards?"

"The same; and before I knew where I was, I got a blow—you see the marks?—that sent me reeling like a top.

"As luck would have it, the force of the blow sent me staggering against a table, upon which stood an empty quart pot. I thought four to one rather long odds, so I laid hold of it, and as the biggest one of the lot came rushing upon me, I dealt him a blow in the middle of the head, and down he went.

"This settled the affair, for the rest rushing into the house, I sent the quart pot flying through a window after them, then beat a swift retreat, and here I am. The blow on the eye looks ugly; that I'll get painted, and to-morrow I'll go to the villa."

" No, you won't," said Dark Davy.

" Why not ?"

" Because there is danger."

" Why, didn't you advise me ?"

" Yes; but my friend, Richard Martingale, circumstances alter cases. If you feel inclined you can settle a good deal of business to-night, without troubling the villa to-morrow."

" Business, and to-night ?"

" Yes; if you don't shrink from it, the career of your friends, Giles Evergreen and that Irish boy will be settled."

" What do you mean ?" said Dick, excitedly, starting up.

" Mean ?   What I say."

" Where are they ?"

" At the villa.   They bowled me out to-day, so that I owe them a score; and by Heaven I'll pay it."

" But explain this."

" Listen.   Can you at a pinch find a couple of fellows that won't stick at trifles if a sovereign or two is placed before them ?"

And Davy looked anxiously at him.

" I should think I could.   Are they to get into the villa, and——"

Here the eyes of these scoundrels met.

" No, nothing of the sort; listen, Dick.   They came down by the train, and in the same carriage as I did.   I overheard their plan of returning home in the evening by water, in a boat by themselves.   Well——"

" Well."

And Dick stared at him.

" Well, what are you staring at ? That blow has knocked all the sense out of your skull.   There will be four in their boat, ha, ha ! four boys, while in ours there will be four men. We'll let them get well ahead, and then, overhauling them, pick a quarrel (those things are common enough on the water).   Suppose we do bump a hole in their boat, and it should fill, they won't get out of that job so easily as they did with those quiet horses, eh, Richard Martingale ?"

Dick looked sulkily down.

" You see I know something about that, eh ?"

There was a pause of some duration.

At length Dick said—

" The plan is a good one, and shall be carried out.   The men I take with us must not be trusted with our reasons; they must be plied with drink, and the quarrel must appear natural and not an old grudge.   Then, again, we must disguise ourselves, so that they do not recognise us should they escape."

" Escape ! nonsense, it is not likely," was the reply.

" That is not a certainty; they have done it more than once before, and may again."

" Ha, ha, you are losing your nerve."

" Am I; you try it and see.   How is the young one getting on, eh ?"

" Badly; at least, that is the report in the town."

" Ah, that was a bad job, but he brought it all on himself."

" Of course he did; but you got the papers all right.   Where are they ?"

And Dark Davy looked significantly at his companion.

" Where are they ?   Ah, wouldn't you like to know ?" replied Dick.

"Yes."

"So you shall."

"When?" eagerly asked Davy.

"When I like, Davy Close, and not one minute before. Now, then, is this business to go on?"

"Go on! yes, why not?"

"Well, then, you know the lane leading down to the river at the end of the town?"

"Yes, I know it."

"Very well, I am going there; on the right hand, at the bottom, is a court; go straight up until you come to the last house, and knock three times."

"But why not go with you?"

"Because I think we had better not be seen together."

And going to the further end of the room, he threw open a window.

"You go out at the door, I'll find my way out here."

And, so saying, to the great surprise of Dark Davy, the jockey suddenly disappeared!

For a moment he was so surprised that he kept staring at the open window.

Then suddenly rising and looking out he found Dick Martingale had disappeared.

Dark Davy stood in the middle of the room, taking counsel with himself, then, unlocking the door and ringing the bell, prepared to discharge the reckoning.

That affair having been settled satisfactorily, Dark Davy walked out to keep his appointment, and concert measures for the upsetting the boat in which Giles Evergreen, Ted Flan, and Norman Campbell were about rowing to London in.

By this time the twilight was rapidly advancing, and, in addition to it, the clouds looked rather dark and lowering.

Advancing down the narrow lane Dick had directed him to, he found that worthy in close conversation with a man dressed in the old worn-out dress of a waterman.

"Oh! you are there, Martingale, are you?" said Dark Davy. "What did you make your exit through the window in that strange fashion for, eh?"

"Because I wanted to avoid the prying eyes of the waiter, in case inquiries were made respecting me," was the reply.

"Is this the man we were speaking about?"

"Yes; this is old Owl, as he is called in these parts. Ain't that correct, eh, old fellow?"

"Well," said or rather croaked the man, "I am called so by the fools, and those that don't know me. But, what's the game?"

"You know me, I think," said Martingale.

"Yes; but I doesn't t'other. You're called Martingale, and you're groom to the swells up the hill. Well, what do you want done?"

And the old man glanced suspiciously at them.

"You don't beat long about the bush, my friend," said Davy, "in a matter of business."

"What's the use on it?" growled out old Owl. "It's a clear losing of time."

"Well, will you earn a couple of sovereigns?" said Dick, abruptly.

"Ah! that's bisness, and sounds

well. Well, seeing I ain't earned a farden all the week, I think a couple of sovs won't be amiss· I am your man. Now, the work to be done?"

Dick Martingale paused a moment, as if thinking in what shape the matter could be brought about; but Dark Davy, cunning serpent as he was, had got the matter already.

"Look you, my man; a few weeks ago myself and friend were rowing on the river, when we were grossly insulted by three young fellows, and ran down, narrowly escaping with our lives."

"Well, and what was the cause?"

"Nothing at all, not the slightest."

And Davy looked very significantly at Dick.

"A lark, I s'poses. Well, boys will lark, and when fun is carried out properly I like to see it; but upsetting people into the river is quite another affair. What do you want?—out with it!"

"Well, you see, we have heard that they are going up to London to-night, and so we thought we would pay them out in the same coin."

"Quite right; and you want me to help you?"

"Yes."

"And you'll pay me?"

"Yes; a couple of pound."

"But you only want to give them a ducking."

"That's all; there's no harm meant," and Davy gave one of his low, quiet chuckles.

"Well, I shouldn't for a moment think it; you don't look like a couple of persons to do harm," and old Owl (as he was called) chuckled, and knocked the ashes out of his dirty old pipe. "You don't want to put their pipes quite out, I s'pose?"

"No, no," said Dark Davy.

"I thought not. Well, I'm agreeable to give the chaps a Rowland for their Oliver; nothing more for the price."

And the old Owl looked askance into the gleaming eyes of Dark Davy, and in that moment they both understood each other.

"And you'll let them swim for their lives?"

"They did the same by us," chimed in Dick.

"Quite right. I'll tell you what we'll do, for I see we understand each other; we'll get over to Barnes by train; I've got a brother there who will lend us his boat, which is a stout un; there is a nice dark place off there," said the Owl.

"And we can ·shoot out upon them and upset them," said Dark Davy, and the cold-blooded scoundrel rubbed his hands with a quiet, murderous glee. "Do it well, and I won't stand for a pound or two more."

"You won't?"

"No, nor will my friend."

"It will teach them a lesson they will not easily forget," chimed in Dick. "And I'll stand by my friend."

"That's hearty; I like to see friends stick by each other. Well, come along, we've no time to lose; we'll just have a glass together; I s'pose you don't mind standing that to a friend like me?"

"Certainly not, so come along," said Dick. "I wouldn't miss them for a trifle."

And away started the three villains, bent upon their dark deed of murder.

At the villa all was quiet, for as yet the favourable change had not taken place in the condition of Alfred.

The time wore on.

Norman Campbell had left them to find his friend with his boat.

"My dear boys, I wish I could persuade you not to go to London by water; there are so many accidents happen, that I and Hilda will be in dread until we hear of your safe arrival."

"Niver fear, my lady," said Ted Flan, "there is an old saying that those born to die by rope will not be drowned in a wash-hand basin; and by the powers, we'll show them what rowing is."

"Do not for one moment anticipate danger, my lady, we shall be right enough," and Giles took the hand of Hilda, and pressing it tenderly, said, "Hilda will not feel alarmed, will you?"

"Indeed I shall; and I wish you would not go by water," was the answer.

At that moment Norman (who had become a great favourite with Lady St. George) entered the drawing-room.

"Weel, I am just sorry to say that my friend has been obliged to go to London, and so——"

"You will not go by the river, but by the rail," said Hilda, joyfully.

"Weel, you see, my lady, that canna be, because I've brought the boat round; and by my honour she's a beauty, and I promised my friend that the boat should be brought up to London by me, and a Scot and a gentleman don't like to be worse than his word."

"Well, I see it is in vain to combat the resolution you have taken; but let me send for an experienced waterman to go with you."

"Ha, ha, ha!" laughed Giles and Ted; "we don't want a waterman, my lady."

"I ken every part of the river, as weel as if I had been on it half my life, and can handle the yoke lines with here and there one," replied Norman.

"And we can row any one of our own weight and size; and, with the 'United Kingdom' in the boat, who is to bate us? Oh, the Rose, Thistle, and Shamrock for ever and a month after."

Lady St. George saw that further expostulation was useless; and all being in readiness, both she and Hilda walked down to the landing-stairs at the end of the wall.

"You will let us know by telegram the moment Alfred recovers consciousness, my lady?" said Giles.

"Certainly, my dear boys; and, when he recovers, I hope that you will all be better friends."

"By the powers, I hope so; there's nothing friendly in being bitter enemies. Now, in my own dear country, an illigant fight now and then makes us the best of friends, and it's considered a striking proof of friendship to knock a man down."

The whole party laughed heartily at Ted Flan's wit and humour.

The last beams of the brilliant setting sun were flinging their streams of golden light upon the waters, and the gaily painted pleasure boats, with their happy, joyous freights, flitted about in almost every direction, when the three boys took their seats in the boat.

Adieus had been kindly given, and tears stood in the eyes of the countess and her daughter, as they looked upon the bright, happy faces, and handsome forms of their favourites.

The tide was racing down, and a slight breeze breathed across the waters, as Norman Campbell, with his well-practised eyes, saw that all was ready.

"Give way," he called out.

At the word, the oars fell in the water, and the boat shot forward like a high-mettled racer towards the goal with the speed of light.

The countess and her daughter waved their handkerchiefs until the boat was no longer visible, and then turned sorrowfully towards the villa.

An old boatman, who had been standing close by her, touched his hat as they passed.

"Beg pardon, my lady, is them 'ere young genelmen bound for London?"

"Yes, Joe, they are," was the kind reply. "Why?"

"Nothing of consequence, my lady. I hope they'll get there safely, that's all."

"Safely, what do you mean? Is there danger? I will send after them."

"They must be good hands, and mighty strong arms that would reach them. I never saw boys pull like them afore. It's only the weather I'm afeared on. We shall have a storm, my lady," and the old man, who had weathered many a tough gale, pointed to a mass of black clouds that were rolling up from the north, that looked anything but pleasant.

"A storm!" and the countess looked up at the threatening danger.

At that moment a low, rumbling sound, but at a great distance, sounded in her ears, as the last ray of the sun faded, and sank from the heavens.

"Follow me into the house," said the lady, hurriedly.

"Aye, aye, God bless you! I am always good for something there," said the old waterman.

Again the low rumbling noise, and a faint flash of lightning springing through the dark mass in the heavens.

The boat went flashing through the waters, and at times, as they shot past some jovial party, they gave a merry, ringing cheer, which was heartily returned.

A rowing match was going on, and the cluster of boats was so great that they were obliged to cease rowing.

While so resting on their oars, the distant thunder broke upon their ears.

"Eh, sirs, but there's a storm brewing," said the cautious Scot, "and I think we had better return."

"What for, Norman? Are you afraid of a wet jacket?" said Giles.

"Hoot awa, mon," said Ted, grinning; "we're not sugar or salt, that we shall melt. Are we all clear?"

The rain had by this time begun to descend in torrents, causing the many boats rowing about to make speedily for the banks on each side.

"Thistle of glorious ould Scotland, are we clear?" shouted Ted.

"Clear as ma conscience," answered the Scot.

"Then give way with a will," called out Giles, cheerily.

And away went the boat through the waves like a meteor.

The storm began now to rage in right down earnest, the thunder roaring, with occasional flashes of lightning, vivid and fierce, while the rain poured down enough to wash them out of the boat.

But not for one moment did this diminish or slacken the exertions of the "gallant oarsmen," or their no less cool and brave cox'son."

Under a clump of trees, whose branches nearly kissed the rapid flowing stream, lay a boat, hidden by them.

The three men seated in it kept occasionally putting a small stone bottle to their lips, and then, pulling their coats tightly round them, bent a searching look up the river.

"I should hardly think they'll be such fools to venture out such a night as this," croaked out the man known as the old Owl.

"Well, I shan't give up yet," savagely said Dick Martingale. "It don't matter now, for I am soaked to the skin."

"So say I, Dick. Mind, you will refund the money if the bargain's not carried out. No tricks upon travellers, my friend."

And Dark Davy scowled at him.

"I don't know what you mean by tricks," growled the old Owl. "I think the tricks are with you. Now, mind; you say you can steer?"

"Of course I can—any fool can do that," snappishly replied Mr. Davy Close.

"Of course they can, in their own opinion; and if any fool can do it, you'll do it well. And you can pull?"

"Like the old one," replied Dick.

"Well, then, get ready, for here they come, a-racing down like steam. Now, then, pull with a will, and we shall just cut them off."

Of went the boat for the middle of the stream.

This was not unobserved by Norman Campbell, and the clear-headed, clear-sighted Scot saw something suspicious in it.

Giles and Ted had for the last mile greatly diminished their exertions, and were "taking it easy."

"I'll thank you to put on extra steam just to head those fellows, who seem inclined to run us down," said Norman.

A few strokes, and the gallant boat flew like the wind, clearing the intended collision by about three boats' lengths.

"What do you mane by that, you thaves of the world?" shouted out Ted.

"We'll soon let you see," said a voice in reply.

"Och! murder! it's the villain, Dick Martingale. Pull, Giles, for it's murder they mane."

"You scoundrel, I'll punish you for this," shouted Giles, bending to his oar, Ted pulling like a giant.

The boys had been much excited at the pull they had already had, but the easy way with which they had been taking it had brought back their strength, and they kept ahead of their intended assassins easily.

Still the strength of the others was greater; they were men in the vigour of life, the one a skilled waterman, the other, Dick Martingale, from his early habits of life, muscular and powerful, and they pressed the leading boat very closely.

But the steering in the one boat was widely different to that of the other; Norman knew all about it; Dark Davy not an atom, and so the chase went gallantly on.

The thunder, lightning, and rain had disappeared, but the wind had increased, rendering the water very rough; still, with undaunted hearts, the boys pulled on, not giving way an inch, while their pursuers seemed to slacken most materially their speed.

The deep and bitter execrations they poured upon the heads of the three heroic boys were answered by loud cheers and hearty laughter, and so on they went, at a speed that was fast bringing them to Battersea Bridge.

Here Norman Campbell was perfectly at home, and they shot through that disgrace to the navigation of the river like a rocket.

Not so Mr. Davy Close; his sight was not the best, and, thinking he was going right, he steered exactly the other way.

With a bitter curse the old Owl shouted to him.

This made matters worse.

Dark Davy lost his presence of mind, and, with an awful crash, the boat ran against one of the piers, and in one instant had parted in half as though cut with a knife.

The three villains were in the waves battling for life!

Now, in his youth Dark Davy had never taught himself, or been educated, in the noble art of swimming, and, in a desperate struggle for existence, a drowning man would cling to a broken reed.

Dark Davy clung like grim death to the old Owl, while the wretched man so named fought him with desperate madness to get free of him.

It was to no purpose.

No human power could have loosened that death grasp.

No human power slackened the clutch for life.

They shrieked forth prayers and blasphemy.

It was all in vain.

They sank together with an appalling, despairing cry, and the waves of the river went rolling on, heedless of the souls that had gone to their dread account.

For some time it was not known what had become of Dick Martingale; but all supposed he had gone down with the rest.

The speed with which Giles and Ted were rowing, prevented them knowing anything of the miraculous accident that had saved them.

They soon gained Searle's famous yard, where their boat was to be left, and then, jumping into a cab, were quickly conveyed to Gower Street.

Springing into the house, they were cordially welcomed by no less a person than " Lawyer Tough Mutton."

Rushing with extended arms towards

them, he clasped the boys to him, but quickly sprang back at finding they were saturated with wet; while Giles, Ted and Norman, laughing at his astonished face, rushed up stairs to their respective rooms.

CHAPTER XXVIII.

FARMER JOLTER RETURNS TO THE COUNTRY.

THE visit of the good old Lawyer Sheepshanks to London was connected with several most important matters of business connected with our hero, Giles Evergreen, Ted Flan, and the renowned family of the Jolters.

It was sudden and unexpected, but excessively welcome to that amiable lady, Mrs. Wilson, who began to tire of the Jolters under her roof.

More than twice or thrice Tommy and Suke had rolled from the top to the bottom of the stairs, quarrelling and fighting like two angry cats, so that the poor lady was kept in a continual state of tribulation and fear, daily and hourly expecting that some calamity would befall them, and that a coroner's inquest would be held in her best drawing-room upon one or both of their bodies.

The farmer and Mr. Walmisley had struck up a very extraordinary piece of croneyship, and were out all the day at the market, &c., and generally returned home in a cab " considerably refreshed " at night.

Then, again, the angry altercations between Suke Jolter and Susan Flipper were daily becoming more serious, so much so that the latter young lady had given her mistress a month's warning, and a gentle hint that she thought of " bettering her condition," and that service after all was black slavery under another name.

The pudding or poultice had considerably soothed and healed Tommy's head, and the thumping legacy left him by his uncle had so bewildered him, that he was, if possible, still more eccentric in his manners and ways; whereas, on the contrary, Suke not having come into possession of any legacy at all, had grown more vixenish in her temper, and expressed her intention of again revisiting the farm, a proposal which Mrs. Wilson would gladly have seconded by paying the fare for her.

This was the state of things in Gower Street at the time of the lawyer's arrival, bringing with him his clerk, Mr. Steelpen, who, when he again met Suke, was received with a loud laugh.

" I say, lawyer's clerk, what dost thee say to another ride like the last upon Swish-tail? Ecod, thou didst look a funny soight wi' thy hat o'er thy eyes, thee didst—yah !"

" Well—ah !—'pon my word, Miss Jolter, it was—ah !—strange sight; hope you didn't feel any ill effects from the—ah !——"

"Yah! not I. I ha' been on Swish-tail's back a score times. Well, what fool's errand hast thee come upon, eh? Thee'll find Lunnon a queer place, and thee wilt make another queer one in it. Lor'! what brought thee and old Tough Mutton up to Lunnon, I wonder?"

Mr. Steelpen could have told her what brought him up to town, if he had been so minded, but he kept the secret locked in his own breast.

He knew that old Jolter was very rich, and that a large slice of the plum pudding must fall to Suke's share, and although her manners were not cast in a Belgravian mould, yet he thought that if they were covered with gold-leaf, it would be better than many others with no gold-leaf at all.

So Steelpen began to lay siege to Suke's money bags.

The morning after the desperate race on the river, breakfast being ended, the lawyer sat in a private room with Giles and Ted Flan.

He listened with great attention to the account of their many and various adventures in London.

And, when Giles had concluded, he leaned back for some time, thoughtfully, in his chair.

"I shall have occasion to wait upon the Lady St. George in the course of a few days, in order to clear up the mysteries of the hatred shown to you by Alfred Ravensborne, and that detestable scoundrel, Dick Martingale; and my visit to you is partly on that account."

"Indeed, sir," said Giles, with great surprise.

"Yes, on your account!"

And the lawyer laid a marked emphasis on the words.

"May I ask, sir——" said Giles.

"Not just at present; but this much you may know. You are aware that I am the executor under your aunt's will, the conditions of which are somewhat singular; in becoming her executor, I likewise became so to your poor father."

"My father, sir?"

And, thrilling with emotion, Giles started to his feet.

"Yes; you have no recollection of him."

And the lawyer looked kindly on the agitated boy.

"Alas! no, sir. I was too young to——"

"Miss him. At present we will leave him. At the death of your aunt, a vast quantity of property came under my care, and for many years has remained unnoticed. Rummaging among a mass of papers the other day, I came across a bundle that so excited my surprise that, neglecting other matters, I came up to London to protect you from——"

"Whom, sir, whom?"

"The jockey, Dick Martingale," was the reply.

"Indeed! then calm your fears, sir, for he must have perished in the boat last night. So says the account that Norman Campbell brought us— 'that a boat struck against the piers of Battersea, and sunk with all in it.'"

"Ah, we shall see; the death of the fiend Martingale I don't think will ever be achieved by water."

"P'r'aps by a trifle of flax well

twisted together," chimed in Ted Flan.

"That is nearer the mark, Ted. No, no, my brave lads, I think we shall hear a little more respecting Mr. Richard Martingale."

At this moment the door was hurriedly opened, and in walked Farmer Jolter, followed by Tommy and Suke.

"Eh, what, Lawyer Tough Mutton !" exclaimed the farmer; "but I be main glad to see thee."

And he grasped the lawyer's extended hand as though it were the paw of a bear.

"Yah ! what beest thee glad to see him for ?" said Suke. "Ain't we had enough of him ? Didn't he send us to this plaguey place, where they give decent people dinner when they ought to be in bed ?"

"What's that to do with thee when people grub ?" replied Tommy. "Thee art always a-growling and snarling and wanting to get back to the pigs, the only company you're fit for."

"Ha, ha, ha !" laughed the lawyer, "affectionate as usual, I see. Well, Suke can go back to her companions when she likes; all the law business will be settled to-morrow."

"Yah ! law business ! What have I to do with law ?"

"Not much, Suke," replied he.

"Yah ! I should think not; if folks had a grain o' sense in their noddles they'd never touch the law."

"By the powers, Miss Suke," said Ted, "the law won't be much richer by what Uncle Tommy left thee; it was like my countryman's fortune."

"Yah ! and what was that ?"

"Why, it could never be found," said Ted, grinning.

"Yah ! You stop till I get thee down at the farm; I'll show thee a trick or two."

"What, monkey tricks ?"

"Yah ! I'll pay them ere monkeys out afore I leave Lunnon, take my word for it."

"Leave London, Suke," said the lawyer; "are you tired of it ?"

"Yah ! sick and tired ! I long to be among the fowls and pigs. What sayest thee, feyther ?"

"Say, gal ! I wish I could start to-night," replied the farmer. "Drat that next of skin."

"All can be arranged without your presence any longer, Jolter; you can start for the farm whenever you like," said the lawyer.

"Can I ?" shouted Jolter, starting up. "Then blowed if I don't start to-night."

"Bother the farm," said Tommy. "I ain't going to follow plough-tail any more wi' forty and five thousand pounds."

"Yah ! the fool; you want to be spending it like a great donkey," said Suke.

"I'll do as I like, Miss Carrots, and not ask you."

Here a battle-royal would, in all probability have taken place, but the lawyer interfered.

"Tommy's property and himself will be placed in Chancery and a scheme drawn up for his future welfare."

"Blowed if I didn't think the lawyers would get hold of it," grumbled old Jolter.

"DARK DAVY'S DOOM."

No. 15.

"The best thing too," said the lawyer, rising. "You must excuse me now. I have most important business to transact for Giles Evergreen, and which will necessarily shorten his visit to London."

So saying, beckoning to Giles and Ted, he left the room.

The rest of the party followed, luncheon being announced, Steelpen paying the most polite attention to Suke, while Tommy whispered to Jones that he hoped that all the jam tart had not disappeared, as he was wonderfully peckish and main hungry.

And so for the present the party separated; as Lawyer Tough Mutton had said, the law business having settled all the Jolters' troubles, they were at liberty to depart.

Few things could be more welcome to the ears of the Farmer and Suke; during their short stay in London they had been continually in trouble, and a great source of annoyance to Mrs. Wilson.

It was therefore arranged that the night train should convey Jolter and Suke down to the farm under the personal superintendence of Mr. Steelpen.

It did not take long to pack up the family chest; and, such was the general joy of the household on the matter, that Mrs. Wilson was just in time in saving Flipper from rushing out to have the old "Bloomsbury bells" rung.

At last the hour approached that was to take Jolter, Suke, and Steelpen away.

"Well, good-bye, marm," said the old man. "Sorry you have had so much trouble; but you can excuse that, for London be enough to craze Old Nick himself."

"Yah! what are you talking about? You arn't got nothin' to beg pardon about. You've paid your way to she and what more does she want? Yah!"

"Well, I never in all my life——" said Flipper.

"Yah, hold thy tongue! Thee haven't forgot the Blue-bottle that thee went flying downstairs with, have thee? Best be quiet, or else I'll——"

Here the announcement of the cab that was to take them away stopped any further altercation.

Old Jolter got in, Steelpen mounted the box, while Tommy stood at the door with Suke.

Bestowing a slap upon Tommy's face, she made a desperate onslaught on Flipper's cap and streamers, and succeeded in getting and tearing them up; then she sprang into the cab, and, as it drove away, she thrust her body half out of the window, and said—

"Yah! Flipper, good-bye; thee hasn't had any the best of Suke Jolter. Yah!"

And away went the cab, to the great relief of Mrs. Wilson, while Flipper, being tightly held by Jones, was prevented rushing after it, and, the door being closed, shut in her indignant cries of "Police! police!"

And so, to the great relief of all concerned, the Jolter family (excepting Tommy) had gone back to their "rural amusements."

The arrangement of the lawyer, in accordance with the will of Tommy's uncle, was that he was to receive what he, the uncle, never had, "a good education."

And so, as soon as the effects of the "monkey tricks" had vanished from the exterior of Tommy's cranium, all care and attention was to be bestowed upon the interior; until then Mrs. Wilson, Butler Jones, and the Flipper, were to have Soft Tommy under their especial care and attention.

All this having been arranged, and a great weight taken off Lawyer Tough Mutton's mind, he set zealously about finding out whether Dick Martingale was still in the land of the living.

Directing Giles Evergreen, Ted Flan, and Norman Campbell to be ready at a moment's emergency to accompany him to Lady St. George's villa, where Alfred Ravensborne still lay in a state of only partial consciousness, he proceeded to consult Messrs. Faithful, Son and Steady.

When he had concluded, the former pointed out a paragraph in the *Standard* newspaper.

It was to the following effect:—

"THE DREADFUL ACCIDENT AT BATTERSEA BRIDGE.—We find upon inquiry, that one of the men who was in the boat when it struck against the bridge was saved, and carried ashore."

"One of them, but which?" said the lawyer.

"That must be ascertained," was the reply; "you must go to Battersea."

"I don't know the place, and should be like a fish out of water," said Tough Mutton.

"Humph! just so. Wait a moment, friend Sheepshanks, I think we can get over the difficulty."

And, so saying, he left his sanctum, returning again in a few moments.

"I have sent for a man who will be your guide in this matter; he'll be the very thing for you if we can catch him. Amuse yourself with the paper, my worthy friend; my clerk is an active fellow, always on the bustle, and won't be long."

And, so saying, Mr. Faithful directed his attention to some papers.

A short time elapsed, and a knocking at the door announced the return of Mr. Faithful's active clerk, and entering the room, he introduced the man he had been in search of.

It was our old acquaintance, Shambling Jack.

He was somewhat better dressed, and appeared as though the "light of other days" was again beaming upon him.

He was briefly informed of what was required of him.

"Battersea!" he said. "Why, Lor' bless you, sir, I know every inch of the ground there, cos, you see, I was born there, and so, you see, had no occasion to go and get cut for the simples."

"I'll be bound not," said Tough Mutton, looking at him very narrowly. "And so you think you can assist me?"

"Assist you! I'll find the man if he's upon terra firma. Sad accident, but very natural. It ain't everybody can shoot the bridge; but I'm your man, sir."

A cab having been procured, they started, Shambling Jack taking his place by the side of the driver.

There was a little delay at times, and a stopping more than once; at first the driver thought a shoe was loose, and pulled up at a public-house, into which Shambling Jack quickly disappeared; again something was wrong with the harness—that occurred opposite a public-house, and Jack made another exit: a third and last, the horse fell down on his knees, and Jack disappeared once more.

At last Battersea was reached, much to the lawyer's satisfaction.

And Mr. Sheepshanks, directing the driver to pull up at a respectable tavern, entered the coffee-room, followed by the " Shambler."

In answer to his inquiries he was informed that two of the bodies had been recovered by the aid of the drags, and they were now lying for identification at the dead-house.

Hither Mr. Sheepshanks repaired, followed by Jack.

Arrived there, and mentioning the nature of his business to that all-important functionary, the beadle, he was at once shown into the awful place.

There lay two bodies covered over with some sacks.

" I think," said the beadle, " there must have been foul play in this 'ere tragedy, sir," and motioning to the grave-digger, the sacks were removed.

The instant Jack cast his eyes upon the body he started back, and shook in every limb.

" Dark Davy, by all that's glorious !" he said.

" Hulloa ! what's that ?" said the beadle. " Do you know them ?"

" I know one of them as well as I know myself," was the reply.

" Which on 'em ?" said the beadle.

" The one that has got his hand twisted in t'other's neck handkercher. Aye ! aye ! it's like him; leave Dark Davy alone, for once getting his grip on a man, nothing but death would make him leave go; but in this case blest if he hasn't kept a tight hold all through the affair."

Jack was right ; in the awful struggle for life, Dark Davy had fastened his fingers in the old waterman's handkerchief, and with such a convulsive tenacity that the fingers had dug themselves into the wind-pipe, and refused to let go their hold.

Thus they went down into the waters of death together, and thus they were dragged up to the light that they will never behold again.

" Neither of those persons I want. Cover the horrid sight up. Was there not one saved ?" asked the lawyer.

" Yes; and just in time. Slimy Bob, the dredger, threw his hooks safe enough, and they fastened in the poor fellow's shoulder, tearing away the flesh; then he got a crack upon the head, that the doctor says is a percussion of the brain, and so——"

" And where is the other now ?" said Sheepshanks.

" Oh ! Bob took him to his house," replied the beadle.

" And where is that ?"

" Oh ! close by. He was taken there as a matter of conwenience like."

" Will you show me where, my friend ?"

" With pleasure, sir," for the beadle's face appeared radiant with joy, for the worthy lawyer, knowing the prevailing weakness of mankind, had slipped a small yellow piece of shining metal into his hand, "for you're a gentleman."

"Humph! it appears that is a title easily purchased. Come, lead the way, for I am anxious to see if the man saved is the one I want."

"Lock up the house, Mat Mold. As for you," he said, addressing the Shambler, "I shall want you; you know one on 'em. He can't be a friend, for you don't appear at all sorry."

"Well, I never cries if I can prevent it," replied Jack; "and upon this present occasion I doesn't see any necessity. Aye, aye, Davy Close, your old namesake has got you at last," he muttered.

"You'll attend the inquest, my man?" said the beadle.

"With all the pleasure in life," said Jack, "if I have my expenses. Ah! Mr. Gray, happy to see you. You knew our dear departed friend!"

The detective smiled.

"But he's given you the slip," said Jack, grinning, and the party turned their backs upon the "dead-house."

Walking on, they came to the entrance of a narrow court, principally inhabited by that class of persons that may be justly called the "scavengers of the Thames," that go crawling up and down the river, dragging up all sorts of things—coals, pieces of wood, dead bodies, queer-looking bundles, the contents of which the world are never made acquainted with, any more than they are with the odds and ends found on the poor disfigured corses.

Up this court they went, until they came to a wretched hovel, at the door of which sat the owner, sorting a lot of strange-looking articles, the strangest-looking of which was the owner of them himself.

"Where's the man you picked up last night?" asked the beadle, "eh, Bob?"

"In there," said Slimy Bob, taking the short black pipe from his mouth, "with the doctor and the ould hooman."

They entered the room.

There, propped up in a chair, his face hideous with pain, and eyes discoloured, sat a figure, partially undressed.

The light shone full upon him.

"That is Dick Martingale; the man I want," said the lawyer, in a low tone.

"And so do I, sir," whispered the detective. "We're both on the same track."

"Are you?" said the old lawyer. "And pray, sir, what track is that? and who are you?"

The detective whispered to him.

"Oh, indeed! Ah, well, although I didn't send for you, still you may be of service. But what is it you want with him?"

"Why, there is little doubt that he is the perpetrator of the outrage upon the Honourable Mr. Ravensborne; circumstances have lately transpired to bring the guilt more closely home to him."

Here the mangled face and body of the jockey gave a convulsive movement, which caused the surgeon to hold up his finger by way of warning that he desired silence, and then he whispered them to leave the room.

The intimation was promptly attended to, and the lawyer followed by the detective and Shambling Jack, found themselves standing in the close, reeking court, and old Slimy Bob still seated at the door.

"Well, what do you make on him, eh?" said that worthy. "Is he worth anything, eh?" and he looked up very knowingly with his one eye at the whole party.

Old Tough Mutton (we must cling to that name) had seen and noticed the various phases and habits of men all his life, and he was rather struck by the singular look which the man gave him.

"He ain't a son o' yourn, is he?" said Bob, "or a nevvy? He ain't a huncle, I knows," and here he gave a hoarse laugh that smacked strongly of the old river fogs.

"He is no relation of mine," replied the lawyer; "but I take a great interest in him for all that."

"Oh, you do? Well, I'm glad the poor fellow has somebody to look arter him. It was nearly all over with him when I grappled him, and it was as nigh as a toucher that he didn't pull me into the blessed river. Didn't he kick!"

"A narrow escape, my friend. Mr. Gray, do me the favour of sending this telegram; take this man with you and give him a good dinner. I will be with you in a very short time."

He handed a paper he had been writing upon to the detective.

"Certainly, sir," said that worthy. "Everything shall be done as you wish, and this man——"

"Oh, I am with you," said Shambling Jack. "I think you said dinner, sir?"

"Yes, certainly, and anything else in moderation. I leave it all to you, Mr. Gray."

"All right, sir," and touching his hat to the lawyer, he walked off, followed by Shambling Jack.

"And so," said the lawyer, "you saved that unfortunate man from drowning?"

"Yes; but I don't think he'll thank me, for, you see, these sort o' things"— and he held up the grapnels—"don't care wot they lays hold on. I thinks as how you said you had a hinterest in him?"

"Well—yes—a little."

"Ah," and the one eye gleamed up at him again, "that means a lot."

"I have known the man."

"Ah, and you knows him now, and you has a hinterest in him. Wot's the hinterest worth, eh?"

"What do you mean?"

"Well, here, sit down a moment"— and he turned up an old tub—"and I'll tell you; but you wait a moment."

And so saying, Slimy Bob rose from his seat, an old basket, and walked into his den, returning almost in an instant with a bottle and glass.

"Look you," he said to the lawyer, "before I enters upon any bisness I always lickers up," and he poured out a glass of spirits, handing it to the lawyer, "so down with it."

"Well, my friend, I am not in the habit of——"

"Never mind that; off she goes. Ha, ha! that's right; you're an out and out one, like myself, but you are nation tough. What do you make sich a face for, ain't it good?"

"Well, for the matter o' that," said the lawyer, as well as he could for spluttering, "it may be good, but it's very strong."

"Strong, ha, ha! Well, that's a good un; why, it's as mild as milk."

And the old fellow sucked at the bottle as though it were water.

"I fished it out of the river, close agin the Custom House (sink the Custom House), and if ever there was a drop of good Hollands, by all the fish in the sea that's one."

"Ugh! what a wretch," said the lawyer, in a whisper. "Well, but what about the man, and——"

"Ah, that's the pint I'm coming to," and again he put the bottle to his mouth; "you takes a hinterest in him, I forgot. Well, you see, sometimes men follerin' this wocation picks up strange things. When we hauls a body in, articles will drop out, and we can't help it, do all we can. Well, in this case——"

"You found something."

"Well, you see, if I said we didn't, I should be lying, and it's a thing I hates and detests. We did find a summat."

"And you want a price for it?"

"Just so; you've hit it cleverly; one would think you were a lawyer, and ——"

"Never mind about that. Well, what is it?"

"What is it? Why, it's a matter of a oil-skin case which he had fastened round his body, and I thought perhaps that it might be serviceable to some-body, so I——"

"Took care of it, eh?" said the lawyer.

"Well, no, I threw it in the water again."

"The devil! Why, what a fool you must——"

"Ah, just so; I've been a fool all my life, since I was a blessed baby sixty years ago. But I've met a good many like me since then—ah, dear me, a great many."

"Well, but about the case, you say you threw it in——"

"No, I said I meant to do it."

"Well, then, you have got it?"

"Have I? How do you know that?"

"Well, but you said——"

"Well, what did I say?"

And the old dredger, with his one eye, looked into the cold, clear eyes of the lawyer, and the trial of skill was a very excellent one, but Tough Mutton knew how to get the best of his adversary.

With an affected carelessness, and a perfect indifference of manner, he placed his hand in his breast pocket and pulled out a well-filled porte monnaie.

"Well, you said——"

And the old lawyer balanced it carefully in his hand.

"You said that——"

"Ah, I remember I said I had it."

And again the eyes came into play.

"Look you, my man, I shan't go beating about the bush with you."

"No, don't," replied Slimy Bob, "because it would be time thrown away."

"Would it? You saw that man in black that went away with the other?"

"Yes. What of him? Who is he?"

"Only a policeman in disguise—a detective," said the lawyer, looking keenly at him.

There was a visible change in Slimy

Bob's face, bronzed as it was with the weather and the dirt, and there was a convulsive twitching about the mouth.

Old Tough Mutton saw that he had hit the mark.

"Well, what o' that? I ain't done anything wrong, and don't care for he."

"We shall see about that. If you detain anything belonging to that man, I am afraid the law will say that it amounts to stealing."

"Will it; but I arn't going to keep it. When the chap gets well I shall hand it over to him, and if he should go t'other way, why, then, I shall give it to the crusher, unless you——"

And the one eye gleamed again up at the lawyer.

"Unless what?"

"You'd take charge of it; you seem to know him."

"I know him well and will take charge of it: and as you had a great deal of trouble in saving the man's life, you shan't go unrewarded."

"Ah! that's summat like; directly I clapped my eye upon yer, I knew you was a gentleman, and I arn't mistaken. I'll get yer the article, and leave all the rest to you."

And so saying, the old man went into the place, and quickly returned, bringing with him a small oil-skin packet.

"There you are, sir," he said, "and I arn't sorry to get rid of it."

"Is this all he had on his person," said Tough Mutton, "when you searched him?"

"Lor bless yer, I didn't search him,

not I. When I pulled him into the old boat, the belt which he had round him broke, and this fell out; and other boats came rowing up, and we brought him here as the nearest place, and then the doctor came, and that's all I knows on the matter."

"Very well, there is a five-pound note for you, to pay you for all the trouble you have had," said the lawyer, "and there is my card."

"Ah, well, the latter arn't of much use, cos, you see, neither I nor the old hooman can read; but the five-pun note is a real out and out God-send, because the old boat wants patching up, and then we're rather bac'ard in our rent, and——"

"Well, make a good use of it, that's all."

And the lawyer prepared to depart, when at that moment the surgeon coming out of the place he joined him, and, after a few words, the two departed together, Slimy Bob going with them to the end of the court, and staying there until the two gentlemen were out of sight.

"Ah, well," muttered the old fellow to himself, as he walked back to his den, "it arn't been such a bad piece of work. There warn't any 'casion to speak of the watch and the purse, becos I call them rightful parquisites; and then the pin in the handkercher ain't worth much, and it's always been a maxim of mine through life, that the least said is the soonest mended."

And Slimy Bob disappeared in his dwelling.

CHAPTER LAST.

Two evenings had elapsed after the previous events narrated in the last chapter, when, in the drawing-room of Lady St. George's villa, there are assembled a number of persons, upon whose countenances the greatest anxiety is visible.

Giles Evergreen is seated by the side of Lady Hilda, and Ted Flan and Norman Campbell are close beside him.

In the room there are two large sofas, and, upon one of them, with his head propped up by pillows, lay Alfred Ravensborne, in a state of half consciousness; at the head of the sofa is seated Lady St. George, while at its foot, sitting on it, is an eminent London surgeon.

On the other sofa, with his eyes closed and apparently asleep, lies extended the dying form of Dick Martingale, the once famous winner of the " Blue Riband of the turf," and whose last race was fast drawing to a close; at his head stands Mr. Gray, the detective, and the surgeon who attended him.

Between the two sofas is seated Tough Mutton, the lawyer, with a small table before him covered with papers, and the oil-skin case belonging to the jockey.

Alfred Ravensborne had only partially recovered from his fearful fall from the room over the stables, and the accident had entirely obliterated the circumstance from his memory, and the slight consciousness which he had shown, the surgeon said, was only temporary, and would in all probability end in " mental darkness " for the remainder of his life.

The accident had entirely altered the whole of his ideas; he had been lying all that day in a heavy sleep, and it was a matter of great uncertainty when he awoke whether he would wake with reason or not, such was his lamentable condition.

His fine face and throat were as pale as the purest marble, and the black velvet skull cap which he wore tended to throw out more strongly the sharp, well defined features. Tenderly watched with all a mother's care by Lady St. George, and skilfully attended by the surgeon, he lay calm and placid as an infant.

When the lawyer departed with the surgeon from Slimy Bob's house, he questioned him as to the state of Dick Martingale.

" My dear sir," he answered, " if he lives three days it will be more than I can hope for."

" Can he be moved as far as Richmond ?" asked the lawyer.

" Well, such a thing might be done," was the answer, " under the influence of chloroform, and it might be accomplished without having any effect either way upon the man."

" It is important that he should be got there, and I should like you to cooperate with me in the matter. All your time and trouble shall be liberally paid—and——"

"My dear sir, I will assist you all in my power; what little you have told me has interested me exceedingly; favour me with your company to dinner, and we will arrange the affair."

"I have some little matters to arrange with the persons you saw with me, and then will join you with pleasure," and shaking hands heartily with each other, they separated.

Towards the close of the afternoon, after this interview, a large boat, with four stout, fast-rowing men, was lying off the stairs at Chelsea; at the bottom of the boat were half-a-dozen thick blankets. The men had not to wait long, when a body of persons were seen approaching the stairs.

Four men carried on the bottom of an old sofa a man, carefully wrapt in some thick covering.

Approaching the boat, he was carefully placed at the bottom of it, and then the men being dismissed, the detective and the surgeon took their seats.

The oars dipped in the water, and the tide running up strongly, the boat, with its freight, was rapidly making its way to the villa at Richmond.

Little did the man lying at the bottom of it dream that he was passing over the spot where he struggled for his life, and over those waters where a foul and cruel murder was to have been perpetrated.

The lawyer was already at the villa, and prepared all the inmates for their intended visitors.

"My dear boy," he said, addressing Giles Evergreen, "you will soon learn now why such unceasing hatred was shown to you by Dick Martingale."

"I never gave him cause," answered Giles.

"Not you, but perhaps others did; this night you will know all."

"I'll be sitting on fish-hooks until I hear the rayson," said Ted Flan.

It was full half-an-hour after they had all assembled when the powerful opiate administered to Dick Martingale had ceased in its effects.

A loud groan, and then a convulsive shudder.

"Help—help!" he screamed out. "Oh, God! I am sinking!" and then tried to spring up, but was held down by the detective.

Nothing could exceed the awful look of terror which he cast around, and the change that came over his countenance on finding that he was not going down under the water.

"Where—where am I?" he said in terrified accents. "Is it a dream?" and he sank back, hiding his face in the blanket.

"Raise him up," said the lawyer, solemnly.

It was done by the detective and the surgeon.

"It is no dream, Richard Martingale, and so you will learn. A long life of villany and craft is about to close. Listen," he said to Giles; "your father, Giles Evergreen, and the father of Alfred Ravensborne, were boys together, and educated at the same school, but the superiority of the former over the latter was so great as to raise a deadly feeling of jealousy and hatred in his bosom, and went on increasing as they progressed in years. Evergreen, on attaining his majority, came into possession of a splendid fortune, and bethought himself of settling down upon and looking after his estates himself.

"But on a visit to London he met a lady of superior attractions of mind and body, and fell desperately in love with her.

"Here, again, that was unfortunate, for the Honourable Mr. Ravensborne had long loved and sought the lady.

"It was not to be. After a brief courtship, she was married to Evergreen, and it was then a deep and fearful oath was taken by the rejected suitor to ruin the successful one.

"At that time Martingale, then a stable-boy, came into the service of Ravensborne, and——"

"Aye, aye. I remember it all," said Martingale, in a low voice.

Without heeding him, the lawyer went on.

"He soon ingratiated himself into the confidence of his master, by pandering to his every bad wish, and between them both a deep plan was laid to ruin Evergreen.

"The one great failing in his character—a love of horses and racing—was to be the first upon which the ruin was to be effected.

"It was a long time before any chance occurred; but at last it came, and then was not lost sight of.

"Evergreen's jockey was killed by being thrown from an unruly and vicious horse, and Dick Martingale, as arranged between him and his master, presented himself and was accepted, Evergreen not then being aware of the great intimacy existing between them.

"From that moment a continued run

of ill-fortune pursued him. Urged on by his jockey, he betted heavily upon his horses, and when everybody reduced his winning to a certainty, he lost.

"His losses were so tremendous that, in a short time, every acre of his land was mortgaged, and the timber would have been felled to the ground but it was strictly prohibited.

"Appalled at this state of things, his wife implored him to give up the accursed thing that was bringing them all to ruin, but in vain.

"Rendered by his losses maddened and desperate, he rushed deeper into the fearful vortex, until at last when you were about four years of age, Giles, the doating wife and affectionate mother died of a broken heart.

"You were then placed under the care of your aunt, your father's sister, and you never saw your father again."

"Never," said Giles, sorrowfully, while the tears stood in his eyes.

Ted Flan silently pressed his hand, while Hilda passed her arm round his neck, as if to mutely comfort him.

The eyes of Alfred wandered from one to the other as if striving to make out the meaning of the strange scene.

"The climax of the ruin was fast approaching. The Great Northern Race was coming off, and Evergreen's horse, a splendid animal, was the favourite.

"He had backed his horse to such an extent, that if he won——"

"Why, he would have won back twice as much as he lost, and that wouldn't have done," said Martingale, with his old malignity. "Ha, ha! He lost! The horse couldn't do it, not he."

"'Tis false, villain, the horse was

winning easily until you held the noble animal in with all your strength, and then it was too late to recover the lost ground !"

" And my father was ruined by that villain !" said Giles, indignantly, starting up and pointing at the trembling wretch, who was fearful that Giles was about to spring at him; but seeing him restrained, he recovered his former audacity.

"Aye, aye, he lost clear enough, not only his money to every pound, but likewise his senses," said the villain.

"And in his rage he nearly killed you, you scoundrel," said the lawyer, "for immediately the race was over he proclaimed your villany, and on the public course thrashed you nearly to death."

" Yes; and for that I swore to revenge myself upon him and all his race, and more than once would have settled him, but——"

" You feared the hangman !" said the lawyer. " It was of no avail, the race was adjudged lost, and your father, Giles, was a loser of more than ten thousand pounds beyond what he could pay."

" And all done by me and the man he wounded in the tenderest point," said Martingale. " Aye, aye, it was a glorious revenge ; we first tried to hocuss the horse, but couldn't manage it. I never forgot his blows, and never will, and I'll have my revenge yet."

" Miserable man," said the surgeon, " are you aware that your hours are numbered, that mortification has set in, and——"

The awful tidings seemed for the moment to paralyse him, then he yelled forth cries of fearful agony.

"Die !" he shouted. " I won't—can't die. Who says so—you ! Liar !" and he aimed a blow at the surgeon. " Die ! Ha, ha ! I'll ride another race and win. Bring my scarlet jacket—there, there I have it on, and I am ready. Off we are, and I've got the lead and nothing can touch me ! Hark to the shouts ! 'The Boy in Scarlet wins the day !' See how the hats fly up in the air, and the hurrahs seem to rend the heavens !"

Here he waved his hand over his head, and frantically hurrahed, then he glared round the room and his eyes fell upon Giles.

"Ah ! I'll have his blood !" and springing up, he was rushing upon Giles, when he fell back senseless on the sofa.

" Let him be carried from this room," said the surgeon. " He has but a few hours to live."

His orders were obeyed, and he was carried from the apartment.

Before the hour of midnight sounded the soul of Dick Martingale had fled its earthly tenement.

During this scene, Alfred had been a silent, sorrowful listener, terrified and appalled at the fearful revelations of villany.

" Let me finish this tragical story," said the lawyer. " Nerve your heart, Giles, to hear the sequel. My lips had best tell you, for you will, perhaps, hear it from others. Your father, maddened by the ruin he had brought upon himself, died——"

" In the hunting field ?" said Giles.

"No, my dear boy—by his own hand!"

Giles, staggered at this awful announcement, would have fallen to the ground, but was supported by poor Ted Flan, whose spirits seemed to have completely abandoned him at what he had just heard.

For a moment there was a deep and solemn silence.

"Giles Evergreen," said a voice, and all started at the sound. It was that of Alfred Ravensborne. "Come here, Giles. My father murdered yours," and his face became bathed in tears. Covering his eyes with one hand, he held out the other. "Can you forgive the son? I have been a wicked, bad boy, but if I live I will make amends by an unalterable friendship."

"Oh, Alfred, in my dark hour of sorrow this is indeed a gleam of comfort. Forgive you!" said Giles, sinking on his knees. "Freely with all my heart and soul, dear Alfred!"

Ted and Norman approached, and kneeling, clasped the hand of the penitent boy, and thus the four schoolfellows were united in the holy bonds of a never-dying friendship.

"Let me add my share to the sunshine," said old Tough Mutton. "Every acre of land, the fine old mansion, and all its splendid contents, were mortgaged."

"And lost," said Giles; "but I'll win more and a great name."

"Not lost," said the worthy lawyer, rubbing his hands. "They were all mortgaged to your aunt, and by her will they are all yours, on one condition."

"And that is——?" said Giles.

"That you shun the whirlpool that destroyed your father."

"Oh, sir, do you think I could——"

"No, I do not; but come, let us to supper, and bid adieu to gloom and sorrow."

"Bad luck to it!" said Ted Flan. "May it be like my countryman's pig; march the wrong way and be always a month's march behind us."

*   *   *   *   *

A few weeks after there are assembled at the fine old building known as Evergreen Hall, a happy party.

A brilliant sun set was lighting up the splendid woods belonging to it, and shining upon the white tents on the lawn, filled with the happy tenantry, their wives and children.

Manly sports were going on in different parts; cricket, climbing the pole, rowing, fishing on the lake, and dancing to the enlivening strains of a band of music.

All was sunshine and happiness.

On the broad stone steps stands Giles Evergreen, the youthful squire, and on one side Alfred Ravensborne; dear old Ted Flan, Norman Campbell, and many other of the boys of the dear old school; aye, and there was the worthy Doctor Birchenough; Lady Hilda and her mother are there too, and Tommy Jolter, with his red hair sprung up again like a new crop of carrots, and Suke and Steelpen, and old Jolter, among the farmers, with his pipe and tankard.

Tough Mutton, the good-hearted, honest lawyer, had put Giles in full possession of his fortune.

"May you be happy, Giles," said they all.

"Thanks, dear, dear friends, and may I always have the greatest pleasure of life, that of conferring happiness on others."

The sun goes down, and night descends upon the earth; the sports are over, the merry music ceases, the loud shouts of joy and the cheering song is heard no longer, and yet they linger long upon the lawn, unwilling to say, as I sorrowfully do,

FAREWELL.

THE AUTHOR.